A Clash of Fangs

◆

A Clash of Fangs

◆

Roger Hyttinen

Writers Club Press

New York   Lincoln   Shanghai

A Clash of Fangs

Writers Club Press
an imprint of iUniverse, Inc.

For information address:
iUniverse
2021 Pine Lake Road, Suite 100
Lincoln, NE 68512
www.iuniverse.com

ISBN: 0-595-20713-8

Printed in the United States of America

To Michael for his constant confidence in this dream.

New In Town

◆

Danny Reed was a short, well–built young man with pasty white hair, a massive nose and wide, sunken dark brown eyes which made him frighten those he passed on the street. He wore a faded jean jacket, ripped black Levi's and being that the temperature was hovering around zero with a wild wind whipping off of Lake Michigan, he was cold. He knew he also should not have been walking out in the open but couldn't quite remember why. Through his foggy memories he seemed to recall that someone was looking for him—someone that he knew shouldn't find him. Was it the cops? Damn, he couldn't remember. Hell, he had a hard time remembering anything.

The alcohol that flowed through his veins warmed him slightly but not enough. In spite of the cold, he smiled. He liked being buzzed. Yeah, life was damned fine. If only it wasn't so damned cold out.

He lifted up the collar of his jean jacket to break the wind. Then started to sing:

She'll be coming round the mountain when she comes
She'll be coming round the mountain when she comes
She'll be coming round the mountain, coming round the mountain
She'll be coming round the mountain when she comes

He stopped his song and laughed loudly. Stupid ass song. What in the hell does it mean, anyway?

He walked on as the cold enveloped him like a tight sweater. He thought about having a cigarette but decided against it, not wanting to expose his hands to the bracing night air.

"It is fucking cold out!" he yelled at the top of his lungs. The echo of his voice bounced off the nearby buildings. He laughed again, then shivered. He then thought that if somebody was looking for him he probably shouldn't be yelling.

"Where in the hell is everybody?" He yelled as loud as he could. No answer. He knew where his buddies were—home in bed, passed out like a bunch of pigs. He wished he were home in bed. He shivered. His friends were a bunch of whimps anyway. They could never keep up to him—nobody could. Every party he went to, he was always the last one awake, the last one to keep drinking or snorting. He never understood how people pass out so fast. They're puppies, that's why. A bunch of goddamned puppies. He rounded the next corner and the wind stung his face like a sharp slap.

As he walked, the thought struck him—why wasn't he sleeping like his friends? Why didn't he stay at Ramiro's like the others? They were at Ramiro's, weren't they? He wrinkled his brow as he tried to dredge up the events of the last half hour. No, it must have been longer than that. How in the hell long had he been walking?

The pressure in his bladder could no longer be ignored. Drunk as he was, he knew better than to just piss out in the open. Especially if it was the cops who were looking for him. He grabbed his crotch hard and winced. Then to his right, he saw a dumpster a little way down the alley. Good a place as any.

He quickened his stride. His insides tingled with relief as his bladder emptied on the snowy ground. He groaned with pleasure. Then the sweet, rancid smell of garbage assaulted his nostrils and he wrinkled his nose in disgust. He tried not to think about it and just concentrate on pissing. He had just about finished when someone touched him. He turned around so quickly he almost fell over.

There was nobody there.

"What the fuck..." he said, rapidly stuffing himself back into his jeans, his heart beating wildly. "Scare the fucking shit out of..."

As he rounded the corner of the dumpster, a hand grabbed his throat. He looked up at the face of a handsome man, who looked younger than himself. Danny could feel the air being squeezed right out of him as the man slammed him into the dumpster. Pain shot down his back. He grabbed the man's wrists in an effort to pull himself free but the stranger was too strong. While Danny struggled to get his breath, the man leaned over and tenderly kissed Danny on the cheek then flicked his tongue across the boy's smooth skin. He rubbed his face in Danny's hair and took a deep whiff. He kissed him again. Danny managed to strike the man in the face but it didn't seem to have any effect. He knew that the little air he was able to suck into his lungs was not enough. He fought to retain consciousness. The stranger's lips parted in a smile.

Long, needle-like teeth now protruded over the stranger's unnaturally red lips. Fucking Fangs! The guy had fangs like some kind of an animal. He wasn't human! Danny tried to scream, but couldn't.

I don't want to die.

Then the stranger's grip lessened just enough to allow Danny to whimper, "Please don't."

The stranger smiled, nodded, then looked at the boy in mock pity. He lessened his grip a little more. Danny gasped as he sucked in air as quickly as he could. For a moment, Danny thought the man was going to let him go. The man threw his head back and laughed like a hyena. His fingers once again tightened around the boy's throat.

I want to live.

The stranger's expression then became somber, and he slowly bent his head toward the boy's neck. Danny writhed violently, making one last effort to escape his tormentor. Then, in one swift move, the stranger removed his hand from the boy's neck and sunk his teeth into the tender spot underneath his jaw. Danny felt a sharp, cutting pain as the teeth broke his skin then buried into his throat. His blood splashed into the stranger's mouth.

Danny screamed, then made a choking noise. His face twitched horribly. His body arched as the life was slowly drained from him. His eyes rolled back, and he stiffened. A few moments later he went limp. The stranger eased the boy's body onto the ground, still sucking at the wound in his throat.

The man lifted his head from the now lifeless boy on the ground and licked his lips. He closed his eyes and smiled, as if revisiting a pleasant memory. He scooped up the body and with one swift movement, flung it into the dumpster as if he were tossing away a light bag of trash. He wiped his bloodstained face with his sleeve—and smiled again.

"I think I am going to like Chicago," he said. He turned, and then sauntered down the dark alley, whistling as he walked.

First Date

◆

Steve Mitchell was sitting alone at a small bar table, contemplating the evening's events when the stranger walked in. Steve became aware of his presence almost immediately, looked up and locked eyes with the new patron. The man's stare was captivating, almost hypnotic and it was with only the greatest effort that Steve was able to break away. Catching himself, Steve turned his head and looked down at his beer. The stranger brushed past him and took the table behind him. Steve couldn't get the image of the man's eyes out of his head and turned around in what he thought was a discrete manner to get another glimpse of the handsome stranger. The man at the small table was placing his order with the cocktail waiter. His voice was soothing and sexy, almost angelic. He looked to be about twenty-three or twenty-four, with short, black hair neatly slicked back. His complexion was a creamy white which reminded Steve of freshly fallen snow and the features of his face were perfect—not one single flaw that Steve could notice. He was dressed in a large, bulky blue sweater with a white t-shirt underneath and blue jeans. The man looked away from the waiter and at Steve. The intense green eyes once again drew Steve in. The man smiled.

Steve half-smiled then, embarrassed by his own rudeness, quickly turned around so as not to stare at the lone man too long. He picked up his beer but could hardly hold onto it because of his now trembling hands. He breathed deeply then took a full-size swallow from the bottle. He all at once felt the strong need to get out of the bar as quickly as possible.

"Perhaps you would like to have a drink with me at my table? I would be most honored."

The voice threw him instantly back to reality. He recognized it as belonging to the beautiful young man at the table behind him. Steve turned to glance at the stranger now standing behind him. He was even more handsome close up than he had been at a distance. The collision of their eyes sent Steve's reasoning into a whirlwind.

"I'm sorry. I was drifting. What did you say?"

The man smiled warmly. "You did appear to be in deep thought. I would love it if you should join me at my table for a drink."

Steve hesitated, then, "I'm not sure. It is getting a bit late."

The young man smiled. "Nonsense! The evening is just beginning. And the way I see it, there is no sense in both of us spending it alone."

Steve found himself unconsciously nodding his head in agreement.

The young man smiled again, reached over and picked up Steve's drink. "Wonderful!"

Steve's hands were trembling now more than ever and he hid them behind his back as he approached the man's table. The man pulled out a chair and gestured with his hand.

Steve took a deep breath and sat down. "Thanks," he muttered and he pulled the chair closer to the table. His right leg began to tremble.

"So—what is a handsome young man like you doing all alone in a place like this?" He grinned at his cliché and without waiting for a response, smiled and said, "My name is Erik."

"I'm Steve." Steve's eyes darted from the left to the right, then to the clock above the bar.

"Are you expecting someone?"

Steve shook his head. "I just stopped here for a quick drink after work to unwind a bit." He drummed his fingers on the table.

"Good," Erik said, watching Steve's busy fingers. "I am relieved to see that I have you all to myself then. It is not easy to make friends in the city, especially when one is new to the area, such as myself."

"You just moved here recently?" Steve asked.

Erik nodded. "A couple of months ago. I decided that I needed a change and felt Chicago would be the perfect place to set up house for awhile. I find it a most beautiful city with a lot to offer. I must try to get out more to take advantage of it."

Erik's voice was so soothing that it seemed to lull Steve into a relaxing trance. Steve noticed that he had stopped trembling, as the calming effect of Erik's voice seemed to work magic on Steve's nerves.

"I think you'll like it here," Steve replied. "I've become quite attached to Chicago in the last couple of years. Never thought that I would end up living in the Midwest with the nasty winters and all."

"Ah! So you are not a Chicago native as well. Now I do not feel like such an outcast. Where do you come from?"

Steve smiled, reached over and took a deep drink of his beer. "Born and raised in Boston, Massachusetts."

Eric raised his eyebrows. "Boston. How interesting. So how is it that you ended up so far from home?"

Steve frowned. "Love, believe it or not."

"Love?" Erik said, then sighed. "You are already spoken for then? How disappointing." His eyes danced wickedly.

Steve looked down, trying to avoid Erik's penetrating gaze. "No, it's nothing like that. I moved here with my ex-lover a couple of years ago," he paused, "but we're no longer together." His eyes returned to meet Erik's. The trembling returned.

Erik nodded sympathetically. "Ending a relationship is never easy. I call tell from your expression that the break-up was difficult for you."

"Yeah, but I'm over it now," Steve replied, fidgeting with his napkin. "That was a long time ago and I've made my own life since then. I just want to forget the whole thing ever happened." He took another sip of his drink, then crossed his hands in front of him, rethought his action and placed his crossed hands on his lap.

Their eyes locked together. Steve had the oddest feeling that Erik was looking right into his soul and reading it like it was an open book exposed for the world to see. A light shudder crept up his spine.

"At least I am assured that I do not have any competition at the moment." He hesitated, then flashed Steve a toothy grin. "Or do I?"

Steve involuntarily tensed up. His emotions were in a flurry as he desperately tried to think of something to say.

"I hope I did not offend you," Erik said in a soft voice, ending the uncomfortable silence. "I would not wish to cause you any discomfort."

Steve forced a smile. "You just caught me off guard, that's all." Steve paused, licked his lips then continued. "So what do you do?"

"I do whatever I feel like doing."

Steve creased his brow. "Huh?"

Erik laughed. "What I mean is earlier in life, I was fortunate enough to have achieved financial independence so that now, money matters are of little concern to me. I can do whatever I feel like doing, whenever I feel like doing it. It is quite nice actually." He picked up his glass of wine and took a small sip. "I do sell and buy antiques to occupy my time. It is more of a hobby than anything else."

Erik smiled. It was soft warm smile and Steve sensed that he had nothing to fear from this young man. His reserve began to deplete itself and Steve became confused by his emotions. He had only known Erik for a few minutes but he felt so comfortable with him. He tried to remember if he had the same feeling when he had first met Jack but couldn't recall. It all seemed like so long ago.

"So you're not only good-looking but you're rich as well," Steve said teasingly. "Quite a catch for someone." His heart sped up as the words left his mouth.

Erik chuckled and bowed his head. "You are kind. I do not believe that I have ever been referred to as being a 'catch' before. I like it. But I am holding out for someone special." He paused, then said, in a much softer voice, "Someone like you perhaps?"

Steve's mouth again went dry and he blushed. "You hardly know me. I could be an ax murderer for all you know."

Erik's green eyes twinkled with delight. "An ax murderer you are not. I can sense certain things about people." He looked down just for a moment, then, "and I sense that I would like to spend some time with you."

"Sense certain things?" Steve stammered absent-mindedly, again looking about the room.

"What I mean is that I am usually a very good judge of character. A gift of mine, you might say. Now back to the subject of spending time together…"

Steve leapt up. "Excuse me. I'll be right back."

He was glad there was nobody in the rest room. He splashed cold water on his face and ran wet fingers through his hair. He should have just gone home when the guy approached his table. He should have lied and said that he was meeting someone later on.

He took a deep breath and glanced at his reflection in the mirror. He looked like a frightened child. "Jack," he said out loud. "maybe it's finally time to get you out of my system for good. This shit has gone on way too long."

He ran his fingers through his hair again, tucked his shirt back into his pants and strode towards the door. He glanced at himself once more in the mirror, smiled, then shut the door behind him. No reason to be nervous. He wasn't going to sleep with this guy after all. At least not yet.

"I would like that very much," Steve blurted out before he had a chance to stop the words. He sat down at the table and met Erik's eyes.

Erik's eyes narrowed. "Pardon me?"

"What you said before about spending time together." Steve paused. "But I have to tell you up front that all of this is new to me. The dating scene I mean. I have been out of it for so long that I'm not even sure I know how to act around another guy." He broke the gaze and looked down. "It's a long story but I guess what I'm saying is that I'm a bit nervous and may end up making an ass out of myself."

Steve felt a light tug on his arm and looked up. Eric's hand was resting on his sleeve.

"You need not worry," Eric said in a velvety voice. "For I must confess that I am unaccustomed to this as well."

"You have got to be kidding," Steve said, shifting uncomfortably in his chair. "I'm sure someone as hot as you is constantly being chased by hordes of good-looking men."

Erik laughed. "Do I give you such an impression? In actuality, I do not get out too often. Much to my dismay, I have become somewhat of a recluse although I have tried as of late to participate more in the community. Dating has not been an activity that I have actively pursued."

Steve nodded then blinked. All at once, cigarette smoke attacked his eyes and they began stinging and watering. He wiped his eyes on his sleeve and squinted at Erik.

"I did not intend to make you weep," Erik said, a wicked grin on his lips.

Steve laughed, picked up the damp bar napkin that was underneath his drink and wiped his eyes again. "It's the smoke. It always kills my eyes after awhile."

"Yes, it is rather smoky in here." Erik looked around the bar as if to make sure that they were not being watched. "Perhaps we can go somewhere else where we can continue our conversation—undisturbed?"

Steve said, "I live only a couple of blocks from here. We could go to my apartment."

Erik beamed. "That sounds perfect. I would enjoy that."

"Do you have a car with you?"

Erik shook his head. "No, I walked. I use the car only for special occasions. I find that living in the city there is little practical use for an automobile and find it to be more of a nuisance than anything else."

Steve nodded in agreement. "I couldn't imagine having a car in the city. Not that I could afford one anyway. The parking costs alone are enough to send you to bankruptcy court."

Erik laughed, stood up and gestured with his hand. "Shall we?"

Steve quickly gulped down the rest of his now warm beer, stood up and followed Erik out of the bar. Nobody noticed them as they left.

Getting To Know You

◆

Erik and Steve talked little on the way to the apartment. The bone–chilling Chicago night air bit into Steve like the teeth of a shark. Everything was completely still, a testament to the extreme coldness of the night. The sidewalks sparkled like a northern star–filled sky and the moonlight glowed softly off the snow in the trees. A blanket of thick frost draped the windshields of the parked cars, the reflection of the moonlight making it appear as though it was several inches thick.

Steve shivered. He wished he had remembered to bring his gloves with him. After only a few moments, he found that he could barely move his fingers, even though they were crammed deeply into his coat pockets. By the time they arrived, Steve's cheeks burned red-hot with cold, which reminded him that he had to buy a scarf this week, something he kept neglecting to do.

"Here we are," Steve said as he stopped abruptly in front of a light gray apartment complex. The sign above the door informed them that they were standing in front of the Wayward Apartments.

Erik smiled. "How fortunate you are to live right in the center of everything."

"I decided that if I was going to live in Chicago, I wanted to live were all the action is."

Erik let out a soft chuckle. "I like to be where there are plenty of happenings as well and Boystown seems to be just the place."

Steve held open the door then said with a mock Transylvanian accent, "Enter freely and of your own will."

Erik gave Steve a startled look and appeared shaken. Steve's brow wrinkled in confusion at Erik's unusual reaction. He then shrugged it off and led Erik up the narrow staircase to the second floor where they stopped in front of Apartment 23. The smell of pizza filled the hallway.

"Here is my humble abode," Steve said. He unlocked the door and waved Erik in.

Erik entered the apartment and Steve followed. Once inside, Steve took a hurried glance around to ensure that everything was in order. As he seldom received company, magazines, newspapers and notebooks tended to pile up in the living room where he worked during his free time. Luckily, he had cleaned that very morning.

Erik scanned the room and nodded with approval. "What an elegant apartment! I love this style of furniture. My home is decorated similarly to this." He turned to look at Steve. "I do find it unusual to see such furnishings belonging to a young man like yourself."

Steve looked around, laughed and said, "Young man? You can't be more than a couple of years older than me."

Erik ignored his remark and continued to walk about the apartment as if he were carrying out an inspection.

Steve took a mental inventory of his possessions. Erik was right about the apartment. The decorating was not typical of a single man in his early twenties. The apartment emitted a flavor of refinement of which Steve was proud. The decor was a mixture of French Victorian and Baroque and, though two different styles, the smart choice of furniture and decorations allowed the two genres to peacefully coexist in the apartment. Rather than the cramped look which is inherent to homes filled with antiques, the positioning of the furniture made the room appear spacious, even though in reality it was a bit small. Soft light from lamps with hanging crystal droplets illuminated the room and a recently restored blue satin couch was positioned in the corner.

Opposite the couch was placed a built–in bar, constructed entirely out of oak. Although modern in its appearance, Steve felt that it fit in nicely with the rest of the items in the room. Dark purple drapes shut out any light from the outside and added a majestic presence. Set off from the living room was a small dining room, equipped with an overly large oak table which had now begun to show its age, although was still nevertheless impressive. At the table were four high–backed French style chairs in excellent shape. Only upon close inspection could one tell that they did not originally come with the table. On the wall next to the kitchen doorway was an antique China cabinet that contained an inexpensive set of stemware and china.

Erik walked to the window and peeked behind the drapes. "How privileged to have a view such as this."

"I don't even have to leave the apartment during the Gay Pride Parade. I can watch the entire thing from my window."

Erik grinned. "Have you been a collector of antiques long?"

Steve beamed. "Only for the past two years. I know it's stereotypical. Although I think I liked this type of furniture even before I knew I was gay so you can't blame it on that."

Erik laughed. "That is the stereotype, isn't it?"

"I like the look that old things give a house," Steve said. "It's funny. The first time my family came to visit me here they all had the impression that I had become suddenly rich since I moved to Chicago." He sighed. "Unfortunately, it's all show. I've accumulated most of this stuff from antique shops, flea markets, consignment shops and estate sales. You can find some pretty good bargains." He threw his coat over a chair. "I think the place feels comfortable. I just hate the modern look. In my opinion, it feels sterile, like nobody lives there."

Steve pointed to the couch. "Have a seat and make yourself comfortable."

They both moved toward the sofa, Erik leading. He sat down while Steve remained standing.

"And you live here alone?" Erik asked.

Steve nodded. "I like my privacy. I enjoy being able to come home and do what I want."

"I can certainly appreciate that," Erik replied, nodding. "To me, privacy is essential."

"Can I get you something to drink? I have beer and some red wine. Or if you prefer…"

"Some wine would be perfect."

In the kitchen, Steve pulled the last bottle of wine from the wine rack and noticed that he was once again trembling. He opened up three different drawers, looking through their contents. Damn. Where in the hell did he put that corkscrew? Every time he cleaned he could never find anything afterwards.

After he finally found the gadget, he opened up the bottle of wine and filled two glasses. His hands shook as he poured and he could feel his heart thumping in his chest. His mind drifted to Jack but he quickly pushed the thought from his head. Why did he have to think about that jerk when there was a staggeringly handsome man is his living room waiting for him? He made a silent vow to stop dwelling on past events and promised himself that he would give the guy in the other room a fair chance. After all, not everyone was an asshole—or at least he hoped that was the case. He composed himself, took a deep breath, then picked up the two glasses and strolled briskly into the living room.

"Here you go," Steve said with a smile and handed Erik a glass of wine. Their fingers touched briefly and Steve was surprised by the coolness of Erik's skin. He probably has cold feet when he gets into bed too, Steve thought and almost giggled out loud as he put his wine on the table. He sat down on the couch next to Erik.

Erik took a sip of his wine then licked his lips. "Delicious. I love a good Bordeaux."

Erik was looking directly into Steve's eyes and Steve felt his insides go runny.

"You have the most striking eyes," Steve said, his voice containing a slight jitter as he spoke. "They really are incredible. It's what I first noticed about you in the bar."

Erik smiled. "Thank you for the kind compliment. They must be prominent since people always seem to be commenting on them." He paused. "And you," he murmured quietly, "are beautiful as well."

Steve's face turned crimson then he grinned sheepishly. He stood up, perhaps a little too quickly. "It's much too quiet in here. How about some music? My furniture might be old but my taste in music is definitely modern."

Without waiting for a response, Steve stumbled to the stereo, almost crashing into a small end table near the couch. "What do you like? I have Bowie, R.E.M., Billy Joel,…"

"David Bowie has always been a favorite of mine."

Steve knelt down in front of a wooden CD rack and picked out the "Let's Dance" CD, plopped it into the CD player and returned to the couch. The music began to roll softly in the background.

"Much better," Steve said as he plunked back onto the couch, this time a little closer to Erik than before.

"So tell me about yourself," Erik said. "What you like, what you hate, how you earn your living, your hobbies, interests—I want to know everything."

Steve grinned. "That's a lot of ground to cover."

"We have all night," Erik said, glancing at the pile of papers and books on Steve's desk. "Are you a college student?"

Steve smiled. "Not anymore. I graduated shortly before I moved to Chicago with a degree in English. I was planning on going to graduate school but that all changed when I met Jack."

Erik raised his eyebrows. "Jack?"

"My ex."

"Ah," Erik replied. "The man who broke your heart."

Steve creased his brow. "Yes, my first and only boyfriend."

Erik narrowed his eyes. "The relationship no doubt had a strong effect on you."

"You could say that. When I first met Jack, I thought he was the perfect man—charming, intelligent, good looking. I pretty much fell in love with him right away. We had only known each other for three months before we moved in together."

"You were together long?" Erik asked.

"Not quite two years. Although it was over well before that. It didn't take us too long before we realized that we both wanted and needed different things."

"In what sense?"

Steve shrugged. "I envisioned warm, cozy nights with the two of us wrapped in each other's arms and nightly dinner on the table—the whole white picket fence thing. Jack accused me of being too domestic and informed me that my idea of a relationship was nowhere near the same as his. It was only a year before things started going sour."

"You still remained with him for nearly another year after that?"

"I loved him so much that I denied that there was anything wrong. Then the cheating started and that's when it ended. I confronted him about it and he admitted sleeping with other people since the beginning. 'Love is meant to be shared, not hoarded,' he told me. He declared that he never did love me and then left for good. I'd never experienced a break–up and I had a hard time afterwards."

Steve thought back to the break–up and remembered the depression into which he fell. He didn't recognize what it was at the time as he had never been depressed before. For two months he stayed in bed and cried on and off. At the time, he was certain that the world was ending. It all seemed so surreal now.

Erik nodded sympathetically. After a moment, Steve continued. "That's what I hinted at when we talked at the bar. I haven't been with anyone since then. I guess I was determined not to let any more assholes destroy my life so I kept my distance from men. Weird, huh? I know it was irrational thinking on my part. So I just concentrated on my work and put any thoughts about men out of my head."

"A broken heart is not a matter to be taken lightly. Wars have been started over such matters of the heart."

Steve jerked his head up as if coming out of a trance and met Erik's gaze. "Oh man, I'm really sorry that I went on and on about this. I just broke the cardinal rule of dating, didn't I?"

Erik looked confused. "And what so called rule might that be?"

"Never, ever talk about your ex," Steve said, smiling. "He really is out of my system. I don't know why I got carried away like I did. I really didn't mean…"

Erik waved his hand. "No apology necessary." He lowered his eyes to meet Steve's. "And it makes me happy that you referred to this evening as a date."

Steve wiped off his damp forehead with the back of his hand. It was beginning to get uncomfortably warm in the apartment.

"It's roasting in here. I'll turn down the heat a tad."

Steve looked at Erik before he got up. Curious. He didn't look warm at all. He seemed perfectly comfortable in spite of the thick sweater he was wearing. Steve crossed the room and adjusted the thermostat.

When he turned around, he noticed that Erik had taken off his sweater and tossed it onto an empty chair. Steve's eyes grew wide when he saw Erik's white t–shirt, clinging to his well–defined body. He could see the ripple of Erik's stomach muscles underneath. Hard biceps protruded from the sleeves. Steve all at once felt self–conscious about his own body. He promised himself that commencing tomorrow, he would begin working out. He rejoined Erik on the couch.

"So where were we?" Steve asked.

"You were thinking about going to graduate school," Erik answered with a sly smile.

Steve sighed. "So I was planning on going to graduate school but then I met Jack and you know the rest. Unfortunately. He got transferred to Chicago, I went with him, we broke up and here I am." Steve took a deep breath. "It was pretty rough at first but I'm all right now. In fact, I'm much better off than when we were together. It was a destructive relationship."

Erik nodded in silent agreement. "So what do you do for a profession?" He shifted closer to Steve.

Steve frowned then looked down. "I'm a waiter at the moment."

"I sense distaste in your voice," Erik said. "You are not happy with your line of work?"

"It's not that I hate being a waiter," Steve answered. "It's just that I didn't plan on doing this for as long as I have. I thought it would be a cinch finding work in my field after I graduated from college. It was not supposed to turn out this way. After three years of job hunting, here I am, still a bloody waiter." He raised his head to look at Erik. "So you see, this is only temporary—only until I can find a real job."

Erik smiled. "What sort of employment are you looking for?"

"Journalism," Steve answered, excitement welling in his voice. "I wish that's what I would have gotten my degree in rather than English. As I've discovered, it's not easy to break into the field with only an English degree. I was pretty confused about what I wanted to do when I was in college. I started out majoring in Nursing and discovered shortly thereafter that I couldn't stand the sight of blood. Then I switched majors to Psychology and discovered that wasn't my cup of tea either so I ended up in English."

Erik smiled, as if amused. "Couldn't stand the sight of blood? How interesting." He paused, then cleared his throat. "What did you plan on doing with your English degree?"

A quizzical look crossed over Steve's face for just a moment, then he continued. "I wasn't sure at the time. I knew that it would involve some sort of writing. It was later that I found out that I loved journalism and struggled to hook up with some publications. I've done some freelance writing and have sold a few articles here and there, mainly to small magazines. My dream is to work for a big publication as a reporter. But until that happens, I guess it will be 'would you like fries with that?'"

"I am sure that success will eventually come your way," Erik said. "I can tell that you are an intelligent individual. You just need the right opportunity."

"If it ever comes."

"You must be careful not to become complacent. It is too easy to become satisfied with one's present station in life and to push one's dreams into the background. There are unfinished novels and half–written songs in too many drawers." He looked at Steve and smiled lazily. "I would like to read some of your writing if you would allow me."

Steve grinned. "If you want. I've mainly written about Gay & Lesbian issues like coming out as a teenager, being Gay in Corporate America and so on."

"You are an activist then?"

Steve laughed. "Not really, although I am open about who and what I am. When I came out, I blew the closet door off its hinges. I'm not the militant type though. I'm a little too low key to become involved in protests and sit–ins. So I take a different approach—the pen."

Steve reached down and took another sip of his wine. He was starting to feel woozy from the booze but at the same time felt more comfortable around his new friend.

"So how about you?" Steve asked. "Are you out to your family?"

Erik placed his hands underneath his legs and sighed. "Regrettably, I am the only one left."

Steve's eyes grew wide. "You mean you have no living relatives?"

Erik shook his head. "All of my relatives are deceased."

"What about your parents?" Steve continued.

"Dead as well."

"How did they die?" Steve regretted the words the moment they left his mouth. Before Erik had a chance to respond, Steve quickly added,

"I'm sorry Erik. I didn't mean to ask that. I get carried away sometimes and don't think before opening my mouth."

Erik inclined his head politely and gazed at his companion. "Yes, it is a subject rather difficult for me to talk about." He reached over and poked Steve in the ribs. "Besides, we were talking about you, remember?"

Steve jumped then broke into a smile. "But I want to get to know a little about you too."

"You will. I actually hope you get to know me very well," Erik said, moving closer to Steve. "As well as you want to know me, that is," he added in almost a whisper. He reached down and took hold of Steve's hand and held it tightly. He slowly moved his head towards Steve.

Their lips met.

Steve fell deeply into the kiss and let out a light groan as their lips pressed together. Erik's lips were quite cool as was the inside of his mouth, which Steve discovered when their tongues met. He had never experienced such an intense kiss before, a kiss that overflowed with heat and passion. Erik's mouth tasted faintly salty, like tears. He pulled Erik closer to him. It felt so good to have a body next to his. No, that was wrong. It was not just any 'body' which felt good, but it was Erik's body. The feeling of Erik's lips and mouth on his own drove Steve wild and he became completely immersed in the erotic kiss, which seemed to go on and on. Erik placed his hands on Steve's face as he continued to explore Steve's mouth with his tongue. The coolness of his hands again startled Steve. Steve wondered if his dick was cool too. Steve almost laughed in the midst of the kiss at the wicked thought.

The kiss broke and Erik began exploring Steve's body with his hands. He reached under Steve's shirt, caressed his back and then moved to Steve's chest. The cool hands were sending Steve into a frenzy. He had completely forgotten about his earlier resolution of not sleeping with Erik. Two years of pent–up, unbridled passion broke though and he grabbed Erik, kissing him hungrily on the neck and face.

Erik pulled away. "What do you say we move to the bedroom?" he said, breathing heavily.

It was not a question but more of a command and Steve was ready to obey. Without a word, he took hold of Erik's hand and led him into the meticulously clean bedroom. Steve strode over to the king-sized bed and turned on the small lamp sitting on the nightstand. A soft red light illuminated the room. Unobtrusively near the doorway stood a huge oak dresser, the top arranged neatly with several bottles of expensive cologne, a jewelry box and a tall silver candlestick which contained a not-yet-burnt yellow candle. Off to the right of the bed was a huge walk–in closet, the contents of which were impossible to see as it extended so deeply in the wall. Several posters of shirtless young men draped the wall, which slightly embarrassed Steve when he caught sight of them.

Erik grinned in the soft light and grabbed Steve. Their lips met once again and they staggered, lips still locked, to the bed. Erik gently pushed Steve on the bed.

"You are beautiful," Erik said, his voice barely audible. He tenderly undressed Steve, undressed himself then stretched out on top of Steve. Steve shuddered beneath him.

"You do have the coolest body," Steve said.

"I think your body is pretty cool too. Fantastic, even."

"No, no, no," Steve replied snickering. "I mean the temperature of your skin is really cool. Almost cold. It's kind of weird."

"So you find me peculiar?"

Steve firmly held onto Erik and squeezed. "I didn't mean it that way. Your skin—I've just never felt such cool skin before."

There was a pause. "I am simply cold blooded."

"I guess I'll have to warm up your skin for you then."

"I guess you will."

They resumed kissing, which then led to a complete exploration of each other's body. Steve was like a newly unleashed wild animal. He attacked Erik with a fervor which surprised himself as much as it did Erik. By the time they had finished making love, neither had missed an inch of the other's body.

Afterwards, with Erik's arms wrapped around him, Steve snuggled up close. "I feel so comfortable with you," he whispered into Erik's ear.

Erik purred and pulled Steve closer. There was a stretch of silence as the two held each other. Erik nudged Steve in the neck with his face, than lightly ran his tongue on Steve's salty skin.

Erik abruptly pulled away, grabbed Steve's face and looked into his eyes. "I certainly am the fortunate one. Not only are you beautiful, but you are magnificent in the bedroom as well."

Steve giggled. "I bet you say that to all the fellas."

"What fellas? You are my first. I wanted to tell you earlier but I did not…."

"Yeah right—and I'm the Queen Mother," Steve said. He grabbed Erik's sides and began tickling. Erik was still.

"Not ticklish?

Erik shook his head.

"I'm going to have to work on finding your weak spot. I know you must have one."

"I think I may have just developed such a weak spot," Erik replied in a whisper.

Steve said nothing. Even though the room was dimly lit, he could see Erik's eyes looking deeply into him. Too deeply in fact. It felt almost uncomfortable. He snuggled up as close as he could to Erik, savoring the feeling of the man's body.

"Erik?"

"Hmm?"

"I really like you too."

Steve wondered if Erik liked omelets and then drifted off to sleep.

The Next Morning

◆

The sun smacked him full force in the eyes. Steve grumbled and covered his face with his pillow. He had been dreaming about gangsters running amuck in his neighborhood, slaughtering people indiscriminately. He couldn't remember too much else about the dream except for the end, in which he was sleeping and was unexpectedly awoken by a deafening crash in the living room. Before he could get out of bed to investigate, one of the gangsters was standing right next to his bed, holding a Norman Bates style butcher knife. The sunlight bounced off of the knife and flashed in Steve's eyes, temporarily blinding him. He tried to scream and move away from the man but found that he could do neither. He then noticed that the sheets were wet. He turned away from the man just for a moment and saw that they were indeed soaked—with blood! Not his blood, but Erik's! It was then he woke up with a start.

In his groggy state and his attempts to recall the disturbing dream, he had initially forgotten about meeting Erik the night before. He abruptly rolled over. The space beside him was empty. Steve flew to full consciousness.

He bolted out of bed, threw on a pair of white underwear and dashed to the kitchen. Then to the living room. Then to the bathroom. All empty. Erik was gone and there was no note to be found.

Steve walked back to the living room, stood in the middle of the floor, and looked around with a confused look on his face. How could

Erik have left like that? Why didn't he wake Steve up before leaving? Shit, they had not even exchanged phone numbers. Steve could feel hot tears welling up in his eyes as he glanced around the empty apartment. He noticed the two empty wine glasses sitting on the coffee table. After all this time, Steve meets a man he really likes and what happens? He just leaves. Gone without a trace.

"Find 'em, feel 'em, fuck 'em and forget 'em," he said out loud, his teeth clenched.

He turned abruptly, shuffled into the kitchen and sat at the table, propping his elbows up on the wooden table and resting his head in his hands. He wiped his eyes with his bare arm then sighed.

"Now what in the fuck am I going to do?"

He almost laughed at his words. Do about what? Things were no different now than they were yesterday. He got laid last night, nothing more. Although at the time, it sure seemed like something more—a lot more. Did Erik lie to him? He said that he liked Steve and Steve had to admit that he had experienced the best sex he has ever had with the man.

He dragged himself to the coffee pot, fighting back a second wave of tears. He reached in the cupboard, grabbed a can of coffee and a pack of coffee filters, filled the filter with coffee and slammed it into the machine.

"Fuck!" he yelled. "Last night was a fucking one night stand, that's all it was."

He walked back to the kitchen table and roughly sat down. He looked at the small clock on the kitchen counter. Shit, it was almost noon. He would have to go to work in a few hours. How was he going to face his coworkers in the mood he was in, much less his customers? He thought briefly about calling in sick but decided against it. He needed the money too badly. There was no way he could afford to take off a night from work, especially a Saturday night. On weekends, he could walk out of the restaurant with at least eighty dollars in tips in his pocket and wasn't about to give up that kind of money for a silly bout of the after-sex blues. No, it was silly to get upset about this. It was a fun night, he had a great time with Erik but now it was over.

He had just taken the first sip of his coffee when the telephone rang.

"Hey big guy," a voice breathed into the phone. "What are you up to?"

"Hi Jamie," Steve answered groggily into the phone. "I just got out of bed not too long ago. In fact, I'm still on my first cup of coffee."

He shouldn't have even answered the phone. He really didn't feel like suffering through one of Jamie's long-winded chats at the moment, a good a friend as he was.

"My, my, my. Aren't we just being Mr. Decadent today. Sleeping until noon. That's out of character for you, Steven. How about getting your tired ass dressed and joining me for a cup of coffee before work?"

"I'm already having coffee."

"So you said," Jamie snipped back. "You certainly are crabby as hell today. Come on lazy bones. It will do you good to get out of the apartment."

Jamie did have a point there. He couldn't spend the rest of the afternoon brooding about Erik. Getting out might make him forget about his woes.

Steve groaned. "Okay, let me get cleaned up first. I'll meet you at the Coffee Depot in about forty-five minutes."

"Great hon. See you then." Jamie chirped. "Oh, I almost forgot. Have you read the paper yet this morning?"

"I just got up. Remember?"

"There was another one of those vampire murders last night."

"Vampire murders? What are you talking about?"

"You know, the ones where the victims all turn up a few quarts low with a gash in their throat. Just thinking about it makes me squirm."

"I think I remember hearing something about them. I haven't really paid too much attention." Steve thought about the pile of unread newspapers stacked neatly in his broom closet. "I'll have to check out today's paper."

"Christ hon, for a wanna be journalist, one would think you'd be more up to date on what's happening in the world."

"Jamie, don't even think of fucking with me this morning. I am not in the mood for any shit."

"Lighten up girlfriend," Jamie said sharply, obviously feeling hurt. "You sure are touchy this morning. What's up your craw anyhow?"

"I'm sorry," Steve replied, "I didn't mean to snap at you. I just have a lot of things on my mind."

"Why don't we get off the phone so you can shag your ass down to the Coffee Depot and tell me all about it."

Steve snickered. "It is kind of silly to be talking on the phone when we're going to be meeting. I'll see you then."

"Bye-Bye—and don't dilly-dally like you usually do."

"I'll be there in less than an hour."

Steve hung up the phone. Jamie was just much too perky today.

He walked back to the kitchen table, put down his cup of coffee and started thinking about Erik again. All at once he remembered what Jamie had said about a new murder and went to the hallway to retrieve the morning paper. To his relief, nobody had stolen it yet.

Once inside, he unfolded the newspaper. There it was, right on the front page of the Chicago Tribune.

Vampire Murderer Strikes Again on North Side

AP—Another body was discovered early yesterday morning in a dumpster on Chicago's North Side. The murder victim has been identified as 28-year-old Jeffrey Howard. Howard, allegedly a member of one of Chicago's notorious gangs, was wanted for the October homicides of Richard Rodriguez and Leonard DeNardi, both rival gang members. There are no suspects as of yet, but police believe there is a connection with last week's murder of

Alfredo Lacconi, a known male prostitute. Both bodies were completely drained of blood. No blood was found at the discovery site of the bodies. This is the eighth such slaying since November, where the first victim has been identified as Danny Reed of the near Northwest side of Chicago. Police have no suspects but are continuing their investigation.

Steve read the article and shuddered. Jamie was right. Having the blood drained from you was a horrible way to go. Who could do such a ghastly thing? And why? Probably one of the rival gangs. Those guys were pretty nasty these days. Kind of strange that the gangs would target a hustler though. Although if the hustler was gay, then it could have been a hate motivated crime.

Steve reread the article looking for additional clues but nothing jumped out. Naming the killer or killers 'Vampire Murderers' was in bad taste, Steve thought. Vampires, of all things. The journalistic wheels in his head began turning and he rushed to the broom closet, and began digging through his old newspapers. Maybe he could look into this on his own. Who knows? If he could crack this story, it could be the big break he had been hoping for.

He sat contemplating the case for several minutes and then suddenly looked at the clock in the kitchen.

"Oh shit! Jamie!" he said, and flew from the table and dashed into the shower.

While showering, he continued to think about the murders. Even if he doesn't come up with anything, it will at least add some excitement to his otherwise mundane existence. Mundane that is, until last night. He felt sadness descending again but shrugged it off. He quickly dried off, dressed and darted out the door to meet Jamie.

* * *

"You're late as usual," Jamie commented, looking at an imaginary watch on his wrist, as Steve joined him at a table near the window.

"Sorry," Steve said, still out of breath from the brisk walk. The deep-freeze that had slammed the Chicago area still lingered and according to the weather forecast, there was no relief in sight. It was more bitterly cold today than it was last night and although bundled up in a thick knitted hat, a robust winter sweater and a bulky wool coat, the few minute walk had chilled Steve to the bone, causing him to shiver uncontrollably. He sat down, removed his gloves and blew on his hands.

"Boy, is it freezing out! Remind me to buy a scarf on our way home," Steve said, rubbing his hands together.

"You still haven't gotten that damned scarf? I swear, you are the worst procrastinator I know."

"Guilty," Steve said, and laughed. "Although it's more like absent-mindedness than procrastination."

"So what took you so long? I started to think that you had gone back to bed and I would have to come over there myself to drag you out."

"I got involved with that article you told me about."

"So you did read the paper after all. How literate of you." Steve's expression changed to a frown. Jamie quickly added, "Just kidding dear. You have got to learn how to take a joke and not be so touchy about everything. One would think that after knowing me for two years, you would have gotten used to my sense of humor by now."

Steve ignored Jamie's comments and continued trying to warm up. He was still rubbing his hands together.

"I find this whole thing very perplexing," Steve finally said.

Jamie looked confused. "Dear, what on earth are you talking about?"

"The murders. Now what would gang members and hustlers have in common?"

"They are both very bad boys for one," Jamie replied, not looking at Steve. "Undesirables, according to some." He looked around for a waiter, then reached into his pocket and pulled out a cigarette.

"Undesirables," Steve mimicked. "But why would someone target them?"

Jamie looked at Steve and took a deep puff of his cigarette, blowing the smoke above his head. He shrugged. "Who knows? Maybe it's some kind of super hero out to make the world a better place." He turned, still attempting to catch the waiter's eye. "Just think. A super hunk in a cape and tights. Don't you just love a man in uniform?"

Steve snickered. "You could have a point there. It might be some sort of fanatic vigilante who has taken it upon himself to rid the world of crime."

Jamie looked irritated. "I wouldn't exactly call hustling a crime."

"Not in the sense of violent crime maybe, but it is still illegal—and dangerous."

Jamie raised his eyebrows. "Dangerous? And how do you figure that?"

"Dangerous to the people they trick with. I would imagine that they are walking virus banks, infecting everyone that they come into contact with."

Jamie rolled his eyes. "You disappoint me Steven. I didn't think you would be so narrow-minded. The fact of the matter is that most hustlers are very AIDS aware and insist on protected sex. Referring to them as virus banks is both unfair and uninformed."

Steve sighed. "Okay, I'll admit that I don't know all that much about hustlers since I don't know any personally. But the point is, why would somebody drain them or gang members of their blood? That's pretty sick and twisted."

A frown crossed over Jamie's face for a moment, then disappeared.

"Have you ever considered the possibility that it might be a real vampire?"

"Come on, Jamie. A vampire? I'm trying to be serious here."

"And just why in the hell not? Stranger things have happened. Who's to say that there aren't real vampires lurking about? Can you prove that there aren't? People have written about them for centuries. It's possible that there's some truth to the folklore. I, for one, believe in keeping an open mind."

Steve knew that Jamie was a horror buff and that his favorite monster happened to be the vampire. How many times Jamie had subjected him to bad vampire movies Steve couldn't remember.

"I'm all for open-mindedness but I think the vampire thing just might be pushing it a little bit too far. I think you've been watching far too many horror flicks. I suppose the next thing that you're going to tell me is that you believe in werewolves as well. And let's not forget goblins and ghouls."

Jamie stuck his tongue out at Steve then gave him a sarcastic grin. "You can really be a shithead, you know that?"

"I'll take that as a compliment."

"It wasn't meant that way."

Steve stuck his tongue out at Jamie. They both laughed.

"In answer to your question," Jamie said, "I do not believe in were-wolves and I never said that I actually believe in vampires. I'm just implying that it is a possibility. Nobody has ever proven that vampires don't exist. Plus how do you explain the bodies that were drained of blood? How would someone be able to do that? Stick a siphoning hose in their neck and suck it out like they were draining gasoline from a car? Doesn't sound very likely to me. From everything I've read about it, I wouldn't be too quick to discount an actual vampire as being the killer."

Steve heard giggles coming from the table behind them. He turned around and saw two young guys, both in their early twenties, whisper-ing and sniggering while watching him and Jamie. They had obviously been eavesdropping on their conversation, which wasn't too difficult to do since Jamie's voice was not what one would call subdued.

"Where's that fucking waiter?" he said loudly. "I sure could use a cup of coffee."

He then turned around again to face the young couple, a scowl on his face and glared at them, mustering up his best "evil eye." They quickly averted their eyes and looked down at their breakfast.

"Patience dear," Jamie said as he stirred his cappuccino. "I'm sure he'll be here soon. It is busy in here after all. Wait until you see him by the way. He is drop dead gorgeous!" Jamie rubbed his chin and creased his brow. "Come to think of it, he'd be perfect for you. Young, handsome,…"

"Jamie, don't you start with that crap again."

Jamie had decided to take a personal interest in Steve's love life, which irritated Steve to no end. He knew that deep down Jamie had good intentions but tended to meddle a bit too much—strange considering that Jamie never talked about his own love life with Steve.

"And why not? You need a man in your life. Everyone knows it. Maybe then you wouldn't be so darn bitchy."

"For your information," Steve said smugly, "it just so happens that I met a man last night."

From the look on Jamie's face, Steve was instantly sorry he had mentioned it.

"*What?* And we've been sitting here all this time and you haven't said a thing? Come on girlfriend, out with it! And I want all the morbid, low-down, dirty, gruesome details!"

Steve was saved by the waiter's arrival.

Just has Jamie promised, he was good-looking. Every hair was perfectly in place, no doubt layered down with several inches of hair spray and styling gel. Although Steve couldn't be sure, it also looked as if he was wearing make-up.

"Sorry it took me so long to get here," the waiter apologized. "We're busier than hell this morning." He turned to look at Steve. "Can I get you something cutie?"

"I'll have a Café Latté," Steve said curtly.

"Jeff, this is my cute friend Steve that I was telling you about," Jamie interrupted. "And he's completely unattached and available." He looked at Steve, smiling. "Steve, meet Jeff."

Steve wanted to wring Jamie's neck.

"Nice to meet you Jeffrey."

The waiter looked Steve up and down, then flashed him a broad smile. "Nice to meet you too, super hunk." He winked, then left the table.

Steve threw his napkin at Jamie.

"Don't you ever do that to me again!" he said sharply. "I told you, I'm not interested in anyone, especially in some prissy waiter with an attitude. Plus he's a blow-dry ditty."

"Now don't go getting yourself into a tizzy," Jamie said giggling, obviously enjoying his friend's embarrassment. "You should give people a chance. Jeff is a very nice guy and you can't deny that he is a doll!"

"Jamie, he's wearing make-up for God's sake!"

"So what's the big deal? A little dab of mascara here and there doesn't hurt anything, especially if you're as cute as Jeff is. It brings out one's eyes. One must always look one's best for the public you know."

Steve groaned and smacked his forehead.

"Don't you think he's even a little cute?" Jamie asked.

"Okay, okay, you win. He isn't bad looking. He just isn't my type, that's all. And, as I've told you time and time again, I don't need you matchmaking for me."

"That's right!" Jamie squealed. "The man you met last night! Come one, fess up. I want to hear all about it."

Steve shrugged his shoulders. "There's not much to tell. I met him at the bar, we chatted for awhile and he came home with me."

"He came home with you?" Jamie said, surprised. "If I wasn't hearing this directly from the horse's mouth itself, I would never have believed it. Steven Mitchell honestly took someone home? This guy sure must have been one hunka hunka burning love."

Steve blushed. "Keep your voice down a bit, will you?" He glanced around the restaurant. The obnoxious young couple who was sitting behind them had left, thank goodness. "As a matter of fact, he was extremely attractive." Then in an afterthought, "an Adonis, actually. He was also the best lay I've had in years."

"Dear, the only person you've had in years is yourself," Jamie reminded him. "I suppose anyone else besides old handy would have to be a good lay." He giggled loudly.

"Just exactly how do long do you want to live?" Steve asked in mock anger.

"Well, it's true, isn't it?" Jamie replied matter of factly. He propped up his elbows on the table and rested his head in his hands, looking directly at Steve. "So tell me more about this man. Top or bottom?"

"Now that's none of your business!" Steve said sternly. "You sure have nerve, you know that?"

Jamie laughed. "Okay, if you don't want to share the juicy details, at least tell me everything else about him. What does he look like? What does he do?"

Steve sighed. "I really don't know too much about him. I know he's not from Chicago. And as for the looks department, definitely the tall, dark and handsome type. More like stunning, actually." He paused, in deep thought. "Funny, I remember asking him to tell me about himself but he never did."

"Oooh, a mystery man!" Jamie shrilled, then clapped his hands. "I just love a man with secrets."

"I didn't say he had secrets. I just said that he never got around to telling me about himself."

"I'm sure he didn't," Jamie said teasingly. "Why waste time on useless chatter when there are other things to occupy one's time?"

Steve ignored his comment. His face lit up as he continued. "But you wouldn't believe his eyes! They were incredible! They were definitely enough to make you melt."

"They must have been if they could make an old iceberg like yourself take notice," Jamie uttered. "So when are you going to see him again. Tonight?"

"I doubt that we'll be seeing each other again."

"What do you mean? Why in the hell not?"

Steve's expression grew solemn. "I woke up this morning and he was gone."

"You didn't get his phone number or anything?"

Steve shook his head. "We never got around to that."

Jamie looked bewildered. "So what you're telling me is that you brought home this supposedly hunky guy, spent a great evening together, had fantastic sex and you didn't so much as get his phone number?"

"I didn't think he'd slip out in the fucking middle of the night like some damned cat burglar," he snapped. "We had a wonderful time and he told me that he really liked me." He paused, then sighed. "I believed him too. Next thing I knew, he was gone." Steve fought off tears.

"Easy killer. I didn't mean to upset you. He must have been something special for you to carry on like this. I don't blame you for being upset, but Hon, that's the way the dating scene goes. It's happened to me dozens of times."

"More like thousands of times," Steve said with a weak grin.

"Bitch!" Jamie replied, and stuck up his nose feigning hurt. He then buried his head in his hands, and emitted several loud, fake sobs. "You're always so mean to me," he wailed. "You never have any concern for my feelings, my needs."

Steve laughed then noticed the other patrons in the restaurant were glancing over at them, a concerned look on their faces.

"Okay Jamie, stop it before you get us thrown out of here."

Jamie looked up with a big grin on his face. Just then, the waiter arrived with Steve's coffee. He looked at Steve deeply in the eyes as he placed the coffee on the table. Steve could feel his face turning red.

"Here you are," Jeff said, his eyes still not leaving Steve's. "Can I get you," he paused for a moment, "anything else? Anything at all?"

"Yeah, he needs to get laid," Jamie said with a snicker. "He's been way too ornery lately."

Steve flashed Jamie the glare of death.

The waiter smiled sweetly at Steve. "Is that true sweet thing?"

Steve quickly averted his eyes and began stirring his coffee. "No, it's not true." He flashed another death stare at Jamie. "He's just being a bitch, as usual."

The waiter snickered and glanced over at Steve one last time before leaving the table. "If you need anything else cutie pie, just give me a holler," he said as he walked away.

"Jamie..."

"Don't even try it," Jamie said with a wicked grin on his face. "That's what you get for insinuating that I'm a slut." He lit up another cigarette. "Plus you know that I'm never going to give up until I find you a good husband."

Steve raised his hands and shook his head in frustration.

Jamie snickered. "Speaking of husband, what are you going to do about tall, dark and handsome from last night?"

"What do you mean what am I going to do? What am I supposed to do?"

Jamie shook his head as if he couldn't believe what he was hearing. "You're not just going to let him walk out of your life, are you?"

"It's not like I have much choice in the matter."

"Steve, you give up much too easily. Where did you meet him?"

"At Buddies."

"Then go back there tonight. You never know, he just might show up again."

Steve shook his head. "I doubt it. I go there fairly often after work and I've never seen him there before. I'd say the chances of him being there again are pretty slim."

"He might show up to look for you. He may feel the same way you do, you know. Have you thought about that?"

"If that's the case, why did he leave the way he did? No note or anything." Steve felt the earlier emptiness in his chest return. "I think it's fairly obvious that I'm being blown off."

Jamie eyed his friend, a serious look on his face. "What would be the harm in trying to find him? You never know how things could turn out. By the way, what's his name?"

"Erik," Steve replied almost dreamily.

Jamie thought for a moment. "I don't think I know any Eriks. Wait. There is that cute little guy who works at Treasure Island whose name is Erik, I think. He's an absolute doll although he's a little to short for me. He can't be more than 5'2 or 5'3 but he's adorable!"

Steve shook his head. "That wouldn't be him. My Erik is well over six foot."

Jamie giggled. "My Erik?"

"Don't be a smart ass."

Jamie laughed again. "Do you know anything else about him at all?"

"Not really. Like I said, he didn't tell me much." Steve paused, took a sip of his Café Latté and looked at his friend. "There was something about him that was a bit odd though. I don't know. I can't put my finger on it but he had the most peculiar effect on me. When he looked at me, I felt as if he knew everything about me. It was kind of eerie."

"Uh-Oh," Jamie answered. "Sounds like love to me."

"I'm being serious. There really was something strange about him. Maybe it was the way he spoke."

"What do you mean?"

"He had a really formal way of expressing himself, like he might have been from another country or something. He didn't seem to have an accent though. I suppose it could have been my imagination. Maybe it's been so long since I've been with someone that I'm getting suspicious of everyone."

"Maybe," Jamie mumbled as he drank the last of his coffee and took a deep puff off of his cigarette. He waved his hand in front of Steve in an attempt to move away the smoke which was drifting towards his face. He knew that Steve didn't like cigarette smoke but never complained about it when he was with Jamie. "He sounds very interesting. I would love to meet him."

Steve chuckled. "So you can sink your evil claws into him? No way Jose! If I ever find him again, I'm going to make sure that I keep him far away from the likes of you."

"We certainly are a witch today, aren't we?" Jamie said. "One would think that getting a little tail last night would have put you in a better mood." He glared at Steve. "Besides, I'm quite capable of getting my own dates. I wouldn't want any of your old hand-me-downs anyway. What do I look like? Second Hand Rose?"

Steve and Jamie both laughed. "One can never be too careful when it comes to men." Steve gulped down the last of his coffee. "What do you say we get out of here? It's just about time to start heading homeward and get ready for work."

"Did you have to bring up work? Leave it to Steve to ruin a perfectly pleasant afternoon."

Steve snickered, and got up. As he bundled up his coat, he asked, "Are you doing anything tonight after work? Maybe we could go out together for a drink or something. I don't think I'm going to feel like returning to that empty apartment tonight."

Jamie averted Steve's eyes. "Sorry Hon, I really can't. I'm busy tonight."

Steve looked at Jamie and creased his brow. "What is it exactly that you always do after work? You always seem to have something going on. You can't have a hot date every night of the week!"

"Says who? Just because you live the life of a monk, doesn't mean everyone else does too."

They left the cafe. On the sidewalk, they said their good-byes as they lived in opposite directions. Steve walked briskly, a sense of urgency in his stride. The temperature seemed to be falling, so Steve increased his step. It was noticeably several degrees cooler than it had been when he had first gone to the cafe. The icy wind whipped against his face, bringing tears to his eyes, reminding him that he still had not stopped to buy a scarf. No time for that now. He'd have to try to pick one up tomorrow.

By the time he got home, he was deeply chilled. He didn't relish the thought of having to venture out into the cold again. As he removed his coat, he once again pondered the possibility of staying home from work today. It was on nights like this that it would be nice not to have to go anywhere, to just stay home and curl up with a book and a cup of hot chocolate. He quickly shook the idea from his head, knowing that calling in sick was out of the question, since he had spent the afternoon with Jamie. Knowing him, he was already on the phone babbling to everyone about their conversation at the cafe. He would have to go to work. He couldn't begin developing bad habits now. He will simply have to force himself to be nice to everyone. No doubt, it will be a colossal effort.

As he began getting dressed, he looked over at the unmade bed, focusing on the pillow next to his own. With a pressed white shirt in his hand, he walked over to the bed and sat down. He brought up to his face the pillow on which Erik had slept and inhaled deeply. His scent was still strong, causing Steve to drift back to last night, with Erik lying next to him, his arms around Steve. Erik's body felt so pleasing next to his— cool, yet passionate.

"How corny can I get?" Steve said and flung the pillow against the wall. Jamie was right. He was going to try and find Erik. He wasn't going to let this man slip through his fingers without at least attempting to find him. He might never hook up with him again, but at least he will have given it his best shot. But where to start? The bar was his only option. He would go back to Buddies tonight after work, and every other night after that if necessary. With a strong reserve and sense of purpose, he got up, finished dressing and left the apartment.

✳ ✳ ✳

"The soups tonight are Chicken Gumbo and French Onion. The specials are Veal Marsala and Orange Roughy. We also have a new cheesecake tonight—Amaretto Cheesecake and it's going for $4.75 a slice so make sure you push it. And," Gary the head waiter continued as he looked at his fellow waiters and waitresses gathered around him to hear the specials before the door to the restaurant opened, "I want to see everyone bring out the dessert tray, regardless of whether the customer says they are interested in dessert or not. You don't ask, you just bring out the tray. What the eyes see, the heart desires. Remember that people. Don't forget, the higher the bill, the more your tip will be. So people, push those appetizers, drinks and desserts."

Steve all at once realized that he had long ago stopped listening to Gary and tried to refocus his attention. It was too late. The speech was over. He'd have to get the specials from somebody else. The group dispersed and the doors to the restaurant opened. Customers began pouring in.

It turned out to be a busy night, unusually busy and Steve ran back and forth incessantly all evening. He sat down in the kitchen and rubbed his aching feet through his shoes. He pulled out a wad of money and counted his tips—close to ninety-dollars. A good night! He was glad he had come to work after all. He might be able to actually get rid of a couple of bills. Things were starting to look up.

He was happy the night was almost over. He was exhausted but dying to get to the bar in hopes that Erik would be there. His heart beat faster as anticipation and excitement crept over him. The kitchen door flew up, interrupting his meditation.

"Oh Stevie," Gary said, as he strode into the kitchen. "Up and at it, slack boy. You have a solo on table twelve."

"Shit," Steve muttered under his breath, low enough so Gary couldn't hear him. He was hoping that he wouldn't get any more customers tonight. It was almost eleven o'clock and he was overly anxious to get to the bar. Instead, he was going to get stuck here—for a solo, of all things. He always thought it was strange that someone would go to a fine dining establishment by themselves. Don't these people have any friends?

"Gary," Steve called out just as the headwaiter was leaving the kitchen. "Could someone else possibly take it? I was kind of hoping to get out of here on time tonight. I have plans."

Gary sneered. "Plans or no plans, the table is yours. Besides," he added with a sneer, "it's a request." The doors closed behind him.

Usually Steve considered it an honor to be requested. A request meant that the customer liked him well enough to ask for him again. It always helped if they were big tippers too. There were some waiters and waitresses for whom the majority of their customers consisted of requests. Steve was not one of them. He was always friendly with his customers but never got warm and fuzzy enough with them so that they would specifically request him the next time they ate at the restaurant. He never felt comfortable being chummy with complete strangers, even a 'fake chummy'. He sighed. A solo should go pretty fast. If he rushed, he still might be able to get out of there by eleven-thirty or eleven forty-five.

He reluctantly grabbed his pad and tray and waltzed out to the dining room. The place had for the most part cleared out except for a few stragglers. The smell of cooked fish weighed heavily in the room. Most of the waiters and waitresses were already at the bar having their 'after-shift' cocktails.

Steve rounded the corner and approached table twelve. He arrived at his destination and looked up to see who his lone patron was. The green eyes boring into him almost caused him to drop his tray.

"I was wondering if you would like to go out dancing," Erik said with a big smile.

A Night Out

◆

Steve was tongue-tied.

"Well, what do you say?" Erik said, putting down the menu and smiling. "Are you game for a little dancing this evening?"

"Dancing?" Steve said, trying to regain his articulation. "Sure. I guess so." A permanent smile plastered itself on his face. "How did you find me? I don't remember telling you where I worked."

"It took a little detective work. But definitely worth the trouble."

Steve blushed. "You really surprised me by coming here." He swung his head around to ensure that nobody was listening and lowered his voice. "What happened to you this morning? I thought I'd never see you again. I woke up and you were gone."

"I am dreadfully sorry about leaving so abruptly," Erik said, his eyes never leaving Steve. "I had a prior obligation to be somewhere early this morning. It was only later that I remembered I had neglected to give you my telephone number or to get yours." He paused, a serious look on his face. "Last night was not a one night stand Steve, if that is what you were thinking."

Steve sat down at the table, facing Erik. "I have to admit that when I first woke up and you were gone, the thought did kind of cross my mind. What else could I think?"

He resisted the urge to reach across the table and grab Erik's hands. Steve couldn't get over how incredibly handsome Erik looked. The soft

42

light of the restaurant softened his flawless features and his green eyes glimmered. He seemed to be melting into the surroundings.

"No more thinking," Erik said, smiling. "So, about going dancing…"

"I'll be off work in about fifteen minutes or so. This is, unless you're going to order dinner."

"No dinner," Erik replied chuckling. "I came in only to see you." He then winked at Steve. "Finish up what you need to do and we'll go out and kick up our heels. It is Saturday night, after all and I am ready for a little fun."

Steve skipped off with a big smile on his face. He couldn't wait to tell Jamie! It was too bad that he had already left. He would have liked for him to catch a glimpse of Erik.

While finishing his clean-up duties in the kitchen, he thought about Erik and what the night would have in store for them. He felt like he was going on a first date and was just about as nervous. He hurriedly wiped down the counters, filled the salad dressings and then dashed to the employee lounge where he changed clothes. He always brought a change of clothes with him to work as he could never bring himself to walk out the front door dressed in his waiter's uniform. He hated the damned outfit and certainly was not going to wear it anywhere but at the restaurant. Hopefully, soon he wouldn't have to wear the thing at all.

He threw on a t-shirt, an oversized gray wool sweater, a pair of black jeans and light brown construction boots. He checked his hair one more time in the mirror, splashed on a bit of cologne, tucked the t-shirt into his jeans and exited the lounge. He was about to walk through the kitchen into the dining room to join Erik when Jake, one of the other waiters, cornered him. His breath already reeked of stale beer.

"So what's the story with the hunk with the eyes on table 12?" Jake asked. "Everyone at the bar is talking about him. You two seemed mighty friendly. Do you know him?"

Steve was in a hurry to join Erik and didn't want to waste his time talking to Jake, especially about something that was none of his business. He didn't care too much for Jake and as far as he knew, most of his other coworkers didn't either. Jake was a vicious gossip and had, on more than one occasion, caused strife among the other employees due to his rumors. Steve himself had already engaged in more than few head-to-heads with Jake.

"Yes, I know him," Steve said reluctantly and tried to squeeze past. Jake blocked his path.

"Tell me more," he continued, evidently getting excited by the prospect of walking back to the bar and filling everyone's ears with juicy gossip. "Who is he?"

"Someone I know."

"What's his name?"

"Erik"

"Is he gay?"

"Yes."

"How long have you know him?"

"Awhile."

"Is he available?"

Steve smiled the sweetest smile he could muster up and looked at his annoying companion. "No, he's not available. At least not to anyone else. He's my lover."

Leaving Jake wide-eyed and open-mouthed, he brushed past him, and strolled into the dining room.

Before reaching the table, he glanced at the bar. Jake was already there, naturally, and was whispering excitingly to everyone. Steve almost giggled. Of course, this meant that he was going to have to face a deluge of questions on Tuesday when he came back to work. He wasn't going to worry about it now.

"Are you ready to go?" Steve asked, hoping they could escape before anyone questioned Steve in front of Erik. That could be disastrous.

"I am all set." Erik eyed Steve up and down, then broke into a smile. "You look nice, Steve." His voice was deep and sensual. For no apparent reason, Steve suddenly felt vulnerable.

"You sure picked a hell of a night to go out dancing," Steve responded, ignoring Erik's comment in an attempt to shake off this strange feeling. "You do know it's eighteen degrees below zero outside, don't you?"

It was true. The freeze which had all but immobilized the Chicago area for the last few days had reached its peak, as the mercury continued to dip down to unthinkable temperatures. Someone at work had mentioned earlier that Chicago city residents would see a penetrating thirty-two degrees below zero temperature before the night was over.

Erik stood up and laughed, buttoning up his coat. "No need to worry my chilly friend. I have my limousine and driver tonight to take us to wherever our hearts desire."

"Your limousine?" Steve asked, as they walked to the front door of the restaurant. "No way! You have got to be kidding!" He paused. "Aren't you?"

"I am quite serious," Erik replied, flashing a big grin. "I thought it would be a nice treat for us, especially on such a frigid night as this."

"But how did you know that I'd even be working tonight?"

"I took my chances," Erik said, opening the front door for Steve. Steve glanced over his shoulder to face the crowd at the bar and waved sweetly to Jake. He couldn't resist.

Sure enough, just as Erik promised, there in front of the restaurant was parked a black stretch limousine. This was not a typical limousine that one would rent for an evening at the prom but was luxurious and flashy, extending the length of at least three cars—the kind of vehicle one would expect to see parked in the Rockefeller's garage. In spite of himself, Steve gasped.

"This is really yours?"

"A weakness of mine, I must confess. I take pleasure in treating myself to an extravagant purchase from time to time."

"I'd call this a little more than an extravagant purchase. My idea of splurging is buying a new pair of boots every other year."

As they approached the monstrous vehicle, a tall chauffeur quickly got out and opened the back door for Erik and Steve, his head bowed down as if in reverence. Steve couldn't see his face very well but guessed that he must have been around his age.

Steve was already shivering from the arctic air as they got in and sat down in the back seat. To his delight, the inside was toasty warm. The fresh smell of new leather filled the limousine, an odor that Steve found to be rather erotic, and he inhaled deeply. Erik sat beside him and closed the door.

"So what do you think?" Erik asked. Even though it was dark inside the car, his eyes seemed to shine. "Approve?"

"This is fantastic!" Steve replied, still in awe. The window separating them from the chauffeur was completely darkened, as were the other windows of the limousine. It was also equipped with a full bar, a television set, stereo and a laptop computer. "I still can't believe that you actually own a limousine. This is just way too cool! I've never ridden in a limo before but I'm sure most of them aren't like this."

"I am glad that you are enjoying yourself," Erik whispered as he moved closer to Steve. His chilly hands grabbed the sides of Steve's face and Erik lowered his lips to his. They kissed deeply. Erik reached his arms around Steve, pulling Steve's body hard against his own as the kiss continued. Steve's head was whirling. The limousine came to a stop.

"Here we are," Erik said, releasing Steve from the embrace. "Time to get out and have some fun."

"But I was already having fun."

Erik tickled Steve's sides. "There shall be more of that later," he said mischievously. "I can assure you of that."

The back door opened and they got out. Steve felt like Cinderella on her way to the ball, waiting to meet her prince—although his prince was already right there on his arm. Music filled Steve's ears and he noticed they were in front of one of the most popular gay dance clubs in Chicago. It has been many years since he had gone out dancing—long before he met Jack. Jack hated dancing. Come to think of it, Jack hated most everything. Now when Steve did go out, he mainly frequented small, neighborhood bars. He was never much for crowds although he did miss dancing. Tonight, however, he was looking forward to being part of the excitement, especially with a man as stunning as Erik at his side.

Erik paid the cover charge and they entered the bar. Being Saturday night, the club was packed with attractive young men. An adrenaline rush filled Steve as the beat of the music pounded in his ears. Multi-colored lights flashed on the dance floor as the music roared and the crowd bunched together to move their bodies to the raging song. The disc jockey's voice echoed from the glass box above the dance floor, commanding everyone to dance, dance and dance some more. Around the dance floor stood a black guardrail about three feet high, all along which people were standing by themselves, trying to catch each other's eye or attempting to start a conversation with the person next to them. The small round tables spread spaciously throughout the bar were all filled. Past the dance floor was a dimly lit hallway leading to the back, which Steve guessed gave way to another bar. The disco was massive and Steve felt excitement fill his veins as his eyes and ears drank in the sensations.

Erik grabbed Steve's hand and drew him up to the crowded dance floor. While they danced, their eyes never unlocked and they smiled at each other sporadically. Slowly, a thick fog was released on the dance floor. It grew thicker and thicker until Steve could barely see Erik. It seemed as though Erik was melting into the fog and was becoming part of the heavy mist itself. Steve poured his soul into the music, feeling more pumped up than he had ever remembered experiencing. Even though Erik was now barely visible, Steve could still feel the strong connection between the two of them. Abruptly, the tempo of the music stopped, the lights dimmed, and the crowd on the dance floor began dissipating as a slow love song started to whine out of the oversized speakers. Erik stepped out of the fog and Steve suddenly felt his powerful arms encircle him and pull him close. Erik snuggled to Steve's neck, brushing it with light kisses as they danced. The feeling of Erik's cool lips sent a chill down Steve's spine. Steve pulled himself closer to Erik. Erik then lifted his head and crashed his lips down on Steve's. Their tongues met and the two men swirled slowly, embraced by the fog. The room seemed to be spinning and everyone else in the bar disappeared as Erik and Steve continued the dance, their lips locked together. Steve was oblivious to everything but the feeling of his new friend as their hungry mouths explored each other on the dance floor. Finally, the fog thinned. The music came to a gradual stop and the dimmed lights began to gain in brightness. Erik pulled his lips away. Everything started coming back into focus for Steve as he discovered that they were at a dead stop in the middle of the dance floor. The song was over.

Steve looked at Erik and murmured, "Wow."

Erik threw his head back and laughed. The lights once again flashed with energy as the pulse of the music accelerated.

"Come," he said. "Let us search out a cocktail and take a break from the dance floor."

Steve followed Erik off the dance floor into the mob, his head still swimming from what he had just experienced. They worked their way up to the bar. Each ordered a glass of red wine and stood side by side together, watching the crowd. Erik reached down until he found Steve's hand and coiled his fingers around Steve's. They held hands tightly, neither of them finding it necessary to utter a word. Steve moved closer to Erik so that their bodies were touching while still clinging tightly to Erik's hand. Unexpectedly, Steve heard a familiar voice from behind him.

Steve spun around, searching the crowd with his eyes. A few feet away from him stood Jamie, talking to a man considerably older than himself.

"It's my friend Jamie," Steve told Erik. "Jamie!" Steve yelled, waving his arms.

Steve caught Jamie's attention and to Steve's surprise, a disturbed, almost horrified look seemed to spread, just for a moment, over Jamie's face, as he recognized Steve. It quickly dissipated into a nervous smile. Jamie grabbed his companion's hand and started towards Steve and Erik.

Jamie reached them with what looked to Steve to be a fake smile plastered on his lips.

"Why as I live and breathe! If it isn't Steve Mitchell in the flesh! Actually out in the real world! Silly boy, you didn't even tell me you were going out to be coming *here* tonight."

Jamie looked at Erik, then shifted his eyes back to Steve, giving him a sly, knowing smile.

"It was as much a surprise to me as it is to you," Steve said. "I wasn't planning on coming here either." He looked at Erik and gave him a grin.. "You could say that it was a last minute decision."

Jamie turned his gaze back to Erik. "Aren't you going to introduce me to your friend?"

"Oh, sorry," Steve stuttered. "Jamie, this is Erik. Erik, my friend Jamie. We also work together."

"Ah—*Erik*," Jamie exclaimed, with a big smile. "The mystery man," and he extended his hand to Erik.

Steve's face flushed with embarrassment. Erik and Jamie's hands met, and a shocked looked came over Jamie's face as they made contact. After a swift shake, Jamie pulled his hand away quickly. "Damn, your hands are cold."

Steve, paying no attention to Jamie's comments, looked over at the man at Jamie's side. He was a short, stocky blond man who Steve had never seen before. He was about 5'6 but looked considerably taller due to his muscle-packed body. He possessed sharp, defined cheekbones, which Steve always found attractive, and a pronounced nose. From the size of his neck, arms and chest, it was obvious that this man spent a lot of time at the gym. He was attractive and masculine looking and Steve guessed that he must be fifteen, if not twenty years older than himself and Jamie. He looked out of place standing next to Jamie, whose lanky and effeminate body was in direct contrast to his partner's beefy frame. Steve shifted his attention back to Jamie.

"So Jamie, aren't you going to introduce us to *your* friend?"

Jamie blushed. "Oh sure, This is…um…" He looked desperately at his friend.

"Brock," the blond guy said. "Pleased to meet you."

The name fit him perfectly. As Steve and Brock shook hands, Jamie looked nervously around the bar. Steve guessed he was attempting to hide his discomfort at having forgotten Brock's name.

After the introductions were finished, Jamie turned his regard to Steve. "So Mr. Sleuth, have you solved the vampire case yet?"

Erik quickly glanced at Steve. Steve couldn't help but notice the unusual expression on his face. Erik's features had suddenly become very hard and serious—it almost resembled a look of fear.

"No, not yet," Steve answered, still studying Erik's face out of the corner of his eye. He then gave Jamie a quick tickle. "I haven't had much time to think about it since this afternoon. We worked all night, remember?"

"Vampire case?" asked Erik, eyeing Steve suspiciously. "To what vampire case might you be referring?"

"This afternoon, Jamie and I met for coffee and we talked about the murder that was in today's Chicago Tribune," Steve explained. "The one where the guy was found in the dumpster and had almost no blood left in his body. There have been several other ones just like it as well. The media has named the killer *The Vampire Murderer*." Steve looked at Jamie and grinned. "Jamie seems to think that it is a real vampire who is responsible."

"Now don't you go twisting around my words, Mr. Steven Mitchell," Jamie butted in. "You know very well that I never said that it was a real vampire. I only said that one should consider all the possibilities and be open-minded about the whole thing. I'm just saying that it's possible that the killer could be a real vampire."

"What a nice neck you have," Brock said in his best Transylvanian accent as he buried his head on Jamie's throat and began making exaggerated sucking and gurgling noises. Jamie giggled, trying to push the older man away but Brock held on tightly.

Finally able to release himself, Jamie glared at his partner. "Now I'm being serious Brock. Aren't you willing to accept that it's at least a possibility? I mean look at the evidence."

Brock shook his head. "I guess I haven't thought about it much but no, I don't believe it's even remotely possible. The whole thing was invented by Bram Stoker way back when—the early 1900's I think."

"In 1897," Jamie interrupted

"Okay, so in 1897. But it's nothing more than fiction, a story—the imagination of a writer. Besides, if I believed in vampires, I'd have to believe in werewolves, witches, zombies, ghosts, gnomes, hobbits and ghouls as well."

Steve leaned over to Erik and said softly, "We had this identical conversation this afternoon."

Erik paid no attention to Steve, as we watched Jamie and Brock with a spellbound interest.

Jamie glared at Steve, then turned back to Brock. "Ah, but that's where you're wrong. Dracula was not the invention of Stoker but was rather based on the life of an actual person, Vlad Tepes, more lovingly known as Vlad the Impaler. Stoker just took this ancient madman and gave him vampiric qualities. And the idea of the vampire wasn't from the author's imagination either. Stoker's concept of the vampire stemmed from centuries of old legends of bloodsuckers that rise from the grave and take the blood from the living. These are actual legends although they have not, as far as I know, been scientifically proven or disproven. But if you would happen to do any research on the subject, you would find that almost every country of the world has a legend of some sort of vampiric creature—Greece, Israel, Russia, just to name a few."

Brock crossed his arms. "Yes, but doesn't every country have stories about ghosts and zombies as well? Just because there are similar legends around doesn't mean that they are fact. People in nearly any country fear death. Out of this fear of something that we don't understand comes the ghost and vampire stories, perhaps to help us better deal with death or help us convince ourselves that death is not the end of our existence. With something as frightening and uncertain as death, it's not surprising that legends of immortal creatures would pop up."

"What do you think Erik?" Steve asked his partner with a grin on his face. "Do vampires exist? Could it have been a real vampire who committed the murders?"

"They might exist," he answered coldly, almost uncomfortably. "But if they do walk among us, neither you nor I shall ever know of it."

"What do you mean?" Jamie asked.

"If the legends are true that vampires can live for centuries and possess certain powers, then they would be certainly much too clever to be caught by mere mortals or even allow their existence to be known. Think of it. If your existence depended upon your invisibility, would you go around leaving drained bodies in dumpsters for the world to find? If it was a vampire who killed those people, it was indeed a very stupid vampire."

Steve laughed.

"Good point," Jamie responded, contemplating Erik's comments. "That could also explain why there's never been any documented cases of vampires. It makes sense that a creature who is several hundred years old would possess the cleverness not to allow itself to get caught and would have capabilities far beyond our comprehension."

"So then you admit then that it wasn't a vampire who killed those people?" Brock asked.

"Nothing of the kind," Jamie responded.

"Wait a second, Jamie," Steve said, "Now you just said…"

"I said that a vampire would be too smart to allow anyone to discover his secret. That's bearing in mind that he wants to keep his secret hidden. Maybe this vampire wishes to get caught."

"Why would a vampire want to get caught?" Steve asked.

Jamie shrugged his shoulders. "Tired of life? Who knows? Maybe he went insane. Or maybe the drained bodies are a message to someone—or something else. He might even be trying to make his presence known to another vampire."

"Enough of this Dracula talk," Brock said impatiently and grabbed Jamie's hand. "Let's go dance."

"Okay," Jamie agreed, hesitant to leave his companions. "Nice meeting you Erik." He turned and winked at Steve, as Brock dragged him off to dance.

"Likewise," Erik responded after they had left.

Steve and Erik stood alone for several minutes, neither of them saying a word as they watched the people around them. It was Erik who finally broke the silence.

"Steve, exactly what interest do you have in these murders?"

"It was a thought that I came up with this afternoon," Steve said. "I told you that I was interested in journalism. So, when Jamie and I were talking about the murders earlier today, I got the idea that I might investigate the case myself and see what I can come up with on my own. A high profile case like this would be the perfect kind to bust open—and provide me a story that could finally get me some notoriety. It could be the big break that I've been waiting for."

"I would not get involved," Erik said matter-of-factly, staring straight ahead.

"What do you mean?"

"From everything that the newspapers have revealed, this is extremely dangerous business. You could end up getting yourself killed. I would leave the solving of crimes to those who are trained in such matters. Why not just write a story about it when it is all over?" He had an air of quiet severity.

Steve looked at Erik for a moment, dumbfounded. "That's what journalism and investigative reporting is all about Erik. It's necessary to take risks from time to time. It goes with the job. I've been waiting a long time for something like this and like I said, who knows? If this could be my big break, I certainly have no intentions of passing it up."

Erik frowned, and wrenched his hands together. "I see at the moment there is no changing your mind."

His face softened. He reached over and grabbed both of Steve's hands. "I am only concerned for your safety, Steve. I just do not want anything to happen to you. Even though we have just met, I am starting to care about you very much."

Steve's body tensed up and his mouth went dry. Without responding, he took a step forward and wrapped his arms around Erik.

"Don't worry," he whispered while they were embracing. "I wouldn't put myself in any danger. I'm always careful."

Erik pulled away after a few moments. "The hour is getting late. What do you say we leave this place?"

Steve nodded. "I'm ready to go too." He rubbed Erik's side. "Would you like to come over to my place for sandwich or something?"

"I'd be delighted."

They retrieved their coats from the coat check and left the bar. Steve shivered the moment the outside door opened and he felt the blow of the cold air strike him. He smiled when he saw that the limousine was still parked outside.

Moments later, they arrived at Steve's apartment. After they got out of the car, the driver backed it into a parking place, turned off the lights and waited. Steve sighed with disappointment. It didn't look like Erik would be spending the night.

"What would you prefer—a cheeseburger or a grilled cheese?" Steve asked once they got inside.

"I am not particularly hungry," Erik answered. "But please go ahead and make something for yourself."

"Are you sure?"

Erik nodded. "I dined before I came to the restaurant."

Steve's stomach rumbled, as it had been doing for the past couple of hours.

Erik smiled. "Sounds like you need to fix yourself a sandwich though."

Steve blushed. "Damn, you have good hearing. You sure you don't mind?"

Erik nodded. "A man who is weak from hunger is not very entertaining."

Steve squeezed Erik's shoulder. "I guess not. I haven't eaten since lunch time so I am pretty ravenous."

Steve prepared himself a grilled cheese then munched it down quickly while Erik made small talk.

"I had a wonderful time tonight," Steve said after he swallowed down the last bite of his meal. "Although it's going to be worse than the Spanish Inquisition when Jamie gets a hold of me."

Erik creased his brow. "How so?"

"Remember I told you that Jamie and I met for lunch today?" Steve looked at the kitchen clock. "I guess it was actually yesterday. Anyway, I told Jamie about the wonderful man I had met the night before. Being the typical Jamie that he is, he drilled me for information about you." Steve took a gulp of his Pepsi. "He's taken it upon himself to watch out for me. Guess he likes playing the big brother role. I told him that you had left this morning before we had the chance to exchange phone numbers and that it was unlikely that we'd be seeing each other again.

So then we show up together at the bar. Jamie definitely is going to want some details."

Erik chuckled. "You two are close then?"

"Jamie is a good friend. We get together a few times a week for coffee, a movie or shopping. I met him when I first started working at the restaurant and we've been more or less inseparable ever since." Steve paused for a moment. "I've gone through some pretty rough times over the last couple of years, with the breakup with Jack and all, and Jamie has always been there for me. He's helped me out a lot."

"Your Jamie seems to be a very devoted companion."

"He is." Steve's eyes met Erik's. "He kind of reminds me of you in a way."

"Me?"

Steve nodded. "Yeah, secretive and mysterious. I can hardly ever get him to talk about his personal life. Like the guy that he was with tonight, this Brock character. He didn't even tell me he had a date. He's always rather vague about what he does after work."

"Everyone needs their privacy."

"I suppose you're right. But the funny thing is, he never lets me have mine." Steve smiled, picked up the dirty dishes and put them into the sink. "How about heading into the living room? I'm sure the couch would be more comfortable than these hard kitchen stools."

Erik followed him into the living room. Steve sat down on the couch and Erik slid in right beside him. Steve remembered last night and the first kiss they shared on this couch. Erik reached out and snatched Steve's hand. Steve was briefly startled once again by the coolness of his flesh. *This guy really must be cold-blooded. This is going to take some getting used to.*

Erik looked at Steve deeply, a somber look on his face.

"Steve, I want to once again apologize about last night. I did not intend to run off the way I did."

"I was wondering about that."

Erik looked down momentarily and turned his regard back to Steve. "I just want you to know how special last night was to me. And I am not just saying that to appease you. I mean it. I had a wonderful time with you and have been able to think of nothing else but you since then." He paused, squeezing both of Steve's hands. "I do not want you to have the wrong impression."

"After tonight, who could have the wrong impression?" He grinned. "You more than made it up to me. The most important thing is that you came back." Steve swallowed hard. "I would like to see a lot more of you. That is, if you don't mind."

A broad smile spread out on Erik's lips. "The same thought was on my mind as well."

Erik reached over, wrapped his arms around Steve and held him tightly. Steve hugged him back and slowly began nibbling on his muscular neck.

"Ummm...that feels good," Erik purred. "You certainly do have a way with men."

Steve snickered and stopped nibbling. "You're quite the charmer yourself," then continued kissing and licking Erik's neck. He ran his mouth slowly around the contours of Erik's throat, licked behind his ears and chewed lightly on them. Erik grabbed him by the face and pulled him away. Steve looked hurt for just a moment, until Eric's lips collided with his own.

"Erik," Steve said, breaking the kiss, "I am off from work tomorrow. How would you like to spend the day together? Maybe we could go to a museum or a movie. We could even stay in bed all day, for that matter." He gave Erik a wicked grin.

A peculiar look shadowed Erik's face. "I'd love to—except that I'm busy during the day. Business you know. It unfortunately occupies most of my free time during the daylight hours. I will be available tomorrow night though. I would love to see you then."

"Oh. Sure. That's fine." He frowned without realizing it.

"Please do not be upset." Erik said. There was a note of concern in his voice.

"I didn't mean to give you that impression. I guess I was hoping that we could spend the day together tomorrow. Tomorrow night will be great though. Come to think of it, I have some work of my own that I need to take care of tomorrow."

Erik took a deep breath, seeming to resemble a sigh of relief.

Steve reached over and squeezed Erik's knee. "I still know hardly anything about you."

"I assure you, we shall get to know each other in time," Erik answered. "Why rush things?"

Steve jerked back for just a moment, then lowered his eyes to meet Erik's. "It's almost as if you're avoiding the subject. You seem to be pretty good at that sort of thing."

Erik laughed. "I feel that the most satisfying part of a relationship, of meeting someone new, is getting to know them slowly—to learn more about them as time passes." He reached over and tousled Steve's hair. "If we both told each other all about ourselves the first night, we would have nothing to discuss during future encounters."

Steve forced a grin. "I guess so. It's just that I'd like to learn more about this handsome and mysterious man who so abruptly wandered into my life."

"I am not that mysterious, really." He lowered his voice. "Just cautious."

"I can relate to that," Steve said.

"Good. I am pleased we have an understanding," Erik replied. "For now, let us just enjoy each other's company."

His eyes penetrated Steve's. Steve felt that funny feeling again and shivered. All at once the long day was beginning to take its toll on Steve and he let out a wide yawn.

"I'm sorry," he said, covering his mouth a little too late. "I guess it's been a long day. It must be almost morning."

Erik bolted to an upright sitting position. "Whatever time is it?" he asked. Concern weighed heavily in his voice.

Steve squinted at the clock on the VCR. "It's a little past 5:00. Boy, the night sure flew by. I can't believe that…"

"I am sorry Steve, but I must be going," Erik said as he stood up abruptly. "It is getting late."

Steve was startled by Erik's sudden abrasiveness. "Oh. I was wondering if perhaps you'd like to spend the night? We could tell your chauffeur and I could set the alarm for what time you need to get up and…"

"That is impossible. Perhaps next time. I unfortunately must depart now." He started walking towards his coat.

"What about tonight?"

Erik stopped. "Tonight? Oh yes. How about 7:00?"

Steve creased his brow as he watched Erik. "Seven is fine. Would you like to come over? I could make us some dinner."

"Dinner would be lovely," Erik murmured absentmindedly as he put on his coat.

He walked over to Steve, seeming to drag his feet as he moved forward. He gave Steve a quick peck on the lips and headed for the door.

"Thank you for a wonderful time," he muttered, as the door was closing. He was gone.

Steve stood looking at the closed door, his mouth opened wide. He tried to figure out what in the hell had just happened. Erik practically had pushed him out of the way to fly out the door. He couldn't think of anything that he might have said that could have offended Erik. Had he pushed the getting to know you thing a little bit too hard? As he turned away from the door, he began to wonder if Erik would even show up tonight at all. There was now no doubt in his mind—Erik was definitely one strange cookie.

He threw himself back down on the couch. All at once a realization hit him and he shook his head and groaned.

"Shit! I still didn't get his phone number!"

On the street, Erik flew into the limousine. "Quick! Get us home!" he bellowed to the driver.

With a squeal, the car peeled out its parking place.

Home At Last

◆

It was almost 5:30 by the time they arrived home.

The black limousine pulled into the garage. Without saying a word to each other, the two men exited the vehicle and shuttled quickly towards the house.

"Cutting it a bit close, aren't you Erik?" the chauffeur asked as they moved along. "I was ready to start searching the apartment building for you."

Erik said nothing and continued rushing towards the house. He already noticed how heavy his legs felt and how each step he made became increasingly more difficult. Within a matter of minutes, it would be practically impossible to move any part of his body.

He had indeed cut it close this evening. He was usually so careful about this sort of thing. So cautious, so aware. What had happened tonight to cause him to become this careless? The boy. It was because of the boy. Erik found that Steve had the most unusual effect on him, quite a pleasant effect actually, something he did not recall experiencing before this. When he was with Steve, he sometimes, almost—forgot.

The chauffeur grabbed the doorknob and held the door open for Erik. Erik entered the house and sighed with relief as the door slammed behind them. He looked at the clock in the hallway. He had made it, with even some time to spare. He dragged himself to the living room, strutted over to his favorite chair and tossed himself into its soft cushions. He stretched out his legs.

The chauffeur took the chair next to him and stared at Erik. For a moment neither of them spoke. The ticking of the clock echoed loudly from the hallway. It was Erik who broke the silence.

"Say what is on your mind, Mitch."

"I'm sure you know what's on my mind."

"Naturally. But I would prefer if you would bring up the subject yourself."

"Very well. I don't mean to pry…"

"I am sure you do not."

Mitch cleared his throat, hesitated for a moment, then began again. "May I ask what is going on between you and that boy?"

"His name is Steve."

Mitch nodded although Erik didn't see him as he was looking straight ahead.

"I am not quite sure," Erik said.

Mitch looked confused. "I take it you didn't feed on him tonight then?"

Erik glared at Mitch for a long moment, then his face softened. "No, I did not." He wrung his hands together tightly. "Nor do I have any intentions of doing so."

"You're not going to feed on him?"

"No."

"You've been with him before tonight?"

"Yes."

"Did you feed on him then?"

"No."

"Oh. I see." Mitch looked at the floor, then moved his stare to Erik's still outstretched legs, then up to his face. "Erik?"

Erik sighed. "Yes Mitch?"

"I'm not sure that I understand."

Erik chuckled and turned his droopy eyes to Mitch. "I guess that makes two of us, my friend. I am feeling rather confused as of late myself."

Silence.

"Are you becoming romantically involved with him?"

Erik hesitated for a full minute before answering, appearing as though he were in deep thought. Finally, a long sigh escaped him.

"I believe so."

"I see," Mitch said again. An apprehensive frown grew on his face. "Do you think that's wise Erik? Don't you think that getting involved with a human could be dangerous?"

Erik swung his head around to face Mitch. His eyes burned red.

"No, it is not wise. Not in the least. And dangerous you ask? Damned right it could be dangerous. For myself as well as for him. But that is nothing new for me, is it Mitch? My entire existence reeks of danger. Danger is the essence of my being. Danger to anyone who unknowingly crosses my path. Every time I feed I expose myself to danger, the fear of being discovered and destroyed."

"I'm sorry Erik. I didn't mean to…"

"I know Mitch." Erik paused for a moment, then, "It is I who should apologize to you." He let out another long sigh. "You are entirely correct and have every right to be concerned. I am sure to you it seems as if I am making a mistake carrying on this way." He paused. "Perhaps I am making a grave error in getting involved with the boy but it is a chance I am willing to take. I feel a very strong attraction to this Steve Mitchell— something I have not felt since—before."

He laughed and looked at Mitch, smiling. "And just when I thought all of my emotions had shriveled up and died." The words became increasingly more difficult to get out and the weight of body was exhausting him.

Mitch tensed up, then glanced out the window at the gray sky which threatened to turn orange within minutes.

"Erik, it's time."

Erik nodded and without a word, rose and climbed the stairs. He trudged down the long hallway until he reached the door to his room. He let out a long sigh as he reached in his pants pocket, retrieved a ring of keys and unlocked the four locks on the door. He could feel the sleep coming on him quickly—too quickly. He was not ready for his night to end. He felt a tug at his chest as he thought about Steve. More than anything, he wished that he could have stayed with him, that he could have woken up in the boy's arms and watched the morning sunrise together. The morning. What an unusual notion. The morning had not been his for decades and he would never again know it nor be able to share it with anyone. But at least the night belonged to him.

He slowly undressed and looked around the windowless room. Drab as all hell, he thought. Morbid, actually. Especially with the coffin lying against the far wall. He looked at the object with disgust. The coffin wasn't necessary for his survival. Not being exposed to the deadly rays of the sun, however, was. It's just that—well, it was a tradition. Vampires were supposed to sleep in coffins after all. It is how he started out, and since Erik was a strong believer of tradition, he continued the practice throughout the years. Of course, the coffin did add an extra measure of safety as well, with a nearly impenetrable lock that he had placed on the inside.

Throwing on a baggy t-shirt and a pair of gray jogging pants, he dragged himself to the coffin and raised the lid. Another fun-filled day, he thought to himself and felt an unwelcome wave of depression drape him. He entered the coffin and closed the lid, lying there in total darkness. He had a few minutes yet before the dreaded coma would come.

His thoughts again drifted to Steve. Then Mitch's words rang in his ears. What exactly was he doing with the boy? He was falling in love with him, that's what—a human, whom until now he had mainly regarded as food and with whom he had avoided all but necessary contact. It was not always this way. Even after he changed, he found that he enjoyed the company of humans and learned much from them. But when one is a creature such as himself, it is nearly impossible to retain friendships. People just would not understand, not that he would ever willingly expose himself to anyone. For nearly seventy years, his secret has been safe and now for the first time, it was being threatened. He was endangering the boy's life as well as his own by allowing himself to get involved. How could he continue seeing Steve while hiding his true identity? It was obvious that if the relationship was to progress any further, he would eventually have to tell Steve the truth, tell him that his boyfriend is a vampire. It is not like being a vampire is something that one can simply hide and hope one's partner never finds out. Steve would begin asking questions sooner or later. They were starting already. Erik shuddered in his coffin at the thought of the day when the inevitable questions would arise. *How come I never see you during the day? What do you do during the day? Why can't we ever spend the night together?*

He would have to tell Steve the truth, before he discovered it on his own or started to put the pieces together for himself—which could very well turn out to be the case. Steve had, after all, said he wanted to investigate the "Vampire Murders." Who knows what he might come up with should he start digging.

All at once, a horrible thought crossed his mind. Depending on Steve's reaction, there is the possibility that he would have to kill him. Steve could panic and run right to the police at the news. But would they believe him? They might. Especially in light of the recent killings. Erik quickly tried to get the thought out of his mind. He could not bear the idea of having to kill Steve.

He stretched out and his body grew heavy. His eyelids fluttered as a tremendous, familiar darkness swept over him. Ah, peace had finally come, he thought and closed his eyes. The coma swept him off into oblivion.

The Investigation Begins

◆

Steve awoke the next morning to the sound of the phone ringing. He covered his head with his pillow, in the hopes that if he ignored it long enough, it would just go away.

No such luck.

"This better be good," he said gruffly into the phone.

"Uh-oh. I didn't wake you up, did I?"

"Jamie, this is getting to be a very bad habit of yours."

Jamie snickered into the phone. "If it wasn't for me, you'd sleep your life away. So stud, are you alone?"

Steve looked at the empty spot next to him, and remembered Erik's swift, if not rude departure the night before.

"Yeah, completely alone. Totally alone. You wouldn't believe how bloody alone I am. I am so alone that…"

"Uh-oh. Somebody does not sound too happy this morning. What happened to your mystery hunk?"

"He left."

"Hon, don't you know it's considered rude to boot out hunks in the middle of the night?"

"I didn't boot him out. He left entirely of his own free will."

"Maybe that's just his style."

"Maybe."

"I'll give you credit for one thing Steve—you have excellent taste in men! He certainly is a looker. And those eyes! A true dreeeeam!" Jamie voice squealed over the phone.

"Yeah, I guess he is pretty hot," Steve grumbled.

"You guess he's pretty hot? Come on dear, you're being so non-chalant about the whole thing. You don't get laid in years then all of a sudden you show up at the bar with a dream man on your arm that everyone at the bar would just die for!" Jamie giggled. "Leave it to Steve to hold out for the best."

Steve sighed. "I'm not so sure that he really is the best."

"That can't be disenchantment I hear? So soon? Why you've only been on a couple of dates. The honeymoon can't be over already."

Steve was becoming annoyed. "I just don't know if he's the right guy for me, that's all. I don't want to make the same mistake that I did last time with Jack."

"Oh, Jack again. When are you going to forget about that piece of shit once and for all?"

"Jack isn't the issue here."

"You brought him up, I didn't."

Steve said nothing.

"So then what exactly is the issue Steve? Why do you feel that this extraordinarily handsome man is not husband material?"

"I'm not really sure."

"Well, if you don't want him, feel free to send him over my way."

"Don't be an shithead, Jamie!"

"Okay, okay. I was just kidding. So what's up with him?"

Steve was still trying to wake up and grumbled something into the phone.

"I can't hear you Hon, you're mumbling again," Jamie said.

"Sorry, I was still sleeping when you called, as most people do early in the morning on their day off."

Jamie ignored Steve's sarcasm. "Late night, huh?" He had a sing-songy teasing tone to his voice.

"Not that kind of late night, if that's what you're getting at. We didn't sleep together. He left before I had a chance to seduce him."

"Sorry to hear that. Did you two have a snit or something?"

"No, nothing like that. It was really strange. One minute he was telling me how much he liked me. We were all cuddled up on the couch and the next thing I knew he was rushing out the door."

"For no reason? What were you talking about? Maybe you said something to piss him off—or scare him off."

"Nothing that I can think of. We were having a nice conversation. It really was the oddest thing. He just stormed out of here like he was late for an appointment."

"Maybe he had a rendezvous with another lover," Jamie teased.

"Don't be rude."

"There are people like that, you know. God knows, I've encountered plenty of them."

"I'm sure you have."

"What's that supposed to mean?"

"Nothing at all."

"I bet. Bitch!"

They both laughed into the phone.

"Seriously," Steve said, "I don't think that Erik is that way. He doesn't seem like the type to run out because he has another date. He seems very sincere."

Jamie sighed. "They all do at first."

"I'm trying to be serious Jamie."

"Any plans to see him again?"

"Tonight. I'm making dinner. At least I think he's coming over. We made the date as he was sprinting out the door."

"At least you made another date this time. That's a step in the right direction."

"Not much of one. Oh Jamie, I just don't know about him. He is the most exciting man I have ever met and he definitely has an air of mystery about him, which I'm not sure is good or bad. He's just so strange! There seems to be something about him that's not quite right."

"Knowing you Steve, I would guess that you're trying to find any excuse you can not to get involved with him. Every time a man shows the slightest interest in you, you hightail it out like your ass is on fire. So what if he's a bit strange? We all are. God knows you have your share of eccentricities. Shit, he's the one who should be nervous."

"Maybe you're right," Steve said. "Perhaps I am just looking for faults. I have to admit that I am starting to get involved with him and it's scaring me. I don't know. But there is something about him though."

"I'll say there's something about him. It's called hunkiness."

Steve laughed. "Hunkiness?"

Jamie snickered. "By the way, how did you hook up with him last night? I thought you didn't have his number or anything."

Steve told Jamie the story about how Erik just showed up at the restaurant out of the blue.

"And you're sure you never told him where you worked?" Jamie asked.

"I'm positive. I told him that I was a waiter but never told him where."

"You must have made quite an impression for him to hunt you down like that. How romantic!"

"Yeah, it is kind of romantic, isn't it?"

"I say go for it."

"You always say go for it."

Jamie laughed. "So what's on your gay agenda for today?"

"I haven't had a chance to think about it. Since I'm having Erik over for dinner, I'll have to run out and get some groceries. Other than that, nothing much."

"I have a few dollars that are just burning a hole in my pocket. What do you say we go do some shopping? Maybe you can finally get yourself that scarf you've been crabbing about ever since it got cold."

Steve looked at the sink full of dishes and the clutter that had built up just in the last day. No wonder Erik took off in such a rush. The place was a sty.

"I'm going to have to take a rain check. I've got to clean this place up and run some errands."

"Okay, suit yourself. Give me a jingle tomorrow and let me know how your date went."

"I'll do that."

"Oh Steve?"

"What?"

"If it's any consolation, I thought he was strange too."

✳ ✳ ✳

Steve spent the early part of the afternoon straightening up his apartment. He was feeling a little apprehensive about this evening and had no idea what to expect from Erik, especially after his abrupt departure the night before. Life was much simpler without men. As Jamie says, "Men—can't live with'em, can't live without 'em."

He had to admit that he was falling for Erik though probably a little too hard and too fast, in spite of his resolve to take things slowly. What the hell. Might as well just go with the flow and see what happens. If it doesn't work out, then it doesn't work out. No sense in dwelling on it. Steve knew by now that worrying about "what if" serves no useful purpose whatsoever. He was going to enjoy the time he gets to spend with Erik and keep things light. But it did feel good to be dating again, to honestly have something to look forward to.

He finished his household chores and glanced around. Everything looked fine. Now at least the place was presentable. Seeing as there were several hours yet before Erik was due, he decided that some fresh air might do him some good. It would clear his mind, if nothing else.

After bundling up for the deep-freeze outdoors, he left his apartment, stopping outside the door to pick up the newspaper. His eyes scanned the front page then he ruffled quickly through the rest of the paper. No new murders today. That's a relief. He threw the paper back down in front of his door then strode towards the elevator. As he walked, he recalled the conversation last night at the bar. Erik certainly didn't seem to like the topic of the vampire murders at all. There were some people who had no tolerance for anything having to do with the supernatural and perhaps Erik was one of them. It was probably best not to talk about it when he was around.

He did find the conversation last night interesting. Although Steve didn't quite agree with Jamie about the existence of vampires, Jamie was right about one thing—it was important to keep an open mind.

He giggled to himself when the image of Barnabas Collins, the friendly (and sometimes not so friendly) neighborhood vampire on the old daytime horror soap opera "Dark Shadows" popped into his mind. He had not thought of that show in years. When he was a kid, he would watch it faithfully every day at 4:00 to see what would happen that day to his hero. His mother, being an overly religious woman, did not approve at all of the daytime serial and did everything she could to discourage Steve from watching the show but her attempts were in vain. He and his mother would go around and around about it, arguing practically on a daily basis. She insisted that the show was something that children should not be watching and that being exposed to evil creatures such as vampires and werewolves would somehow harm him in the long run. Luckily for him, his father always stepped in. "Let the boy watch the show," he would say. "When I was a kid, I never missed a Dracula movie that was playing at a local theater and it hasn't affected me badly."

"That's *your* opinion," his mother would retort, and would walk away in her usual huff. That would be the end of the conversation—for the moment.

How Steve had loved that show! Every morning, he would dash to school to see his friend Raymond and the two boys would spend their entire recess period and lunch hour discussing the previous day's events on Dark Shadows and speculate as to what would happen on the next episode. That show was his first exposure to vampires and since then, he tried not to miss any new vampire movies that came out, not unlike his father. A regular chip off the old block, he was.

Thinking about vampires brought Steve's curiosity back to the surface as he remembered his plan of investigating the murders himself. But how and where to start? A thought then struck him—The Marlboro Man. He was a friend of Jack's—someone Jack had met through an acquaintance at work—but was still one hell of a nice guy. Steve and the Marlboro Man got along quite well whenever he would come to the house, which turned out to be relatively often, and they became quite good friends. Steve had not seen him since he and Jack broke up. It took Steve a minute to think of his real name—Jon Rickman, that was it. He was one of the few openly gay cops that Steve knew of and everyone else at the bars referred to him as The Marlboro Man. It didn't take too much to figure out where the nickname came from. Every time Steve saw him, he had a cigarette dangling from his lips, a Marlboro to be exact. Rickman was a young guy, only in his mid-twenties and was already a chain-smoker. From what Steve could recall, this man possessed not one effeminate bone in his body, another quality which perhaps helped contribute to his nickname. He was also quite attractive. Steve would pay him a visit.

Steve glanced at his watch. It was still early and he had plenty of time to get ready for tonight. With a relentless stride, he directed himself towards the Police Station in the hopes that Rickman would be on duty. He had no idea what the young officer's schedule was.

He entered the building and walked up to the front desk, and faced an overweight policeman with a beet-red face who was busily working on a stack of papers.

Steve cleared his throat. "Um…excuse me."

'Yeah?" the officer said without looking up, a hint of irritation in his voice. His nametag informed Steve that it was Officer Peale who he was addressing.

"Is Jon Rickman on duty?"

The chubby cop looked up at Steve. "Who wants to know?"

Steve felt to urge to simply say, "I do," but resisted. "Steve. Steve Mitchell. I'm a friend of his."

Officer Peale gave him a suspicious look, which Steve could have sworn was almost a look of disgust.

"Yeah, he's here Steve Steve Mitchell." Officer Peale turned around and yelled, rather loudly, towards the back room located behind the desk. "Hey Rickman! There's a Steve Steve Mitchell here to see you."

The entire office turned around to look at Steve.

What an asshole.

Within a minute, Rickman came stumbling from the back room, sans cigarette.

He flashed Steve a bright smile. "Holy Shit! Steve, my man! What a surprise! What in the hell brings you here?"

He was even better looking than Steve remembered. His curly black hair was longer than the last time Steve had seen him—almost shoulder length now. Unable to help himself, Steve glanced up and down at Rickman's body. At 6'3, he had a perfect physique. Being an undercover cop afforded Rickman the luxury of not being required to wear a police uniform. Rickman was dressed in a pair of skin-tight jeans, black pointy-toed cowboy boots with small chains wrapped around his ankles, and a green and black checkered flannel shirt, with the top three buttons undone, revealing rolling tufts of curly chest hair. He had his usual five o'clock shadow, making his sea-colored blue eyes stand out even more.

Steve looked over at Officer Peale who was glaring at the both of them, an obvious scowl on his face. Steve blushed, wondering if the cop noticed how he had checked out Rickman.

"Can we go somewhere where we can talk in private?" Steve asked.

Rickman followed Steve's gaze which led to Officer Peale, then glanced back at Steve, a wide grin plastered on his handsome face.

"Sure, come on in the back. How's Jack? Haven't seen him for a coon's age."

"We broke up awhile ago." Steve said.

"Gee, that's too bad. He was kind of a jerk though, if you don't mind my saying so."

Steve noticed that Rickman and Peale both gave each other a sneer as Steve followed Rickman past the desk.

"Not the friendliest fellow, is he?" Steve asked in a low voice once they had entered the back room."

"Peale? Nah, he's a bigoted jerk. He can't stand the fact that he has to work with a queer cop. Makes him crazy. Actually, he's an equal opportunity bigot. He doesn't just hate gays, he hates everyone. Just an all around prick." Rickman laughed. "Here, have a seat."

Steve looked at the cluttered desk then down to the chair at which Rickman was pointing. Like the desk, a huge stack of unpiled papers was strewn upon it.

"Oh, sorry," Rickman said. "Let me get those out of your way." He rushed over to the chair, bent over, picked up the assemblage of papers and threw it on the floor.

Steve sat down and moved the overflowing ashtray out of his way. Rickman reached in his shirt pocket, pulled out a cigarette and lit it up. Remembering his manners, he pulled out the entire pack and extended it to Steve.

"Cigarette?"

Steve shook his head. "No thanks. I quit over a year ago."

Rickman looked at the cigarette in his hand and sighed. "Yeah, I gotta get rid of the damn things myself one of these days before they kill me." He thrust the pack of Marlboros back into his pocket, then leaned over, placing his elbows on a small pile of papers in front of him.

"So my handsome friend, what's on your mind?" Rickman asked.

"I'm working on an article and was wondering if you could help me out."

"That's right. I almost forgot. You're a writer, aren't you? I saw your article in the Tribune a few months back on the gay bashing in Chicago. Great stuff! Think I even put it in one of my files. It certainly evoked a lot of strong letters from the public."

Steve smiled. He had sent in that article after months of painstaking research and was surprised when the newspaper agreed to run it. Unfortunately, he had published nothing since then.

"Thanks," Steve said. "I'm glad you noticed it. I had a lot of fun putting it together. If nothing else, it at least made the public aware that gay bashing is a real and serious problem not only in this city but around the country, with innocent people getting beaten or killed for no reason."

Rickman nodded. "And you'd be surprised how many victims of bashings never report them. Guess they are too afraid to come to the cops, especially when they have to deal with the sort of intolerance that our extremist friend Peale at the front desk exhibits." He paused, taking a deep puff off of his cigarette. "One of these days, they're going to get rid of that jerk, I swear. So what kind of article are you writing now?"

"It's about the vampire murders. I was wondering what you know about them."

Rickman nodded his head and laughed. "Vampire murders. You wouldn't believe how many crank calls we get about them. Damned media. They're the ones who coined the fucking phrase." He hesitated,

then blushed. "Whoops. No offense my friend—about the media comment I mean."

Steve laughed. "None taken. I don't really consider myself part of the
media anyway. Just a freelance writer. Please go on."

Rickman nodded in acknowledgment. "We get people calling here
night and day telling us that Count Dracula is living next door to them,
draining bodies and throwing them into dumpsters. One guy even
offered to send us over a truckload of crosses and wooden stakes with
which to arm the police force." He rolled his eyes and continued. "I've
also had plenty of calls from nuts claiming that they themselves are
vampires. All of this vampire crap is pretty embarrassing for most cops,
especially since we haven't nabbed the real nutcase yet."

"Do you have any suspects or leads?"

"Between you and me, not much. We've investigated some of the
gangs in town but they seem scared shitless themselves about the whole
thing, especially since the murderer seems to be targeting gang members and street hustlers. They all accuse their rivals but each gang is
equally frightened. I highly doubt that it was a gang related murder."

"How about the mob?" Steve asked.

Rickman shrugged his shoulders. "Can't tell you too much about
them. The majority of people still deny that the mob actually exists.
Even if by some miracle we were able to nail down some names of mob
members, it wouldn't be the easiest thing in the world to question them.
As you can well imagine, they wouldn't take too kindly to being interrogated by the police." Rickman looked down then creased his brow. "I
find it highly unlikely that the mob had anything to do with it either. I
can't see how small time gangs or gay hustlers would be a threat to
them. Their operation is of a much bigger proportion than that. The
mob is usually very clean and discreet about their killings. Draining the
blood from the victims and tossing them into dumpsters just isn't their
style."

"So as of yet you've found no correlation between the murder victims?"

"None except the obvious. They both hang out on the street, making them an easy target and are both considered by most to be underground societies. It could be some loony trying to clean up the streets of Chicago although draining the victim's blood certainly is an extreme way to do it."

Steve sat in silence, hands clasped. Then, "I wanted to ask you about that. The paper said the victims were drained of blood. Were they completely drained? Do you guys have any idea how it was done? Were their throats slit?"

Rickman's smile faded. He glanced around to ensure that there was nobody listening. "Okay Steve, this is just between you and me. Okay? This has to be off the record." He looked at Steve with widened eyes.

"You got it," Steve whispered excitedly.

"Just like the paper said, the bodies were drained. There was practically no blood left in them at all. What's so strange about this, is that the throats were not slit. They were ripped open."

"Ripped open?" Steve asked. A slight shudder ran up his back.

"Yup, wide open. It was like the victims were attacked by some sort of animal—a wolf or a tiger or something like that. The Coroner says the only explanation is that it was in fact some sort of wild animal as, according to him, only a set of fangs could have ripped open the throats like that. It definitely was not any kind of knife or razor sharp object."

Steve's eyes grew wide. "A wild animal on the streets of Chicago?"

Rickman shrugged his shoulders. "Yeah, I know. Kind of hard to swallow, isn't it? But there's more strangeness. If these people were really attacked by an animal like the Coroner says, they would have been covered in blood, right? Think about it. If blood gushed from their throats, their clothes should have been drenched. That was not the case though. There were only a couple of droplets of blood on the clothes. That's it. It's almost like the blood was sucked out of them. And not to mention that the bodies were tossed into a dumpster. I don't think any wild animal could have killed them, washed them off, changed their clothes then tossed them into a dumpster." He smiled.

Steve swallowed hard. He began to feel a wave of nausea sweep over him but luckily, was able to quickly suppress it.

"Could it be possible that the throats were ripped open after the blood had already been drained?"

"Not according to Mr. Coroner man," Rickman said. "He said the throats were positively ripped open when the victims were still alive." He narrowed his eyes then looked at Steve directly in the eyes, his face holding an expression of urgent seriousness. "But there's one more thing."

"What's that?"

He glanced around him, as if someone could have snuck into the office when they weren't looking. "You have to promise me you won't tell a soul. I mean nobody, Steve! This cannot get out."

"I promise. Whatever you say will be just between you and me."

"I believe you Steve." Rickman cleared his throat and reached for another cigarette. After lighting it, he inhaled deeply, blowing billows above his head. "The Coroner's office found some sort of strange saliva in the wounds. I'm not sure of all of the specifics, but I do know that they weren't able to identify the DNA in the saliva. What I mean is that it wasn't human saliva and they couldn't match it with any known animal. They've now sent it to some big time top-secret labs for testing and from what I've heard the results are the same. Nada."

Steve looked at him, afraid to speak. Unthinkingly, he crouched in his chair. "That's incredible," he said finally, shifting himself upright again. "A strange sort of saliva…"

"That's about all I can tell you about that."

Steve was afraid to ask the next question. "Jon, can I ask you something without you thinking that I'm crazy?"

Rickman wrinkled his brow. "I have an idea what you're going to ask. But go ahead."

Steve swallowed. "Do you think it's possible that a…a real vampire could have committed these crimes? I mean is the possibility being even remotely considered?"

Steve expected Rickman to either laugh at him or kick him out of the Police Station. Luckily, he did neither.

"When the papers first started calling the killings the Vampire Murders everyone made fun out of it, us included. Now I think there might be a little less joking going on. There are just too damned many unexplained things about this case." He paused, then smiled. "But a real vampire? Nah, I doubt that anyone is pursuing that angle. That's just too far out. Our main concern right now is to find out from what or from whom that saliva comes. And what the fuck it was that ripped open those throats."

"What do you personally think?"

"About the saliva?"

Steve shook his head. "No, about the possibility of a real vampire being involved." Steve felt silly asking such a question but he had to get it off of his chest.

Rickman raised his eyebrows. "I just don't know Steve. It's way too over the top to even contemplate. I'd like to say that it's possible. That would make the case a hell of a lot easier to solve. That way, at least we'd know what we are dealing with. But on the other hand, I don't even want to think that it's possible. You know what I mean?"

"I think so," Steve replied.

"I'm sure when the case is solved there will be a logical explanation."

"*If* the case is solved, that is," Steve muttered.

Rickman laughed. "I see you have a lot of faith in your Chicago PD."

Steve's face flushed red. "Sorry, I didn't mean to make it sound like that. What I meant was…"

"No need to explain," Rickman said, adding a soft chuckle. "I know what you meant. I was just giving you shit. But you're right. It is true that a lot of cases never do get solved. There's just not the manpower to handle them all." He paused. "I have a good feeling about this one though. Especially now that the big boys are involved."

"The big boys?"

"The Federal Bureau of Investigation, my friend. Affectionately known as the FBI. After the last body was found, they decided to step in—or maybe somebody asked them to help. Who in the hell knows? They haven't been too cooperative with us and keep pretty much to themselves. Of course, they have never had the reputation of collaborating very well with the local police. Probably think they're better than us lowly street cops. But that's another topic for another time."

Steve chuckled. "Wow. The FBI. Is it unusual for them to get involved in a case like this?"

"Not really, considering the nature of the killings. They ordinarily don't get involved in your everyday run of the mill murder cases. Usually it takes something like a serial killer for them to show any interest. Of course, all the far-out press that the murders have received could have played a part in it as well. The FBI loves the glory of being in the papers after successfully solving a case. After all the bad publicity they've had lately, they could use some positive coverage—and they know it."

Rickman shifted in his chair then glanced at his watch. Steve took ·this as a hint that the interview was coming to an end. Steve, in turn, looked at his own watch.

"Whoops," he said. "I have to get going. Jon, thanks a million for taking the time to help me out on this. I really appreciate everything you've told me."

Rickman flashed a big grin at Steve. "It was my pleasure. Glad I could be of assistance. But remember, the majority of what I said is just between you and me, right?"

"You bet," Steve said as he stood up. "Mum's the word."

Rickman rose, walked around the desk and gave Steve a friendly squeeze on the shoulder. "Next time, don't be such a stranger, hey? I wouldn't mind hearing from you every now and then." He hesitated for a moment. "Perhaps we could go out for coffee or dinner or something. Or maybe even get together for a nice neighborly game of cops and robbers?" Rickman winked and then reached down and gave Steve's ass a quick pinch.

Steve jumped in response to the unexpected tweak. "I'll keep in touch," he said blushing.

He is cute, Steve thought. If this thing with Erik doesn't work out, just maybe....

They once again strolled down the dimly lit hallway towards the main office. Officer Peale flashed them both the evil eye when they walked past the front desk. Steve happened to be looking at Rickman and noticed that he gave Officer Peale a wink as they walked past the desk. Steve giggled.

"He hates it when I do that," Rickman said, smiling. "What can I say? It's a weakness of mine—taunting bigots."

Steve noticed a blond officer sitting at a small desk looking at them curiously. It first struck Steve as peculiar that the cop was watching them so intently. Then Steve felt something else. He had met this guy before, he was sure of it. But where? He couldn't remember but there was no doubt in Steve's mind that their paths had crossed somewhere. Then it hit him. He looked a bit like Erik's chauffeur from last night, although Steve couldn't be sure, being that he didn't get a very good look at the driver and it was dark. But still—there seemed to be a strong resemblance. A cop moonlighting as a chauffeur?

"Hey Jon," Steve said softly as not to be overheard, "Do you know anything about that blond cop over there sitting at the desk on the right?"

Rickman glanced over. The blond looked away.

"Oh yeah," he answered, "Blondie. He's pretty hot, isn't he?"

Steve nodded. The blond was in fact quite cute. "I guess so. Do you know if by any chance he works as a chauffeur?"

"A chauffeur? You mean like a limousine type of chauffeur?"

"Yeah, exactly. He kind of looks like this chauffeur that I met."

Rickman shook his head. "I doubt it. He doesn't seem like the chauffeur type to me. He's new on the force, a rookie who just was hired on a few months back. A real quiet guy. I've been trying to figure out whether he's 'family' but haven't been able to peg him yet. He certainly isn't bad looking, that's for sure. Hell, I'd do him."

"It's probably not the same guy," Steve answered. "I only did see him once and it was dark."

Rickman flashed a wicked grin. "That sounds like a story that I'd like to hear sometime—a rendezvous in the dark with a chauffeur. You little devil, you!"

Steve laughed. "It wasn't anything like that! But I do agree with you about the cop, he is attractive. But then, I've always been partial to blonds."

Rickman sighed and ran his fingers through his black hair. "Guess I'll have to pay a visit to my hairdresser. I wonder what I would look like as a blond?"

Steve laughed. "Don't you dare! I don't think blond hair would suit you at all. You're hot just the way you are." Steve blushed moments after the words left his lips.

Rickman's face brightened, then he winked. "Thanks," he said. "Like I said, if you're ever up for a friendly game of…"

"Yeah, I know. Cops and Robbers. You never know. I just might take you up on that."

Steve glanced back at the blond cop. He was once again watching both of them. Upon noticing that Steve was looking at him, the cop quickly shifted his gaze. Steve turned back to Rickman.

"What's his name by the way?"

"Mitch."

Mitch didn't take his eyes off of them until Steve had left the Police Station.

Concern

◆

Darkness had arrived early in Chicago. By four-thirty in the afternoon, the city was already blanketed with deep blackness. This was a dreaded time of year for many—a time when the winter blues would settle in hard on those who rarely saw the daylight. One leaves for work when it's dark and returns home when it's dark. Such is the lifeless schedule of winter. It is during this time of year that the suicide rate is at its peak— the time of the year when people yearned to live in the Land of the Midnight Sun—or at the very least to see the bright orange ball in the sky occasionally. It was not unusual for weeks to pass by without the fireball so much as even making a guest appearance. But there were some who welcomed the wintertime. There were those who waited for and anticipated this time of the year. Wintertime meant fewer hours of daylight.

Shortly after the sun set, Erik came back to life. The daylong coma had slipped away and his eyelids fluttered a few times, then popped open as he took his first conscious breath of the night. Ah, the evening, he thought, as life slowly began to once again creep into his body. It has been 70 years since he had seen the light of the day, as it was impossible for anything to wake him from his daytime coma. It was when he was at his most vulnerable but at the same time, the safest. Not even the most seasoned physician would guess that there could be any life in the body of the apparent corpse. Erik's heartbeat slowed down to such an extent that it was virtually undetectable and his breaths were small and silent, each one spaced out several minutes apart. For all intents and purposes, Erik was dead during the day. There was only one thing that could shake the death sleep from him—the sunlight, with the result of any such contact being his immediate death. Fire would have the same effect but as far as Erik was concerned, they were one and the same.

Once fully recovered from his sleep, he undid the latch in his coffin and raised the heavy lid. He sat up and breathed deeply of the night air, rubbing his eyes. He got out of the coffin, walked downstairs and sat in his favorite chair. At least the hunger wasn't there. Thank goodness for that. He would be good for a couple of weeks yet—maybe longer, depending on how strong his willpower would be. When the hunger was strong within him, any living and breathing human being would be in immediate danger if he or she crossed Erik's path. He shuddered as he thought about Steve. Would he be able to control himself around Steve? Even though he was now fully satiated, he could smell the thick, young blood flowing through Steve's veins whenever he was with him. What would it be like when he was in the grips of the hunger, in all its force? Would he be able to resist? He would simply have to, wouldn't he?

He avoided feeding upon innocents—feeding all the way that is, although it has happened far more often than he would care to admit. He had never gotten emotionally close enough to a human when in the state of hunger to test his strength—his ability to resist. There was no doubt about it—he was getting close to Steve. He wasn't quite sure how it happened. He had fed the night he met Steve—and fed well. Too well. It was one of those unfortunate nights, for the young man involved, a night when he had gone *all the way*. Tears filled his eyes at the memory, the memory of what had occurred earlier that evening, the memory of a young man's death. He still could not understand what had occurred. He had not taken that much. Maybe a little over a pint. Perhaps two. He had been so careful, for so long. But the next thing he knew, the sleeping youth went into a spasm. His heart slowed to the point of near death. It would only be a matter of moments before life would leave the youth. A sad, unexpected reaction. As Erik could do nothing for the dying boy, he then drank his fill, draining him in between sobs.

After leaving the young man's apartment and disposing of the body, he had returned home to burn the clothes which he had been wearing during the feeding—the slaughter. There must never be any evidence around to remind himself of what he really was. He hated being what he was, a stalker of humans, a parasite in human form. He could never even bring himself to say the word or words, as there were several, to describe his condition and he forbade Mitch to ever mention any of them in his presence. So he had burnt the clothes and like almost every other time he had taken a human life, he began seriously entertaining the idea of terminating his own. It would be quite easy actually. A leisurely stroll down by Lake Michigan right about the time the sky first begins to turn pink would do the trick. He would feel the coma start to overtake him and would no doubt fall to the ground in a deep sleep— that is, until the first rays of the dreaded sun hit him. He was always curious as to what would happen next. Sunlight would destroy him, he knew that much, but would it kill him instantly? Would he wake up before he died? Would the coma leave him as he burst into flames? Perhaps he would just succumb to the coma and never feel or become aware of his own death. Then, there would be simply oblivion—the end of his tortured existence.

On the night of his last feeding, the thought of putting an end to his unnatural life dominated his thoughts. He had left the house—to think and to contemplate. How he ended up at the bar, he could not remember. Maybe a need for contact with people, people who now had nothing to fear from him. He had just only entered the establishment when he noticed the unsuspecting Steve Mitchell. There was something about the boy that immediately intrigued him, almost as if he was drawn to this boy. It might have been the way he walked or the way that he looked around at everyone. He was careful to avoid meeting anyone's eyes, yet curious to see who else was in the bar, his gaze holding a certain naiveté like a child on his first visit to the carnival. Erik knew that Steve had been attracted to him as well. He could sense it. Once when the boy had turned around to scan the bar, their eyes met briefly—actually slightly longer than briefly. Steve had stopped cold and held his stare. That was when Erik felt it—that something he had not felt for many years, although he could not put a name to it at the time. His remorse from his earlier adventure had nearly vanished from his consciousness and he had begun concentrating on the young man seated at the bar—the young man who had caused such a strange feeling to stir within him. Steve had been apparently concentrating on him as well as he noticed the boy stealing several glances at Erik in the mirror. Erik then did something he never would do unless he had intentions of feeding. He had walked up and talked to the boy.

Erik smiled at the memory. He was aware from the moment their eyes first locked together that there was something special about Steve. An innocent quality perhaps? He was not sure. He never really thought about innocence being attractive—especially to him. On the contrary, he usually looked for the complete opposite when out hunting. But he was not out hunting when he had met Steve. What was he out for that night? Planning his death? Saying good-bye to the humanity which had sustained his existence and letting them know that it will once again be safe for them to walk the streets at night? He did not know. The vision of Steve's youthful face and bright innocent eyes filled his thoughts. He had to admit it. He could not wait to see the boy again.

He heard the click of the seven locks on the front door being undone. Mitch had entered the house.

"Mitch?"

Erik didn't have to ask. He could smell that it was Mitch long before he had even reached the house.

"Hello Erik," Mitch sighed as he entered the sitting room. He sat on the chair opposite of where Erik was seated. Worry wore heavy on his face.

He could sense that Mitch had something to tell him.

"Are there any new developments?" Erik asked.

"No late breaking news in the case, if that's what you mean. The saliva results came in from the new lab though."

"And?"

"They are admitting that they are unable to recognize the strain of DNA. They say it's something that they've never run across before. From what they could tell, it seems to be an extremely disease resistant strain but have been unable to pinpoint what species of animal it belongs to. They are calling in specialists to investigate further."

Erik shuddered at the word "animal." "Do you have any idea what kind of specialists?"

Mitch shook his head "I'm guessing that it's most likely the FBI but I can't be sure. Those on the case are pretty tight-lipped about it." He paused shifting himself in his chair. "I have to say that I'm getting a little concerned though. I've heard people finally start whispering about the possibility of the supernatural in connection with the killings. They pretend they're joking but I can detect a serious undertone. I think that some of them are considering the possibility of a real..." He hesitated, cleared his throat, nodded and looked at Erik.

Erik sat silently, hands clasped in his lap. He creased this brow, then nodded. "Why do you think this is? Because of the unrecognized DNA?"

"I would guess that would play a big part in it. Maybe they're getting desperate. Who knows? The nature of the killings defeats any rational explanation. You can't blame them for starting to pursue these new routes. Everyone is frustrated and feeling defeated. But there's no need for real concern. I don't think they're quite ready to completely accept the premise of the supernatural—not yet, anyway.

Erik was silent. A troubled look settled in on his face. He looked over at Mitch who, upon meeting Erik's stare, shifted uncomfortably in his chair. Erik broke the glance. Neither said anything for several minutes.

It was Mitch who broke the silence.

"Erik? Can I ask you something?" His voice trembled as he spoke.

Erik's eyes narrowed as he moved his eyes toward Mitch. "Certainly you may."

"It's about the other night."

Erik looked perplexed. "And to which night in particular are you referring?"

"The night that you," Mitch swallowed before continuing, "went out alone. I assume you went all the way?"

Now it was Erik's turn to shift uncomfortably. "You know I never discuss such things with you. How dare you even ask me such a question?"

"I was here when you came home. I saw you. Your clothes were covered in blood."

Erik glared at him. "And your point is?"

Mitch cleared his throat and looked down. "I was just wondering, that's all. I wanted to make sure there was no chance that the police…"

"They won't," Erik said sharply. "The body was disposed of properly, if that's what you mean. It will not be traced back to me."

"Are you sure? I mean absolutely sure?"

Erik's face was hard as he stared at Mitch, then his glare softened. "I am always exceptionally careful." He turned away from Mitch. "There is no need for concern on your part. I just need you to keep an eye on the progress of the murder investigation and keep me informed about what they come up with.

Mitch was contemplatively silent for quite some time.

"There remains something else on your mind?" Erik asked, not looking at Mitch.

"Yes." Mitch took a deep breath to gather up his nerve and continued. "Another uncomfortable situation seems to have arisen."

Erik raised his eyebrows and looked over at his companion. "What do you mean?"

"Your new friend paid a visit to the police station today."

Erik's eyes grew wide. "Steve? Are you certain?"

Mitch nodded. "He came in to talk to one of the officers working on the case, Officer Rickman. They went to his office and were in there for quite some time."

"Do you have any idea what they discussed?" Erik's voice displayed the slightest tremor.

"I managed to sneak back and listen outside the door for a few minutes. From what I could hear, they were talking about the murders."

"You are positive of this?"

"I'm afraid so. It was difficult to hear everything that was being said, but I distinctly heard them discussing the case."

Erik was visibly shaken. So Steve had decided to take it upon himself to investigate the killings after all. Erik shuddered.

"What was said?" he asked.

"Rickman seemed pretty loose lipped with your friend. That's how I found out about the saliva. I also got the impression from their conversation that they know each other rather well, that they are friends."

"He is friends with a cop," Erik said in a monotone, staring straight ahead. "This is not at all good news." He began wringing his hands. His brow darkened with worry. "Did you hear anything else of interest?"

"That was about it. I had to be careful that nobody would see me so I didn't dare eavesdrop too long. But your friend did ask the cop one question that I found interesting."

"Well, what was it?" Erik said impatiently.

"He asked Rickman if he thought it was possible that the murders could have been committed by a real...vampire." Mitch swallowed the words, his voice quavering as he spoke.

Erik visibly tensed up at the word, the lines on his forehead protruding slightly. "And how did this Rickman respond?"

"He never gave a clear answer but I got the impression that he is not entirely discounting the possibility."

"I see," Erik muttered out loud, then quickly gathered himself back into the conversation. "I would like you to tell me everything you know about this Officer Rickman."

"I've never had any personal dealings with him. He's involved with the case, I know that much. To what extent, I'm not sure. He is also gay which explains how he might come to know your friend. I've heard the other cops making private jokes about Rickman and his penchant for young men. It doesn't seem to bother him in the least. He's very outgoing and one of those kind of people who doesn't give a shit about what anyone thinks about him or his sexuality. He can also be a little crass at times."

Erik chuckled at Mitch's description of the cop. "He sounds like a very intriguing person." Then a disturbing thought crossed his mind. "Did Steve see you?"

Mitch nodded. "I'm afraid so."

Erik placed his head in between his hands and groaned. He looked back up at Mitch. "Did he recognize you?"

Mitch could hear the tension in Erik's voice. "I'm not really sure. He glanced over at me a couple of times on his way out and I believe he and Rickman were talking about me. What was said, I couldn't tell you. It could have been good-natured cruising for all I know."

Erik said nothing, his head still buried in his hands.

"I don't think he got a good look at my face last night," Mitch continued. "I made certain of that."

"If he stops in again, you must make every effort not to get close to him and to avoid all eye contact. I do not want to take the risk of him recognizing you." Erik said coolly. "Damn it anyway!"

He rose from his chair, walked across the room and looked out the window. "Naturally, we shall have to avoid using the car for the time being. We simply cannot take any chances."

"Erik," Mitch asked cautiously. "I've never been one to meddle in your personal affairs and excuse me if I'm out of line, but I really don't think you should continue to see the boy."

Erik found it amusing that Mitch used the term "boy" as Steve and Mitch were about the same age.

"You are correct. You are out of line." Erik paused, still looking out the window. "But your opinion has been noted."

"But Erik," Mitch continued, "Don't you realize that you're risking exposure to yourself, especially now that he's involved with Rickman?"

Erik didn't like the sound of 'involved with Rickman' and a shade of jealousy passed over him, but just for a moment. He knew right then that he had intense feelings for Steve. It was time to tell Mitch the truth. He strode back to his chair and sat down, crossing his legs. He looked directly at Mitch. "I have decided that I want Steve for my mate."

"*What?*"

"It's been a long time since I have had feelings like this for anyone. I truly did not think it possible for me to feel anything anymore. But I have fallen in love with Steve and have decided that I want him." Erik lowered his head. "Being with someone that I love may make this existence a little more bearable."

"You're crazy!" Mitch couldn't help himself. "I can't believe you're actually considering this!"

Erik's eyes burned in anger. "How dare you talk to me in such a manner?" Erik blurted out, his hands shaking. "I have a right to have a mate just like anyone else."

His own temper flaring, Mitch said, "You're not thinking clearly! Do you realize what you are saying? Think about it Erik. He's a human being for God's sake! What kind of relationship could you possibly have with him, with you dashing off to your coffin every day minutes before the sun rises. And do you think he would understand when you tell him that you need to go out and drink the blood of his fellow humans? How do you know he would ever accept you for what you are? He might very well turn you into his friend at the police station or try to destroy you himself. Have you thought seriously about any of this?"

Erik, trying as best he could to stay calm, forced himself to speak in a soft voice. "Of course I have thought about it and I am willing to take that chance. I love him Mitch and my decision has been made. He is all I have been able to think about since we met. He loves me too."

"Has he said this?" Mitch asked.

"I can sense it. If he does in fact love me, he will be able—and willing to accept my state."

The words cut into Mitch like a sharp knife.

"Would you transform him?"

"Never! You know my feelings on that issue. I have never created another such as myself nor would I ever consider it. No, he would be my human mate."

"And just how do you think this will work? You are not as he, Erik, accept that fact. How can you expect him to accept being with a mate who is only alive a few hours every day? And what do you think will happen when he begins to age, and you do not? Will your love for him be just as strong then?"

"If all anyone ever did was dwell on the future and worry about what might happen or what could happen, our existence would be meaning-less. If there is one thing I have learned over the years, it is to live in the now and savor what life offers in the present. Whatever happens, I shall cherish every moment that I get to spend with Steve."

Mitch rose and walked over to where Erik was sitting. He knelt in front of him, placing his hands on Erik's knees.

"And what about me?"

"You?"

"Yes, me. Where do I fit into all of this?" Mitch said, eyes glaring at Erik.

Erik looked away. "I assure you I would never desert you, if that is what you are worried about. You will always have a place in my life, you know that. Your years of dedication mean everything to me. Anyone else coming into my life would have to understand that."

"But how do you think this whole situation makes me feel?" Mitch blurted out. His eyes dampened. "If you are so damn good at sensing things, then it should be clear to you how I feel. You know that I love you and have always loved you. I have given you every part of me and would do anything for you. What's more, I have unconditionally accepted you for what you are. Yet you turn your back on me and choose another human mate who doesn't even know what you are." By this time Mitch's cheeks burned red with anger. Without waiting for a response, he got up and walked back to the couch, hands trembling.

Erik was amazed at his own insensitivity. He knew that Mitch loved him and had done so ever since he had met Erik at the tender age of seventeen. It wasn't long after they met that Mitch confessed his feelings to Erik. Erik gently informed him that although he cared for Mitch immensely, the feelings he had for the youth were more paternal than those of a lover. After many long and tearful discussions, it was finally decided that they would remain friends and Mitch was welcome to stay with Erik for as long as he wished. Mitch took on the personal responsibility of protecting Erik during the day when he was most vulnerable to the world. It has been years since the subject was brought up. Obviously, Mitch's feelings had not dissipated.

Erik looked over at Mitch with a look of shock on his face. The shock then turned into a deep concern.

"Mitch, we had this discussion a long time ago and nothing has changed since then. I told you at the time how I feel for you. I love you deeply and care for you. I just do not love you in the way one would love a lifetime mate. You must understand that you mean the world to me and I cherish every year that we have spent together. But if it is as lover that you want to be with me, I must tell you that it simply cannot happen. I told you once that I want you to stay with me as long as you are willing and as long as you are happy being with me. If Steve or anyone else comes into my life, they will have to understand that you come as part of the package. Do you understand that?"

Mitch could no longer fend off the tears that he was so desperately trying to hide from Erik. He got up from the chair, walked around the room rearranging the plants which sat on a small card table near the window. His back was turned to Erik. "I understand all too well what you are saying. I just needed you to know how I feel. I too have enjoyed the years we have had but that doesn't change the fact that I do love you and have all along." He was silent for a moment then, "I just don't want to lose you. I am afraid for you."

"We shall not lose each other, I can assure you of that. I need you to deal with the fact that I love Steve and plan on doing everything in my power to gain his trust, in the hopes of building a relationship with him."

"And what if he's not willing?"

"I will deal with that if such a time would ever come," Erik said matter of factly.

Mitch turned around and walked towards Erik until he stood directly in front of where Erik was sitting.

"If he doesn't accept the fact that you are what you are, you do realize that there would remain only one option, don't you?" He hesitated and cleared his throat. "You would have to dispose of him."

Erik rose from the chair and roughly pushed Mitch out of the way. "I do not want to discuss that possibility." He then moved directly in front of Mitch, so close that Mitch could feel his hot breath on his neck.

Mitch took a couple of steps back, never losing eye contact.

"But you've got to face the reality of the situation. How many humans would react kindly to the fact that their lover is a vampire and lives off of human blood?" Mitch began to shake and moved a couple of more steps back. It was the second time that evening that he had said the word that was taboo in the house and feared he may have pushed his luck too far this time. But still Mitch stood firmly, hands still trembling at his side. His eyes locked with Erik's as he waited for the worst.

"I know damn well what I am!" Erik bellowed. "And I do not need you to remind me. I told you that I will deal with it if and when the time comes—and it will be dealt with in the most appropriate manner."

Daringly, Mitch said, "I just hope that if it is necessary to destroy him you will have the balls to do it."

Erik said nothing. All at once, there was an intense blast of air and the front door slammed shut. Mitch looked at where Erik had been standing a second before. The place was empty. The room was empty. Erik was gone.

He shuffled over to the couch and sat down, releasing a long sigh as his body made contact with the piece of furniture. He was still shaking and tried to calm himself down. He lied back until his head met the couch pillow and closed his eyes, praying that sleep would come.

The Stranger

◆

"God, I hate this fucking city," Neil said out loud as he ran a key across the side of a parked car. He loved the scraping sound that the key made as he raked it across the vehicle. Without even checking his handiwork, he continued keying the next car that was parked along the side of the empty street. What to do. His black motorcycle boots dragged on the pavement as he walked. He was bored tonight. Bored to fucking death. Where in the hell was everyone anyway? Usually some of the guys could be found hanging around looking for a little action. What in the hell was the point of being in a gang if nobody was around?

He continued walking, his key scraping against the few remaining cars. He was still groggy from the night before. A bad case of leftovers. He and his buddies had a major score the previous evening so they had spent most of the night hungrily partaking of the nose candy. The money was flowing in and it was a cause for celebration. It was great— all the money, the blow, his friends. But for Neil, there still was something missing. He needed something more. Perhaps it was that he was itching to kill again.

The first time he had killed it was purely accidental and had taken him completely by surprise. He had never thought of the possibility of actually taking somebody's life before. A nearby gang—major assholes—was poking around where they didn't belong. Stupid fuckers. They should have known better than to think that they could butt in on the action in Neil's territory. Not a very smart thing to do. For them that is. He and his boys finally hooked up with the daring intruders. If they weren't willing to leave his territory on their own then they would need to be *convinced* of the importance of staying on one's own turf. Invading someone else's domain was like stealing food from their kitchen table. And nobody likes to have their dinner taken away from them.

They had been effective in communicating to the other gang that their territory was not to be messed with. The war was quick and effective, lasting only a few minutes. Nobody had guns at the time as both gangs were completely thrown off guard by the presence of the other. A battle ensued—the good old fashioned kind where flesh meets flesh. The fists flew. While pummeling the face of one kid, another had jumped on Neil's back trying to pull him off. A grave mistake on his part. It was at that point when Neil reached inside the pocket of his too tight Levi's and produced his trusty virgin switchblade, his pride and joy. Before the kid could react, Neil had plunged it into his soft belly. It sunk in like a spoon in a dish of Jell-O.

Neil took a step back. The first noticeable effect of the stabbing was the bright red blood dripping off the blade of the knife. Very nice. Just the sight of it released adrenaline throughout his body. He looked at the kid clutching his stomach and groaning in pain. Neil couldn't help but smile. Poor kid. He obviously wasn't participating in Neil's high. Ah, what the hell, Neil had thought and walked over to the kid, got down on his knees, and plunged the knife four more times into the wounded boy, this time in his chest. Within moments, the kid lay on the street, dead, blood pouring out of his young body, staining the concrete as it flowed. Neil stepped back in amazement, and stared as if he were an artist studying a painting. He hadn't known that blood darkened so quickly. His adrenaline rush continued for several more moments. If only he had known before that killing someone would feel so damned good! Shit, it even gave him wood. The power he all at once felt was like an aphrodisiac. He glanced over at the numerous bodies strewn in the street, many members of his own gang. He stepped back from his kill, still in a daze. He then heard the gang leader yell, in response to approaching sirens, "Let's get the fuck out of here!"

Since then, he had killed several times, and each time it gave him more and more pleasure. Sometimes he would actually crave the feeling of his switchblade entering the body of some unsuspecting enemy. He always loved the look on their face as the knife made its first plunge into their flesh. He once admitted to one of his gang members that killing often made his dick hard. The guy had looked at him with such a mixture of astonishment and horror, that from then on, Neil kept his lust for killing to himself. It was obvious that the others just wouldn't understand. It would have to be his own little secret.

He moved up rapidly in the ranks of his gang, mainly due to his sheer courageousness which he had demonstrated time and time again. If there was a battle to be fought, Neil was always ready to dive in head first, switchblade bared to take on any offending gang. His gang leader showed the utmost respect for Neil and often used him as an example as how the others "should be." This pleased Neil enormously as he had never been shown any respect or encouragement in the other aspects of his life. His parents didn't give a flying fuck about him, that he knew. Especially his old man. Neil hadn't seen or heard from him in years. Shit, the bastard never even called him on Christmas or his birthday. As far as Neil was concerned, that was just fine with him. And then there was his mother, the bitch whore. She was too busy screwing her ever growing number of trashy boyfriends to even care what her kid was doing. Sometimes as much as an entire week would pass by without him seeing her at all. It was nice not to have the old lady breathing down his neck anyway. When he quit school at sixteen, she really didn't show too much concern. None for that matter. She had never once asked him about school or even shown the least bit of interest in what he was learning so why in the hell should she care if he quit? When she did find out, all she told him was that he would now have to get his lazy ass out on the street and find a job because she wasn't about to support a no-good-for-nothing bum living under her roof. Or something like that.

He had done just that. He found a job and it was a great job. Shit, he made more money than the bitch whore would ever see in her entire lifetime. Working with the gang was more lucrative then he had ever imagined it could be. Of course, he could never let the bitch whore know how much he was making or where it was coming from. It was none of her fucking business. Being the righteous bitch she was, she probably would go to the cops if she found out what he was doing. Anything to get him out of her hair once and for all. As if he'd give her that satisfaction.

He hadn't heard from any of his buddies yet today and frankly it was starting to piss him off. His head still pounded from all the blow he snorted last night. He could really go for some more tonight. It might at least ease his boredom. He crossed the street and headed over to their usual hangout. Nobody was there. Everyone must still be fucked up from last night. Actually it was more like this morning. He vaguely remembered stumbling in sometime after 8:00 a.m. A headache was still a small price to pay for all the fun he had. It would have been more fun if they could have tangled with a rival gang or something. It had been several weeks since their last fight and he was just about due for a good one.

He glanced around. The streets were completely deserted except for a few randomly parked cars here and there. He keyed a few more cars, then put his key back into his pocket. He was bored with this already. He kept walking, hoping that something interesting would cross his path or that he would run into some of the guys.

"Fuck everyone!" he yelled out loud, just to break the silence.

All at once he caught sight of a tall young man walking ahead of him. He was very well dressed, wearing some sort of a suit and walked slowly. Too slowly. It was almost as if he wanted Neil to catch up to him. What in the hell was a businessman doing in this neighborhood? From the looks of him, Neil guessed that he probably had a bit of dough on him. Maybe the night wouldn't be a waste after all. A lost businessman. Yeah, this was gonna be fun. Neil would have to teach this sad fuck that he shouldn't go into areas of the city that he wasn't familiar with.

The man turned into an alley, which Neil knew was a dead end. The man stopped and turned around with a look of confusion and saw Neil staring at him, arms crossed.

"Oh, hello." The man glanced around again and scratched the top of his head. "Oh dear, I must have taken a wrong turn somewhere. Could you tell me which way it is to Michigan Avenue?"

Neil laughed. "Man, you are in the wrong fucking neighborhood. You're not going to find Michigan Avenue anywhere around here." He reached into his pocket and wrapped his fingers around the cool switchblade.

"I guess I must be lost. I have no idea how I ended up here. If you would be so kind, could you please point me in the right direction? At least I will know which way to start walking."

Damn, this guy is dumb. Here he was in the worst side of town, standing in an alley with a stranger and he didn't even seem to be the slightest bit nervous. Neil would have to put a stop to that.

"How much money do you have mister?" Neil asked. His heart was beginning to pound with excitement.

The man looked as if he didn't understand the question.

"I beg your pardon?"

"I said how much fucking money do you have!"

The man nonchalantly shrugged his shoulders. "On me? On my person, you mean? Several thousand I would guess. I have not counted it recently. Why do you ask?"

Neil laughed out loud. It was definitely confirmed. This guy was dumber than a load of bricks. Could anyone really be this stupid?

He placed his hands on his hips and glared at the stranger. "Because I want it, that's why!"

The guy studied Neil for a moment, a dumb perplexed look on his face. "Oh, I do not think that…"

"I don't care what you fucking think, man! Hand over the dough."

Neil pulled out the knife. It made a menacing *click* as he pressed the small button on the side. The blade, still stained with dried blood from the last stabbing, pointed threateningly at the man.

The stranger didn't move and still didn't appear to be the least distressed by his situation.

"I am terribly sorry young man, but I suggest you obtain your own money. You will appreciate it so much more if you earn it yourself. My father always told me that. Now, as for those directions to Michigan Avenue."

"Jesus Christ, you are a dumb fuck, you know that?" Neil screamed. "Maybe you just don't get it. You see, if you don't hand over the money, I'm gonna fucking slit you wide open. You hear me?"

Neil planned on killing him anyway but couldn't let the man know that. It's always fun to play with them first—to see the fear fill their eyes. This guy was ruining it though. He didn't seem the least bit afraid. Neil couldn't understand it. There was something strange about this man. It was his eyes. They had a profoundness to them, a deepness, which caused the skin on Neil's neck to prick up.

The man squinted his eyes as he looked at Neil.

"I do not think so," he said matter of factly and began approaching Neil, as if he simply intended to walk around him and be on his merry way.

This is it. Time for the dumb bastard to die. As the man came closer, Neil raised his knife and brought it down quickly, aiming for the man's chest. Just as the bloodstained blade was about to make contact with the man's chest, Neil felt a hand tightly gripping his wrist. The grip was vice-like.

"What the…"

"You stupid little idiot!" the man said, and with a strength Neil had never before encountered, heaved the boy right over the man's head back into the alley.

Neil found himself sprawled on the ground. The pain in his back was searing. He moved his arms and legs. No broken bones that he could notice. He shook his head to clear his thoughts. What in the hell happened? How could this guy have thrown him like that, as if he were a paper airplane? Neil was more pissed off than ever. Where was his knife? As he glanced around desperately, his eyes locked with those of the stranger.

"Are you looking for this?" the man said, a terrifying grin plastered on his pale face. He tossed the knife over to Neil. "Here is your little plaything. It is of no interest to me."

The knife landed a couple of feet from Neil. He moved as quickly as he could to retrieve it but before he could even take a couple of steps, the man was there, holding Neil several feet in the air by the front of his t-shirt. "Who in the fuck are you?" Neil asked, in between gasps of breath. "What in the fuck are you?"

"Your death, my young hoodlum."

The man then parted his lips. To Neil's horror, two pointy white fangs began slowly protruding from the man's mouth.

Neil screamed.

"Whatever could be wrong my little one? You do not want my money anymore?"

"Please, please let me go. I'm…I'm…sorry mister. I didn't mean to. Really."

Neil wished more than anything he had his knife right now. The man grabbed onto his shirt even tighter and pressed him against the hard brick wall.

"Hindsight is 20/20. That is how the modern expression goes, does it not?"

The man lowered the fang filled mouth to Neil's throat.

"It is unfortunate that we all learn things too late," he said in almost a whisper.

As the man's mouth met the skin, Neil felt a sudden sharp stab of pain. The fangs sunk easily into the soft throat. Neil's warm blood filled the man's mouth. The man drank deeply, locking his entire mouth over the wound, then sucking with great force, like a newborn baby nursing from its mother. As Neil's life fluid slowly left his body, his struggle became weaker and weaker. He finally stopped kicking and a blank, glazed look crossed over his face.

The man removed his teeth from the throat, leaving a several inch long gash where this mouth had been. He threw the empty body onto the ground and began wiping his blood-smeared face with his shirt-sleeve. As usual, he was covered in blood. The first puncture always made such a mess. Very tasty, though. Quite full-bodied.

He glanced around and noticed a bright green dumpster at the end of the alley. He breathed a sigh of relief. No sense in breaking tradition now.

He bent over and effortlessly picked up the young corpse at his feet. With one hand, he tossed the corpse into the dumpster, then peered in to look at the dead boy lying amongst the trash. He smiled.

"You really are a dumb fuck, you know that?" he said, threw his head back and laughed.

He covered up the dead boy with garbage and closed the lid. Under normal circumstances, he would never discard a victim in such a manner, where the body was sure to be discovered the next morning. But these were not normal circumstances and he had his reasons.

He took a few steps away from the dumpster. He felt wonderful as the boy's fresh blood coursed through his veins. The exhilaration and strength he suddenly felt, though it was the same after every kill, beggared description.

He ran his tongue across his fangs and smiled. "It's almost time to look up an old friend," he said out loud.

In a flash, he was gone.

The lone bloodstained switchblade lie on the ground, its blade pointing towards the dumpster.

A Theory Confirmed

◆

"So how did dinner go the other night?" Jamie asked, unlacing his sneakers and kicking them off.

"Not bad," Steve said. "I made my infamous lasagna."

"Oooh, I love your lasagna. I remember you make it that really weird way—with the hard boiled egg in it. Don't get me wrong, it's really good like that." Jamie smiled. "I have to admit though, that the first time you made it for me I thought it was a bit odd."

"It's my grandmother's recipe. I figured that for dinner, I was going to play it safe and make something that I knew I wouldn't fuck up since I've made the lasagna hundreds of times. I didn't even burn the garlic bread this time."

Jamie laughed. "So have you two picked out a china pattern yet?"

"For your information, we aren't even near that point yet. We're still working on the wedding invitations, for crying out loud."

They both giggled. Jamie reached for the ashtray that was on the floor but just barely out of his reach and made a grunting noise as he stretched his body to grasp it. They were both sprawled out on the living room floor in stocking feet, drinking ice tea which Steve had prepared earlier. They had decided to get together at Steve's apartment before work and just hang out, as they had both put in a lot of hours at work lately.

"So what exactly is up with you and Erik?" Jamie asked, stirring his ice tea just to hear the clanking of the ice cubes on the edge of the glass. "Are you two officially an item?"

Steve shrugged his shoulders. "Who in the hell knows? I like Erik a lot but he is so strange. I might be wrong, but I get the distinct impression that he's hiding something. He also does things that are out of the ordinary, things that I don't understand.

"Like what?"

"He still has not spent the entire night with me for instance. He waits until I fall asleep and then takes off. I have yet to wake up in the morning and find Erik still here. And if we do stay awake, he always ends up leaving in a rush. There's a sense of urgency about his insistence on leaving. Now what could be that important at 5:00 in the morning?"

"Got me on that one." Jamie sighed. "Have you ever come right out and asked him?"

Steve frowned. "I guess not. I figured until now that it was none of my business but now that we're getting more serious, I think it's time to start making it my business. What kind of long-term relationship could I have with a guy who won't even sleep over?"

"So now we're talking long-term relationship?" Jamie said, in a teasing tone of voice. "I never thought I'd see the day when my once celibate friend would be walking down the wedding aisle."

Steve blushed. "I'm talking about possibilities, that's all. Who knows where this could lead?"

Jamie flashed Steve a big smile. "I am quite happy to see you dating again. But just be careful, okay? I don't want to see you getting hurt again. There are a lot of creeps out there, as you know from experience. I'm not saying that Erik is one of them. I'm just suggesting you keep your guard up a bit until you get to know this guy a little bit better."

Steve said nothing as he drifted into deep thought. His meditation was interrupted by the sound of the phone ringing. He jumped up and ran to the phone, hoping that it would be Erik at the other end. Instead, Steve was greeted by a deep, yet familiar voice on the other end.

"Steve?"

"Yes?"

"How are you doing super hunk? You didn't think I'd forget about you, did ya?"

It took a moment for Steve to recognize the voice as that of the Marlboro Man.

"Jon!"

"I told you that I'd be hooking up with you. I was wondering if you'd have some time today to get together. Maybe grab a cup of coffee?"

Steve hesitated. "I do have to work this afternoon but I have some time before that."

"Great! Can you meet me, say in about a half an hour, at the Melrose?"

"Sure. All I need to do is throw on a coat and I'm off," Steve said.

"You might want to bring your notepad with you."

"My notepad?"

Rickman cleared his throat on the other end of the phone. "I have some more information. I can't talk about it now. I'll fill you in when we meet."

"I'll be there in a flash." Steve hung up the phone and smiled.

"Okay Mister, now who is this Jon?" Jamie asked, looking at Steve intently. "And just how many men are you seeing?"

Steve grinned and walked back over to where Jamie was sprawled out. "The Marlboro Man." He had already told Jamie about his conversation with Rickman a few days back. "He wants me to meet him for coffee—says he has some more information about the vampire murders."

"So you're still pursuing your Nobel Prize winning article?"

Steve grabbed a pillow off the couch and flung it at Jamie. It missed him but landed right in the ashtray. Ashes and cigarette butts went everywhere.

"Now look what you've done!" Jamie squealed, laughing. "You made the mess, you have to clean it up."

Steve ignored his comment. "As a matter of fact, Mr. Smartass, I am still pursuing the story. Ever since I started doing this, I feel at least like I have some purpose in life. Remember dear, I didn't go to college so I could spend the rest of my life as a waiter."

"Why not? A waiter is a perfectly noble profession. Sheesh...that certainly says a lot about me."

"It has nothing to do with you. It's just not for me." Steve said flatly.

"Oh, I see. So you're better than everyone else."

Steve threatened him with another pillow. "Don't be funny Jamie."

Jamie got up, brushing the ashes off of his t-shirt. "How is the case coming along, by the way?"

Steve had mentioned his visit to the Police Station only briefly to Jamie.

"Not too well, I'm afraid. There hasn't been anything new since the last time I talked to you and as far as I know, there haven't been any new murders, which is a good thing, I suppose." He plopped himself down on the couch. Jamie followed. "By the way, did you happen to see the article in the Enquirer? 'Ancient Vampire continues to stalk the streets of Chicago.' It was hysterical."

Jamie shook his head. "I missed that one. Leave it to the Enquirer."

Steve stood up. "I don't mean to be rude, but I have to go meet the Marlboro Man. I'm just dying to find out what he has to say. You can hang out if you want. I shouldn't be too long. That way we can walk to work together."

Jamie stretched his arms and yawned. "I just might take a nap anyway. Have fun and don't do anything that I wouldn't do. From what I hear, the Marlboro Man is quite a stud."

"I have no interest in him except as a friend," Steve said as he put on his coat and hat. "He is cute though. I wonder if Erik would get jealous."

Jamie giggled. "Maybe if you got him jealous, he'd be more willing to stay the entire night with you instead of dashing off."

"I don't think I'm going to push my luck on that one." Then, in an afterthought, "I sure hope that I didn't give Jon the wrong impression the other day."

"The wrong impression? What exactly went on that day between you two?"

Steve smiled at his friend. "Nothing really. He just flirted a little bit with me and I guess I kind of flirted back."

"You guess?" Jamie shook his head, then looked up at the ceiling. "Uh-oh. I smell trouble brewing on the horizon."

* * *

The bright sunlight caused Steve to squint as he left the apartment building. What a great sight! Everything was finally melting. The nasty cold snap had finally come to an end. Being only February, he knew that the end of winter was still a long way off and there was bound to be more cold weather ahead but it was nice to get a little break from it nonetheless. Nothing quite like a January thaw in February to lift one's spirits. The streets were bustling with people, many of them wearing light coats rather than the massive bulky ones he had gotten used to seeing. There were even a few brave souls wearing no coat at all. Steve shook his head in disbelief. One day above freezing and people start thinking it's summer. It was warmer, but definitely not warm enough to go without a coat.

Rickman was already there when Steve arrived. He smiled when he saw Steve and beckoned him over. He had a cigarette in his hand and there were already three butts in the ashtray. He had chosen a seat in the back of the restaurant where it was relatively quiet. It also just so happened to be the smoking section.

"Steve, my man," Rickman said as Steve approached the table. "Glad you were able to come. Nice to see you, as always. How about this weather? Bitchin, huh?"

Steve threw his coat and hat in the booth against the wall and sat down. "I didn't realize how warm it actually was out here today. Sure am glad the cold is finally over"

Rickman laughed. "Don't get too used to it buddy. I'm sure that Old Man Winter will be rearing his ugly head again in no time at all."

A waitress appeared a few moments later and Steve ordered a cup of coffee. Rickman crushed out his cigarette before the waitress grabbed his ashtray and immediately reached in his pocket to pull out another one. She was back within moments with a clean ashtray and Steve's cup of coffee. The smell of the coffee made Steve think of those Maxwell house commercials in which a handsome guy in a flannel shirt was brewing a fresh cup of coffee in a mountain cabin somewhere. Or maybe it was Rickman that made him think of that. Steve inhaled the aroma of the coffee before cooling it off with milk. He wondered if Erik liked coffee.

Steve looked over at Rickman after placing his spoon on the table. "So Jon, what's up?"

Rickman smiled a toothy grin. "I just wanted to take another look at that incredibly handsome face of yours."

Steve blushed. "I bet you say that to all the boys. If fact, knowing you, you probably do."

"Actually, you're right. I do." Rickman said, and then laughed so hard that he ended up coughing.

Steve tried to sip his coffee but it was still too hot to drink. He poured some more milk into it, and stirred. "You mentioned that you had some news for me?"

Rickman nodded. "The last time we spoke, you were inquiring about the dumpster murders. Are you still interested in that?"

Steve nodded. "I haven't come up with too much. Nobody seems to know anything and the murderer has been quiet lately—or at least the newspapers haven't mentioned anything. The National Enquirer seems to think that there's a vampire on the loose in Chicago."

A grim look passed over Rickman's face. He looked around the restaurant then his gaze slowly returned to Steve. Then, under his breath, "That may very well be the case."

Steve dropped his spoon.

"I beg your pardon?"

Rickman wiped his brow with his hand. "There's been another murder. Yesterday morning, a young kid was found in a dumpster on the West Side. Same thing as the others. His throat was ripped out and he was almost drained of blood."

"You're kidding! I checked the paper and didn't notice any mention of a new murder."

"The body was found late yesterday morning. The papers just had a small article about it. You see, the police department is trying to pass this one off as a gang related murder. The kid was a well-known member of one of the gangs and a pretty vicious little fuck too, from what I hear. With the media running amuck with this vampire thing, we're trying to keep the publicity to a minimum. That's all we need right now is people taking to the streets armed with crosses and wooden stakes."

"Surely nobody is actually taking this vampire angle seriously?" Steve asked in amazement.

"After this last murder, they just might. You see, this one was a little bit different that the previous killings. We believe the kid was killed right in the alley where his body was found. With the other ones, we had a difficult time explaining what happened to the blood in the bodies so we came to the conclusion that the murders occurred elsewhere. In this case, we know that the kid was killed right there but there was hardly any blood at the murder scene. Shit, you get more blood from a nose-bleed than what was found in the alley. I mean if this kid was murdered right there in that alley, what in the fuck happened to all of his blood?"

"I know this sounds strange Jon, but could they have drained him right there? I mean could it be some strange religious cult who cut his throat and caught his blood in a bucket or siphoned it out with a hose or something? There are a lot of sickos out there."

Rickman shook his head. "Your theory isn't that far fetched. We have already thought of that but there are some problems. For one thing, just like the others, his throat wasn't cut but rather ripped out by those same fangs or at least by something resembling fangs. I was one of those who investigated the crime scene this time. From the nature of the gash, there should have been blood splattered all over the place. Nothing. We also found that strange saliva in the wound again—the same shit as last time. Nobody has still been able to figure out what species it belongs to. So—if you have a ripped out throat with saliva in the wound, that can only mean something—or someone had its mouth on the dead kid's throat. The only conclusion that one can draw is that whatever tore this victim's jugular to bits seemed to have drunk his blood as well."

"Drunk his blood?" Steve's head was whirling with what Rickman had just said.

Rickman grinned at Steve's wide-eyed look. He took a deep puff off of his cigarette, blowing out the smoke through his mouth and nose simultaneously.

"I'm afraid so. There just doesn't seem to be any other explanation and all the evidence points to the fact that the kid's blood was con-sumed directly from his body."

Steve sat in silence for a moment, just staring at Rickman. His voice trembled as he spoke. "So you're saying that The Enquirer might be right, that maybe there actually is a vampire walking the streets of Chicago." He shook his head and continued. Rickman watched him silently. "You know Jon, I have always prided myself on being extremely open-minded but I am having a difficult time accepting this—a really difficult time. I suppose that's a normal reaction. But just the thought of some undead creature attacking someone and sinking its fangs into their throat. It goes against everything we were brought up believing."

Rickman watched Steve, his face expressionless. "I know what you mean buddy. I'm having a hard time buying it myself."

"What makes you think that the murder happened right there in the alley?" Steve asked.

"There was evidence of a struggle in the alley—bits of torn clothing from the kid. We also found a switchblade knife with the kid's finger-prints on it. It was open, something unlikely to occur if it had simply fallen out of his pocket. Maybe he threatened his attacker or tried to defend himself. The interesting thing about the knife is that there was another set of prints on it as well. We're having them checked out now. We're hoping that somehow the attacker got his hands on the knife."

"What about the kid? You mentioned that he was in a gang. Could he have been killed by one his rival gangs?"

Rickman shook his head. "Very slim chance. We questioned most of the members and everyone seems to have a pretty strong alibi for that night." Rickman hesitated and creased his brow. "It was strange," he continued, "usually they are about as uncooperative as you can get as far as answering any questions from the police. This time, they seemed more than anxious to help. Shit, they were even willingly volunteering information that had nothing to do with the case. They are actually afraid. I suppose that's natural considering that the murderer seems to be focusing his attention on young gang kids as of late. With all this hype about vampires, I think these kids are really starting to watch their backs—or their throats, if you will."

Rickman chuckled at his own joke. Steve tried to smile but found the entire situation distressing.

"Do you know anything else about the kid that was killed?" Steve asked. "Was he involved in anything shady?"

Rickman let go of a deep throaty laugh. "Steve, all those kids are involved in something or another that's shady. This one was no exception. Nothing out of the ordinary for a member of a street gang. Some of his friends said he seemed maybe a little more ruthless than most. Although they never came right out and said it, but I got the impression that many of them were terrified of him. I'm guessing that he was probably one mean little dude."

"What do the other cops think?"

Rickman sighed, then frowned. "Remember last time I told you that everyone at the station was joking about the media and their vampire hype? Now everyone seems to have stopped making light of it. There's too much strange evidence that one cannot simply explain away." He lowered his voice to almost a whisper. "Shit, last week I noticed a stack of books next to my supervisor's desk. I was able to catch a glimpse of some of the titles—'Dracula', 'The Vampire Companion', and some of those books by Anne Rice. Vampires are no doubt on everyone's brain. Our common sense tells us it's impossible. But is it a myth or is there actually some truth to it? According to everything we have come up with, the only conclusion that makes any sense is that there is indeed a vampire or some sort of vampiric creature stalking the streets of Chicago."

Rickman gulped down the last of the coffee that was left in his cup and made a face as it went down his throat. He was so busy talking that his coffee had gotten cold.

"So let's say for the sake of argument that this creature really is a vampire," Steve said. "How would you catch him?"

Rickman narrowed his eyes then shrugged his shoulders. He let out a soft chuckle. "Catch him? I just wonder what in the hell we would do with him when we found him! But you're right. That is another question. Just how do you fight a vampire? As far as I know, there have never been any documented cases of anyone bringing down a vamp."

Steve frowned. "According to all the books and movies I've read on the subject, crosses and wooden stakes seem to be the weapons of choice."

Rickman smiled and nodded. "Right. But that's exactly where they stem from—novels and Hollywood movies. It comes from the imagination of fiction writers and who knows if there could be any truth to the old standard methods of killing a vampire. If you read any of the modern vampire novels, these creatures can now enter churches and walk during the day. Sure, it would be great if you could pop a crucifix out of your coat pocket and have the mean 'ol vamp instantly burst into flames. But who's to know if any of this shit would really work. I personally am hoping that a bullet in the head would bring the fucker down."

"Now I don't know what to think," Steve said. His voice quivered as he spoke and he seemed to avoid eye contact with his companion. "This is all so crazy. I know we talked about the possibility before but that's all it was—a remote, unlikely possibility. Now you're telling me that you actually suspect that a vampire is involved?" He looked at Rickman and forced a weak smile. "If I didn't know you better, I'd say that you were completely cracked."

Rickman laughed loudly. "Yeah, I've been beginning to wonder the same thing myself. I know this is all pretty far fetched and believe me, I've had an extremely difficult time coming to terms with it myself."

"Does the media know anything about the Police Department's suspicions?"

"No, and we plan on keeping it that way for as long as we can. If it is in fact such a creature that's killing these people, we would like nothing more than to solve this case quietly without ever letting the public know about its outcome." Rickman's voice was almost a whisper.

"Is that ethical? If you believe that a vampire is actually on the loose, shouldn't the public be made aware of this so that people can take precautions to protect themselves?"

Rickman frowned, then nodded. "I understand what you're saying, I really do. But there are several issues to take in consideration when contemplating communication to the public. People hold certain beliefs about the world around them and put their faith into that which is rational. We need to hold onto these beliefs to try and make sense out of this already fucked-up world. If these deep-seated beliefs were to be shattered, chaos would result. Let's say that everyone suddenly found out about the existence of vampires. What then? If vampires exist, why not werewolves, ghosts, mummies, witches, ghouls, and so on and so forth. Those who believe in a god would begin to question their beliefs, maybe even reject them altogether. Once we begin to deal with issues of the supernatural and immortality, things outside of the supposed normal world, we begin to question the rules that we have always known that keep society in order. You get what I'm saying? We just don't think it would be wise."

"I think so. Believe me, I'm having a hard enough time accepting this myself. But as for the issue of witches and werewolves and…"

"Don't even go there! I don't want to get near that discussion!"

Steve was finally able to smile. "Me neither. Okay, let's say that it was a vampire that killed those people. How do you go about finding him and catching him?"

"Or her."

"Huh?"

Rickman snickered. "Who's to say that it's not a lady vampire? One must not be sexist you know."

Steve laughed. "You're avoiding the question. Pardon me, let me rephrase. How do you go about finding him or her?"

"The department is putting a plan together. I hope you understand but there are some things that I simply cannot tell you."

"I won't push it." Steve said and looked at his watch. "Shit, I'm gonna be late for work if I don't get moving."

Rickman looked disappointed. "Late for work? I thought I could talk you into a quick roll in the hay." He winked. "Kind of a payment for all the information I've given you."

Steve blushed. "Sorry, I'll have to take a rain check. Gotta make a living you know." He was hoping that Rickman was just kidding but had the feeling that he was serious.

Rickman perched out his bottom lip as if pouting. "I do take IOUs."

Steve pushed his coffee cup towards the center of the table and stood up. "I'll keep that in mind. By the way, I really appreciate the information. Really I do."

"Even if you can't use it?"

"Can't use it?"

"Even if the case gets solved and it turns out that it is an actual vampire involved, this is something that we cannot ever leak out to the public."

Steve nodded. "I'm counting on the fact that it isn't a real vampire."

"And I hope to God you're right. But whatever the outcome might be, just keep in mind what I said. Also, you've got to promise me that you won't breathe a word of what I told you to anyone—not your mother, father, friends—not anyone."

"I promise. I would never do anything to jeopardize your career."

Steve extended his hand to Rickman. He grabbed Steve's hand and held onto it firmly. "One more thing Steve. I think it's best that you don't get too involved in this. I know you're on the hunt for the big story and I'd really like to help you out with your career, but this is getting dangerous. I promise I'll keep you informed on what's going on but I'm asking you not to get directly involved. I don't want to find your body in a dumpster, transformed into a bloodless heap. Okay?"

"You got it," Steve said softly. "Now can I have my hand back?"

Rickman beamed at Steve. "Oops, sorry. By the way, did I tell you how exceptionally hot you look today?"

"You are absolutely incorrigible!"

"I'll take that as a compliment."

Steve reached over and squeezed Rickman's shoulder. "I really have to run. Thanks again Jon for everything."

Rickman winked again. "You'll be hearing from me, studly."

Steve left the restaurant and walked abruptly back to his apartment. He was already late for work and he knew that Jamie would be furious with him for not coming back. When he arrived, the apartment was empty. There was a note on the kitchen table.

If you're fucking him, I'm going to tell Erik.
Hugs and Kisses,
Jamie

.

He had to think of something to tell Jamie. Rickman had sworn him to secrecy and he would never break that trust. He just might have enough information for an article. He would start on it right after work tonight. How to approach the subject? He'd have to veer away from the vampire angle—that much was certain. But how to do it?

He rushed to the bedroom, threw on his work clothes and headed out the door. He had a lot to think about. Rickman's words were ringing in his head, *"our only conclusion is that there is indeed a vampire or some sort of vampiric creature stalking the streets of Chicago."*

Flinging on his coat, he darted out the door.

The Hunger Returns

◆

Erik sat in an overstuffed chair, contemplating the night which lay before him. For the first time since they met weeks ago, Erik would not be seeing Steve tonight. It wasn't that Erik didn't want to see the boy. The opposite was true. He was in love with Steve. There was no use in denying that and he believed that Steve loved him too, although neither of them had actually come out and said it as of yet. But Erik knew that he was also hurting Steve. Not intentionally of course, but out of necessity. He had vowed to himself that he would tell Steve the whole story but he hadn't figured out quite how to approach the subject and the more attached he became to Steve, the more difficult the task became. How do you tell someone, "Dear, I'm a vampire—but I love you just the same." Erik had tried to come up with a speech that would somehow soften the blow. Such things needed to be worded ever so carefully. Although he was getting to know Steve better and better every day, he still could not even fathom what the boy's reaction would be to such news. Would Steve be able to accept him for what he was? That was asking a lot and Erik knew it. The time was drawing near when Steve must be told the truth. It was not going to be tonight though. There was something much more important on Erik's mind, something much stronger and more compelling.

The hunger.

He had been fine for the past couple of weeks. His last victim had seen to that. But now the urge had returned in full force. The need for blood pounded in his drying veins and gripped at his insides, worse than an addict's craving for heroin. When the hunger was upon him, his mind clouded and dulled, with rational thought almost an impossibility. The hunger had been creeping upon him already for several days but had been weak enough to ignore. Until now.

It always arrived slowly, starting with an increased awareness of his senses. As he weakened, his already excellent vision would suddenly become as sharp as that of a jungle cat and his sense of smell would be enriched to the point where being around any humans was torturous. It was blood that he would smell, gripping him, beckoning him to drink. Living among humans, he had grown accustomed to the constant smell of blood coursing through their bodies and had reached a point where, under normal conditions, he barely noticed it. But when the hunger came, it was so overpowering that he could hardly endure it. The aroma of blood followed him everywhere he went.

He could distinguish the differences in people's blood—some smelled sweeter than others. There were also those whose blood was putrid. This was the vile stench of diseased blood—a warning of imminent death. During the hunger, Erik could barely contain himself while walking down the street, as this mixture of all of the different blood aromas filled his nostrils, the onslaught of scents commanding him to feed. At times, the smell grew so strong and overpowering that his retractable fangs would protrude on their own. Under normal circumstances, he could control them and not allow his canines to expose themselves until he was ready to sink his teeth into some poor unsuspecting soul's flesh. But when he no longer had any control over when his two razor-sharp teeth would make their appearance, he knew that feeding could be put off no further.

Such was case last night when he was with Steve. He had risked Steve's life by going to his apartment in the condition he was in. The hunger was already overpowering but Erik was sure he could contain it. He loved Steve, after all. Wasn't love stronger than anything? It wasn't until Steve opened the front door that he realized he had made a serious error in judgment—a potentially fatal error. The smell of Steve's blood was incredible. It was the sweetest smell he had ever encountered. The fragrance was that of youth, strength and purity all rolled into one, with a singular sweetness that sent Erik's senses reeling. He had never noticed the smell of Steve's blood as he did then. When Erik entered the apartment, his mind began spinning, and after a quick peck on the cheek, he had excused himself to the bathroom where he quickly tried to compose himself and mentally will his canines to remain where they were.

The rest of the evening, as short as it was, was agony. He could barely concentrate on Steve or anything that he was saying. All he could think about was how wonderful, how enticing Steve's blood smelled. At one horrifying point, he had actually begun considering the possibility of sneaking 'just one little taste.' It was then he knew that he could not spend an entire evening with Steve and made an excuse to end their date early. The wounded look on Steve's face wrenched at his heart. Erik made a hasty retreat.

Soon you will understand, Steve. Everything will be clear.

He snapped back to the present and trembled slightly as he sat listening to Bach. The music brought some relief as it filled his ears. He closed his eyes, trying to relax his troubled spirit. Usually, Bach could tame the thirsty beast within him and allow him, at least momentarily, to forget his troubles. But not tonight. He would succumb to the hunger this evening. He would partake of the life fluid upon which his existence depended. He could put it off no longer.

The music ceased to exist as he began making his plans for the evening. Even though he had fed thousands of times during his extended lifetime, each time when the hunger hit and he was ready to go out on the prowl, he was faced with an agonizing decision—to kill or not to kill. Killing someone meant draining them completely, drinking until the heart slows, and then stops. The advantage of killing the victim was a prolongation of the period when the hunger was not present. Erik has gone as long as three weeks without needing to feed after killing a victim in such a manner. But there was a second option. He also had the choice of just taking a pint or so, thus sparing the victim. This method typically involved seducing a young man and, during his sleep or unconsciousness induced by Erik himself, taking just enough blood to curb his hunger for the moment. This could be tricky as the chance of discovery was great. There was always a risk that his victim would awake during the time when Erik's teeth were planted firmly in a vein and his mouth was drawing blood out of the victim's body. Over the years, he had developed a technique, an almost infallible system. He kept a bottle of chloroform and a dry rag in his coat for just this purpose. After a bout of lovemaking he would wait for his intended prey to fall asleep. Erik would then sneak out of bed, retrieve the rag and chloroform and gently place it over the sleeping man's face—lightly enough as not to wake him, but firmly enough to put him under. Then he would drink. The next day, the victim would awaken as usual, feeling perhaps a little tired and headachy from being a pint or so low, but alive—and unaware of what had occurred the night before.

Such a procedure does not always work, however. There have been times when Erik inadvertently killed his victim or came extremely close to it. The human body of the average male contains about six quarts of blood. A pint can be removed without any repercussions. Removing two pints was getting into dangerous territory as a person would often go into shock and long-term damage was done. Having fed almost weekly in this manner his entire life, Erik could tell when he had drawn his allowable limit, where taking any more would jeopardize the victim's life. The difficult part was trying to pull himself away. Simply stopping was not easy. When the hunger is upon him in all its force, his instincts tell him to drink until the hunger is no more, and he loses himself in the sound of the victim's heartbeat and in the warm life-giving blood filling his throat and restoring his strength. At the point when Erik has already removed a pint or so of the life giving nectar, he must muster every bit of his willpower to cease feeding before the victim's heart began to slow. For Erik, this is the worse feeling in the world—the stopping of the flow of blood into his mouth. Numerous times he had gone too far and his victim had gone into shock. At this point, the only remaining option was to finish the job he had started, and then dispose of the body. The remorse he felt when his victim died was intense and he secretly grieved inside for the death of every innocent young man for which he was responsible.

But there were times when Erik left his house with the full intention of killing, although such instances were rare. After months of taking only enough blood from his victims to temporarily dull the hunger, he craved for a complete feeding, the indulgence of draining his victim completely dry. The best way to do this is a wound to the throat, where there is little chance for recovery. When intent on participating in this sort of feeding, Erik made sure that it was not an innocent who would face his demise. He would walk through the worse part of town by himself, hoping to get attacked by someone who was alone. Not always an easy feat to accomplish as most attackers travel in packs. Often it took him several nights of prowling before he found his victim—or rather before his victim chose him. Although Erik justified his kill by choosing someone who would have most likely killed him first had he been mortal, he was still visited by enormous guilt after each occurrence. But when his prey turned out to be a so-called fag basher, someone who tried to kill him because he assumed Erik was gay, his guilt was minimal. Being gay all of his life, he considered those who would harm or kill others for no other reason than because of their sexuality was something Erik could not tolerate. His remorse when one of these such people fell beneath his fangs was slight.

Erik snapped back to the present. How long ago the music had stopped, he didn't know. He got up and looked out the window, trying to muster up the strength to do what needed to be done. The night was dark and chilly and out there was the blood he needed. He was weakening rapidly but his decision was made. Tonight he would find a young man who would satisfy his hunger but Erik would spare his life.

A wave of guilt swept over him as he began formulating his plan. He had forgotten to figure Steve into his feeding arrangement. His routine of having sex with a young man, then feeding on him afterwards seemed no longer acceptable given that Steve was now part of his life. Would sleeping with another man be considered cheating, even if it was done out of necessity? Most likely. But he also knew that morally, cheating on one's boyfriend was not as bad as slaughtering someone. Murder was forever and sex was just sex. He just hoped when the time came for Erik to explain himself that Steve would understand. Accepting this relationship would not be easy for Steve.

Erik left the window and once again sat down. The house was silent and he could feel his own heart pounding rapidly in his chest. The rest of his body was in a state of pain, the searing agony associated with the intense, unfulfilled hunger. The front door slammed and all at once the house filled with the scent of sweet, fresh blood. Mitch was home. He had come to know this smell well over the years. Like Steve's, Mitch's blood smelled virile and strong but it was blood which had never once passed his lips. He would never allow himself to nourish himself from his companion, even though Mitch had offered himself upon several occasions during Erik's periods of extreme weakness. As difficult as it was, he had always refused. Never feed on those who would protect you. This was his own rule to which he held firmly. Jeopardizing Mitch's life to satisfy his own immediate needs was unimaginable.

He heard the click of the closet door as Mitch hung up his coat, then the opening and closing of the refrigerator. Even though he was in the other room, the scent of Mitch's blood slammed his senses. The fragrance was so overpowering that he knew he would have to leave the house soon and tend to his business.

Mitch walked into the room and stopped short when he laid his eyes upon Erik.

"You look like shit," he said.

It was true. Erik looked horrible. When he was in a state of hunger, his usual composed, calm self disappeared and was replaced by a wild-eyed, desperate looking creature. His skin tone would become unearthly pale, resembling someone with an extreme case of anemia. Dark circles would develop under his eyes and his normally tight skin would begin to sag ever so slightly. The rapid aging process would then commence.

"I do not feel so good," Erik said. He attempted a weak smile. "I shall be going out tonight."

"Alone?"

Erik knew that Mitch was wondering if he was going to be seeing Steve. Ever since Erik's declaration of love for Steve and Mitch's reiteration of his love for Erik, a noticeable tension existed between the two men.

"Alone," Erik repeated as he stood up.

Mitch unconsciously took a couple of steps back. This never ceased to surprise Erik. The only time Mitch seemed actually afraid of him was when he was in grips of the hunger. Erik felt that after all this time, Mitch should know that Erik would never harm him. But human instincts are stronger than reason.

Erik walked to the front room to gather his coat. Mitch stopped him.

"Erik," he said with a slight tremble to his voice, "I'd be especially careful tonight if I were you. More so than usual."

Erik looked at Mitch, a curious expression on his face. "Meaning?" His voice revealed irritation.

Mitch stepped back. "I've been hearing a lot of talk around the police station the last couple of days since that last kid was found in the alley. From what I can gather, the higher ups on the case are treating the murders as official," he paused, "vampire slayings." Mitch swallowed hard after he said the words.

Erik sat down in the chair next to the door, still holding his coat in his hand. He glanced up at Mitch, a distressed look on his face.

"They have come right out and said this?"

Mitch nodded. "More or less. I have overheard some conversations. They have been doing research on vampire folklore and from what I understand, now consider a vampire as their prime suspect."

"There is no possibility you could be mistaken?"

Mitch shook his head. From the look on his face, it was evident that he felt uncomfortable about towering over Erik.

"I'm afraid not. What's more, they are now discussing strategies to battle a vampire and researching what it would take to kill one. I heard they are manufacturing some special type of weapon. I don't know any of the details though."

Erik pondered this for a moment, then laughed. "Battle a vampire? They would not have a clue on how to battle a true vampire should they come across one. They have no idea of the power we possess. I imagine this weapon is of the sort that it would fire wooden stakes at the creature? Or perhaps crosses? Maybe even garlic?" Erik's smile faded as his voice trailed off.

Mitch looked startled, then frowned. "I wouldn't underestimate the resources of the police…" He paused, meeting Erik's glance, "or get too overconfident. There are still limits to what you can endure."

Erik broke the stare and looked at the floor. He grabbed Mitch's hand. "Mitch, you will have to excuse my behavior as I am not quite myself tonight."

"I understand," Mitch said flatly. "I just wanted to make you conscious of the potential danger."

Erik smiled weakly. "My friend, I've been facing danger for over 70 years now and I think I can handle pretty much of anything your police friends can come up with." He creased his brow. "I do find it incredible that this investigation is leading to the supernatural, though. I never thought I would see the day when humans would actually admit that a creature, present only in folklore, could possibly exist among them. This may change things for me in the future."

"Just be extra careful tonight, okay?"

Erik smiled, then the blackness of discomfort settled on is face. He abruptly stood up, startling Mitch. He brushed his lips on Mitch's cheek. "We shall have to talk more about this later."

He threw on his coat and was gone.

* * *

The fresh night air augmented his hunger. He breathed deeply and walked, not yet sure where he was going to end up or what was going to happen. All that he knew was that feeding could be postponed no longer. He was getting weaker every moment and dared not take the risk of losing control, which was always a possibility in his present, crazed state.

The street was relatively quiet. He passed a young woman with urgency in her step and inhaled in the aroma of her blood. He heard her heart quicken as she passed. He salivated. His legs weakened. He needed to act quickly.

On trembling legs, he walked past Roscoe's and could feel the vibration of music emanating from the popular club. Once one of his favorite hunting grounds, he no longer dared frequent the bar. He had to find an establishment where the chance of accidentally running into Steve or one of his companions was minimal. Charlie's would be a good choice. A recently opened Country and Western gay bar, Erik had gone there a few times and had actually done quite well. It was a quiet place during the week, which made him a bit nervous, as he preferred to blend into a large crowd. But Charlie's would be a wise choice as he remembered Steve telling him that he abhorred Country and Western music.

When he reached the bar, he stopped at the front door and tried to compose himself. He must appear calm and natural—human-like, and not have the air of a cheetah who has not partaken of a meal in several days. He took a deep breath and opened the front door. An unusually strong odor of stale beer and cigarettes floated out of the bar, mingled with the sharp scent of human blood. His groin stirred and he became hard. His hands trembled. He swiftly walked to the bar and sat down.

A good looking blond bartender in a leather vest and brand new cowboy boots hurried over to him, flashed Erik a full-size smile and offered to take his order. Erik ordered a beer and glanced around. He really did like this place. The fresh smell of the wood and leather was still strong, as if the bar had just opened the day before and the shiny gleam of the polished steel running along the bar confirmed its newness. As it was still early, the tavern contained only a few patrons. He noticed an attractive young man sitting quietly at the other end of the bar. Erik guessed his age to be about twenty-two or twenty-three and, from the way he struggled to hold up his head, it was evident that he was quite drunk. Erik sensed that the young man had the deliberate intention of becoming as intoxicated as he possibly could. Jilted by a lover, no doubt. The intoxicated man's thoughts were too jumbled to tell for sure. He would pass on this one. He knew that when someone's blood alcohol content was as high as this young man's was, the blood would be bitter, and would cause him to experience a slight drunkenness himself accompanied with extreme nausea. He had learned this well the few times he had fed upon inebriated victims. A wave of the kid's blood assailed his brain. The smell was harsh and bitter—more so than that typically associated with drunkenness. This young man was ill as well.

Erik slowly sipped his beer and much to his relief, the craving temporarily subsided, allowing him to drift into deep thought. He should just forget about Steve and end the relationship. At least he would not have to try to figure out how to explain his situation to him and deal with whatever reaction he would have to Erik's news. Of course, there was another option…"

"Hey good-looking," a deep voice next to him said.

Erik was startled by the presence of another human. He had been so wrapped up in his thoughts, that he had not noticed the man plop down next to him nor had he heard the door behind him open and close, unusual considering his present overly keen senses. He turned to look at the new arrival. He was young, mid-twenties perhaps, wearing tight Levi's and cowboy boots. A t-shirt with the words *How dare you assume I'm straight* clung to his well-developed, tight body. A thick head of well-styled but natural looking, curly black hair hung loosely on his collar. This man was very masculine, the exact kind that Erik loved. His blood smelled fresh and healthy and was mixed with the odor of inexpensive cologne and stale cigarettes. A pleasant mixture all in all. Erik felt the hunger once again rise to the bottom of his throat.

"You certainly are a charmer." Erik replied, forcing a friendly smile. His gaze momentarily drifted to the man's throat.

The young man beamed. "I try. It's a dirty job but someone's gotta do it."

"I am glad that you took it upon yourself to fill the position. There is an unquestionable lack of charmers in the world these days."

The man smiled at Erik's comeback. "So, are you waiting for someone?"

"We are all waiting for someone, are we not?" Erik replied, forcing a smile.

He laughed. "I guess we are." His eyes searched for the bartender. "Hey Billy! How about a beer over here?"

The bartender placed a frosty bottle of Miller in front of the man. He raised the bottle to his mouth and took deep drink "Ah, that shit is good. I needed a beer after the day I had today. What were we talking about?" He reached into his pocket and pulled out a cigarette.

"Waiting for someone, " Erik replied, becoming intrigued with this rugged young man.

"Oh yeah. How we're all looking for someone. Even when we find someone, many of us are still waiting and looking." He took another long swig of his beer.

Erik felt a tinge of guilt as his thoughts shifted to Steve. He shook the image away. "And yourself? You are alone tonight?"

The man looked over both of his shoulders and then back at Erik. He took a drag off of his cigarette. "Looks like I am now. The crowd of men that was following me must have disappeared."

"Hmm," Erik said, creasing his brow, "they must have taken off with the crowd of men that was following me." Erik found the man's arrogance attractive.

They both laughed.

"Don't you hate it when that happens?" the man asked, smiling. "So what's your name?"

"I am Erik. And you?"

"Pleased to make your acquaintance Erik," the man said and bowed his head. "This only goes to show that my confirmation is correct."

"And what confirmation might that be?"

"That all Eriks are hot by nature. I still have yet to meet anyone named Erik who hasn't driven me up a fucking wall. The name suits you well."

Erik smiled. "I shall take that as a compliment. I still did not catch…"

"What do you say we get out of this place? The man gulped down the remaining contents of the bottle and placed the empty container on the bar. "I've got some nice cold beer in my apartment."

"I would like that very much," Erik replied, his heart rate suddenly increasing. "I am not much for taverns anyway."

He stood up on his trembling legs. The handsome stranger joined him.

The bartender watched the two men leave. He shook his head. He walked over to one of the patrons at the bar. "Can you believe him? That bastard scored again. I just knew he would end up leaving with that guy with the sexy eyes."

"What, are you jealous?" the bar patron asked.

"Me? Jealous? Of Rickman? Not a chance. It just would be nice if the shithead left some men for the rest of us," the bartender said smiling. He walked away and went back to washing glasses.

A New Friend

$\blacklozenge$

The clanking of dishes in the kitchen was driving Steve crazy. His head had been pounding all evening and he swore that if one more person asked him if he was on the rag, he would have simply have to deck them. These damn headaches would spring out of nowhere, and often were dehabilitating, causing him to wince in pain from the slightest noise or light. From the small window in the kitchen, he could see Jamie standing outside, having a cigarette. It would be a good time to take a break himself. The fresh air might help his pounding temples.

He tossed on his coat and went outside. Jamie looked surprised to see him stumble out the kitchen door.

"What's up?" Jamie asked. "You start smoking again?"

"I just needed a break. Thought the fresh night air would help my headache a bit. God knows the aspirins haven't done any good."

"You still have that pounder?"

"Yup. I've had it since yesterday. This one is as wicked as hell."

Jamie threw his cigarette in the snow, reached in his pocket and lit up another one. "Haven't had a smoke in hours." He inhaled deeply. "Can you believe how busy we were tonight? My feet are killing me! How did you make out by the way?"

"Not that great. I had a hard time being nice to customers and my tips show it. It didn't help that I kept getting assholes to wait on. This one guy was really a jerk. He and his girlfriend had completely finished eating. Their napkins were crumpled up and thrown on their plates. When I went to remove their dishes, he told me that if I touch his fucking potato he was going to break my hand, and went off on this tirade about how he was sick of being rushed wherever he went and that I never even bothered to ask him if he was finished with his potato. I wanted to cram the damn thing right down his throat until he choked on it!"

Jamie cracked up laughing. "Did he leave you a nice tip?"

"Are you kidding? Not a cent. Not that I expected one. I told him that he can take all night to gnaw on his potato if he likes, threw down their check and never went back to the table."

Jamie laughed again. "What are you up to after work? Seeing loverboy?"

Steve shook his head. "Not tonight. He had something he needed to take care of, some business I guess. It's the first night since we've started dating that we're not spending together."

Jamie grinned. "So Stevie's free tonight! Great! I was kind of feeling like going out tonight. What do you say?"

"I don't think I..."

"A man's got to have a night out by himself every now and then," Jamie interrupted, "without the old ball and chain."

"I wouldn't exactly call Erik a ball and chain," Steve answered, pretending to be offended. "I happen to enjoy spending time with him."

"You know what I meant, you silly, silly boy. So what do say we go out dancing at Roscoe's?"

Steve shook his head. "No way Jamie. My head is pounding too much to put up with that loud music. Plus you know that I really don't like that place."

"I thought you loved Roscoe's. Isn't that where you met the man of your dreams?"

"No, Buddies. I'm just not in the mood tonight for the crowds or the noise. Besides, since when do you want to go out after work? Just about every time I've asked you to go out for a drink with me, you've always had something to do or some hot date lined up. I've always wondered what you did after work that was so bloody secretive."

Jamie blushed. "I can't spill my secrets. A man's gotta have some air of mystery about him."

Steve rolled his eyes. "I'm going to follow you some night and see what you're up to."

Jamie snickered. "Okay, Roscoe's is out. How about Buddies then?"

"Actually Jamie, I think I'm going to stay home tonight. After being with Erik every night, I'm just going to take an evening for myself and maybe curl up with a good book. If I can get rid of this headache, that is."

"Every party has a pooper, that why we invited you," Jamie began singing.

Steve snickered. "I hope you realize that your horrid singing just made my headache worse."

Jamie smiled wickedly, then, "I didn't even get a chance to talk to you tonight. So how are things going with your little hunk? I hope he's not the cause of your headache. I know I've dated a few men that definitely gave me a pain. Can't necessarily say that it was in the head though."

Steve laughed, then winced. "Ouch."

"So tell me. How are things going between the two of you? Will there be wedding bells in the near future?"

"Not bad, I guess."

"You guess? Come on, what's up? Is it true love or not?"

"We are getting serious. But there's still so much I don't know about him yet. Shit, I don't even know where he lives."

Jamie shrieked in fake horror. "What? You haven't seen his place yet?"

Steve shook his head.

"My dear, you have to see his abode before you even consider taking any marriage vows. What if he has it decorated in Early American? Or what if he lives in—*gasp*—a trailer?"

Steve giggled. "I'm thinking of inviting myself over to his place. I think it's been long enough."

"Sounds like a good idea. Why don't you just come out and ask him everything you want to know about him if that's what's eating away at you? Since you two are dating, you do have that right you know."

Steve sighed. "It's not that easy. He has this uncanny ability to change the subject whenever the topic of conversation turns to him, without me even realizing it."

"Maybe he's hiding something—perhaps a wicked and torrid past. Maybe he's a child molester or a serial killer or a gangster or…"

"Stop it! I don't think he's a murderer or anything like that."

Jamie kicked at the snow. "So have you two said those three little words to each other yet?'

"What three little words? Oh, you mean 'want to fuck'"?

"Nice try," Jamie said. "You know damned well what I'm talking about. So? Has he said it yet? Have you?"

Steve laughed. "We haven't gotten that far yet. I'm taking things super slow this time. At this point in my life, I'm going to ensure that I really know the person well before I make any major commitments."

Jamie looked at his watch. "We better get back inside before Gary has a conniption. You know how he is about taking too long of a break."

"I'm starting to get chilled anyway."

The two went back inside. Steve took care of his last couple of customers. If he didn't have such a headache, he wouldn't have minded closing tonight. He was feeling a bit guilty for dashing out early every night to be with Erik. But his head was really pounding by this point and his routine clean-up tasks were torture. He felt bad that he turned down Jamie's offer to go out. He had been neglecting Jamie ever since Erik had come into the picture. He would have to make a point of spending more time with him.

Slowly he filled the ketchup bottles, wrapped up the desserts, wiped down all the waiter trays and filled and covered the salad dressings.

"I sure hope I don't have to do this forever," he said, accidentally out loud, immediately thankful that there was nobody else in the kitchen to have heard him.

Unfortunately, there didn't seem to be any light at the end of the tunnel at the moment. Just last month alone he must have sent over fifty resumes and query letters and hadn't received one response—one positive response, that is. He got plenty of the basic form letters 'we have reviewed your qualifications and regret to say that…blah, blah blah.' Steve referred to them as 'fuck you letters.' He had drawers full of them. He'd been successful at getting several of his articles published in local newspapers but that didn't seem to help him at all in his job search. He'd nearly finished his article on the vampire murders though. Hopefully, he'll be able to find someone to publish the darn thing. He'd been true to his word to Rickman and approached the story from a different angle—that of a serial killer, a vigilante out to cleanse the streets of hustlers and gangs. It was quite a switch from the recent garbage in the papers about vampires. Too bad he didn't have any real evidence.

He all at once realized that he was unconsciously taking his sweet time finishing up his side work. Usually he just flew through these mundane duties, especially when he was in a hurry to get out of there and be with Erik. A wave of emptiness came over him with the knowledge that his handsome young lover would not be waiting for him tonight. He didn't realize until now just how much a habit seeing Erik after work had become.

He sighed then hung up the damp rag with which he had wiped down the kitchen, on the side of the dish cart. The rag was drenched with Thousand Island dressing, spilled milk and cheesecake crumbs and felt slimy in his fingers. He grabbed it and tried to rinse out the stains in the sink but it was to no avail. The rag ended up in the laundry bag next to the back door. The owner was such a cheap bastard that he insisted they use the damn rags until they were almost in shreds. We must keep the laundry bill down you know.

After changing his clothes in the employee lounge, he popped a couple more aspirin, then walked through the dining room and up to the front bar. Several regular customers, who came to the restaurant every Friday and Saturday night to hear the piano player, were already seated at the bar. Steve decided that he was going to splurge and have a beer before going home. It might not help his headache any, but what the hell.

"Bill, can I get a Beck's?" Steve called out to the bartender.

Bill sluggishly waltzed over and placed the beer in front of Steve. "What's the occasion? Not running off tonight?"

"Just felt like sitting and unwinding a little bit. Tonight was a bitch."

Bill grinned at Steve and rested his elbows on the bar. "Your new boyfriend didn't dump you already, did he?"

"What boyfriend?" Steve asked, trying to look as if he were truly perplexed by what Bill was saying.

"Don't play dumb with me, Stevie boy. Everybody knows that you've been dating that cute guy with the eyes who was in here awhile back. Pretty serious too from what I've heard."

Steve narrowed his eyes. "That Jamie has such a big mouth."

Bill laughed. "So where is your new beau tonight?"

"He has something going on. Kind of glad he does because I have the headache from hell. It feels like my head's going to blow up any second now."

Bill's eyes grew wide. "I have something that will take care of that." He reached behind him and produced a rather large shot glass then filled it up with the contents of a bottle that was hidden underneath the bar. He placed it in front of Steve. "This will fix you right up."

"What is it?" Steve asked.

"The perfect headache remedy."

Steve shrugged his shoulders and held up the glass. He gulped the liquid down, then made a horrible face. He quickly brought his hand up to his mouth. "Yuck! What in the hell is this?"

Bill laughed. "Chartreuse—guaranteed to cure the worst of headaches."

"Yeah," Steve answered, wiping his mouth with the back of his hand, "you'll be so busy puking that you'll forget all about your headache."

Bill was still grinning. "Ah, come on Steve. It's not that bad. Guess you just have to get used to it. It's an acquired taste."

Steve gulped some of his beer to wash the taste of the horrid liquid from his mouth. "So, is it true that you're dating the daytime busboy? What's his name…Tim?"

Bill flashed him a wicked grin. "Now who on earth went and told you something like that?"

It was Steve's turn to smile. "Let's just say there's been a rumor floating around here to that effect. So is it true?"

"Let's just say…he makes great French toast."

"Why you scurvy dog!" Steve said and grinned. "Leave it to you to get your evil claws into that innocent young kid."

Bill threw his head back and laughed. "Yeah, right. He's not as innocent as you might think."

Bill left to go check on his customers. Steve took a couple of swigs of his beer and noticed he was feeling slightly light-headed from the Chartreuse. He really should have eaten something earlier. All at once, he had the distinct feeling that somebody was watching him. He glanced over at the end of the bar and noticed a young man with straight dishwater blond hair staring at him. Steve felt a sudden chill roam up his spine and quickly looked away. He took another sip of his beer, trying not to glance at the guy. For some strange reason, the man reminded him of Erik, even though they looked nothing alike. It was the eyes—that was it. The man slowly got up and strode over to where Steve was sitting. Steve watched him out of the corner of his eye.

"Is this seat taken?" The blond man asked smiling, and pointed to the empty stool next to Steve.

"No, go ahead," Steve answered, with a quiver in his voice.

The man was actually very good looking. He was tall and slender but in very good shape. He was wearing a tight fitting white dress shirt that allowed one to see the contour of his pecs. He was overly pale and had deep ocean blue eyes. Yes, the sharpness of his eyes definitely reminded him of Erik. His chiseled facial features indicated that he was of European decent and flashed a bright mouthful of white teeth when he smiled. His age was difficult to discern, oddly enough. Steve guessed him to be in his mid to late twenties. Maybe older.

The blond man sat down and placed the bottle of Heineken that he was holding on the bar in front of him.

"My name is Victor," the man said coolly, and extended out his hand.

"I'm Steve," said Steve, taking Victor's hand in his. The temperature of Victor's hand startled him and Steve quickly withdrew his own. The skin temperature was the same as Erik's. Unusually cool.

Victor's eyes locked to Steve's and Steve found it strangely difficult to break the stare. The man's initial friendly expression had changed.

"I am quite aware of who you are," Victor said in a hollow voice. "I've been wanting to meet you for quite some time. I came here especially to see you." He pushed the bottle of Heineken away from him.

He stared at the stranger, studying him. "I'm afraid I don't remember meeting you. Where do I know you from?"

"Nowhere." The man flashed a toothy grin and moved in closer to Steve. "But I'm sure we'll have an opportunity to get to know each other very well. I believe we have a mutual friend. I understand you know an attractive young fellow named Erik?"

Now it made sense. This guy must be a relative of Erik's, maybe a brother or something. That would account for the similarities in their skin temperature.

"Yes, I do know Erik. Are you a relation?"

The man's smile dropped off his face. "We are just very good friends from way back. Unfortunately, we have managed to lose contact over the years. A shame, really. It saddens me." He reached for the bottle of

Heineken, glanced at it with disgust and placed it back on the bar. "I recently moved to Chicago and you could well imagine how delighted I was to learn that Erik was living here as well. An acquaintance informed me that Erik was dating a fellow named Steve who worked at this restaurant. It will be lovely to see Erik again after all these years. I am so very much looking forward to our reunion."

Steve's senses screamed. There was something about this man that he didn't trust. In fact, Steve had the impression that everything he had just said to Steve was a lie, although for what reason the man would lie to him, Steve couldn't begin to guess.

Steve looked at him suspiciously. "Sounds like you got the right person. I am dating Erik. May I ask how you know him? How good of friends were you?"

Victor seemed irritated by the question. "We were exceptionally close when we lived in New York. I now would like to renew our friendship."

"Were you lovers?" Steve stammered.

Victor smiled and then laughed very loudly, so loudly in fact that the other patrons at the bar turned their head to see from where the laughter was originating. The bartender flashed a curious look at Steve. Steve shrugged his shoulders and blushed.

"No reason to be jealous my little friend," Victor said. "We were not lovers in the sense that you mean. We shared—a different kind of bond. A much deeper, special kind of bond." He paused, then asked, "Erik has never mentioned me?"

Steve avoided his gaze. "No, he hasn't. We haven't been going out for very long though and I really don't know too much about his past as of yet."

"I would be more than happy to fill you in, my new friend!" Victor exclaimed, with an odd expression on his face that Steve did not like one bit. "We shall have to get together for a drink sometime." He glanced at the clock above the bar. "Unfortunately, I have a most pressing engagement and do not have any more time to chat with you. Do not fret, however. I will definitely be in touch. Oh—and please do tell Erik that Victor is in town and is just dying to see him." With that, he snickered.

"I don't have his address or phone number," Steve said. "Otherwise, I'd offer to give it to you."

A wave of darkness passed over Victor's face. "I assumed that was the case. That is why I did not ask." He eyed Steve up and down one final time, pushed the full bottle of beer to the edge of the bar, and stood up.

"Is there a way Erik can reach you?" Steve asked, stung by his last comment. "I'm sure he'll want to contact you."

Victor lips formed into a tight smile. "I will contact him when the time is right." He laughed again. "Of that, he can be certain."

With that, he turned his back and briskly walked through the crowded lounge and disappeared into the night. Steve blinked his eyes. He could have sworn the man had disappeared before even reaching the front door. Steve turned around, grabbed his beer and took a long gulp, emptying the bottle. A small burp escaped him.

"Bill, can I get another?" Steve said, holding up the empty beer bottle. His voice was trembling.

Bill returned promptly with a full bottle of Beck's. "So who was the cute blond? Looks like he was trying to pick you up."

Steve had a distant look in his eyes and at first appeared not to have heard the question. "A friend of Erik's," he replied in a monotone.

Bill picked up the full bottle of Heineken and poured it down the drain. "Your boyfriend sure has some hot looking friends." He tossed the empty bottle into the garbage can. "There was something weird about him though. I thought he was kind of creepy."

Steve raised his eyes to meet Bill's. "You got that same impression too?"

Bill shrugged his shoulders. "Yeah, he seemed kind of out of it. Like he was on something. Didn't even touch his beer. Rude too. Why is it that the cute ones are always so damned off the wall?"

"Good question," Steve said but Bill had already left. Another shiver ran up his spine as he thought about Victor. The conversation made no sense at all but he felt that there was a lot more to Victor's relationship with Erik than he had let on. The next time he saw Erik, he would force him to come clean about his past—especially as far as this Victor character was concerned.

Steve took another sip from his beer and stood up. "Night Bill," he called out as he started walking to the front door. All of a sudden he realized that his headache was gone.

* * *

Victor was already at home by the time Steve left the restaurant. He threw his jacket over a chair and glided into the living room and sat on a French loveseat. He then stretched out, placing his hands behind his head, a smile plastered on his face.

"Such an attractive young thing you have Erik," he said out loud. "You have done very well for yourself, very well indeed." He stared at the ceiling. "I think he shall make a fine specimen, a nice addition to our little family."

He rose abruptly and directed himself towards the window, where he stood gazing at the blackness. "It is a pity that you will not be around to witness the transformation!" His hands were balled up into fists, rendering his already pale skin even whiter from the intense pressure he was applying. His blue eyes blazed so red with fury and hatred, that if anyone would have accidentally made eye contact with him at that moment, the pour soul would have most certainly dropped dead from instant cardiac arrest.

The Revelation

◆

Jon Rickman became aware of the offensive taste in his mouth before he opened his eyes. Lying in bed, he contemplated this noxious sensation. His mouth tasted of cotton balls that had been drenched in rubbing alcohol. What in the hell had he been drinking last night? He tried to think back. Nothing except for a few beers. His eyes still closed, last night's events slowly began to reappear inside of his foggy brain. Oh yeah, there was the guy he brought home last night. Tall, dark and handsome. He didn't remember doing anything out of the ordinary with the dude. A little blow job action that's all and if he remembered correctly, he only had one beer after they arrived at the apartment. So why in the hell did he feel like such shit?

He opened his eyes and quickly closed them again, the onslaught of sunlight too painful. His head began to pound. Since when did a couple of beers give him a hangover of this caliber? If he wanted to, he could usually drink at least a twelve pack and walk steady on his own two feet. He must be coming down with something and whatever it was, it was kicking his ass. Good thing he didn't have to work today. There was no way he could have made it through an entire day judging by the way he felt now.

He opened his eyes again, this time more slowly in order to allow them to adjust to the light. He stayed in bed for another ten minutes, trying to clear his cobwebbed mind. With a Herculean effort, he finally managed to lift himself up from the bed and place his feet on the cold wooden floor. As he erected himself, he lost control of his knees and plummeted downward. He grabbed a hold of the nightstand with both hands, narrowly avoiding contact with the floor. He turned his body around and sat back down on the edge of the bed. Shit, he must have one nasty bug. He breathed deeply several times, as if it were lack of oxygen that was causing his dizziness. He had to at least get to the bathroom to get some water. He felt dehydrated and needed to rinse away the ghastly taste from his mouth. A good douse with Listerine should do the trick.

He had never lost his balance before or experienced such a total loss of strength. A few years ago, he had come down with the flu for the first time in his life and it had hit him hard. He was in bed for four days, delirious most of the time. That was the first and only time as far as he was concerned, that he had ever been really ill, although his mother insists that he had experienced the same virus when he was about eleven years old and had slept for three days straight without so much as even going to the bathroom. She had recounted the story to him many times. At the end of the third day, she had become so worried that she had finally called the doctor. When she informed the doctor that her son Jon had not so much as even stirred in three days time, he supposedly became hysterical (one of his Mother's favorite words) and said, *"Mrs. Rickman! Get some water into the boy immediately! He must be dangerously dehydrated by now!"* She then forced her son, in his delirium, to consume some water and on the morning of the fourth day, supposedly, he had ventured downstairs in a complete daze, unsure of what day it was. That is how she told it. Personally, he had no such recollection of ever having the flu as a child and never believed his Mother's long-winded tale. But then, he didn't believe a lot of what she said.

Right now, he felt worse than any illness, childhood or adult, had ever shown him. He was shaky and his energy was depleted. He took another deep breath. He had to give it another try. He wasn't about to sit on the edge of this damned bed all day. Steadying himself on the night-stand, he brought his feet to the floor and, still holding on, rested his entire weight on his bare feet. So far so good. His knees still felt shaky but he was doing better than before. Maintaining this hunched over position for several seconds, he finally erected himself and let go of the nightstand, standing straight up. Still a little wobbly, he put one foot in front of the other. Okay, he was at least maintaining. He thought of the six-pack of Pepsi he had purchased the day before and directed himself to the kitchen instead of the bathroom. Pepsi is what he needed, some-thing chuck-full of sugar and caffeine. Still wary of falling, he took his time reaching the kitchen, stopping whenever he began to feel dizziness overcome him. After what seemed to be an eternity, he finally reached the refrigerator. He leaned his entire weight against it, took several deep breaths, and then moved back to swing open the door. After having retrieved the much-needed Pepsi, he stumbled to the kitchen table where he abruptly threw his weight on one of the creaky wooden chairs surrounding it. Opening the soft drink with the frenzy of a man whose very life depended upon the contents of the aluminum can, he emptied the container in one long gulp, the cold, sweet liquid dampening his parched pipes. He let go of a deep burp and pounded the empty can down on the table. He was starting to feel much better. He thought of the Blueberry Pop Tarts sitting in the cupboard above the sink and his stomach rumbled, but he decided that it would be best to wait a few more minutes before daring to journey across the kitchen.

The aroma of rubbing alcohol, now gone from his mouth, pene-trated his nostrils. This horrid smell was obviously not doing his headache any good. Resting his head in his hands, he tried to remember anything he could have done or consumed the previous night that could be the cause of this internal medicine-like smell he couldn't get rid of. Last night's events all seemed so hazy, as if they had been a bro-ken dream which was becoming more and more difficult to reconstruct.

He creased his forehead as he thought. Okay, first he brought home that guy. What was his name? Derrick? No, it was Erik. They had a beer and talked very little. He remembered the guy was very quiet and seemed nervous. On second thought, not nervous, more like evasive. He seemed like a nice enough guy though. The sex hadn't been too bad although the guy was a bit hesitant at first. There was something else. The guy had felt strange somehow. Now he remembered—his skin. It was almost cold to the touch. The thought had crossed his mind that this guy was somehow sick and was suffering from a low-grade fever. He had seemed perfectly healthy in every other way—just cold. They had sex—safe sex, of course. Rickman had made sure of that. But what had happened after that? Nothing that he could recall. He must have fallen asleep after that. When he awoke, the guy was gone and he felt like absolute shit.

He stood on his wobbly legs and hobbled back to the refrigerator to retrieve another can of Pepsi. The thirst was back already. Now conscious of his growling stomach, he maneuvered himself to the cabinet and retrieved the box of Pop Tarts. Although he usually liked them toasted, he wasn't going to mess with it today and would just eat them cold, right out of the package, like he did when he was a kid. He did feel better than he had when he first awoke. Looks like that was all he needed—massive amounts of sugar.

His thoughts drifted once again back to last night's visitor. This Erik was quite a hot number if he remembered correctly. Too bad he took off without them exchanging phone numbers. All at once, he realized that this guy could have ripped him off for all he knew. Where did he leave his wallet? His pants pocket. He hoped it was still there. He had been ripped off before by jerks that he brought home and it pissed him off to no end. This Erik didn't seem like the type who would roll you when you were asleep. But you never know. His experience as a police officer had shown him that anyone is capable of anything at any time.

Finishing his soda, he walked slowly back to the bedroom. This time the trip was much easier although the lightheadedness remained. He was weak and felt drained. He picked up his pants that had been thrown over a chair the night before and retrieved his wallet. Everything was there, including all of his money. For a fleeting instant, he felt guilty for suspecting this Erik of ripping him off, but the feeling passed almost as quickly as it came. After all, he didn't know him from Adam. They talked very little and he didn't know anything about him, not even his last name. It didn't take long at all for Rickman to get him into bed. He smiled to himself as he remembered the ravenous way in which the man had attacked him once they plopped into the sack. He may have been soft-spoken but was an animal in bed. At first, it was doubtful that Rickman was even going to score with the guy, as he had seemed so wishy-washy about messing around. He sure had him pegged wrong. He should have known better. It's always the quiet ones who are the wildest.

He sat back down on the bed, debating whether or not he should try to get some more sleep. He still felt tired. He glanced at the digital clock next to the bed. Shit, it was 2:30 in the afternoon! Calculating in his head, he realized that he had slept for almost thirteen hours. He had to be sick. Six hours of sleep a night for him was considered lucky, even on his days off. He had never been able to sleep for long periods of time— his mind was always too busy working on whatever case he happened to be on at the time. Some of his colleagues had suggested to him that perhaps he took his job a little too seriously. Maybe he did. But for him, being a cop was his life. Lately, he had been sleeping even less than usual. The vampire case was on his mind constantly these days and he had been able to think of nothing else, except perhaps, of an occasional roll in the hay. The fact that the department suspected that a real vampire committed the murders caused his already overworked brain to churn night and day. Initially, he had a difficult time accepting this premise, but the more he worked on the case, the more he began to agree that it was a possibility. If even the seasoned cops on the force were starting to consider it, who was he to argue? Although everything he believed in was being challenged, he had no choice but to eventually listen to his logic. He shivered when he tried to picture a vampire with its teeth buried in someone's neck, sucking out all the blood like some kind of goddamned leech. But was this case really so much different than the other lunatic murderer cases he had come across over the years? These fuckers will kill without reason but always end up getting careless. This bastard was bound to eventually make a mistake. The only question that remained, was when we find him, how in the hell do we kill him?

Deciding not to go back to sleep, he walked towards the bathroom. Maybe what he needed was a nice hot shower. A good shower has been known to cure even the worst of hangovers. He just had to be careful not to lose his footing.

He pulled open the glass door and stepped inside, steadying himself on the shower wall. He made a mental note to himself to buy some more of the slip-proof decals to put on the bottom of his bathtub. The ones he had put down a couple of years ago were now mostly shredded. You could hardly tell anymore that they used to be fish. He bent down to turn on the shower. A good majority of his strength had come back and he was feeling a little less lightheaded. The hot water felt great pounding on his exhausted body and he slowly felt life creep back into his veins. The steam from the shower penetrated his nostrils and he could notice the rubbing alcohol odor starting to subside. He grabbed his washcloth and a bar of soap and had just begun lathering up his body when he felt a sharp, stinging sensation on his right leg. He looked down and saw two rather large marks on his leg, encircled by a bright purple bruise. Through the steam and the soap, it was difficult to get a good look at them but from what he could make out, they appeared to be some sort of bite marks. Without finishing his shower, he turned off the water, quickly dried himself, then sat down on the closed toilet seat to take a closer look. About three inches from his crotch were two large holes about an inch and a half from each other, both resting on the vein of his right leg. If those were in fact bite marks, they must have been made my one hell of a honking big spider. They were about half the size of a dime but seemed jagged, as if some sort of serrated object made them. A scab had already formed on both the marks. Rickman stared at the wounds in amazement. He had no memory of either injuring himself or getting bit and judging by the size of these marks, if it was an insect that had decided to take a chomp out of him, he certainly would have felt it. Irritated by the hot water and soap from the shower, the wounds were stinging even worse now. He pressed on the bruise and let out a yelp of pain. He was perplexed. This must have happened last night—he certainly would have noticed it before. But when? In his sleep? If something big enough to make these kinds of marks had bitten him, he no doubt would have woken up, especially being the light sleeper that he was. It didn't make any sense.

He stood up on the cool tile floor, the steam from his shower finally starting to dissipate. He was just about the leave the bathroom when for the first time that morning he caught a glimpse of himself in the mirror and stopped dead in his tracks. Dark circles surrounded his eyes and the skin on his lips was chapped and broken. He looked as if he hadn't slept in weeks. What startled him most, was the color of his skin—or the lack thereof. He had never seen himself look so pale. He inched himself closer to the mirror and traced his face with his fingers then stepped back, almost in horror.

"What in the hell is going on here?" he said out loud. He continued staring at this reflection and glanced down again at the glowing red marks on his leg. Towel still in his hand, he dashed off to the bedroom and threw back the covers. There on the sheets were several deep red spots, already darkened, of what appeared to be blood–and now there was little doubt in his mind that it was his own blood on the sheets. He sat down on the edge of the bed. His hands began to shake uncontrollably.

"Holy fuck," he said out loud. "I think I've found the vampire!"

Confrontation

◆

The loud knock on the door caused Steve to jump, dropping his book to the floor. He had become so engrossed in the publication that he had lost track of time. He had spent a majority of the day in front of his computer trying to put together another article on the vampire murders. He was amazed at how much information was available on vampires and was even more surprised at how serious many people were about the subject. He had figured that the Internet would be a good place to start and after entering the word *'vampire'* in one of the many Internet search engines, his screen became flooded with more information than he would ever have had time to look through. He visited many of the World Wide Web sites listed, printing out as much information as he could find out about the subject. One of his most surprising discoveries was a list of Message Boards who all shared the common theme of vampires. He had logged onto one of them and literally spent hours browsing the various forums. Many of the posted messages were by people who actually seemed to believe that they themselves were vampires, countless of them claiming to be hundreds of years old, some even thousands, each comparing stories of the previous night's feast. Some of these online fiends had given themselves names from popular vampire novels. Steve found the messages to be entertaining yet frightening in a way. What if some of these people actually believed that they were vampires and tried to live the exact lifestyle of such a creature?

Maybe some psycho would even push it so far as to drink human blood. Wasn't there a case a few years back of a guy who had killed someone and drank the corpse's blood because the murderer believed he was a vampire? It seemed to him that he had read something about it but no longer remembered when or where. He would have to pop to the library later to see if could dig up some information about the crime. He also made a mental note to give Rickman a call and discuss it with him. But then there was the other stuff that Rickman had brought up—the saliva, for one. That would be difficult to explain.

As he got up to answer the door, he frowned when he realized what a mess he had made of his apartment. There were computer printouts outs strewn all over the living room along with several books relating to vampires, all evidence of his day's work. When he was expecting Erik, he made a point of ensuring that his apartment was immaculate. He sighed. Too late to worry about it now.

After tucking his shirt into his pants, he opened the front door. His lover stood there with a huge smile on his face. Steve was struck by Erik's appearance. Radiant was the only word which came to mind. His green eyes flashed brilliantly, full of life, and his skin had a velvety glow to it. Steve had observed that Erik was looking weary and pale the last few days as if he weren't getting enough sleep or perhaps coming down with something. Whatever the reason, he certainly had recovered. He looked wonderful tonight.

"I missed you," Erik said as Steve continued to stare at him. He strode into the apartment and wrapped his cool arms around Steve. As Steve buried his face in Erik's neck, a pleasant aroma filled his nostrils—an aroma that he couldn't quite pinpoint. It had a sweet scent to it, almost like that of fresh lilacs but not quite. It was not like any kind of cologne he had ever smelled. He nuzzled Erik's neck and hair, breathing in the pleasant scent.

Erik broke the embrace, placed his hands firmly on Steve's face and lowered his head until their lips met. Steve's lips parted, allowing Erik's tongue easy entry into his mouth. Steve felt himself melting into the kiss. At that moment, his mind held no other thoughts except for those of the handsome man he was kissing. Steve felt Erik's hand slip under his shirt and run gently along his back, caressing Steve's skin as they kissed. The familiar cool sensation of Erik's hand caused Steve to shiver slightly. Steve kissed him harder and more passionately.

Steve finally pulled away, almost out of breath. "I have to spend a night from away from you more often," Steve said. A wide-eyed grin was planted on his face.

Erik grabbed his hand and led him toward the couch. "I just wanted to show you how much I missed not seeing you last night."

When they reached the couch, Steve bent over to pick up some of the papers spread over it and threw them on the floor.

"What is all of this?" Erik asked, pointing to the pile of computer printouts and books. "It seems someone has been busy."

"Just research," Steve said.

"Research?"

Steve hated to bring it up, remembering Erik's brusque attitude the last time he discussed the killings with him.

"I've been working all day on the dumpster murder story. You wouldn't believe how much information there is about vampires. Just about everything you can think of." He pointed to the stack of books on the coffee table next to the couch. "Have you ever read any of these?"

Erik frowned. "I am not much for horror novels. Besides, I came over to see you, not to discuss—vampires." A forced smile returned to his face and his eyes once again scanned the papers.

They snuggled up on the couch. Steve reached out and began rubbing Erik's chest. He loved the feel of his hard body underneath the t-shirt.

They were silent. Steve's mind churned. It was time to clear the air. He took a deep breath, trying to build up his nerve. It was now or never.

"I met a friend of yours last night," Steve said.

Erik turned his head to look at Steve, a confused look crossing over his face. "A friend of mine? Who?"

"He said his name was Victor. He stopped in at the bar at work. Name ring a bell?"

Steve was startled when Erik abruptly pulled away from him. He was visibly shaken. He grabbed a hold of Steve's shoulders and looked him right in the eyes.

"Are you certain he said his name was Victor?"

Steve nodded.

Eric continued. "What else did he say? What is he doing here? How long has he been here? What did he tell you about me?"

Steve stared at Erik warily. "Looks like this Victor guy upsets you."

"Steven, please. It is essential that you answer my questions." Erik genuinely seemed angry.

Steve pursed his lips and crossed his arms. "He didn't say too much at all really. He asked me if I was dating you and told me that you two were old friends back in New York. He also said that he would be in touch with you. I have to admit that he gave me the creeps."

Erik rose abruptly, walked around the apartment then returned to the couch where Steve was still seated. He stopped in front of him.

"Are you sure that is all he said? Steven, it is extremely important that you remember every word that was said."

"Well," Steve paused, "he did say something that I found rather strange. When I told him that I didn't have your address or phone number, he implied that he wasn't surprised. What was that supposed to mean?"

Erik ignored the question. He sat back down on the couch and grabbed both of Steve's hands.

"Steve, if he ever shows up again, do not talk to him. Stay as far away from him as you can. I mean it Steve, do not go near this man." His eyes flashed as he spoke.

Steve nodded, feeling almost afraid to speak. "Okay, but I think you have a little bit of explaining to do. You owe me that much. Who is he anyway and why is it so important that I stay away from him?"

Erik sighed and slumped backwards. "He is somebody from my past—somebody that you do not want to get to know, trust me." He hesitated, looking at Steve. "I met him when I lived in New York. A relationship developed between the two of us but ended on a very bitter note."

"Ah ha! So you two were lovers!"

"I would be hard pressed to call what we had any sort of romantic relationship." Erik paused for a moment, then, "Victor knows nothing about love." His voice was angry and bitter.

"What was your relationship with him then?"

"More that of mentor and student," Erik said, watching Steve. "What I do know is that he is extremely dangerous," he added.

"Dangerous?"

"More than you realize. I quickly discovered that he was not completely sane. I am very serious about this. You must avoid him at all costs."

Steve looked at Erik with no expression on his face. "I think it's time to talk Erik. I hope this doesn't scare you away, but I need to say this." His voice lowered to almost a whisper. "I love you Erik, I really do. I'm not sure when it happened but it did and I have no idea if you feel the same way about me. I have fallen for you hard. I wish I could have told you this under different circumstances. The point I am trying to make is that I know absolutely nothing about you—where you come from, what your past was like, what your hobbies are—nothing at all. Victor was the one who told me that you were from New York. And this Victor did bring up an interesting item. After all this time, why is it that I don't know where you live or even what your telephone number is? Wouldn't you say that it's strange that I don't? What's up with that Erik? Do you have some kind of horrible past that you're hiding?"

Erik looked at Steve, a look of astonishment on his face. He said nothing. Steve continued.

"If this Victor is as dangerous as you say he is, then I deserve to know what this is all about. I will wait all night if I have to."

The silence that fell between them was maddening. Steve waited, not saying a word. He was finished with his tirade. It was Erik's turn.

Erik swallowed hard and finally spoke. "Steve, first of all I want you to know that you are the most important thing in my life. I have never loved anyone like I love you. You mean everything to me and I would never do anything to hurt you. You do know that, do you not?"

Steve beamed. "I guess I do now."

"My main concern right now is for your safety. Yes, I have been hiding my past from you. I will tell you everything. I promise you that." He sighed. "I have been meaning to for quite some time but have found it difficult to find the right words. The time has come, I realize that." Erik looked down at the pile of papers on the floor, and the word '*vampire*' jumped out at him. He turned back to his companion. "It is late and I will require an entire evening to tell you all. Would you be able to take tomorrow night off from work?"

"I guess so. Okay."

"Perfect. I want you to come over tomorrow night to my home. Then, you will learn everything. All I ask is that you keep an open mind and know that I love you deeply, no matter what your reaction will be to what I tell you."

Steve slowly nodded. At first, he had no response. His mouth became as dry as the Sahara dessert in August and he felt as though he had just been struck by a brick. So there was some sort of horrible secret after all and by the way Erik was acting, it was obviously something big. How would he make it until tomorrow night without knowing what it was?

"What about tomorrow during the day?" Steve asked. "Couldn't we get together then? I have no plans at all."

Erik shook his head. "Impossible. You shall find out why tomorrow night. Trust me Steve. You will know all then."

"If I have to wait until the evening, then I'm willing to do so. The most important thing right now, is that I don't lose you. I suppose one more day won't kill me, since I've waited this long." He smiled weakly at Erik. "I have to admit that I'm kind of nervous about tomorrow."

"You have every right to be," Erik said under his breath, so low that Steve couldn't hear him.

"What did you say?" Steve asked.

"I feel that everything will work out. I love you too much to let you go now." He reached over, pulling Steve close to him. They held each other tightly.

"Erik?" Steve whispered in his hear.

"What?"

"Will you make love to me? I really need you close to me right now. I mean really close."

Erik pulled away and looked directly into Steve's eyes, a big smile on his face. "I was just thinking the same thing."

They both stood up, they eyes never unlocking. Hand in hand, they walked into the bedroom. For the rest of the evening, they made love, slowly yet with an intensity they had not yet experienced with each other. Steve, exhausted, cuddled up to Erik, his head resting on Erik's chest. Neither of them said a word as Steve listened to the steady rhythm of Erik's breathing. He knew that when he awoke in the morning Erik would be gone. He ran his hand over Erik's chest and held him close as he fell into a troubled sleep.

The Truth Be Told

◆

Steve tried to take a nap but couldn't sleep. He was too wound up and too nervous, and the nearer it came to dusk, the more nervous he became. He had mixed feelings about what the night threatened to hold in store for him. According to Erik, tonight he would know all. But the question was, all of what? All day he had tried to imagine what kind of horrible secret Erik could be hiding from him. All he knew was that it had something to do with that creepy Victor guy who, according to Erik, was dangerous. Was he a murderer? Steve's mind conjured up all types of horrible images but he pushed them back.

He sighed and glanced out the window again. The sun was finally setting. Erik had told him not to come over until it was dark, as he wouldn't be home before then. Steve guessed he must have left town during the day, probably having something to do with his antique business, although Steve had the strange feeling that there was a lot more to it than that. How could Erik stay up until almost the crack of dawn every night and then go out of town on business seven days a week? The man would have to sleep sometime.

"I'd say that it's just about as dark as it's going to get," he said out loud.

Steve walked away from the window and checked himself out one more time in the full-length mirror that hung on his bedroom wall. With one final tuck of his shirt into his jeans, he strolled into the living room, stopped at the front closet and retrieved his coat. His heart felt as if it were literally in his throat. For all he knew, tonight could be the end of his relationship with Erik, depending on what Erik would tell him. He once again told himself that he would be able to handle anything Erik would tell him. He felt that with Erik, he had found that 'one true love'—the one that everyone says happens only once in a person's lifetime. He certainly hadn't felt it with Jack, that's for sure and now that it was here, he wasn't going to willingly walk away from it, no matter what. With one final deep breath, he left the apartment.

The house was easy to find, as Steve knew Chicago, or at least his immediate neighborhood, extremely well. He was surprised to learn how close Erik lived to his own apartment. He recognized Erik's house even before he saw the address. It was a huge old place with a Victorian elegance, exactly the kind of place in which Steve expected Erik to live. Seeing how much Erik loved antiques, it would only make sense that he would choose to live in a Victorian mansion. With a gulp, Steve walked to the huge oak door and knocked loudly.

Before he had a chance to move his hand away from the door, it flew open. Erik hugged Steve right in the doorway.

"Hey hunk," Erik said, releasing Steve.

Steve followed his lover through a long hallway which led through the dining room and finally into a small, yet cozy sitting room. Steve was in awe. The house was decorated in antiques and furniture which no doubt must have cost a fortune. A huge crystal chandelier swung in the dining room above a wooden table equipped with eight high-backed chairs. It was obvious from the furnishings that Erik had money. Steve pictured himself living here then blushed at the thought.

"Have a seat," Erik said with a devilish smile on his face, as if he had just read Steve's mind. There was a slight quiver to his voice, which informed Steve that Erik was just has nervous as he was.

Steve sat down and Erik plopped next to him, crossing his legs and sitting on them. "I appreciate that you took the night off from work. I pray that it did not cause you any unnecessary difficulties."

Steve shook his head. "I just called in sick. It was too short of a notice to find a replacement. They were actually really nice about it. I'm one of the few people who show up for work consistently so they don't give me too much shit when I do call in."

They sat in silence for a few minutes, hands entwined. Steve's heart was beating in anticipation of what was to follow.

Erik reached over and gave him a peck on the cheek. "I guess it is time to get this all out in the open. It is difficult for me to determine where to begin." He stood up and walked to the window.

Steve watched his every movement. "Start from wherever you feel the most comfortable. You have my undivided attention."

Erik turned and smiled at Steve. "You are truly wonderful, you know that?"

"So I've been told," Steve said. He flashed a grin at Erik in return, trying the hide the intense nervousness he was experiencing.

Erik took a deep breath, turned back to face the window and started to speak.

"First let me say how distressed I was when you advised me that Victor had stopped by to see you. It has been many, many years since I have last seen him and in all actuality, was hoping never to lay eyes upon him again. Yet, I knew that he would find me eventually and that I would have to deal with him when the moment arrived. It seems that time has finally come." He hesitated for a moment, then continued. "There is something very important about Victor you need to know. You see, I have every reason to suspect that Victor is the one who has committed the murders which you have taken upon yourself to investigate."

"You mean the Vampire Murders?" Steve asked. The astonishment was evident in his voice.

"The very same. From everything that I know about Victor, there is little doubt in my mind that it is he." His voice faded to almost a whisper. "You see Steve, Victor is a vampire."

There was silence. Erik still stood with his back facing Steve, his eyes affixed to the darkness outside of the window. Finally Steve spoke, his eyes glued to Erik's back.

"A vampire? You're trying to tell me that he's like...a real live neck-biting vampire?"

"That is precisely what I am saying. I know this may be difficult to believe but I assure you, it is the truth. In spite of all the vampire related materials in which you have been engrossing yourself as of late, I hope that you are still capable of keeping an open mind." He stopped for a moment, brushed his fingers through his hair and continued. "I read your article in the newspaper about a serial killer being responsible for the murders. You are half right. Your guess is correct that Victor is a serial killer, but he is a serial killer who is also a vampire."

"Do you have any proof of this?" Steve stammered.

"There is a reason that I am telling you all of this," Erik said, ignoring Steve's question. "You have asked how I fit into all of this and what my relationship with Victor was. That is a long story, which I am about to recount to you. But before I commence, you need to know one important fact." The sound of his sigh echoed in the quiet room.

"Steve, I too, am a vampire."

Steve stared at Erik's back in utter amazement. He wished Erik would turn around and look at him.

"I don't know what to say. I mean if you think you're a vampire, maybe we could..."

Steve never finished his sentence. He had been watching Erik at the window carefully as he spoke, and then next thing he knew Erik was gone and now was sitting right next to him on the couch! He had not seen Erik move from the window.

Steve gasped and instinctively stood up. Without thinking, he took several steps away from the couch and began to shake uncontrollably. He looked at Erik with round eyes, his mouth gaping.

"What the…." His heart was pounding faster than he had ever experienced and it became difficult for him to fill his lungs with the air he so badly needed at the moment. He feared he was having a heart attack. He took a couple of more steps back.

Erik sat calmly on the couch. He began in a soothing voice, "Steve, please do not be afraid. I knew that you did not believe what I was telling you. The only way to convince you of the truth was to show you. I need you to know that I would never, ever hurt you."

"How….how…did you do that?"

Steve could barely get the words out. He was frightened. His instincts screamed to him to run out of the house. Holy fuck! Erik was really a vampire.

"I have the ability to move very quickly—so quickly that the human eye is unable to detect my movement. It is one of my…gifts." Erik's voice was soft and quiet, as if he were lulling a baby to sleep.

In spite of the softness of Erik's voice, Steve was still frightened. Fearing that he would hyperventilate, he crouched over, taking several rapid breaths while still trying to keep an eye on Erik. For the first time ever, he felt actual fear for his life. Everything he had ever learned, read or seen about vampires came rushing into his thoughts. Vampires kill. They are undead. Evil. They drink your blood. They tear out your throat. Trying to catch his breath, Steve looked up at Erik wide-eyed, unable to say anything.

Erik looked as if he were close to tears. "Please Steve, do not be afraid of me. You never have to be afraid of me."

"I'm not afraid," Steve stammered.

Erik looked down, trying to appear as non-threatening as he could. "Yes you are." He paused. "I can sense it."

Steve looked at Erik for just a moment then his head quickly turned to the door, calculating the distance to it from where he stood. Would he have a chance of making it before Erik killed him?

"Steve, all I ask is that you hear me out. When I am finished, you have the option of leaving here and never coming back. I promise you. You will be free to go."

Steve stood immobile in front of the couch, his hands limp at his side. "You're....you're…"

Erik's voice broke his thought. "Steve, there are actually very few differences between you and me. We are basically the same—thinking, feeling, emotional beings."

Steve's eyes met those of the vampire. "Do you drink blood?"

He took several more steps back and was now standing almost in the center of the room. He stared wide-eyed at Erik and unconsciously brought his hand up to his throat, as if to protect it from an imminent attack.

Erik took a moment before answering. "Drinking blood is, unfortunately necessary for my survival. But Steve," he took a deep breath, "partaking of blood does not mean that I have to kill. There are ways to feed without harming the person involved."

Steve shook his head, wordless. He shifted his weight from one leg, then to the other, not daring to unlock his eyes from Erik's for a moment.

Erik continued in a wooing voice. "What I need from you now is to not think of the vampire in the traditional sense. Do not try to compare me with the fictional vampires of Hollywood movies and your mainstream horror novels. Vampirism is more like a disease, one that is unfortunately incurable. I am not some fiend out to drain humans of their blood. I am just like you. I have feelings. I can love, laugh and cry. I can feel pain and sorrow. I feel everything you do."

The adrenaline still flooded Steve's veins as he tried to force himself to calm down. He couldn't help wonder if Erik would still kill him after all.

"Steve, please listen to me. I could not even hurt you much less kill you."

"*You can read my thoughts?*" Steve finally managed to stammer.

Erik nodded. "Only when your emotions are strong, like they are right now, am I able to clearly tell what you're thinking. With concentration, I can pick up some of your thoughts when you are in a relaxed state." He smiled warmly at Steve. "Do not worry though. I refrain from such behavior unless it is necessary. I do not believe in invading one's privacy—especially if it is someone that I care about, or love, like I do you."

Steve's heart rate, although still rapid, was beginning to slow closer to a normal rate. "I," he gulped, "love you too."

Erik breathed a sigh of relief, then smiled.

"I can imagine how difficult this must be for you and I can sympathize with what you are going through right now. I have agonized for a long time about how to tell you. All I ask is that you be willing to hear everything that I need to say. Give me that chance."

Steve nodded, still standing firm in the center of the room.

Erik asked, "Can I get you a beverage before we continue? A beer? You look like you could use one."

Steve smiled weakly, still keeping his distance. "I think I could use a drink right now. Just don't zip in and out so fast that I can't see you, okay?"

"I promise. No more tricks."

Erik got up slowly as not to startle Steve. He unhurriedly walked to the kitchen and returned with two beers. He smiled when he saw that Steve had retaken his place on the couch.

"Here you go," Erik said as he handed Steve a beer. He did not join Steve on the couch but rather stood a few feet in front of it. The boy's fear was still strong.

"May I continue with my story?" Erik asked.

"Can I ask you a few questions first? There's so much I need to know."

Erik nodded. "You can ask me anything you want. I shall be as open and honest with you as I can."

Steve eyed Erik cautiously.

"Can you turn into a bat?"

Erik laughed, then covered his mouth. "I apologize, Steve. I did not mean to laugh at your question. No, I cannot change into a bat, a wolf, a rat or into any other animal. As you saw earlier, I have the ability to move swiftly and for great distances, remaining virtually undetectable. It is almost like being able to fly while still remaining on the ground. However, I cannot fly. All of my senses are razor sharp. I can see in almost complete darkness and hear the most minute whisper and, as I explained to you, have limited ability to read the thoughts of others."

Steve listened eagerly to what Erik was saying, trying to register every last word.

"It is true what they say about not being able to go out in the sun? Is this why you have never spent the night with me?"

Erik nodded sadly. "That is the reason I have never been able to stay until dawn. If sunlight were to come into contact with my body, I would burn. I do not know whether I would survive such contact as I have never attempted to test it. My guess is that I would not.

"That's a relief," Steve said unconsciously.

Erik appeared momentarily horrified.

"A relief?"

"Oh, I didn't mean it like that. I was just beginning to wonder if the reason you always left the way you did was that you had another lover on the side that you were seeing in the morning. It never made any sense to me why you wouldn't spend the night. I just feel better now that I know." A faint smile crossed his lips.

"I suspected that question would arise eventually."

"I hope what I ask next won't offend you, but….do you sleep in a coffin?"

Erik hesitated. "It is not absolutely necessary that I sleep in a coffin but have nevertheless chosen to do so. The main reason is for protection. I can lock myself in from the inside and thus am ensured that I am safe from any contact with the sun. A coffin can be easily disguised and hidden, with a slim chance of being discovered for what its true purpose is. You see, if I were by some chance discovered in the coffin, I would be mistaken for dead. Moments before the sun rises, there is another physical change that occurs. I slip into what I can best describe as a sort of a deep coma. My heartbeat is almost undetectable and there is no response to any physical stimulation—no pupil dilation, no reflex reactions, nothing at all that would suggest that I was alive. There is nothing that I know of that could awaken me from this sleep. It is when I am my most vulnerable."

Steve swallowed and said nothing. Erik walked slowly to the couch, knelt down in front of Steve and grabbed both of his hands. "Are you okay?"

Steve looked into Erik's eyes and held tightly onto his hands. His fear had mostly dissipated. "I'm not sure. You know? I mean this is a lot at once to handle. It's not everyday that you find out that the man you're in love with is a real honest to goodness vampire. I definitely will need some time to absorb all of this."

"I understand that Steve and wish I could give you all the time you need. But there is a more important issue that we both have to deal with. I suspect that you are now in serious danger."

Steve stared back wide-eyed. "Me in danger? You mean because of this Victor?"

Erik nodded. "He does nothing without careful planning, which leads me to believe that his visit to you was an omen that he has some plan in the works—and I have little doubt that it directly involves you."

"I take it he's really pissed at you."

Erik chuckled. "Really pissed would be putting it mildly." He stood up, walked across the room and sat down in a chair facing the couch. "Let me tell you everything, right from the very beginning. It will help you understand what kind of creature Victor is and what we will have to contend with.

"I'm ready," Steve said. "I do want to hear everything." He sat frozen and struggled not to lower his eyes.

Erik nodded. "Very well then. I have recounted this story only to one other person so telling certain parts of it may prove difficult. I beg of you to bear with me."

His eyes contained a sudden flicker of pain. He took a deep breath and then began his story.

Unfortunate Encounter

◆

"My childhood was normal by most standards. Living in New York back then was a lot different than it is now. Times have greatly changed since 1904.

"1904?" Steve asked in amazement. "That would mean you're…"

"Ninety-seven. I will celebrate my ninety-eighth birthday in September. There are certain advantages of being a vampire." Erik smiled broadly and continued. "Much to the disappointment of my mother, I grew up to be very similar to my father, what I guess one would classify today as a troublemaker. Engulfed with lassitude by the time I was eighteen, I was no longer content to work in my father's store. He himself paid very little attention to the family business at this point. Why should he have to when he had a devoted son to carry out all the work for him? He regularly provoked fights in town, would arrive home nightly in a state of drunkenness and ended up in jail more times than I can count. Bitter at being left in charge of the store while he was always gone, I rebelled. I hated everyone and everything, and, not unlike my father, trouble seemed to seek me out wherever I went. It was not unusual for me to crawl home at some ungodly hour of the morning with a bloody nose, a black eye or bruised ribs and had plenty of my own brushes with the law.

"It was also at this time that I slowly began to discover awakenings in me which were, by the standards of that time period, unnatural and perverted. That was at least the way I personally interpreted them. Back in the early 1900's, gay rights and gay pride parades were unheard of. If there were any gay meeting places in existence, I was not aware of them. Homosexuality was something that was not discussed or even mentioned except perhaps when it was interwoven into a fiery sermon by the minister, who swore that people with such penchants had a pre-arranged reservation in hell. When this horrible awakening overtook me, I became all the more restless and troublesome. Fights with my mother and father became more frequent and maintaining even the slightest measure of civility towards our customers at the store became a constant effort. I tried to fight these urges, convinced that the devil himself had surely taken hold of me. This constant battle made me all the more wild and untamed.

"Then the answer to my prayers, or so I thought at the time, entered my life. I was working late at the store one night when the most beautiful man I had ever seen came in for some provisions. The hidden urges which I had been fighting resurfaced, and I put forth not the slightest attempt to thrust them back from where they came. I had felt strong attractions to men before but never anything like this. As he gathered his items, my gaze was drawn to him. The first time that I looked up and our eyes locked, I knew there was something different about him. What it was I could not tell. Without ever talking to him before or knowing the slightest thing about him, I felt as if he knew everything about me, including my horrible secret, and loved me in spite of it. This feeling of complete exposure threw me into a panic and made me want to run from the store, run from him, and not look back. He finally came to the counter and spoke.

"'Is this your store?' he asked, staring into my eyes as if wooing me.

"'It is my father's,' I replied nervously. His gaze seemed to have frozen me for I found myself unable to move. 'I run it for him though as he has not the time, nor should I say the desire, to run it himself. Thus the obligation was handed down to me.'

"The words shocked me as they escaped my lips. I had no idea why I was telling all of this to him, a complete stranger and a customer. It was not in my nature to pour my heart out to anyone, much less someone that I had never met before.

"He narrowed his eyes, then shook his head in agreement. 'That is usually the case with young men such as yourself. Many are taken advantage of in such a fashion. It certainly creates a great deal of resentment between father and son, does it not? Especially when the son had no interest in devoting his life to such a trivial affairs.'

"I was elated. Somebody finally understood me. I nodded vigorously in agreement.

"'Yes!' I exclaimed. 'I am only doing this because this store is what supports the family—my mother and brothers. What I really wish to do is go off to the university and be something, anything besides a shopkeeper. The first chance I get I am….'

"'Your name is Erik, is it not?' he interrupted. I noticed that his eyes gleamed like the sun on ice.

"I felt my eyes widen in surprise. How did this man know my name? I was certain he was a stranger to me. I immediately wondered what else he knew about me and felt my face redden should be aware of my unsavory exploits as of late. Perhaps my first feeling about him was correct. Perhaps he actually did know everything there was to know about me.

"'Yes, my name is Erik,' I stuttered, suddenly wary of him. 'May I inquire as to how you are familiar with my name? Have we met somewhere before?'

"He laughed heartily then smiled. 'If we had met before, I most assuredly would have remembered such an encounter. No, I have heard about you in town. There have been stories of the shopkeeper's beautiful son who has an incurable thirst for adventure and conflict. I am most delighted to finally make the acquaintance of one so well-known and so similar to myself.'

"I was speechless and could feel the hot color returning to my cheeks. I could not find the words to respond as he held me in his impenetrable gaze.

"'Who are you anyway?' I was finally able to stutter.

"'I am called Victor,' he said simply. He leaned closer until I could feel his hot breath upon my face. His voice lowered to a soft whisper. 'And what they say is true—you are a most beautiful boy. I should be delighted to get to know you better.' He leaned over the counter and kissed me lightly on the cheek.

"Without waiting for a response, he smiled and left the store, abandoning the food which he had so meticulously chosen from the shelves. I stood alone, gaping and wide-eyed. I had never met such an incredible man. My thoughts were in a frenzy as the urges which I had so desperately tried to suppress, flooded to the surface. My mind could think of nothing else but the beauty of Victor's eyes, the smoothness of his pale skin, the roundness of his lips. I felt that if I should not see this man again, I would surely perish. I dashed out the door after him but the streets were empty.

"I arrived home that night a changed man. I said nothing to my mother as I entered the house. I sequestered myself in my room, not even partaking of any dinner. There were to be no arguments with my parents that night. My thoughts were consumed with Victor, my soul on fire with his memory. I slept a tortured sleep laden with strange and erotic dreams of a man I barely knew.

"As I awoke the next morning, I knew that I would never be the same again, that I could no longer be content with the banal life I was leading. I felt anxious. I needed to act. I must find Victor. Should I have had to survive in my present state for any length of time, insanity would no doubt have overtaken me.

"That evening at the store, I watched the door impatiently, waiting for my beautiful stranger to pay me another visit. The hours miserably dragged by. He never came. I was devastated. By the time I closed the shop, I had convinced myself that I must push Victor out of my mind.

"I locked up the store and walked homeward with a relentless stride, attempting to clear my mind and refocus my thoughts. As I walked, I all at once had the feeling that I was being followed. I stopped and turned around. Silence. Convincing myself that it was only my imagination, I continued my walk home. The feeling of being observed was still very strong. I continued on foot until I was almost certain that I heard the steady click of footsteps behind me. I stopped once again and turned.

"'Is somebody there?' I called out, the slightest quiver to my voice.

"The streets were deserted and all was quiet. I continued marching forward, subconsciously increasing my pace. The footsteps returned, then suddenly stopped. Until now, I had always considered myself to be fearless, but now a strange foreboding took hold of me. I increased my stride once again and then noticed a figure ahead of me—a tall man standing on the street corner with a cigarette in his mouth. His posture revealed that he was expecting someone. I no longer heard the footsteps behind and lowered my head, breathing a sigh of relief as I approached.

"'Good evening, Erik,' a familiar voice said to me as I was about to pass. 'A bit chilly tonight, is it not?'

"I looked up. It was Victor. He stood on the edge of the street in a long dark coat and looked even more stunning then he had the previous evening. My heart raced at the sight of him.

"'Victor!' I said, not quite knowing what else to say to him. My delight at seeing him was evident.

"Even in the semi-darkness, his eyes gleamed. 'A cool night, yet perfect weather for an evening stroll. Would you not agree? Care to join me, my new friend?'

"It never occurred to me to ask him what he was doing there all alone at such a late hour or whether he was waiting for me. I was so happy to see him that I thought of nothing else but his presence next to me.

"'I should love to,' I replied happily but he had already started to walk. I caught up to him. 'I was just on my way home from the store.' The words sounded as if they were being spoken by a stranger.

"We walked side by side wordlessly. At the time, the silence did not seem the least bit odd. I felt safe and content at his side. Reaching the river, he stopped on top of the bank and sat down, his hands outstretched. I took his hand and sat next to him. My heart was beating wildly. I was unsure what was going to happen next.

"Without a word, his arms encircled my shoulders and he pulled me close to him. I felt myself snuggling into his body. It was the first time that I had ever been touched by a man in such a fashion. I felt myself becoming aroused and blushed in the darkness. The lurid thoughts had returned and I tried to push them out of my mind, lest they become apparent to my partner.

"I looked up and our eyes met. He was grinning broadly as though amused by my agony.

"'Such a strong and beautiful boy,' he murmured.

"He lowered his face to mine and for the first time, another man's lips came into contact with my own. His lips seemed unnaturally cold as his mouth parted and I felt his tongue invade my own mouth. I dissolved into the kiss, my mind whirling like a top. I broke the kiss and he watched me with a bitter smile upon his lips. His face suddenly seemed so pale.

"'I have never done this before,' I blurted out, 'with a man, I mean. I have thought about doing it over and over and now it has finally occurred. I just do not know if I want it to happen.'

"He laughed softly. 'You are just afraid, my little friend, that is all. Nothing more. To go against one's natural instincts is to go against nature itself. You must let yourself go and be what you are. In fighting your desires, you can only remain unfulfilled.'

"He once again lowered his mouth to mine. What little fight there may have been left inside of me departed. He reached around and held me tightly in his arms. His lips brushed my neck and I could feel his chilly teeth make contact with my skin. His breath was hot and sweet. The kisses he placed on my throat made me mad with passion and I pulled him all the closer to me. He then pulled away abruptly and stood up.

"He saw the confused look on my face and giggled with sudden delight. 'Come, let us walk.' The faintest curl of mockery frolicked on his lips.

"We walked together, my mind still unsure of the feelings that flooded my entire being. Under a bridge, he stopped and gazed at the sky.

"'The night belongs to us,' he exclaimed. 'The world is ours for the taking.' Then turning to look directly at me, 'If you are with me my young Erik, together we can rule such as no two beings have ever ruled before.'

"I swallowed hard. 'I am not sure of what you are speaking. I do not understand.'

"He laughed. 'Of course not. How could you? There are wonders and mysteries that you cannot even begin to comprehend, my naive friend. But I shall show you. I shall teach you all you need to know.'

"He turned to me, grabbed my shoulders and kissed me hard, so hard it hurt. I did not mind the pain. It felt wonderful to have another man's lips upon mine for the third time that night. I loved the way he spoke to me about ruling the world and all the mysteries he had to show me. I thought he was talking about love and the sexual heights to which he would take me. I discovered later that I was quite mistaken.

"He pulled away from the kiss, put both of his chilly hands on my face and looked deeply into my eyes. 'Yes, you will do very nicely,' he whispered fiercely. He ran a chilly hand through my hair. 'You are young, beautiful and strong. Such a perfect mate you shall make.' His words seemed to mount and echo in my ears.

"Perhaps it was the words that he spoke or the manner in which they were delivered, but my brain screamed that there was something wrong.

Unable to pinpoint the reason, I became filled with an unnamable dread. It seemed that Victor sensed this. His entire demeanor abruptly changed and the color drained from his cheeks.

"I nodded weakly to his words. 'But I hardly know you,' I stammered, 'and this is all so very new to me. I need time to sort this all out, time to try to understand myself, time to determine if this is what I truly want.'

"His smile was twisted and strange. 'Time?' he said. He then threw his head back and laughed, roared actually. 'My beautiful one, we have all eternity!' He seized my shoulders in a vice-like grip. 'Wait, and you will learn.'

"With that, he was gone. When I say gone, I mean he had completely disappeared from my sight, like a specter. The only sound that remained was the whistling of the wind underneath the bridge. I swung around like a madman. He was nowhere to be seen. He had been clutching onto me just a moment ago and now he had vanished. My young mind reeled in terror and I ran, moving faster than I had ever thought capable. The wind seemed to be singing my name, calling me, beckoning me, as I dashed towards my house, not daring to look back. When I reached my front door, I was exhausted and out of breath. Luckily, my parents were already asleep and did not have the opportunity to witness the physical and emotional state of disarray that I was in. My hair was wringing wet, my clothing completely disheveled. I fled to my bedroom, locked the door and sat on the edge of my bed. My hands were shaking uncontrollably and I was still unable to catch my breath. Unconsciously, I crossed myself.

"Once having regained my composure, a cutting realization unearthed itself. Victor could not possibly be human, at least not in the sense that my young mind understood a human to be. For people cannot simply disappear at whim, without a trace. He was no doubt some sort of subhuman being. The question was, what kind? My first thought was that he was a ghost of some sort, some unearthly apparition. But that could not be. He was flesh and blood. I had felt his solid body pressed against mine. What else, then, could he be? I had thought I was going to experience for the first time the sexual rapture about which I had so often fantasized and instead I encounter some sort of creature, possibly a demon.

"Finally gathering my self-control, I got into bed and pulled the covers over my head. I hated to admit it to myself, but I was terrified. As I lay there, heart still pounding, the evening's events played fully in my brain. Demon or not, I could not deny the potent attraction I felt for Victor. I wanted him sexually, more than I had ever wanted anything else. I shuddered every time I thought about the kiss, his mouth exploring my own and the feeling of his hard body pressed against mine. A lifetime of concealed fantasies had almost come true. Why he had even asked me to be his mate! Or did he? I no longer remembered. I was confused. My thoughts muddled. After several hours of turmoil, I fell into a light sleep.

"I refused to get out of bed the next day. The events of the previous evening were simply too much for my yet immature mind to deal with and I reluctantly informed my father that I was too ill to mind the store.

"Needless to say, he did not take the news well and attempted to verbally fight with me. I refused to speak any further on the subject and returned to my room. I feared encountering Victor again. As much as I wanted him, my instincts warned me that there was something dreadfully wrong—and dangerous.

"Having slept away the majority of the day, I was wide awake by nightfall. I wondered if Victor had stopped by the store to look for me or whether he was waiting on the street corner as he had the night before. I thought for a moment of fleeing the city, getting far away from him as possible. Yet somehow I knew flight would be a wasted effort. I paced back and forth in my small room, not knowing what to do, yet realizing that another encounter with this creature would be inevitable. I then decided that I needed to get out of the house for some fresh night air in an attempt to ease my troubled mind.

"The crisp night air felt good as it filled my lungs. I sat on the edge of the well in the yard and forced myself to think of nothing else but the beautiful night and the star filled sky. It was then I heard the unmistakable sound of my name. At first, I thought it a trick of the wind but then I heard it again.

"'Erik,' it called in such a sweet tone that it was almost a whisper. 'Erik.'

"I spun around wildly but could see no one. There were not many places where one could hide in the empty yard and I continued to convince myself that it must be my imagination after all. Then I heard it again. This time the voice was clear and distinct.

"'Good evening Erik,' the voice said. I recognized it immediately.

"I jumped up and whirled around. There stood Victor on the other side of the well, smiling broadly at me with the moonlight softly illuminating his pale, yet beautiful face.

"'You!' I cried out, instantly terrified. I took a step back. 'How…'

"He inclined his head politely. 'It is so nice to see you once again Erik. I must apologize for dashing off so quickly last night.' Then, in a near whisper, 'The moonlight brings out your beauty more than I could have imagined.'

"'How did you know where I lived?' I asked, involuntarily beginning to shake.

"His lips formed into a thin smile. 'Why I simply followed you home last night.' After seeing my expression of confusion, he added, 'I was with you the entire time.'

"'But…'

"'But you didn't see me?'

"'You were not there! I am certain of it. I was alone,' I cried, trying not to believe a word of what he was telling me.

"'Oh, I was there. I chose for you not to see me.' He bared his teeth into a grin. 'But you can see me now. That is all that matters.' He laughed, and walked around the well to where I was sitting. I backed away from him.

"'What are you?' I asked, the words barely audible.

"'What am I you ask? I am your lover, your savior, your dark cherub who has come to rescue you from your ordinary, dull existence, this existence that you have come to despise. That is what you wanted, is it not?' His voice had the sweetness and innocence of an angel.

"'You are not human!' I cried out, continuing to back away from him. 'You are a creature, a demon.'

"He clapped his hands. 'Very good. You are correct, sir,' he said. 'I am not human. I am stronger than your fellow humans and I can move so quickly that your dull, weak eyes could never detect my movements.' He paused, then smiled sweetly. 'What is more, I cannot die.'

"'You cannot die? You are *immortal?*' I asked incredulously, trying to decide whether or not I believed him.

"The next thing I knew, he had me in his arms and his mouth came crashing down on mine. With an unbridled passion, his tongue forced its way into my mouth. His mouth tasted sweet and enticing. I relented, and my body grew limp in his arms as the kiss grew deeper. I could feel his erect manhood constraining in his trousers, pushing firmly against my own aroused hardness. Our lips broke apart. His head moved towards my neck.

"'Yes, I am immortal and I offer you the gift of immortality to share with me,' he whispered softly in my ear. 'You will live forever and together, we will live and love as no two have lived and loved before. Join me for all eternity. Be mine, young Erik.'"

Erik noticed a flash of jealousy cross over Steve's face for just a moment. He laughed.

"Steve, this happened over seventy years ago."

"Silly, isn't it?" Steve answered with a weak smile. "But it still bothers me to imagine you kissing someone else."

Erik smiled a contented smile. "I would be concerned if it did not bother you—at least a little."

"So he offered you immortality," Steve said. "Did you have any idea at this point that Victor was a vampire?"

Erik shook his head. "I had no idea what the price of Victor's offered immortality would be. I was afraid, yet intrigued at the same time. The new sexual sensations coursing through me were fully occupying my thoughts so when Victor asked me to join him, my judgment was clouded. I was practically ready to do anything he asked. His hot breath in my ear, the feeling of a man's body pressed close to mine, my mind whirled. I forced myself to pull away from him.

"'I don't know,' I replied, looking at Victor, not yet fully comprehending the enormity of what had just been proposed. 'How can it be that you are immortal? How can it be that I myself could be immortal?'

"Victor creased his brow and smiled. 'How I became what I am is a long story and best saved for another time. But I will tell you this. I have survived for more centuries than your naive mind could ever imagine and will continue to do so. Each century has been filled with wonder and adventure far beyond your simple mortal comprehension. But the time has come for me to take a mate, someone with whom to share this wondrous gift of immortality. I have so much to teach you, my young strong one. So much to show you. I have been watching you for some time and must say that for a mortal, the qualities you possess are impressive. I have admired your strength, your quickness, your refusal to conform.' He eyed me up and down as if evaluating a slab of beef. 'You will indeed make a fine vampire.'

"'A vampire?' I asked in utter amazement, not having enough common sense to be frightened. 'You are a vampire?' My thoughts went to Bram Stoker's novel, "*Dracula*", a book that my parents forbade us from bringing into the house.

"Victor threw his head back in a deep, throaty laugh. 'What? You have never met a vampire before? My friend, how inexperienced you are!'

"He was mocking me and I knew it. 'I never knew such things existed.'

"'I prefer not to be referred to as a thing,' Victor said with a sarcastic grin.

"'I...I did not mean to insult you,' I added quickly, the fear more than evident in my voice. 'I only meant that I have never encountered one such as yourself before.' I desperately tried to remember all of the stories and legends I have heard about vampires. 'Do you kill people?' I asked innocently.

"His smile chilled me to the bone. 'Naturally. And so shall you.'

"I swiftly moved away from him as fear continued to well up inside of me.

"'I could never kill anyone. I would never kill anyone.'

"'My dear, young Erik,' he began, in a voice most condescending, 'once the transformation is complete you will see the world in an entirely different light. You will then realize that every being was put on this planet to be food for another and you will think nothing of partaking of the life-giving substance that is necessary for your survival. Think about it for a moment. Snakes eat rats, tigers eat gazelles, fish eat other fish, everything feeds on everything else. It is the way of nature, my friend. Why would you think that humans should exist on this planet without having a predator when every other being must participate in this chain of life?'

"'And I would live forever?' I asked incredulously.

"'For all eternity. The world will be ours to rule as we see fit. Think of the power you will have! Never to die or age.' He approached me slowly, then ran his fingers gently through my hair. 'You will always be as young and beautiful as you are right now.' His eyes held mine in a deep gaze. Unknowingly, I was succumbing to his will.

"I felt a strange excitement of anticipation and of doubt. My mind reeled from all he was telling me. It was every man's dream come true— to achieve immortality, and here was the most beautiful creature offering this gift to me. My newly discovered sexuality coupled along with an offer of living forever was overwhelming my young mind. I found it impossible to think clearly. Finally I asked him the question that would seal my fate.

"'What do I need to do?'

"He flashed a toothy grin in response. 'We would need to consume each other's blood. A very simple procedure actually. The transformation will be complete in five days time. But it will not be an easy process. Only the strongest of mortals survive it. You will experience an illness, the likes of which you have never known before. You will be feverish and your body will be racked with pain. A small price to pay for immortality.'

"'What if I should refuse?'

"'Then I should have to kill you,' he said flatly, as if commenting on the weather. "Tonight."

"'Kill me?' I exclaimed, a sudden fear gripping me.

"'I most certainly could not let you simply walk away, now that you know my secret, now could I?' he said, his eye glittering.

"He watched me with a bitter smile upon his lips.

"'May I have a day or two to think it over?' I pleaded.

"He creased his brow. 'No. You must decide tonight. Either you will join me and evolve into a new plane of existence or you shall perish.' His brow darkened and he added bitterly, 'Only a fool would pass up a chance to live forever.'

"The full impact of what he was saying finally hit me. I tried to gather my thoughts as he stood facing me, waiting. To attempt to escape him would be in vain, that much I knew. If I rejected his offer, he would kill me. My life would come to an end. There was actually no decision to be made. What else could I do but agree to his proposal? I regret to admit that at the time, it was not a painful decision—to an eighteen year old, the idea of immortality sounded more than intriguing. My heart pounded madly as I looked up and met his cold, dead eyes. I nodded and silently approached him, my arms hanging limply at my side.

"'I accept then,' I said under my breath.

"His face betrayed not a glimmer of surprise. He moved closer to me, so close that I could smell his sugary breath.

"He leaned down and kissed me, this time gently and expertly. I shook uncontrollably, anticipating and dreading what was to come next. I had so many questions that I needed to ask him but was mute. The words welled up in my throat and remained there, unable to escape.

"He lifted his face from mine and spread his rosy lips into a wide grin. What I saw then rendered me utterly immobile. His two incisor teeth began to grow and soon were transformed into sharp, white fangs! My instincts begged me to flee. He gently took hold of my arm and brought it to his mouth while I watched him in awe. Never taking his eyes off of me, he kissed and licked along the length of my arm, his other hand entering into the front of my trousers. My body stiffened in anticipation. Then the pain. The thought occurred to me that he just might kill me anyway but I was powerless to do anything. My body was paralyzed. As he drank of my blood, I began experience an intense dizziness and then felt a coldness, moving up my legs and into my chest. Through my clouded mind, I realized that he was taking too much. I could feel my heartbeat slowing. He was draining me! He was going to kill me after all!

"Just as I was on the brink of unconsciousness, he unlocked his mouth from my wrist and looked up at me, his face covered with my blood. He bared his red stained teeth into a wide grin.

"'Now you shall drink of me,' he said in a voice so low I could barely hear him though the ringing in my ears.

"I watched as he slashed his own wrist with his fangs and brought it to my mouth. His other arm supported my swaggering body to prevent me from falling.

"'Drink and be immortal,' he whispered fiercely. 'But be quick about it. You must drink before you die.'

"Instinctively I opened my mouth to take in the blood which spewed from his wound. It hit the back of my throat with a gush, causing me to choke and sputter at the initial onslaught. Then it flowed down my throat in a continuous stream. I was surprised how pleasant the blood tasted. I should never have guessed it to have such an agreeable flavor. I was all at once aware of a deep hunger wringing at my stomach and I sucked all the harder on his wrist, trying to fill himself with as much of his blood as I could.

"'Enough!' he cried out and pulled his wrist away, wrapping a handkerchief around his wound. Then, more tenderly, 'We are now one.'

"I discovered that I was now on my knees and became acutely aware of a wetness on my face. I shivered in disgust when my mind cleared enough for me to comprehend what I had just done. My face was covered with his blood. I rubbed it onto my hands, staring at it in disbelief. I glanced up at him desperately. He stood there in silence, hands clasped. Then without warning, the worst pain I have ever felt seized me and I fell onto the ground writhing, both hands clenching onto my stomach. My own heartbeat echoed loudly in my ears and I was seized with spasm after spasm of pain. I was certain I was going to die, as his blood fought for control of my own.

"'Help me please,' I whimpered, lying on the ground in agony.

"He looked down at my withered form with approval.

"'There is nothing I can do for you now. Either you will die an agonizing death, or shall evolve into one such as myself.' He flashed me a sarcastic smile and was gone.

"With what little strength I had left, I crawled to the house. The pounding in my ears had become unbearable and just maintaining consciousness was a colossal effort. Once inside the house, I thought of my parents, sleeping peacefully in their room and remembered the dried blood on my face. Thinking back, it now it strikes me as amusing that I should worry about what they would think were they to see me covered in blood, while I was on the threshold of death. I washed myself, a task which took some time to accomplish in my weakened state. I could feel the fever building up inside of me. Just at the point of exhaustion, I disrobed and crawled into my bed where I was to remain for five full days."

Erik paused and cleared his throat. Steve saw two tears roll down Erik's cheek. Erik wiped his face with his sleeve.

"Thus began my transformation."

Transformation Complete

◆

Steve sat wide-eyed in silence.

Erik stared straight ahead, a distant look on his face as if he were revisiting a painful memory.

"Erik?" Steve asked.

Erik shook himself and looked at Steve. He smiled in embarrassment at his young lover.

"I must have drifted off for a moment. As you can imagine, this stage of my life is not easy for me to talk about. This is the point where my human life as I knew it ended and I was reborn as what I am today."

Steve nodded his head solemnly. "So it took you five days to change into a vampire?" He gulped, trying to get the words out.

Erik looked at him with defeated eyes. "Yes, only five short days." He sighed. "It was so long ago, another lifetime really. It does not even seem like it is my own story that I am telling but rather that of a stranger, of someone I knew in the distant past." He was silent for a few moments, then, "The next five days were agonizing. I remember very little about them actually. When my mother discovered me the next morning, I was burning with fever and my body was delirious from the pain. She immediately summoned the local physician but he could do nothing. He had no idea what was causing the fever or the origin of my pain. Today, with a simple blood test, they might have discovered what was occurring inside my body as Victor's vampiric blood slowly destroyed

184

my own. Not that it would make much difference. There is no cure for vampirism."

Steve's eyes widened. "Have you ever been to a doctor? If they knew such a condition existed, maybe a cure could be found."

Erik smiled. "I have pondered it many times over the years, wondering if there could be an end to this curse somewhere, somehow. The problem would be to find a physician that I could trust." He paused. "I am not sure the world is ready to admit that such a being as myself actually walks among them. But let me continue with my story."

Steve nodded in silent agreement, giving his full attention to Erik.

"The fever grew worse as the days passed and I fell in and out of consciousness, not sure what was real and what was delusion. During the brief bouts of wakefulness which the illness graciously provided me, I grew certain that I would not survive the change. The unrelenting pounding in my head became insupportable, pushing me near the point of madness and preventing me from forming any rational thought. I could not say which was worse, the pain in my head or the cramps which sought to squeeze the very life out of me. I feel sorry for what my mother went through with me during that time. She sat helpless at my bedside, listening to my agonizing wails. I could sense that she believed that I would perish as well. There is one amazing aspect of the human mind for which I am grateful—the ability to erase from one's memory most recollection of unbearable suffering. Most of the experience is now only a foggy recollection, as it was when I finally awoke from my illness.

"As Victor promised, my torture ended on the fifth day. Late in the night, I all at once awoke fully alert, as if I had just left a deep hibernation. The first thing of which I became aware was that the pain was gone! I had somehow survived. I sat up erect in my bed, elated at the feeling of health. That last evening that I had spent with Victor seemed like a dream and for a moment, I thought that it possibly was. Perhaps it was simply a conjuring of my feverish brain. As I blinked, I knew there was something wrong. It was not until I rose to my feet that I was certain of it. Everything looked different somehow. I was viewing the world in an entirely new way. Every detail of even the smallest object in my room jumped out at me. I was being visually bombarded. It then stuck me that my room was completely dark, yet I could see a tiny ball of dust resting on the floor ten feet away from me. I tried to blink away what I thought was an illusion but it was to no avail. I sat back down on the bed, trembling as I focused in on these new sensations. Then I felt it—a sudden burst of strength. I had never felt so healthy, so strong, and so robust in my entire life. Eager to experience my newfound vigor, I dashed out of the house. As I stood in the yard and breathed in the night, I felt power surge through my body. I could smell and hear even the tiniest of creatures as they rambled through the grass. I could hear the shifting of worms in the earth. The minutest sound seemed to pummel my eardrums.

"What had happened to me? I was unable as of yet to recall the complete events of my night with Victor five evenings before and like everything else, it seemed to be a distant, blurred memory.

"Without warning, a new awareness took hold of me and screamed in my brain. I knew I was being watched.

"Victor appeared out of nowhere. I leapt back in surprise. It had not been a dream after all.

"'So my newly awakened friend,' he said, 'I see that you have survived. You have done well.'

"He floated over to me and placed his lips gently on mine. Then he kissed me savagely.

"'I knew you would, of course,' he said as he broke the kiss. 'You were strong in your mortal life and are even stronger now. I was correct in my valuation of what an exceptional vampire you would become. You are truly…beautiful.'

"'A vampire? I am now a vampire?' I asked, trying desperately to remember what had passed between us only five short days ago. 'I remember so little. Everything is so cloudy.'

"I stared into his pitiless eyes.

"'Yes, my young one,' he said. 'You and I are now the same.' He laughed shortly. 'Come with me for I have much to teach you.'

"'Am I dead?' I blurted out, rubbing my arms.

"Victor laughed again and then nodded. 'The life that you knew as a human is forever extinguished. It no longer exists for you, as vampire blood now flows through your veins. But dead? No, my young Erik, far from it. For the first time you are truly alive. Can you not feel the new sensations? The new strength? The new awakening?'

"'Yes,' I responded weakly. 'I feel different then I did before I became ill.' I thought for a moment, then added, 'Will my parents notice the change? What shall I tell them? How shall I hide it from them?'

"He looked at me, his eyes glittering and then laughed rudely. 'Do you not realize that you can no longer walk among humans? You are no longer one of them. The life that existed for you as a mortal can never be again. Not only have your senses sharpened, but there has been a physical metamorphosis as well. Your skin is now as pale as the whites of one's eyes and your movements resemble those of the most graceful jungle cat. When the hunger falls upon you, your fangs will protrude without the slightest warning, exposing you for what you really are. You will need to learn how to control these new powers and your new strength for the brief moments that it will be necessary to enter into the human world. But walk among them as a mortal? Never again. There remains very few similarities between what you are now and what you used to be.'

"I stared at him blankly, not quite sure if I was fully grasping the meaning of his words. 'I can no longer live with my parents or associate with my companions?'

"He nodded impatiently. 'Very good. You finally understand. From this point on, you will only associate with your own kind, namely myself. Humans are only to be regarded as,' he hesitated, breaking into an unearthly smile, 'food.'

"An involuntary convulsion overtook me as the complete memory of my last meeting with Victor abruptly resurfaced and the full comprehension of what I had become became apparent for the first time. I looked at him blankly, feeling conquered.

"'I am really a vampire,' I said out loud to myself in disbelief. My own voice seemed different to me, as if the sound had not been produced by my own vocal cords but rather from an unexplored cavern in my brain.

"'Come,' Victor said in a harsh and distant voice. 'It is time for you to leave this place. Say your final good-bye to your previous reality and prepare yourself for your new life.'

"I glanced back at the small house in which I had grown up and could feel tears welling up in my eyes at the thought of never returning—of never again setting my eyes upon my parents and friends. I stared at the house, trying to recapture all of my childhood memories. For me, there would be no further memories made in that house. I felt a rough tug on my arm, which snapped me back to consciousness.

"'Enough,' Victor said harshly. 'We must take leave of this place for a busy night awaits us. The time for useless reminiscing is past.'

"I swung around to face Victor, his hand still firmly gripping my arm. His eyes glowed like fiery red embers.

"'Where are we to go?' I asked.

"'To your new home,' he said, waving his arm above his head. His voice softened. 'Now you must learn to concentrate. You have the ability to move more quickly that the human eye can see. Once you gain speed, it shall be difficult for you to control your direction until you understand how to master the skill of concentration. I will lead you by the arm until you learn to command this gift yourself.'

"'Are we going to fly?' I asked innocently, exited at the prospect of what he was telling me.

"He laughed. 'Not exactly,' he answered, raising his eyebrows. 'Rather it resembles floating forward with great speed.' His grip tightened on my arm. 'When you feel the force of me pulling you forward, you must clear your thoughts and focus solely on moving ahead, following my lead. When you were a mortal, all your movement was accomplished physically. Now you must relearn how to move your physical body, but this time by force of your mind rather than your muscles. Now...' he finished, his voice drifting off.

"All at once I felt a heavy pressure on my chest as I began to move forward at such a rapid rate, I most surely would have fallen had Victor not been tightly holding onto me. As we plunged forward, I tried to concentrate the best I could, attempting to suppress the fear which insisted upon showing itself during the journey. I am certain that my feeble attempt at concentration did little to aid my forward movement, and that Victor had been solely responsible for our journey. Houses and streets blurred by so quickly, that I could barely make out what they were. Before I knew it, we had left the city and were out in farming country, with barely a house in sight as we blurred by. The sharp night air tightened around my body as we leapt forward. The pressure all at once subsided as we slowed down, then came to a complete stop. I found myself in front of an old, but well-kept house a few miles down a deserted road. My legs were shaking from the shock of the trip and I was barely able to remain standing when Victor released his grip on my arm. He grabbed me and kissed me softly.

"'Now that was not so bad, was it?' he said, baring his teeth into a grin. 'Do not fret, you will get used to it in time. After a few such excursions, it will become second nature to you.'

"He led me inside of the old house. I was surprised to discover that the interior was lavishly furnished. Every wall contained a tall bookcase, jammed full of old, dusty tomes. Huge chandeliers swung from the ceiling of every room and a unique assortment of religious statues garnished the halls. I followed him into the living room where a roaring fire was burning in the fireplace. The glitter of all of his possessions was attacking my newborn vision causing me to squint my eyes upon entering the room.

"Ignoring the numerous couches and chairs placed about the room, he sat on the thick furry white carpet in front of the fire and gently pulled me down to him. My senses were overwhelmed, having not yet recovered from the trip to his house. I was trembling. It all at once struck me as strange that I did not even know where I was. We had moved along so quickly on the way here that my sense of direction had been completely lost.

"Victor pulled me close to him and began kissing me all over. The passion that was surging inside of me came flowing through. We attacked each other. It was my first time making love to either sex and was sure that if I had experienced it when I was a mortal, I most surely have been disappointed. The feeling of his naked body pressed next to mine, his hot breath on my neck was more intense than any fantasy I had dared imagine. My senses whirled as Victor introduced me for the first time to the pleasures of the flesh."

Erik paused, eyeing Steve carefully. "I am sure that it is not easy hearing all of this. I know I would not wish to hear about your past sexual escapades but I need to explain every aspect of the entry into my new life to you. It is important to me that you know and understand everything."

Steve nodded wordlessly and a bleak smile spread on his lips. "I do want to hear everything. And like you said, it was a long time ago." He paused. "I am a bit surprised though. From everything that you told me earlier, I had the impression that Victor was some kind of monster but from what you just described, he did seem to have," Steve hesitated, as if trying to find the right words, "somewhat of a human quality to him—so to speak."

"I thought the same thing as well, but discovered all to quickly that I was deceived. The first awakening, that first lovemaking—all of it brought forth an unknown aspect of my being, a pleasure I could not describe. What was to follow opened my eyes to what Victor really was. I do not wish to jump ahead of myself. Let me pick up where I left off and you will understand my meaning soon enough. Deal?"

Steve slumped into the couch, lifting his legs up and hugging his knees. "Sure," he said anxiously. "Please go on."

"After we made love, we held onto each other tightly. Any feeling of guilt or remorse which I would have experienced earlier was absent. I was still savoring the feeling of his fiery breath on my throat and the sensation of his body wrapped in mine when he abruptly pulled away from me as if my touch disgusted him. He gathered up his clothes and quickly dressed himself. I stared at him, not understanding what had brought on this sudden change of behavior and unsure as to what he was going to do next or what I should do next.

"'Get up,' he said with a harsh insistence, and tossed me my pants. 'We have many things to discuss this night.'

"The satisfied feeling passed and I suddenly felt dirty. I gathered up my clothes and joined him on the couch where he had already installed himself. He watched me closely, his eyes blazing cold.

"'Is something wrong?' I asked innocently. 'Did I do something wrong?'

"He laughed hollowly and stroked my arm, his pale expression slightly softening. 'Not at all. I enjoyed our little fuck immensely.'

"I was furious! With that one word, he had degraded the entire experience into something loathsome and disgusting.

"I glared at him and his lips parted into a victorious smile.

"'We must talk at once,' he then said with a sense of urgency. 'As the evening is drawing to a close, I need to quickly explain some things to you. There are preparations which must be made.'

"'Preparations? I do not understand.'

"'Of course you do not,' he added sarcastically, then continued, with a more serious tone of voice. 'In less than an hour, the sun will rise, which signifies the end of our day. The rays of the sun are deadly to us and we must secure ourselves in a safe place during the day where the death-dealing rays cannot reach our skin. But that is not all. The moment the sky begins to lighten we fall into a deep unawakenable sleep, similar to death itself. It is then that we are the most vulnerable to the sun as well as any outside dangers. If any mortal were to ever discover us, they would assume us dead.'

"'This cannot be true!' I cried in utter disbelief.

"'When we are in the sleep,' he answered, ignoring my outburst, 'there are no vital signs. At least none detectable by humans. The death sleep continues until the last rays of the sun have set and night begins.'

"I let out a cry of anguish at his words. I would never again see the sun or be able to bask in its warmth. I would now only see the world in darkness. The beauty of the world lit up from the rays of the sun would now only be a memory.

"Victor glared at me angrily, as if he could read my thoughts.

"'You fool!' he said. 'It is a small cost for the gift of immortality. Nothing comes without a price. You shall learn that soon enough, my young prince.' He gestured wildly with a sweep of his hand. 'It is time for me to introduce you to your resting place. Follow me. I have prepared a safe sanctuary for you.'

"In the kitchen, cleverly hidden underneath a carpet was a trap door, which led to the basement by way of a creaky set of stairs. Victor gestured for me to go first. I descended to the basement and he followed, carefully closing the trap door behind him and ensuring that the carpet slid back over it, concealing its existence. The room was pitch dark and I was again amazed at how well I could see in the almost complete absence of light. The room was empty except for a mammoth wine rack built into one of the walls. Victor smiled at the look of confusion on my face. He walked past me to the wall on the right where he proceeded to insert his fingers into an open gap on the corner and pulled. To my amazement, the entire wall slid back, revealing a large, empty hidden room.

"I watched him as he sauntered over to the huge, dark rose drapery hanging from the ceiling on the far end of the room. His head turned and his eyes locked to mine, a devilish grin on his face as he pulled the drapery back. To my horror, there were two wooden caskets placed side by side in the center of the room.

"'What are those coffins doing here?' I asked, my eyes practically bugging out of my head.

"He laughed loudly, sputtered and choked, then continued to laugh. "'That, my young companion, is where we sleep.'

"I shook my in confusion.

"'It is in these coffins where we will find our daytime sanctuary and ensure our safety,' he said. 'I had one built especially for you, equipped with a lock on the inside to keep out any unwelcome visitors.'

"I could feel disgust and loathing rise in my throat. 'I am not sleeping in a coffin!' I screamed. 'What do you think I am, some kind of ghoul?'

"'You ungrateful wretch!' he said with a sudden explosion of fury. In a flash, he flew across the room to where I was standing and struck me so hard across the face that I found myself flying in mid-air and eventually crashing into the rock wall. Pain tore through my body and I could feel warm blood trickle down my face. I looked up hesitatingly to see Victor standing over me, his face red with rage.

"'I have given you immortality, given you my precious blood and this is how you repay me?' He continued. 'Yes, you are now a ghoul, a stalker of humans, a demon. You must face what you have become.' His face softened and he lowered his voice to almost a whisper. 'Get up.'

"He held out his hand to help me up. Miraculously, the pain that seared though me moments ago had disappeared and I was able to lift myself easily from the stone floor. The bleeding had stopped and I could feel the gash in my forehead already begin to mend itself.

"Victor walked over to the two caskets and lifted both lids, his eyes never leaving mine.

"'You must get in now. You have no choice. If you do not, you will perish.'

"Afraid of once again incurring his wrath, I lumbered in silence to the coffin and reluctantly got in. As I stretched out and placed my hands at my side, an unnamable dread gripped me as Victor began to close the lid.

"'Rest well my young hatchling as tomorrow you shall need to feed,' he said softly as the lid closed. I found myself in total darkness.

"I heard the lid of the coffin next to me close and was certain I heard a laugh coming from the neighboring casket. Tears streamed out of my eyes as I thought of my new uncertain fate. I felt for the lock on the side and fastened it, just as a heaviness that of which I had never before experienced overtook me and dragged me into blackness."

The First Kill

◆

Erik stared silently toward the opposite end of the room. He felt a hand upon his shoulder and looked up into Steve's tear filled eyes.

"I'm really sorry," Steve said in a whisper and wrapped his arms around Erik. "I can't imagine what that first night must have been like for you."

Erik held Steve tightly and breathed in deeply of Steve's familiar scent. Their lips met briefly.

"Once I realized exactly what I had given up to become this—this creature, I knew that all chance for happiness was lost. Especially after what lie ahead to face me on that second night."

"The feeding that Victor mentioned?"

Erik nodded. "I had not thought about it at all that first night. I was too preoccupied with trying to comprehend the extent of what I had become and what my fate with Victor would be. Upon awakening on that second night, it took me a moment realize where I was until the previous evening's events came rushing back to me. Victor had been right about the death sleep. I remembered the heaviness, the extreme fatigue that overtook me moments after I got into the coffin, then nothing. When I recalled that I was in fact lying in a coffin, I threw open the lid and crept out of the accursed thing as quickly as possible. Victor was already awake and was sitting, silently, on the edge of his coffin, waiting for me.

"'Did you slumber well my sweet?' he asked mockingly, with a tight smile upon his lips. 'The night has arrived and is waiting for us. Tonight you shall become a true vampire.'

"I closed the lid of the lid of the casket and sat down upon it, mimicking Victor. I wanted to tell him how much I despised him, how I loathed him for what he had turned me into when all at once, a dreadful cramp seized my stomach. I felt as if I were going to wretch.

"'What is wrong with me?' I asked, barely able to speak. 'What is happening?'

"'You need blood,' he answered flatly. 'You must learn how to procure for yourself what you need to survive. You will learn to stalk and to hunt for your food, as we were meant to do.' He gazed upward, as if in ecstasy. 'The kill is the most tremendous thrill a vampire can experience.'

"'I must actually drink blood?'

"'If you wish to survive. Should you deny yourself this necessity, you will die and it would be a most agonizing death. You see young Erik, once again, you have no choice in the matter.'

"He abruptly stood up, chuckled, and directed himself towards the stairs.

"I followed him out into the yard. It felt good to be out of that ghastly coffin and into the fresh air once again. The pain was still present although it seemed to have somewhat subsided upon leaving the house. From then on, the cramps seem to come in waves, each one more intense than the previous.

"As I clutched onto my stomach, Victor smiled at me mockingly. 'Don't fret. The pain will disappear as soon as fresh, warm blood fills your stomach and a bliss such as you have never known will take the place of your discomfort. You will soon discover how pleasurable drinking blood can be, not to mention the gratification of the kill itself.'

"I drew back in horror.

"'I do not think I could kill anyone,' I stammered, trying to ignore the new wave of cramps which had suddenly seized me.

"He stared at me wildly then laughed. 'You will be amazed at how effortless it will be. Why after the first kill or two, you will look forward to your next one with anxious anticipation, awaiting the moment when your fangs will have their next opportunity to sink into tender human flesh. It is your fate, my young friend.' He licked his lips.

"Before I had a chance to react to his words, his hand took a strong hold of my arm and we were off. Within minutes, we were in the city. The trip was much easier for me this time as I attempted to concentrate on my movement. I actually did feel my body propelling itself forward at the command of my mind. As we traveled, I felt Victor's grip on my arm lessen.

"'You did very well this time,' he said grinning. 'I needed to help you little.'

"I did not answer him, still somewhat dizzy from this mode of travel to which I was not yet fully accustomed. I looked around. We were standing next to a river in an area that seemed deserted.

"'What are we doing here?' I asked.

"'This is the perfect place for a novice hunter to begin his training. Though there are no people here at the moment, one or two will surely wander in—for dinner.' He snickered at his own joke.

"He strode towards a clump of trees and I followed, not sure what to expect next. Then an unfamiliar smell struck me, seizing my body in its grasp. I became even more unsteady on my feet as the odor intensified. Another wave of pain swept over me, the worst I had felt yet. Victor watched me intently, a satisfied look on his face.

"'You smell that?' he asked, fully aware that I did. 'That is the sweet fragrance of human blood. Wonderful, is it not?' He inhaled the air deeply, as if trying to prove his point. 'The enjoyment you experienced from food in your mortal life was nothing compared to what you will experience from partaking of blood.' His lip curled slightly. 'Blood is the essence of our entire being and it is humans who are here to provide it to us. You must think of mortals only as food, nothing more.'

"He marched with purpose and I followed. The smell of blood grew stronger and I felt a squeezing hunger well up inside of me. I was unable to think clearly. All I could do was follow the scent.

"Victor stopped suddenly. 'Quiet,' he said, gesturing with his hand. 'There, next to the small tree.'

"Seated by the river near a small bush were two young men, talking quietly to each other. I guessed that neither of them could be over eighteen or nineteen years old and from what I could tell, they appeared to be very robust young men. As I watched them, the smell of their blood caused my senses to reel. I tried to fight the urge which was growing stronger every moment but felt powerless. My mouth watered.

"'These two shall be perfect,' Victor exclaimed. 'I love hunting young men—they always put up such a fight! You will come to appreciate challenges such as this as time goes on, young Erik.'

"'I will not do this,' I said, but my voice did not sound very convincing. I was weakening rapidly but could not bear the thought of harming these two boys. I wanted to flee as far away from all humans as I could and simply allow myself to be consumed by the morning rays of the sun. Death certainly had to be better than the ghoulish existence that lie ahead of me.

"'Do not be a fool,' he said, grabbing both of my wrists. 'You must feed. You cannot deny your nature!' His eyes were ablaze.

"'It is not my nature to kill!' I exclaimed. 'And you shall never convince me otherwise.'

"I pulled back and returned my gaze to the two young men. My reason seemed dulled as I continued to watch them. Victor turned to me, raised his eyelids and smiled, revealing his sharp pointy white fangs.

"I stepped back in disgust.

"'What do you fear?' Victor asked, then gently rubbed a finger along the length of his newly protruded teeth. 'Your own fangs seem to be quite ready themselves.'

"I reached up to my mouth and discovered that he was right. Sharp canines now pointed downward in my mouth. I had not even been aware that my teeth had changed.

"'This is incredible,' I said, feeling my fangs in disbelief.

"Victor laughed quietly, then a serious expression swept over his face. He parted his lips and stared into my eyes.

"'It is time. Watch and learn from your master.'

"With that, he was gone. I quickly glanced over to where the boys had been sitting. Before either of them had time to react, Victor had grabbed one of them by the throat and flung him against the tree as if he were merely a rag doll, knocking him to unconsciousness. I watched in horror. I had to stop this slaughter. Using my mind, I propelled myself to where Victor had the other boy. When I arrived at the massacre site, I stopped dead in my tracks, unable to move. The smell of the boy's blood was overpowering me, and as Victor gently squeezed the boy's throat, I could see his jugular vein pulsing, full of living blood. Victor held onto the boy's throat just tight enough so that the boy could breathe, although barely. Victor smiled a hellish smile.

"'You do not want to kill them before you drink,' he explained, still holding the youth in the air. 'Blood from the dead will do you no good. Your food must be living.'

"At Victor's words, the boy's eyes grew wide with terror. He tried to scream, but was unable.

"My reason and my morals shouted to me to help this boy but my thirst instructed me otherwise. I was unable to get my mind off the aroma of the boy's blood. Victor seemed acutely aware of my state and flashed me a toothy grin. He lowered his head slowly until his teeth made contact with the boy's protruding vein. With one quick push, his teeth sank easily into the youthful flesh and the boy's blood squirted into Victor's mouth. He widened his mouth until it completely covered the open wound, then clamped his mouth onto the throat. I tried to cry out for him to stop but my vocal chords were numb. Within moments, the boy stopped kicking and his body became limp. Victor pulled away, letting the dead boy's body drop to the ground and glared at me. His face was covered with the youth's blood.

"By this time, the smell and sight of fresh blood had overpowered me to the point where I feared I might lose consciousness. In one quick movement, Victor scooped up the unconscious boy that he had struck moments before and who rested quietly by the tree. He extended out his arms, presenting the youth to me, as if handing me a prize.

"'This one belongs to you,' he gurgled, locking his eyes to mine. Victor's skin had a luster to it like moonlight on a lake. 'He is a beauty, is he not? Of course, it will not be as much fun to kill him as it would were he awake, but for your first time, he will serve well.'

"Any resistance that I might have had was gone. An animal instinct took hold of me as I stared at the boy's throat. I drifted to Victor and the boy. My movements were no longer my own and it seemed I was being propelled forward by an unseen force. I took the boy from Victor and looked down at him. My head descended to his throat until I felt my fangs touch his tender flesh. I knew that with one push the boy would be mine. I hesitated for just a moment, then lunged downward. The flesh broke easily and steaming, rich blood poured into my mouth. I drank hungrily from the boy, savoring every drop of the precious fluid. The taste was indescribable, as was the effect it was having on me. Unlike Victor's unholy blood, this boy's blood tasted pure and thick. I could almost feel the boy's youth enter my own body. A new strength surged through me and my senses seemed heightened even more so than upon my first awakening as a vampire. I drank hungrily and deeply, lost in the taste of the blood and the beating, then slowing, and finally stopping of the heart. The strong flow of blood turned into a weak trickle and the limp body fell from my hands onto the ground. The revelry of my new sensations came to a quick halt as I glanced at the boy's dead body, wide-eyed on the ground, instantly comprehending that I was now a killer.

"I let out a shriek of horror and buried my head in my hands, the dead boy's body at my feet.

"'What have I done?' I cried. 'God in heaven, what have I done?'

"Victor rushed to me and kicked the body on the ground so hard that it flew several feet from where we stood. He glared at me angrily. His voice was shallow and hard.

"'You have done what comes natural, what you must do to survive. Do I need to tell you this over and over until you finally understand? You are a vampire. Accept it Erik!' His voice softened slightly. 'The first time is always difficult, especially if you have never taken a life when you were human. But you will come to enjoy it in time and wait impatiently for each new victim. You will come to relish the act of the kill itself.'

"I looked up at him with contempt. 'Never! How can you believe that killing another human being is natural? These are people we are talking about, not some kind of animals. You were human once or can you not even remember that far back?'

"Victor smiled coldly, and with an air of nonchalance, wiped the blood off of his face with a white handkerchief. 'I was a mortal in another lifetime as were you and that short existence now means nothing to us. Can you not see this? You are no longer human and never shall be again. When you accepted my gift, you gave up your place in humanity with no turning back. You have the choice of accepting what you have become or facing a miserable, torturous eternity.' A sneer quickly replaced his smile. 'We are powerful creatures, possessing a strength far surpassing that of hundred men and a cunning no human could ever attain. Do not be a disgrace to your species.'

"'Accepted your gift?' I exclaimed. 'I did not accept your gift, you forced it upon me. Do you not remember that the only choice you gave me was of this accursed existence or death?'

"'You should have chosen death, then.'

"With that he scooped up the dead boy that he had killed. I stood immobile, sobbing uncontrollably.

"'Pick up your kill and follow me,' he said practically without moving his lips, ignoring my sobs. 'You are about to learn another important lesson. How to dispose of your victims.'

"I picked up the boy upon whom I had fed and looked at his innocent, dead pale face. I felt ripped apart knowing that it was I who had caused his death.

"'What are we going to do with them?' I blurted out through my sobs.

"'We must cut them up into small pieces so they will be unrecognizable, then bury them. I have a special place where I often dispose of my leftovers.'

"With that, we were off. I followed him to an abandoned dilapidated house several miles from civilization. I numbly carried out his orders, chopping up the bodies with blood stained utensils we found in the shed, then burying the pieces in a shallow grave underneath the basement floor. When we had finished, he grinned at me in victory.

"'You have done very well. Perhaps you shall make a satisfactory vampire after all.'

"I turned away in disgust. I could no longer bear to neither look at his wretched face nor hear his foul voice. Without a word, I mustered up every bit of concentration I could and moved myself forward, away from him, until I reached the house.

"I burned the blood stained clothes I was wearing and bathed, attempting to scrub off all remnants of the kill. I returned to the living room where Victor had already situated himself in a chair, deeply engrossed in a novel as if nothing unusual at all had passed this evening.

"Without looking up from his book, he said, 'I am glad you found your way home. It would have been a shame should you had gotten lost, especially with it being so close to sunrise.'

"Saying nothing, I sat down in front of the fire. The strength that I was experiencing was incredible. I truly did feel invincible. But the price of such a feeling! For what seemed like hours, I stared into the fire, contemplating the night's events and dreading the evenings which would follow. My silence seemed not to bother Victor in the least.

"Finally, 'How often do we have to kill?'

"He placed his book on his lap and looked at me with surprise. 'Why as often as possible,' he stated flatly. 'Would not one wish to participate in the beauty of the kill at every opportunity?' He then casually returned to his book.

"I ignored his statement. 'How long can we go without feeding?'

"He looked up at me again, expressionless. 'You could go without blood for two weeks, possibly three if absolutely necessary. By then, the craving would be unbearable and your body would begin to deteriorate. Your strength would diminish quickly and ultimately, you would be unable to lift yourself out of your coffin. But you would not perish at this point. Instead, your rotting body would lie there in eternal hunger, unable to do anything about that hunger. In this state, eternity would be a very, very long time.' He snickered in amusement.

"I shuddered. 'Is it necessary to always kill the victim?'

"He frowned, then flashed me a disapproving look. 'Not necessarily. You could take just enough blood to satisfy your hunger. To accomplish this, you would need to draw blood from somewhere other than the throat as there are not many humans who could survive a gashed jugular vein. You must also bear in mind that your victim would be alive afterwards. Do you think most people would willingly allow you to sink your vampiric teeth into their flesh, draw out their blood, then permit you to politely walk away? Once word got around that a vampire was walking amongst humans, they would waste no time in hunting you down and destroying you.'

"I contemplated his words. So I would not have to kill to survive. There was another way.

"He was suddenly standing in front of me, clasping me roughly by the throat. 'You must never let a victim live. Never! Do you understand me? To do so would be suicide.' Fire gleamed in his eyes.

"I shrugged him off and stood up, fearful for my life. The look on his face chilled the marrow in my bones.

"'I understand,' I said simply, not wishing to make him any angrier. I now realized that he could read my thoughts.

"His face softened and he grasped my face and kissed me deeply, tearing the clothes off my body before I knew what was happening. My revulsion for Victor ran so deeply that he no longer held any beauty for me. I forced myself through the sex act mechanically, praying for it to be over as quickly as possible, yet being careful not to allow him to see my disgust. It was soon completed and Victor retreated to his chair without a word. Trying to act as calmly as possible, I dressed myself and told him that I needed to be alone. With no response from him, I retreated to the coffin room to try to put things into perspective. It was then I knew that I could not spend the rest of eternity with this beast. I vowed to myself at that moment that I would spare my victim's life as often as possible and would eventually escape Victor's control. It was only my second night of being alive as a vampire and knew that I had much to learn before I dared venture off on my own. I needed to learn everything I could from this beast and then flee once the knowledge of my new condition was adequate. I would stay with him and be as docile as possible so as to not arouse his suspicions of my true intentions. Little was I to know that Victor was even more ruthless than I could possibly have imagined and that the time I would spend with him would be a virtual blood bath.

Three's Company

◆

"The months passed quickly with Victor as I struggled to adjust to my new situation. It was true what he had told me about the thirst. I found that I could go for several weeks without the need for blood, although the thirst was always there, silently gnawing at the back of my mind. When not unbearable, I was able to ignore it. Victor, on the other hand, killed whenever possible. He explained that it was not so much the need for blood which drove him, but rather the thrill of the kill. He was convinced that with us, killing was as instinctual as it was for a cat. I, however, did not seem to share this instinct and never arrived at seeing our condition in a similar manner.

"With terror, I anticipated and dreaded each occasion when the urge would become intolerable, when I would weaken, my judgment becoming clouded and dull with the only thought occupying my mind being the consumption of human blood. I would always wait until I reached this insupportable state before I would venture out to the city and seek out a victim. During the first few weeks of my new vampiric existence, I would accompany Victor on the hunt. I needed to learn as much as I could from him. I would watch in horror as he swooped down on unsuspecting young men, ripping out their throat with an unrivaled ferociousness. I tried to spare my victim's any suffering and would kill them as quickly and as painlessly as I could.

"We would not always hunt together. Often he would choose a victim from afar, and then befriend the poor soul, toying with him for weeks at a time. When he had finally gained the young man's complete trust, he would kill him slowly. It was this type of slaughter which he seemed to relish the most.

"The remorse I felt each time I killed was tearing me apart, forcing me to realize that I would be unable to morally justify this accursed existence for long. The vow I had made to myself haunted me. I recalled what Victor had told me on the night of my first kill, that there are ways to feed without it being necessary to terminate the victim's life. With that in mind, I developed a strategy to change my methods of hunting. Of course, this would mean that, from this point forward, I would have to hunt alone.

"When I conveyed to Victor that I would no longer be accompanying him on the hunt, he was enraged but I made it clear to him that he had no say in the matter. He, in turn, made it quite clear to me that he considered me a disappointment, some sort of unnatural mistake and continued to refer to me as an insult to my species. He had harbored these fantasies of the two of us prowling the city nightly, slaughtering everyone who happened to cross our path and upon discovering that this was not to be, took it upon himself to try to make my life as miserable as he could. It may have been then when I realized he was mad, genuinely insane, with an uncontrollable obsession with power. His long tirades about how he and I could take over the earth confirmed of my suspicions. The only thing I could do was stay as far away from him as possible. As you can imagine, our home life had a lot to be desired.

"Being true to my vow, I worked out a new method of feeding. Steve, this may sound barbaric to you, even ruthless, but the only way I could think of to fulfill my bloodlust and spare the victim's life was to knock them unconscious. My methods are more sophisticated now. Knocking them unconsciousness seemed at the time to be the only alternative to killing and figured it would be easy enough to carry out but I soon discovered that there was to be a period of trial and error. On several occasions, having not yet mastered my vampiric strength, I struck the victim with too much force and he died instantly from the impact of the blow. When I was successful, I would pull down the trousers, puncture a vein on the leg and feed. There was another lesson to be learned as well—when to stop drinking. On far too many occasions while gripped in the throws of the thirst, I would take too much blood from my unconscious prey and death would occur.

"In order to mask my true intentions, I would rob my victims. Thus, upon their awakening, they would assume that a mugger had simply attacked them. I was overjoyed at first to learn that I could in fact spare the lives of the young men upon whom I fed. I was also to learn that there was one important drawback to not completely draining my victims. The hunger would return in only a few days time, forcing me to go back out on the hunt to find some more fresh blood. I lived in practically a constant state of hunger, something that I have learned to deal with over the decades. But at that time, I wondered how I would come to survive in this constant state of yearning without going mad.

"Victor noticed that I began going out to hunt more frequently and figured that I was starting to come around to his way of thinking. I made the grave error of enlightening him on my methods. He was furious.

"'Did I not tell you that you must never allow your food to live? Do you realize the danger you are putting us both in? You fool! You absolute fool!' he screamed wildly, his eyes ablaze with fury.

"For reasons I cannot explain, I no longer feared him. A strange transformation had taken place within me. My loathing and hatred for him ran deeper than any remnants of fear. I sensed that he was aware of this change in me as well.

"'No, it is you who are the fool,' I retorted, sneering at him as I spoke. 'And it is you who are an insult to the species, not I. You kill not because you must, but because you want to. You are a selfish monster, an evil being obsessed with power and death. I believe you to be insane.'

"He flew across the room at me with such speed that I did not even see him. He seized me by the throat.

"'I should just kill you now and be done with it,' he said through his teeth, my throat held tightly in his vice-like grip. His mouth spread open wide and his fangs protruded. He lowered his mouth to my throat. I had no idea what would happen if he did succeed in ripping out my throat, but I know that I did not wish to find out. With a strength that I was unaware I possessed, I threw him off of me, hurling his body across the room. I was on him in a split second, holding his arms down. The savage look in his eyes almost made me pull back, but I held firmly. I suddenly realized that somehow, I was stronger than he and the startled expression on his face informed me that he knew it as well. I brought my face right up to his.

"'You may have transformed me into this creature, this thing, but you do not own me,' I said, clenching my teeth. My own fangs were present themselves and I bared them at him. 'My will is my own and I shall not live by your rules. I shall feed in whatever manner I choose and you shall have nothing to say about it.'

"With that, I let him up. I kept my defenses firm, not knowing what he would try next. He rose slowly and brushed himself off, wordless.

"'So be it,' he said quietly and walked to the chair in front of the fire. I watched him closely, not trusting him for a moment and not daring to let my guard down. His face softened.

"'I am your creator. That is true. I chose you to be my mate and still wish for you to remain with me. I have been alone for longer than you can imagine and I do care for you deeply Erik. We can work out our little differences, I am sure of it. After all, there is no law that says we must be exactly the same, now is there?' He rose from his chair with the swiftness of a cat, walked over to me and planted a soft kiss on my lips before I could turn my head. 'You will stay with me, will you not?' There was what I thought to be genuine concern in his eyes.

"I found myself softening and I returned his kiss. I thought that Victor might not have been the heartless ghoul that I had imagined him to be. I struggled to accept as true the words that he had spoken.

"'Very well,' I answered. 'I will stay with you. I just hope that you really mean what you say and this is not another one of your tricks.'

"He smiled a crooked smile. 'I do mean it Erik—every word I speak is true. We will have a wonderful life together, you and I. You shall see.'"

"Was he sincere?" Steve asked.

Erik narrowed his eyes, then shook his head. "Ha! Not in the least."

Steve giggled at Erik's unexpected response. Erik smiled, then a serious look crossed over his face as he continued.

"I thought that things had changed at first. After that night, Victor grew very quiet and there was undeniably less tension between us. Still, I had the strange feeling that he was up to something, although I had no idea what it could be. He no longer flaunted his killings in front of me, nor even discussed them for that matter. My methods of feeding no longer entered into any conversation between us.

"Contrary to what Victor had said, I found to my surprise that I was able to walk amongst humans as one of them, and soon relished their company. I attended plays, concerts and even accepted dinner invitations, although I usually tried to avoid eating among them. Food you see, does absolutely nothing for me and I am unable to derive any nutrition from it nor am I able to digest it. It remains in my stomach like lead, weighing me down and causing discomfort until I force myself to—remove it. I will be kind enough to spare you the details. As I was saying, I began to make a life for myself among humans and nobody seemed to suspect that I was any different from themselves. I never fed upon anyone whose acquaintance I had made. It was only strangers upon whom I would feed and I took every precaution to spare their life whenever possible. For the first time since the transformation, I was truly living and actually enjoying life. The idea of immortality even sounded attractive.

"Unfortunately, things were not to continue in this manner. I returned home one evening and was immediately struck by the smell of blood—blood from a living human. I was furious! Victor had promised that he would never take a victim to the house. I could hear voices coming from the upstairs. I scrambled up the stairs and threw open the door. There was Victor in bed with a very attractive young man, about nineteen or twenty years old. Victor's eyes met mine and they widened in feigned surprise.

"'Why Erik! I did not expect you home so soon. How was your evening?'

"I stood there glaring at him without saying a word. I could feel my cheeks redden with anger. At least the boy was still alive.

"'How rude of me,' he added without giving me chance to respond to his question. 'Erik, I would like you to meet Jason, a new friend of mine. He is beautiful, no?'

"I glanced over at the young man who was watching me with wide-eyed terror. He had no idea that he was in a room with two vampires and that his life was in danger. From his thoughts I learned that his terror stemmed from being discovered in bed with a man. I also sensed that this boy was not so innocent a young man as he looked. He had himself, killed—that much I could sense, and had done it more than once. He was a human version of Victor.

"'A pleasure to make your acquaintance, Jason,' I said coldly and left the room.

"Was he going to kill the boy in the house, after he promised such a thing would never occur, just to anger me? From what the boy's mind informed me, it would be no great loss to humanity if Victor were to kill him. I could have even condoned the murder.

"I sat in the study and waited. I heard the front door open and close. The smell of blood had vanished. He had spared the boy. Victor joined me moments later, ridicule written all over his face.

"'What may I ask is going on?' I said. 'You agreed never to bring a victim to the house. You gave your word.'

"He grinned evilly. 'Victim? To exactly what victim are you referring?'

"I sat silent, glaring at him, arms crossed.

"He raised his eyebrows and studied my face for a moment.

"'Ah! You must be referring to Jason, my new lover.'

"'*Your new lover?*'

"'Can you blame me? You, after all, have not been very receptive. So I have decided to take on a new lover. A very interesting and exiting youth, he is. Reminds me a lot of myself.'

"'You have no intention of feeding on him?' I asked in disbelief.

"'Now why would I want to do a thing like that?' he sneered. 'A dead lover would not be much fun now, would he?' He crossed his legs and clasped his hands in his lap. 'What is wrong my noble Erik? Is that jealousy I sense?'

"'I am not jealous,' I replied. 'I simply do not believe you. This is out of character for you.'

"'How suspicious you always are!' he said, grinning. 'I just decided that some human companionship would be nice for a change.'

"I knew he was lying.

"'Since when do you search out the company of humans?'

"'Since you spend so much of your time in their company, I thought I might try it as well. Why should I not partake, as you do, of all the human community has to offer? They are such interesting creatures.' He lowered his eyes. 'One is entitled to change one's views.'

"'Victor, I am warning you, if you so much as…'

"'I stand warned,' he interrupted, and stood up. 'Now if you will kindly excuse me, I need to go out and hunt.'

"With that, he was gone. He left me sitting there, fuming. He had conjured up some sort of diabolical plan, of this I was certain. But what?

"Several weeks passed without Jason returning again to the house. I prayed that either he had killed him by now or had forgotten him. I was wrong on both counts.

"I returned home one evening after a particularly enjoyable night spent with my new human friends. Dawn was approaching rapidly so I had retired to the basement. When I entered the coffin room, I gasped in horror. There in the room was a third coffin! I must have stared at it for several moments when I heard soft chuckling behind me. I swung around. Victor was standing in the doorway, arms crossed with a demonic smile upon his face.

'There is soon to be a new addition to our little family,' he said cheerily. He walked over to the new casket and rubbed his hand across the top of it lovingly. 'I hope you will be welcoming to him when he arrives.'

"I looked at him wildly. 'You did not!' I exclaimed, wanting to tear his fiendish heart right out of his body. 'That boy—Jason. You have transformed him!'

"He opened the new coffin and got in, crossing his arms on his chest. 'I think he will be quite comfortable in here. What do you think? Or should I add another pillow?'

"I was wild with rage.

"'How could you do this? How could you bring another person into this horrible existence? What the world does not need is another drinker of human blood.'

"He smiled at me, an amused look on his face.

"'What is wrong Erik? Do you feel as if you are being replaced?' He got up abruptly from the coffin and slammed the lid. 'Well you are! You and I could have had it all but instead, you have decided to turn against me and pursue these absurd moralistic values of yours. Pathetic creature that you are! I am sure that Jason will not do the same. He loves me as I love him and will be my new mate for all eternity, a rank which could have been yours, should you have had the wisdom to accept it. Perhaps I did not take enough time with you before I turned you. Oh, do not fret. The three of us will make one big happy family together. Why, you can clean house while we go out killing.'

"A demonic sound escaped his lips and his voice turned into a twisted laughter. I shuddered, realizing that I had been correct in the assumption that Victor was insane. His eyes clearly betrayed his madness.

"'You will not do this,' I cried, grabbing a hold of his shirt. 'I will not allow it.'

"'You will not allow it?' he roared. 'You seem to have forgotten who is master here. I created you. You are in my house and will answer to me!'

"'You did not create me,' I reminded him roughly. 'You forced your accursed gift onto me and I bow to no one.'

"I let go of him, feeling defeated. I could not allow him to bring another vampire into the world, especially one that would surely turn out to be as evil as Victor.

"'Have you already transformed him?' I asked.

"'Tomorrow night is when it shall take place. In a mere five days he shall be joining us.' He stared into my eyes as if trying to seduce me. 'There is no need for concern. We will be happy together, the three of us. You shall see.' He bowed in mock reverence and retreated to his casket.

"In his own twisted way, perhaps he did love the boy or felt a strong bond with the human. Whatever the case, I could sense that Victor's feelings for this boy were strong. But I decided, as I lay in my coffin waiting for the death sleep to overcome me, that I would not allow this to happen. I came up with a plan, I knew what I had to do."

Erik was silent for several moments. He looked at Steve and forced a weak smile.

"I had to kill the boy before he became a vampire."

Steve's eyes grew wild. "You killed him?"

Erik nodded his head weakly. "I had to. It was true that Victor could make other vampires if he wanted to, choosing whomever he wanted.

But this boy was too much like Victor, too bloodthirsty even as a human. The transformation had to be stopped, and the only way I could think to stop it was either kill Victor or kill the boy. Naturally, killing the boy would be a much easier task."

Erik hesitated, clasping his hands together tightly. "In order to complete this mission, I had to be more clever than Victor. Knowing that he would start the process the next night, I carefully followed him when he left the house. True to his word, he led me right to where the boy lived. I returned home quickly, ensuring that I would be there when Victor arrived so as not to arouse his suspicions. He had unknowingly provided me with what I needed to know.

"Victor returned later, an air of triumph in his stride. I said nothing about his proposed plan and luckily, he did not mention it himself. As we sat together, my heart beat wildly. I was terrified that he would somehow comprehend what I planned to do. To avoid the chance of somehow revealing my plan, I kept conversation to a minimum and blanked my mind.

"The next evening, I returned to the boy's home. Trying not to think of the task which lie ahead, I climbed the house and entered through the window into which I saw Victor penetrate the night before. There he was, just as I had expected to find him, overtaken with fever, as I had been nearly a year before. The boy was delirious, which would make the chore all the easier. I looked down at him for several moments, trying to build up the courage to carry out this deed. I believed he recognized me for a moment through his altered state, but I cannot be sure. I hesitated, not yet realizing the enormity of what I was going to undertake. This boy had to die. I could not allow him to enter the world as a vampire.

"I crept to his bedside and looked him in the eye. I slowly lowered my face to his ear.

"'You will never enter the world as a vampire,' I whispered softly. 'I will spare you from this fate. Sleep well and peaceful young Jason.'

"With that, I sunk my teeth into his neck. For being in such a weakened condition, I was surprised at the extent which he struggled for his young life. But he was no match for my strength and quickly succumbed to my deadly bite. I held his drained corpse in my arms then gently laid him on the bed. The deed was done. I disposed of his corpse properly so that nobody in the mortal world would ever discover what had befallen him.

"It was now time to face Victor.

"The slaughter of Jason was bloody. My clothes were drenched. Rather than attempt to hide what I had done, I gallantly sauntered into the living room and stood before Victor. His eyes met mine, and then they searched my blood-doused clothing. There was a flash of recognition, then a fury that I had never witnessed before or since in any being, vampire or human. He knew well the smell of his young lover's blood.

"'*What have you done?*' he roared so loudly that my hands instinctively went up to my ears to protect them from the invading unearthly noise.

"For the first time I knew what actual terror really was—no, the emotion that I experienced then ran much deeper than terror, something I could not even attempt to put into words. My blood froze as he stared at me, hellfire burning in his eyes.

"I took several steps back, then said as calmly as I could, 'I could not allow you to bring another monster into this world. Your fledgling-to-be has been executed.'

"He smiled sweetly.

"'And I, in turn, shall execute you.'

"His face contorted into that of a horrible demon and he flung himself at me, his sharp fangs baring wildly, murder in his eyes. I attempted to cover my face to ward off his attack but he was too quick. He had closed his hands around my throat and I could feel his rancid breath on my neck. Suddenly, his teeth sunk into my throat and he pulled with his fangs, trying to rip my throat to shreds. Blood gushed from the wound, drenching the both of us.

"Aware that I was weakening quickly, I searched desperately for a means to escape a certain death at this fiend's hands. On the table next to me was a glass vase, one of Victor's prize possessions. With his teeth still embedded in my neck, I knocked the vase just enough so that it would plummet from the table onto the floor, shattering as it hit. Victor, surprised by the sound, pulled away just long enough to allow me to reach down and grab a huge shard of the broken vase. I plunged it deeply into his throat. He howled in pain as he tried to dislodge the invading fragment of glass from his throat. I moved as quickly as I could toward the fireplace, grabbed an old book and plunged it into the fire where it immediately burst into flames. I turned just in time to see Victor approaching me, a gaping hole in his throat where the glass had been.

"'You will now die!' he thundered.

"Just as he reached me, I stretched my arm into the fireplace, retrieved the book, then hit him with all my force across the chest with the flaming book. He stumbled backwards from the force of the blow, and then realized that his clothes had caught afire. He screamed and quickly began brushing at the flames as they crawled down his legs and up his back. He threw himself on the floor, attempting to extinguish them. Still holding the book, I flung it at his writhing form on the floor, causing his clothes to ignite further. I watched in horror as he desperately tried to put out the flames. The fire spread rapidly on the carpeting and draperies until the entire room was ablaze. I ran back to the fireplace, and with one final act, grabbed a rod iron poker and jammed it into the chest of the charred vampire on the floor. A piercing scream echoed in the burning house. Fearful of perishing in the fire myself, I dashed out the door. The screams that followed me were to haunt my dreams for many nights to come. *Run! Run far and fast for I will find you! You will never escape me Erik! Never! I have all of eternity to find you. I will be avenged!'*

"The words assaulted my brain as I fled the burning house. I thought I could hear an eerie laughter intermingled with the screams of agony. I did not look back. That was the last time I saw Victor.'"

"Did you know that he didn't die in the fire?" Steve asked in almost a whisper.

"Not at first. I believed there was no possible way he could have survived. He was engulfed in flames with the poker sticking in his burning chest when I left the house. Perhaps the chest wound was not enough to do him in, but I was aware that fire would certainly destroy our kind. Not too long afterwards, I sensed that he was still alive. I cannot explain how, it was a feeling. Perhaps since he was the one who made me what I am and his blood flows through my veins, that I can sense when he is near. I do not know. I just understood that somehow, he was still out there and eventually would make good on his promise." Erik shuddered involuntarily. "And he has now returned to avenge himself."

Neither man spoke for several moments. Steve was trying to digest everything he had just been told. None of it seemed real. His lover was a vampire and another vampire was out to kill Erik, and possibly himself as well.

"What do we do now?" Steve asked.

Erik gazed at his lover in despair. "All we can do is wait. Victor will be back, I can assure you of that and I shall be prepared to do battle with him when the time comes. In the meantime, I want you to stay here with me. During the day, you are safe. He cannot harm you then. At night, I will not let you out of my sight for a moment." He paused, then, "I would never be able to continue living if anything ever happened to you." He stroked Steve's arm, then kissed him on the cheek.

"I have to admit that I'm a little scared," Steve said. "This all seems so unreal."

Erik nodded. "We must both be very careful and always on our guard. I will deal with Victor quickly and effectively when the time comes."

Steve looked at his lover, sighed to himself and wondered what it would be like to be a vampire.

Word On The Street

◆

"Just watch yourself, okay?" the sandy haired young man said to Jamie. They both stood on Halsted Street, braving the chilly night. "In case you haven't noticed, most of the guys are staying off of the streets these days. Shit, if I didn't need the money so badly, I'd do the same."

Jamie glanced around. It was true. The turf was mainly deserted tonight, as it had been the previous night and the night before that. Word had gotten out quickly. A murderer was on the loose and lately, his attention seemed to be focused on the Halsted Street hustlers. Last weekend one of the regulars, a rough-looking but shy boy named Christopher had been discovered dead. It was the same as the others. His throat had been ripped out and he had been completely drained of blood. The vampire murderer. Jamie had been able to think of little else lately, especially since his discussions with Steve.

He reached into the inside pocket of his black leather jacket and fumbled until he pulled out a cigarette. He was nervous being out here and had been especially careful with whom he left these days. Unlike his companion, he didn't desperately need the money to live. He had no bills to mention, no car payment, no mortgage and didn't do too badly from his waitering job. What hustling did provide him was a fast way to make an incredible amount of money, money he diligently put away for his future, for a time when he would have to decide what he wanted to do with his life. But it wasn't just the money. He hustled because he enjoyed it as well. He loved adventure and found plenty of it on the streets. Sure, he had run into the occasional weirdo but for the most part had been lucky. He had never run into a situation that he couldn't get himself out of. Besides, there was that kinky side to his personality that he just loved exploring.

Christopher had not been so lucky. Jamie didn't know him that well but had spoken to him several times. He seemed to be a nice enough guy, a little on the shy side but always friendly. Jamie had also been quite attracted to him. He was most likely no more than twenty with sparkling blue eyes and straight blond hair, clipped short in an Navy style cut—the all American Boy look. He was perpetually tanned with a tight, well-formed body and had a genuine look of innocence about him. Jamie had tried to strike up a conversation with him several times in the hopes of getting to know him better but Christopher was not the chatty type and most attempts to get the boy talking were in vain. Christopher would rarely associate with the other boys on the strip and liked to keep to himself. Jamie eventually concluded that he was most likely straight, hustling only for the money and gave up on his attempts at hooking up with the handsome guy.

Nobody on the strip that Saturday noticed with whom Christopher had left. It was the unwritten law that you don't mess with another boy's john and if someone scores, you keep your nose to yourself and look the other way. Jamie rarely paid attention to any of the other hustlers while he was working. He had his own turf and all that mattered to him was scoring. The other boys felt pretty much the same so Christopher's disappearance that night went unnoticed.

Jamie was taking a chance being out on the street with this vampire killer on the loose and he knew it, but he was never one to cower in fear at anything. He had been a hustler since the tender age of sixteen, one of his best kept secrets, and was well aware of the ways of life on the Chicago streets. It was strange how he had gotten himself into hustling. He had been a busboy at a local restaurant, his first job actually. Jamie was developing into a striking youth who turned the head of both the guys and gals, although he was unaware of it at the time. He had been chubby in grade school and well into high school and because of this, had not developed a very confident attitude about his looks. Then, all at once, or so it seemed, the weight dropped from his body and he was transformed into a handsome young man and became the object of desire of both sexes.

Jamie wasn't interested in both sexes though—only guys. He had been gay for as long as he could remember and explaining to someone how he came out was easy. 'When my friends started noticing girls, I started noticing my friends' was his standard answer. The moment he reached puberty, he immediately accepted his sexuality and explored it every opportunity he could. He never understood the concept of 'coming out' because as far as he was concerned, he was born 'out'. Being completely open about his sexual preference had led to a few problems with some of the neighborhood boys, but he always fearlessly stood his ground. Of course, being considerably bigger than the other boys helped.

Working at the restaurant didn't change his candidness about being gay and luckily for him, the owners were two older gentlemen who had been lovers for close to thirty years and who were totally open about their sexuality. It was at the restaurant that an older straight couple, Eileen and Alan, took Jamie under their wing. They weren't actually that old, most likely in their early thirties, but to a sixteen year old, they were ancient.

It was only Eileen who worked at the restaurant but it seemed that her handsome boyfriend Alan was always there as well, watching her with the devotion of a Cocker Spaniel while she worked. At first, Jamie couldn't understand what Alan saw in Eileen. She tipped the scales at well over 300 pounds and chain-smoked—Salem 100's to be exact. The words that would come out of her mouth would cause even Jamie to blush, and he was not one to blush easily. After getting to know her better, he understood. She was a warm, funny woman with a raspy laugh that was as contagious as the common cold. When Eileen broke into one of her infamous laughing fits, even the sternest, most serious of souls could not avoid cracking at least a smile. One of her favorite stories to tell was about the first time she got the crabs, discovering her affliction at work, and would go so far as to describe in minute detail what the nasty little critters looked like.

She accepted Jamie's homosexuality without so much as a bat of an eye and encouraged him to tell her all about his sexual adventures. Soon Alan would join in on the conversation and edged Jamie on, just as Eileen did, to fill them in on all of the juicy details. He loved them both and began spending more and more of his free time with his two new friends. It was Alan who brought up the idea of hustling.

"Jamie, do you realize how good looking you actually are? Why, you are one of the most beautiful young men that I know."

Jamie blushed, causing Eileen to go into a fit of laughter.

"Thanks Alan. I guess I'm okay looking. I usually don't have any problem getting dates."

"You mean getting laid," Eileen added.

Jamie blushed again.

"What I'm trying to tell you," Alan continued, ignoring Eileen's interruption, "is that you could be making a shitload of money with those looks."

"Money? Like from modeling?"

Alan shook his head. "Hustling my boy, hustling. There are guys that would pay a hundred bucks or more to land a hot guy like you in the sack. When someone is gifted with looks such as yours, it would be a crime to waste them. They disappear so damned fast. Take it from me, I know." He grinned wickedly. "You have a chance to make a lot of dough for doing nothing more than having sex, evidently something that you enjoy very much." He grinned. Eileen watched Jamie intently for a reaction.

Jamie blushed again and creased his brow, obviously in deep thought. Hustling. Now this could be interesting. Making money for doing nothing but sleeping with people sounded right up his alley.

They spent the rest of the evening talking about the possibilities and Alan ended up convincing him that this was one opportunity that he must not let slip through his fingers. He didn't think of it at the time but now wondered how Alan knew so much about hustling? They were definitely a strange couple, Alan and Eileen, and Jamie was saddened to think that he had lost contact with them over the years.

Now, seven years later he was still on the street, cashing in on his good looks. He also followed Alan's advice and took all the money he had made from hustling and stuck it away in the bank. He now had a nice chunk of change waiting for him for the time when his hustling days would be over. He knew that soon he would have to decide what he wanted to do with his life, as the time remaining on the streets for him was limited. More and more guys were showing up all the time, most of them much younger than himself, their presence informing him that his time was running out. Like his friend Steve, he also had no intention of making waitering a permanent career. It was just a temporary resting spot until he decided what he really wanted to do for the rest of his life.

Jamie glanced at his watch and sighed. He had been standing out here for several hours already. He hated nights like this. When he first noticed that so few of the usual boys were showing up, he had hoped that this would mean it would be easier for him to score. Unfortunately, most of the customers neglected to show up as well. It seemed that everyone was avoiding the streets. It probably was reckless of him to be out as well. Why risk your life for a few bucks? Not that he couldn't handle himself. He glanced at his watch again.

"That's enough of this foolishness for one night," he said out loud.

The other young man glanced over at him from the opposite corner. "Did you say something?"

"I'm gonna take off," Jamie answered. "There's not too much going on and it's just too damn cold." He plunged his hands into his pocket.

"Yeah, I don't think I'm going to hang out much longer myself. It seems like pretty much of a waste of time tonight."

"Be careful, okay?"

"You got it," the kid answered with a smile. "Take it easy."

* * *

Just minutes after Jamie disappeared, a tall man turned the corner. From a distance, he seemed rather good-looking. The sandy-haired boy's heart started pounding. Maybe he was going to finally get lucky tonight, although this guy looked too young and too hot to be out looking for hustlers. But, you never know. Some young guys, even the really good-looking ones, have this fantasy about paying for sex. He never understood it—they could have the pick of the crop at any bar in town—and for free. He was getting cold and frustrated himself. To his delight, the handsome man stopped right in front of him.

"Chilly night, no?" the man said, looking right into the boy's eyes. "Much too chilly for an attractive young man like yourself to be alone."

"Chilly isn't the word for it," the boy responded, not really in the mood for small talk. "It's downright frigid."

"So it is."

The boy shuffled his feet. "So what are you looking for?"

"Companionship," the man answered flatly. "Interested?"

"You're not a cop, are you?" the boy asked, not sure if he trusted the man. "If you're vice, you might as well just keep on going 'cause I'm only hanging out. Nothing more."

The man laughed a little longer than necessary. "I am about as far from a cop as you can get." He fished out a thick wad of money from his pocket and began counting it absent-mindedly. "You still have not answered my question. Interested or not?"

The boy's eyes grew wide. "You got a place?"

The man shook his head gently. "Naturally." He moved forward, standing right next to the boy, touched his cheek and then began walking away from him. "Come."

When the boy caught up to the man, the man put his arm around him as they walked. "What's your name boy?"

"Skip."

"Skip. What an interesting name." The man wrapped his arm even more tightly around the boy.

"I am Victor," he said and they disappeared into the night.

Revelation

◆

The smell of freshly brewed coffee filled Steve's nostrils. He had been awake for some time but the strange bed felt so soft and so comfortable against his skin that he hated to get out of it. He had been thinking about everything Erik had told him the previous night. He was dating a vampire. How about that? Steve had always said that he was open to new things but this just might be pushing it a bit. He had a lot to think about, a lot of sort out. Especially about this Victor. This was one dude that he did not want to run into again.

He bounded out of bed and slipped into his jeans and t-shirt.

"Nice view," he said out loud, looking out the window. He buttoned up his jeans. "Quite a place you have here Erik."

Of course, Erik couldn't hear him. He was deep in his death sleep at the moment. Steve did not even want to try to picture him lying in a coffin in some hidden room in the house. He shuddered and sat back down on the bed, staring straight ahead while looking at nothing in particular.

His mind went back to his and Erik's conversation. Definitely some heavy shit. How in the hell was he supposed to be able to deal with all of this? Vampires, of all things! He wished Erik were here now. He was so confused about everything—everything that is, except for his feelings for Erik. He loved Erik, he knew that much, but did he love him enough? Would he be able to stand it when Erik went out on the prowl in the evenings, fangs bared, looking for some innocent guy willing to part with a couple of pints? He didn't know. He had to think. But it hurt to think.

The smell of coffee again filled Steve's nostrils. That's what he needed, a good strong cup of coffee to clear his head. He then heard dishes clanking downstairs. Erik? No, Erik was…sleeping. Then who in the hell was downstairs?

He tucked his shirt into his pants and laced up his sneakers. Tiptoeing, he opened the door to the bedroom then closed it quietly. He crept slowly down the stairs, careful not to make a sound. He could hear movement coming from below. There was definitely someone in the kitchen.

He thought about making a mad dash for the front door and then running like hell. Coward, he told himself. There was nothing to be afraid of. Erik said that vampires could not walk during the daylight, or do much of anything else for that matter. So it was impossible that it was Victor in Erik's kitchen brewing morning coffee. Gathering up all of his nerve, he walked cautiously to the door that gave way to the kitchen. His heart was pounding rapidly. He peered around the corner.

At the kitchen table sat a blond man with his back to the door, holding an oversized yellow coffee cup. He looked young from what Steve could tell.

What was he doing here? Erik never mentioned having a housemate. He cleared his throat.

The man turned around quickly and their eyes met. Shit! It was the blond cop from the police station where Rickman worked!

The blood drained from Steve's face as the young police officer continued to stare at him. Finally the blond man spoke. His voice was soft, yet masculine.

"Do you want some coffee? I just made it."

Not waiting for an answer, the man strolled over to the kitchen cabinet, retrieved a large yellow mug and filled it with the steaming brew.

"Cream? Sugar?"

Steve hesitated. "A little cream, thank you."

The man returned to the table with the coffee and placed it down in front of an empty chair. Steve stood motionless at the doorway.

"What are you waiting for? It's going to get cold. Come on in and sit down. Being timid won't get you very far around here." The man smiled.

Steve dragged himself to the table. His hands were shaking. He prayed he wouldn't be interrogated by this man, although there was little doubt in his mind that this would in fact occur. How was he going to explain what he was doing there?

The man didn't look up as Steve sat down. They sat in silence for several minutes, each sipping their coffee. Trying to rush, he took too big a gulp of the hot coffee. He let out a yelp and his hand flew to his mouth.

"Easy," the man said, looking up at him, a weak smile on his face. "It's hot." He eyed Steve up and down as if examining him. "You are a good-looking one, I'll give you that much."

Steve didn't answer him and continued trying to empty his coffee cup as quickly as possible. The man continued.

"I assume he told you everything?"

"Huh?" Steve responded, startled.

"I asked you if he told you the whole story. Spilled the beans, as it were."

A confused look crossed over Steve's face. He put down his mug, and then rubbed his hands together. "I'm sorry, I don't know what you mean."

"Erik," the man said simply. He rose, poured himself another cup of coffee then returned to the table. "Did he tell you all about himself?"

"We just met recently so I don't know too much about him." Steve put down his empty coffee mug. "I really have to get going now. Errands to run. It was really nice talking…"

"Don't you dare move," the man interrupted, eyes glaring at Steve but looking rather confused as well. "There's no need to be afraid of me. I'm not the enemy you know."

"I'm not afraid of you. I just don't know anything about Erik. Like I said, I only just met him."

The man looked at Steve wide-eyed.

"Why are you lying to me? I know very well that you and Erik have been seeing each other for quite some time already. He told me that he was going to tell you the truth about him. Since you are here, I assume he did." He sipped his coffee then looked at Steve. "You can trust me, Steven. Erik and I are very good friends. We don't keep any secrets from each other."

"Friends?" Steve asked surprised. "I don't understand."

"You don't know who I am, do you?" the man asked, a sly smile upon his face.

"I've seen you once when I went to visit a friend of mine at the Police Station. You're a cop, aren't you?"

The man's eyes grew wider then he burst into laughter so quickly that he had to cover his mouth to avoid spitting out the coffee which he had just sipped. He laughed for several moments, and then regained his composure. Steve stared at him, not having the slightest idea what in the world could be so funny. He was certain that he had not made a mistake and that the man sitting across from him at the table was indeed the blond cop he saw during his last visit to the police station. He tried to remember his name.

"Is that the only thing that you know about me?"

Steve nodded, wringing his hands together.

"So this is what your strange behavior is all about," he said, suddenly warming up to Steve. "You thought that I was a cop and that I was investigating…" He burst into laughter again but this time only for a moment. "Steve," he finally said, "it's not what you think at all. It's true that I'm a cop. But I also live here."

The man sat back waiting for Steve's reaction.

"You live here?" Steve said, mouth agape in surprise. "I don't get it."

"Would you like some more coffee?" the man asked.

Steve nodded. "Yeah, I think I could use a little warm-up."

He smiled at Steve then refilled both their coffee mugs. When he returned to the table, he continued.

"Erik and I have lived together for several years. We have an agreement of sorts. I watch out for him and he watches out for me. He helped me out when I was just a kid and I've been with him ever since. If it wasn't for him, God knows where I would have ended up." He paused for a moment. "Do you remember that night that Erik took you out with the car? I was the driver."

"Ah ha!" Steve said, before he could help himself. "I thought you looked a lot like that chauffeur but wasn't sure. I even asked Rickman if you drove limo on the side. I forgot all about that until you mentioned it."

The man chuckled. "You were right. It was I." The man's face grew serious. "He did tell you everything, didn't he? Erik, I mean."

Steve nodded. He liked this man and hoped that he could trust him but continued to eye him suspiciously.

"Yes, he did fill me in on the details of his life."

"The details of his life? That's an interesting way to put it. Just exactly what details did he fill you in on? I need to know how much he told you."

Steve gulped and avoided the man's eyes. "You mean about being…" he paused, "a vampire?"

Mitch nodded. He smiled, aware of Steve's apprehension. "I'm a friend Steve."

Steve opened his mouth to say something, then thought better of it. He looked about the kitchen.

The young man chuckled. "Erik has told me all about you naturally. Oh, pardon me. I guess we have never been formally introduced. My name is Mitch."

He extended his hand across the table to Steve. Steve rose slightly to shake Mitch's hand.

A contemplative look settled on Steve's face. "There isn't by any chance anything between you and Erik, is there? I mean like—anything romantic?"

A look of sadness was evident in Mitch's eyes. "We're not lovers, if that's what you mean. There is a deep friendship and devotion between us, nothing more." He sighed.

"You feel something more though, don't you?" Steve said. The concern was evident in his voice. "I can tell."

Mitch stared at Steve a moment before answering. "I admit, I do have some strong feelings for Erik. But there's nothing for you to worry about. It's a love that was not meant to be and I accept that. You are the object of his affection, not I and my main concern is for his happiness and safety. I have his friendship and for that, I'm grateful." His voice was distant, but not bitter. "But there is no sense in us sitting here talking about unrequited love. There are more important issues at hand. Mainly, your safety."

"I assume you are referring to Victor."

Mitch nodded. "Don't ever underestimate him Steve or let your guard down. He is extremely dangerous and clever, as I'm sure Erik told you."

Steve smiled lazily. "After what Erik told me last night, I plan on staying out of his way. Far out of his way."

"Let's just hope you'll be able to."

"Have you ever come across him?"

Mitch narrowed his eyes then shook his head. "I consider myself lucky that I've never encountered him. And I hope I never have to. Erik told me all about Victor shortly after I started living with him and he's always believed that Victor would catch up to him one day. It looks like that day is finally here."

"I wonder why he waited so long to come back into the picture? Steve asked. "Erik said that he hasn't seen Victor in over seventy years."

Mitch shrugged his shoulders. "Who knows? Maybe he just couldn't find us until now. We moved around pretty much."

"So Erik spent his whole life hiding from Victor?"

"I wouldn't go so far as to say Erik hid from Victor. I think he would have gladly fought him should the need have arisen but it was much easier to avoid the encounter as long as possible. We've lived in many different cities, never staying in one place too long. Erik never had an explanation when he would tell me that we were to again move, but I always suspected that Victor was the cause of the decision."

"He certainly is creepy."

"Erik?"

Steve frowned. "No, Victor," he answered, almost glaring at his companion.

Mitch laughed and reached over to rub Steve's hand.

Steve smiled weakly. "Sorry. I guess I'm still pretty edgy from everything Erik told me. It's kind of difficult to come to terms with, you know? My boyfriend being a vampire and me being stalked by another vampire."

Mitch nodded in agreement. "I can imagine. I told Erik that you would probably run from the house screaming, never to be heard from again. But you're still here so that's a good sign." He grinned, then in a softer voice, "Erik is a wonderful guy, Steve. You won't find another like him."

"That's for sure," Steve answered, a thoughtful look on his face. "I do love him you know."

"I know."

Mitch rose, gathered up the two coffee mugs and placed them in the sink. "I have to start getting ready for work. You'll have the run of the house today. There are fresh towels in the bathroom and help yourself to any food in the refrigerator. I'll probably be home about 6:00 or so. Erik will be up well before then."

"Actually, I'm going to go back to my own apartment."

Mitch's bright face shadowed. "Do you think that's wise? I'm sure Erik would want you to stay at the house. In fact, he told me to make sure…"

"I'll be fine. Erik said that there was nothing to worry about during the day. I just want to be in my own place right now."

"Just make sure that whatever you do, you get back here well before dark."

"I'm just going to stay in tonight, at my own apartment. But please tell Erik to stop by later on. I'll be home—with the doors and windows locked."

"I really think you should…"

"Please Mitch," Steve interrupted, "I'll be careful. Promise. I just can't stay here right now. I hope you can understand that."

Mitch grunted in frustration. "I see that there's no changing your mind. Very well then." He scribbled something on a piece of paper and handed it to Steve. "Here's my telephone number at work. If anything strange happens, I want you to promise that you will call me immediately. I can be there in minutes."

Steve smiled warmly. "Thanks," he muttered, taking the paper. "I promise I'll call." He reached over and kissed Mitch on the cheek. "I appreciate your concern. Really I do."

After Steve left, Mitch grinned to himself. He liked Steve and could understand why Erik was so attracted to him. He was saddened for a moment at the thought of Steve in Erik's arms, but quickly dismissed the thought. Erik deserved Steve. He had been tortured long enough and if Steve could ease his suffering, that he was all for it. As he left the house and locked the door behind him, a strange feeling of doom came

upon him. He frowned, then silently prayed that no harm would come
to the boy.

* * *

Steve kicked off his sneakers and slammed himself down on the
couch, hugging his knees. He maintained the same position for almost a
half and hour, motionless, just staring straight ahead. He finally shook
himself, shivered, and then jumped up, almost falling as his white socks
glided on the slippery wooden floor. He would just keep himself busy
and not think about any of it. The green glow of his computer caught
his eye. He sighed. He staggered over to the pile of papers he had gathered around his desk and began frantically stuffing them into the black
shredder. The grinding whirl of the machine speared into his nerves as
he watched the tatters of notes on which he had worked so hard flitter
into the wastepaper basket, producing a mound on the bottom of the
container which reminded Steve of a freshly filled-in grave. There
would be no big vampire story. Without knowing exactly why, he was
almost at the point of tears.

The flashing red light on his answering machine all at once caught
his eye. He had not even thought to check his messages. He pressed the
'listen' button and his machine politely clued him in, after an annoying
beep, that three new messages awaited his attention. The first message
began. A distressed voice poured from the machine.

"*Steve, it's Jamie. Please call me as soon as you can. Something horrible
has happened. I can't talk about it on your answering machine. Just call.*"

Steve stood in amazement as he listened. The second message played.

"*It's me again. Where in the hell are you? Steve, please call me. I really
need someone to talk to. Please!*"

The last of the messages revealed only sobbing.

Steve braced himself and picked up the phone. This was not like Jamie at all. Jamie was usually so together, so calm and collected. What could have happened?

The phone rang four times before Jamie's exhausted voice uttered a weak greeting.

"Jamie? I just got home and got your messages…"

"Steve!" Jamie blurted out. "There's been another murder and this time it was a friend of mine. It could have been me! I was talking to him right before it happened. Steve, it really could have been me!"

Steve hesitated, saying nothing. There was dead silence on the line for several moments.

"Steve? Are you there?"

"Jamie, I think we need to talk."

Search For A Vampire

◆

"It's a bite of some kind. I don't recognize it though. Much too big to be a spider bite."

The doctor had a puzzled look on his face as he glanced down at the two bright red marks spread almost three inches apart on the patient's leg. He looked up at the man on the table, then scratched his head.

"I don't think I've ever seen anything like it. Not that I can remember anyway. Other than the marks, how are you feeling now?"

Rickman eyed the doctor. "Better now, I guess. The first couple of days I felt like shit. Drained. No energy. I seem to have recovered now for the most part. Still seem a little drawn but not too bad all in all." He ran his fingers over the marks on his leg, and flinched. "So you don't recognize them, huh doc? No clue what they are?"

The doctor shook his head. "Can't say that I do. We'll have to do some tests to explore them further, especially since you had such a strong physical reaction to them. We also want to make sure there's no infection." The doctor hesitated. "I recommend that you go through a series of rabies shots as well. If it is in fact a bite of some kind, there's always the possibility that whatever bit you could be rabid."

Rickman jumped off the examination table and pulled up his pants. "Thanks doc, but no thanks. I don't think any further examination will be necessary."

"But Jon," the doctor urged on, "you shouldn't let something like this go. It could be serious. If nothing else, at least agree to the rabies treatment. Rabies is nothing to take lightly."

Rickman had to keep himself from laughing. "Don't worry doc. I'm sure the sonofabitch that bit me isn't carrying rabies."

The doctor looked confused. "You talk like it was a person who bit you."

"If you only knew."

Rickman pulled on his cowboy boots and strutted out of the doctor's office. He was right in his assumption that the doctor would have no idea what the marks were. But he knew damned well what they were—and what caused them. And the bastard that made them was going to pay.

He had spoken about this incident to nobody. Who would believe him anyway? Some of the guys on the force might buy it but he wasn't going to take the chance of being ridiculed. If there was one thing that Jon Rickman hated more than anything else, it was to be made fun out of. This was one of his major character flaws and he knew it. An unfortunate incident involving an extremely attractive man he had met at one of the local dance bars was testament to that. It was many years ago—during a rather dark period in his life when Rickman experimented rather heavily with drugs. Speed was his poison then—good old-fashioned Amphetamines. He always carried with him a little plastic baggy with White Cross, Black Cadillacs, whatever the hell he could get his hands on at the time. As long as it would keep him awake, get his blood pumping and allow him to party the night away, he would pop it.

He had been strung out on who knows what the night he met the guy. He had gone out with the express intent to find a man for sex, knowing full well that at times, speed could 'fuck with your nature', although it had never personally happened to him. He had scored quickly that night, ending up at the guy's sparsely furnished loft apartment. Within moments, they had ended up in the bedroom. To his horror, Rickman quickly discovered that he could not get hard. He concentrated, stroked, pulled, pushed, rubbed, pinched, kneaded and finally prayed but nothing. To add to his humiliation, the guy actually made fun out of him. Saying that "perhaps the poor little tiny baby was sleeping" and that "it's always the butch ones who can never get their dick up." It was then that Rickman lost it. Completely out of control, he beat on the guy until the poor fucker was almost unconscious.

"Nobody makes fun out of me, asshole!" he had cried as his fists met with the young man's soft flesh. When he finally regained his composure, he stared at his bloody trick and ran out of the apartment, not fully believing what had just occurred.

There had only been a couple of times in his life when he had lost his temper like that and each time, he never quite remembered what went on in his mind during the attack. It scared him to think that he was capable of almost beating an innocent human being to death in a fit a rage, as he was most of the time a gentle and good-natured man who later became a police officer to protect the community, especially his community, Gays and Lesbians. He saw the guy a time or two after their encounter and the poor fellow, with terror in his eyes, made every effort possible to avoid Rickman. Shit, it should have been Rickman who was afraid of him. The guy could have pressed charges. A battery or attempted murder charge certainly would have put a damper on his future career with the police department.

Rickman groaned as he walked, holding his earmuffs tightly against his ears. Winter was starting to really get on his nerves and he had already had his fill of it. When he reached the station, he settled himself in his office and reviewed his notes on the Vampire Murders.

He felt guilty at the thought that he might be hiding an essential piece of evidence in the case. But what if by some chance he was wrong? It was possible that the guy he had brought home wasn't a vampire after all. He might have just come down with the flu for a couple of days and maybe the marks on his legs were nothing more than some kind of spider bite. But then again, what if…"

He closed his notebook with a bang. He had to keep this to himself. He felt that he wasn't wrong about his suspicion and would find this thing—this Erik—on his own and discover for himself if this indeed is the bastard responsible for all the murders. Remembering how he felt the next day after meeting Erik, Rickman was damn sure he was the one and wasn't going to take any chances with the fiend. He reached down in his bottom drawer and pulled out his 357. He toyed with it lovingly as he held it. He could get in big trouble for carrying this gun as 357's were no longer standard issue for the Police Department. But to carry the standard 9 mm would be suicide as far as he was concerned. If this fucker was indeed a vampire, chances are he wouldn't go down easy. He needed something that would take the bastard's head clean off and this was the baby that could do it.

He put the weapon in his holster after, with shaking hands, he had placed all six bullets in the cylinder. He would find this sonofabitch if it was the last thing that he did. No blood-sucking freak was going to feed on him and live to tell the tale. He would see to that personally.

He suddenly thought about Steve. Shit, the kid was probably still searching for the vampire, looking for his big story. Initially, he had helped the kid, mainly because he had had a crush on him ever since Rickman first met him, but now that Rickman may have actually come into contact with this bloodsucker and was almost certain of its existence, he knew the kid's life could very well be in danger. Shit, he was damn lucky to be alive himself. The other victims had not been so fortunate.

He leafed through his address book until he found the telephone number for Steven Mitchell. He dialed it immediately. On the fourth ring, Steve's crisp voice informed him that he was not at home at the moment but would return his call as soon as possible.

"Steve, Jon Rickman here," he spoke into the phone, trying to mask the quiver in his voice. "Please call me as soon as possible. I have some very important information about the Vampire Murders that you need to know. It's urgent that you contact me as soon as possible."

He hung up the phone, pulled the 357 out of his holster and began toying with it once again. With a final resolve, he slammed the gun back in his holster and left the office.

"I will find you," he muttered under his breath. "You can be certain of that. And when I do, you will die."

The office door slammed behind him.

* * *

Steve had Jamie in his arms, holding him tightly. During the past hour, Jamie had blurted out his entire story to Steve in between his sobs. Well, almost the entire story. Steve felt that there was something Jamie was not telling him and had no idea what is was or why Jamie would keep something from him. All he could get from his friend, was that he was talking to an acquaintance on the street and the next morning, he was found dead in a nearby dumpster, throat ripped out, drained of blood.

"The dumpster was only two blocks from where we were standing," Jamie informed him through his tears. "They said the murder happened about 2:00 in the morning, which was right about the time that I left him. I still can't believe it!"

"What in the hell were you doing on the street at 2:00 in the morning? Especially after everything that's happened lately?"

Jamie's eyes avoided Steve's. "I just happened to be there, that's all. I....couldn't sleep so I thought I'd take a little walk."

"How long were you out there?"

"Awhile."

"Did you notice anyone around while you two were talking?" Steve asked.

"No," said Jamie, shaking his head. "We were completely alone. When I left, there wasn't a soul in sight."

"You don't remember passing anyone or seeing anyone on your way home?"

"Nobody at all." Jamie slowly raised his head so that his eyes met Steve's. "He was only nineteen, Steve. Only nineteen fucking years old! They have to catch this bastard, vampire or not. Why haven't they caught him yet? How many more does he have to kill before they do something about it? Why isn't there more police patrolling? There is a serial killer out there, for Christ's sake!"

Steve tried to calm his friend down. "They'll catch him. I know that for a fact."

Jamie looked at Steve, a look on confusion in his eyes. "What do you mean?"

"Promise me you won't go out alone after sunset, not until he's caught. I mean it. Promise me Jamie."

"What do you mean don't go out after sunset? So what—you now think that it's a real vampire who's doing this?"

Steve hesitated and looked down. "I know it's a vampire."

"*What?*"

"Just trust me, okay? I can't say anything else."

Jamie grabbed Steve by the shoulders. "Just hold on one second, here mister. What do you mean you know it's a vampire? Have you found out something? How do you know this? What do you exactly know?"

Steve broke away. "I can't tell you or anyone else anything more right now. I'll tell you everything later. I promise. Just do as I say and trust me."

"What are you keeping from me Steve? You're saying that you know for sure that it's a vampire but you can't tell anyone about it. Have you gone to the police?" Jamie looked genuinely angry.

Steve shuddered at the thought of Rickman. What if he should stumble upon Victor first? Rickman wouldn't have a chance in hell against him.

"The police can't be involved right now. You'll understand after I tell you everything. I just can't right now. I need some time."

"Don't even think for a second that I'm going to let you walk out of here like this. Just what are you involved in? What do you mean you can't go to the police? This is a fucking murderer we're talking about! You're a waiter Steve, not a private eye or a homicide detective. If you know something about this, you've got to tell the cops. Jesus Christ man, this maniac killed one of my friends last night. He could kill again, and most probably will if he's not caught. Can you understand that Steven?"

He roughly pushed Steve back. His face was red with anger. His eyes were hot with tears.

Steve snatched his coat and stopped at the front door.

"Like I told you Jamie, I can't say anything more. It's too complicated to go into but I do know what I'm doing. I just can't go to the police with this—at least not yet. I'll explain it all later. Just have faith in me, okay?"

Steve opened the front door. Just before leaving, he turned back around to face Jamie.

"And one more thing. You have to stay away from me for now. Hanging around with me could get you killed."

Jamie stood motionless looking at the closed door. His heart was thrashing in his chest and his hands began to shake. He ran to his desk, grabbed a phone book and thumbed through it fiercely until he found what he was looking for.

"I'm sorry Steve but I care about you too much to allow you to get killed." he said out loud. He dialed the phone.

"Jon Rickman, please."

Unexpected Guest

◆

After his visit with Jamie, the day had turned out to be a full one after all. Steve had gone to the Museum of Science and Industry in an attempt to clear his troubled mind. He wanted to think about something else—something other than the tide of recent events which flooded his brain like a runaway river during the first melting of the snow. It had been years since he had visited this museum and had forgotten what an incredible place it really was. For hours he walked along the hallways, deeply immersed in the displays and gadgets that he saw on the way. It was a perfect way to spend a cold, wintry Chicago day. The few hours he spent there were hardy enough to see everything but at least he had temporarily succeeded in taking his mind off of Victor.

He exited the museum and blinked his eyes as he looked up at the gradually darkening sky. Shit! He had not realized it was so late.

The sun was already starting to set. He never did get used to winter when night came so damned early. It was barely past 4:30. Somehow time had gotten away from him. He was a long way from home, at least an hour bus ride at this time of day.

In a near panic, he ran to the nearest bus stop. As he stood waiting, he glanced back and forth from his watch to the setting orb in the sky, shifting his weight impatiently from one foot to the other as the sky threatened imminent blackness.

Where was the damned bus? He took a heavy breath as he finally caught sight of an approaching city bus. The brakes squealed as it stopped and the door clattered open. With a sigh of relief, he boarded the already crowded vehicle.

It wasn't even 5:00 yet but the creaky bus was plump, bursting with the crammed-in passengers who were standing practically on top of each other. For the first leg of the journey, Steve remained standing hoping that a seat would soon become available. His head swam from the wave of different colognes and perfumes which ambushed his overly sensitive nostrils, some almost overpowering, and his feet hurt from walking around in the museum all afternoon. He should have known better than to have worn these pinchy shoes for an afternoon at the museum. He probably had blisters by now.

His panic augmented as the sky darkened, finally enveloping the city completely in night. Erik would be furious if he knew that he was out after sunset. Steve was not that keen on the idea himself. Running into Victor definitely would not be his idea of a good time. His stop finally arrived. The moment his feet hit the snowy sidewalk, he broke into a run. He was scared. As he sped towards home, he realized what must go through a gazelle's mind while being pursued by a cheetah. Out of breath, he reached his apartment building. He threw open the front door and bounded up the steps, not daring to look behind him. Safe at last!

He fumbled with his backpack, trying to get to his keys but the zipper stuck. Almost ripping the bag, he finally managed to retrieve them and flung the door to his apartment open and entered his safe abode. Just as he was about to close the door, an unknown hand stopped it.

Steve panicked.

He had not heard anyone come up the stairs behind him.

He let out a short scream and with all of his strength, he pushed at the door. He was no match for whoever was on the other side and the door flew open despite Steve's efforts, flinging him into the nearby coat rack. With wide eyes, he looked at the intruder as he entered the apartment.

"I thought I made it clear to you that you were to stay at my house and not go out after dark under any circumstances!"

"Erik! You scared me half to death. What are you trying to do, give me a heart attack?"

Erik pointed a finger a Steve who was still on the floor next to the coat rack.

"A heart attack would have been the least of your worries if it would have been Victor on the other side of that door."

Steve stood up, straightening out his disheveled clothes. "I'm really sorry. I went to the museum today and guess I got a little too involved with things. I didn't realize it was almost dark until after I had left."

Erik's face softened but he still looked angry. "Such an error in judgment could have cost you your life."

Without waiting for Steve, he walked into the living room and planted himself on the couch. Steve followed and sat beside him.

"Why did you not stay at my house where you would have been safe?"

Steve sighed and turned to look at Erik. "I know you're pissed and I don't blame you. I," Steve stared at the floor, "I just couldn't stay there."

"Why not? Did Mitch say something to upset you?"

Steve shook his head. "It wasn't Mitch at all. In fact, he was very nice. I just needed to go out on my own today and think things through."

He then recounted the morning's events to Erik about how he mistook Mitch for a police office who had come by to investigate Erik and the murders. Erik laughed and Steve was relieved to see that the angry look which was on his face moments ago had vanished.

"You really must stay with me until I find Victor. Every moment that you remain alone after sunset endangers your life." He reached over and rubbed Steve's arm. "I could never forgive myself if anything happened to you because of me."

"And just how are you going to find Victor if I am to spend every moment with you?"

Erik looked at Steve intently for several moments before answering. "That is a very good point. I guess what I meant to say is that when Victor finds us, and I have no doubt that he will, I do not want you to be alone. I am sure that he plans on enacting some sort of revenge for what I did to him years ago and from what I can guess, that plan includes you. That is the only reason I can think of why he appeared to you first. He does nothing without a reason." Erik paused, then took a deep breath. "If you were per chance unaccompanied when he finds you, you would have no possibility of survival, I can guarantee you that. I am the only one who can protect you."

Steve looked solemn. "In other words, I'm going to have to meet up with this character again?"

"I am almost certain of it."

"What if I were to blow town for awhile? I could always go to Boston and stay with my parents." Steve shuddered at the very thought of it.

"Much too dangerous," Erik replied. "If he is after you, he will find you. Remember, he effortlessly tracked you down at the restaurant. He will track you wherever you go. We cannot take the chance of him finding you without me there to protect you."

Steve sighed. "I guess you're right. I don't think I want to take that chance either."

Erik took hold of Steve's hand. "I am so sorry for getting you involved in this. I never meant for this to happen." Then, in an afterthought, "It was a mistake on my part to pursue you romantically. I should have known that doing so would put your life at risk."

Steve grabbed both of Erik's hands and squeezed them hard. "Don't ever say that or think that again. I love you Erik and if I had to do it all over, I would still choose you. We'll work this out—somehow."

Erik brushed his hand lightly against Steve's cheek, then hugged him. "I got so caught up with Victor that I neglected even ask how you are."

"How I am?"

"I dumped a lot on you last night and I know what I told you was not easy to assimilate. Are you okay with everything we discussed?"

Steve smiled weakly. "I'm coming to terms with it. It's going to take some getting used to. Although when you think about it, it is kind of cool. I mean not everyone has a boyfriend who can leap tall buildings in a single bound."

Erik grinned. "Well, I cannot quite accomplish that."

"Yeah, but you can really run like hell." He paused. "You do have to promise me one thing though."

Erik's eyes widened. "And what is that?"

"After you drink blood, you have to brush your teeth before kissing me."

Erik grabbed Steve and hugged him tightly. He whispered in his ear, "I promise." Erik lowered his face to meet Steve's and their lips met.

Suddenly there was a knock at the door. Steve hesitatingly pulled away from Erik. "How's that for bad timing?"

"Are you expecting someone?" Erik asked, a concerned look on his face.

"Not that I know of. It could be Jamie. He's been known to pop over at all hours of the night unannounced." *Especially after our talk today,* Steve thought to himself. *He should have mentioned it to Erik.*

Erik stood up. "Whatever you do, do not open the door unless you know for certain who it is on the other side."

"What, do you think I'm nuts? This is Chicago, after all." Steve smiled then walked to the door. He looked through the peephole then sighed with relief.

"Erik," Steve called out quietly. "No need to worry. It's a friend of mine. I'm sure he won't stay long."

Erik sat back down on the couch. Steve undid the latches and swung open the door.

"Hey guy! What a surprise!" Steve said as he looked at his visitor.

"Hiya Bud," Rickman said as he strutted into the apartment. "Don't you ever return your damned phone calls?"

He closed the door behind him.

Meeting At Last

◆

"My phone calls?" Steve asked, then blushed. "No, I must have forgotten to check my answering machine."

"Sorry for dropping by like this without warning, but I need to talk to you about something important. It's urgent. I hope I didn't come at a bad time."

"Actually, it is kind of a bad time. I have my boyfriend over right now."

A quick look of disappointment crossed over Rickman's face. "Your boyfriend? Damn! I didn't even know that I was out of the running."

"We've been dating for awhile already. He's really a nice guy. Want to come in and meet him?"

"I'd love to. What I have to say could concern the both of you. It should only take a minute."

Rickman followed Steve down the short hallway, then around the corner into the living room where Erik was still seated on the couch. Their eyes met briefly and a flash of recognition shadowed both of their faces. Erik quickly stood up. Rickman drew his gun and pointed it directly at Erik's head. Steve gasped.

"Sit back down and put your hands on top of your head!" Rickman screamed, holding his gun with both hands, arms outstretched. "Now motherfucker!"

One hand left the gun just long enough to fumble for his wallet and flash Erik his badge. "Police!"

Both hands returned to the gun.

"What in the fuck are you doing?" Steve cried out, rushing up to Rickman.

Rickman brushed him aside. "Stand back Steve and be thankful that you're still alive," he said, his eyes not leaving Erik's for a moment.

Steve's gaze met Erik's eyes, and they locked for just a moment. Steve then turned to face Rickman. "What do you mean?"

"This fucker is a vampire. This here is the rotten bastard who committed all the murders."

"You're wrong!" Steve cried out. "He's not the one you want!"

"Oh, he's the one all right." His eyes narrowed as he glared at Erik. His hands, both still clutched tightly to the gun, began to tremble.

"You sunk your fangs into the wrong guy you freaking blood-sucking motherfucking asshole!"

"You bit him?" Steve said looking at Erik, momentarily forgetting Rickman's presence.

"It was a mistake," Erik said calmly. "I was unaware that he was a friend of yours, much less a policeman." His eyes never left the gun for a moment yet he appeared completely calm. "How strange—I am usually much more perceptive."

"What? You know this creep is a vampire?" Rickman looked at Steve, his eyes burning.

"If you would be so kind as to let me explain…" Erik said.

"You're not going to explain anything! If you so much as flinch, I swear I'll blow your fucking head right off." The gun still pointed at Erik, Rickman turned his attention to Steve. "What are you doing dating this…this thing? He could have killed you like he killed the others."

"Jon, you got it all wrong," Steve said. "He's not the vampire who is doing the killings. If you would just listen to me for one second."

"Are you trying to tell me that there's more than one of these blood-suckers on the loose?"

"Exactly," Erik said. "And I am finding it dreadfully difficult to carry on a polite conversation with a gun pointed at my head."

Rickman tensed his arms, grasping onto the gun all the tighter.

"I wasn't fucking talking to you!"

The next thing he knew, his hands were empty and Erik was sitting on the couch, looking at the gun with wonder, as if it were something he had never seen before.

"What the fuck…" Rickman said, gaping at his now empty hands. His eyes grew wide when he noticed that Erik now held the gun. Terror crossed his face. Wide-eyed, he opened his mouth as if to speak but said nothing.

"I have to apologize but guns make me rather nervous," Erik said cheerily. "I hope you understand. It will be much easier for us to converse this way."

Rickman glanced over at Steve who was smiling. Rickman all at once looked totally helpless and his breath erupted in quick gasps.

"How did you do that? How did you get my…"

"It was very simple actually. The old 'body is quicker than the eye' ploy. Just an example of what we are up against."

"What *we* are up against?" Rickman asked.

"The other vampire." Steve replied.

Rickman focused his attention on Erik. His voice cracked as he spoke.

"You're serious aren't you? About the other vampire. There really is more than one of you?"

Erik sighed and placed the gun on the coffee table next to the couch.

"I am *deadly* serious." He crossed his legs then pointed to a chair across from the couch. "Please sit down, Officer Rickman. I believe we need to clear up a few things."

Steve left Rickman's side and joined Erik on the couch. Both sat silently, staring at Rickman, waiting. Rickman didn't move.

The room was silent for several moments.

"But you are really a vampire?" Rickman said finally.

"That is correct."

"But you didn't do the killings?

"That is also correct."

"But you drink human blood?"

Erik hesitated. "Correct once again."

"Do you kill people?"

"I avoid it if at all possible." Erik paused and smiled weakly at Rickman. "You, sir, are proof of that."

Rickman grimaced at the memory of the marks on his legs and their now clear meaning.

"Why didn't you kill me?"

"I just told you. I try not to kill people."

Defeated, Rickman lumbered over to the chair and sat down. His hands were still trembling and he had the look of a lost child.

"I can't believe I'm actually talking to a real vampire. A bloodsucker."

"You get used to it," Steve said and looked warmly at Erik.

Erik frowned. "If you would be so kind, I would appreciate it if you could refrain from employing the term "bloodsucker." I prefer to think of my condition as being hemo-dependent."

A laugh escaped from Steve before he could stop himself. Erik turned to flash Steve a mock dirty look, but instead smiled at him.

Rickman watched them both in amazement. "You two are...really together?" He turned to Steve, his eyes completely leaving Erik for the first time.

Steve nodded. "We are in love if that's what you mean. I myself only discovered the truth about Erik recently. Yesterday, to be exact." He ran a hand through his hair and continued, "I love him Jon, I really do. So he's a vampire. It just goes to show that nobody's perfect."

A look of hurt crossed over Erik's face then instantly disappeared. He looked at Rickman squarely in the eyes.

"He is correct you know. I am not that much different than you. But the most important thing to me right now is ensuring that no harm comes to Steve. I would risk my life to guarantee his safety."

Rickman creased his brow. "You talk as though he is in danger."

Erik nodded sadly. "I believe that he is in grave danger."

Rickman leaned forward and gazed intently at Erik. "You mean the other vampire you mentioned?"

"Yes," Erik answered. "He has already made himself known to Steve. I have no doubt that he has some hideous scheme in mind which involves Steve."

"But why would he be after Steve in particular?"

Erik turned to Steve. "I think he needs to know the entire story in order to understand."

"I would appreciate that," Rickman said rudely. "I'm still not sure if I'm buying any of this."

Over the next hour, Erik slowly retold his story to Rickman, as he had to Steve the night before. Rickman sat in silence, wide-eyed, occasionally nodding. He did not say one word throughout Erik's entire discourse.

"And this is why I believe that Steve's life is in jeopardy and why Victor must be stopped."

"Holy fucking shit," Rickman said, breaking his silence. "This is way too fantastic." There was a strong distaste in his voice, but an unmistakable hint of fear as well.

"Fantastic, yes, but factual nonetheless," Erik said in an urgent voice. "Victor is not to be taken lightly, as the recent body count has regrettably demonstrated.

Rickman frowned. "You know Erik, you're lucky that I didn't kill you the moment I walked in here. I had you pegged for the murderer."

Erik smiled and fingered the gun on the table.

"There was no chance of that happening. I would not have permitted it." He flashed a toothy grin at Rickman.

"Yeah…right." Rickman wrinkled his brow and then, "If this Victor creature has powers like you, how in the hell can he be caught?"

Erik sighed. "It will not an effortless undertaking, I can assure you of that. We are dealing with a creature who could very well be centuries old." Erik drifted into contemplated thought. "Odd, he never did tell me his true age. But no matter. What is important, is that he is a killer without a conscience, a predator with powers that are no match for human strength. What is needed on our part is exceptional cunning and plain old good luck."

"If I could get together with some of the other guys on the force, we might be able to ambush him." Rickman glanced at the gun on the table and pointed. "That baby will take anyone's—or anything's head clean off."

Erik shook his head. "He is much too clever for that. Remember, he could vanish in a flash without you so much as noticing his departure. He has been avoiding detection by humans long since before you were even born and has gotten to be quite skilled at it. I know I have. Until recently, that is." He smiled at Steve and took hold of his hand. "It is also important to keep in mind that he could kill every one of you so quickly that none of you would so much as even have the time to reach for your weapon. No, it is I and I alone who must face Victor."

"What if he kills you?" Rickman asked. "Then what?"

"He will not," Erik said, his eyes blazing. "I almost did him in once. This time, I shall complete the task."

Steve was not going to let the subject drop that easily. His swung his head around to face Erik. Alarm was evident in his voice.

"But what if he did kill you Erik? It's possible you know. It will be vampire against vampire. Anything could happen."

"My death at the hands of Victor will not come to pass, I assure you," Erik responded, almost coldly. "I have been preparing myself for battle with him for almost seventy years. I will prevail when the time comes."

"How can you be certain?" Steve asked.

"Because I have one huge advantage over him."

"And that is?" Steve said.

"I am much stronger than him, and he is well aware of that fact. I have drunk of his blood twice. First, when he initially transformed me. The second time was when I slew Jason. Victor's blood flowed through the boy's body and was in the process of mutating him into a vampire when I drained him. I do not know the reason for it, but when I drank of the boy, partaking indirectly of Victor's blood for a second time, a change occurred in my body. My strength at least tripled from what it was and I developed what I might refer to as other abilities that I did not previously possess. I have discovered that if I focus my concentration adequately, my body temporarily loses its corporal form and becomes what I can best describe as transparent. Matter can pass through me effortlessly, without inflicting any harm upon me. Unfortunately, I can only maintain this state for a short while."

To demonstrate, Erik stood up and shut his eyes. Within moments, his body dematerialized into a mist-like manifestation, his physical characteristics now barely visible. Seconds later, he was back as he was, whole.

Steve gasped and stared at Erik, mouth agape. "Now that is too cool!"

"Yes, but unfortunately not too useful. I can momentarily prevent a blow but seconds later I am whole once again and it is nearly impossible for me to resume such a state immediately thereafter. The energy required for such a feat is tremendous, and some time is needed afterwards to regain my strength."

It was true. Erik now looked drained, as if his energy had been pulled right out of him. He continued.

"Victor has never mentioned our ability to transform ourselves in this manner, which leads me to believe that he is either unaware of it or incapable of performing the act himself. I only became aware of it myself shortly after I exterminated Jason."

"I have to admit, it is impressive," Rickman piped in, "but will it be enough?"

Erik ignored the question then reached over to the table and retrieved the gun. "You said this gun had the ability to decapitate?"

Rickman nodded. "I doubt that even a vampire could survive a kiss from a 357."

"That remains to be seen. As far as I know, only sunlight and fire can destroy us." Erik then smiled. "But of course, 357's weren't around when Victor told me this. It is unlikely that any creature could survive without a brain. In most cases, our body is able to regenerate itself after almost any wound. But this? I simply do not know. Can you procure me one of these?"

Rickman nodded. "No problem. I have several of them in my apartment. I collect guns in fact."

"Yes, I remember your apartment. You seem to collect a lot of things."

Rickman blushed, as did Steve.

"Do you have any idea how to find him?" Rickman asked.

"It will not be necessary to find him. He will find us."

Rickman glanced over at Steve, then turned back to face Erik.

"What about Steve? This seems like a much too dangerous situation for him to be subjected to. Especially if Victor has his eyes set on him."

"He will be safe as long as he is with me,' Erik said. "As I stated, my main goal is to protect Steve."

Steve cringed. "I certainly hope so."

"I can't just stand by and do nothing," Rickman piped in, slightly annoyed at being excluded. "I am trained in these kind of matters."

'Hunting vampires?" Erik asked.

Rickman frowned. "Hunting criminals, dealing with the scum of the earth, trying to understand how the minds of these creeps work. I think we would have a better chance of surviving an encounter with him if we all work together."

Steve looked at Erik. "He does have a point. The more of us there are, the better our chances."

Erik creased his brow and was silent for a few minutes. "Perhaps you are right. In dealing with an enemy as cunning as Victor, the more positives we have on our side the better. Additionally," he said, pointing to the gun on the table, "your aim with this gadget is probably much better than mine."

"What about some sort of a plan?" Steve asked. "I mean we just can't stand here like sitting ducks waiting for him to pop in and try to kill us."

"Steve's right," Rickman said. "I think we should try to find him and take him by surprise. Can you tell me everything you know about him? His habits, where he could possibly live, how he thinks, anything that could give us an idea on how to start looking for him."

Erik shook his head. "I do not know that much about him myself. Remember, it has been over seventy years since our paths last crossed. I did not even know him that well during the year we did spend together. I have already told you everything that I possibly can."

"I still think we should recruit some of the guys from the force. If we all put our heads together…"

"That is completely out of the question," Erik interrupted. "The last thing we need is media hysteria. I am also unwilling to allow my secret to be known to others." He smiled at Rickman. "This must be something we do on our own. No outsiders."

"You have a point there," Rickman answered. "The guys would probably have me locked up if I asked them to go out hunting vampires with me."

"Don't forget that we do have one other ally in the Police Department," Steve reminded his companions. "I'm sure he could be of some help as well."

Rickman looked confused. "What are you saying? That there is someone else on the force that knows about this? About you?"

Erik laughed. "How could I forget about Mitch? Yes, he could perhaps be of some assistance. He has done a wonderful job of following the case for me thus far."

Rickman shook his head as if trying to ward off the confusion. "Mitch? He knows about you? How?"

"Mitch lives with me."

Rickman creased his brow and ran his fingers through his hair. He turned to Steve, then back to Erik.

"Now this is really getting twisted! He's not…" Rickman cleared his throat, "a vampire, is he?"

"Not at all," Erik said shaking his head. "He is my companion and friend. He has been with me since he was a lad. It was his idea to become a police officer but it actually works out quite well. When one is in my situation, it is always helpful to have a friend on the police force."

Steve chuckled loudly, then covered his mouth with his hand.

Erik glanced at Steve, slightly irritated. "May I inquire as to what is so amusing?"

"I'm sorry Erik. It's just that at times, you tend to show your age. 'Lad' is such an antiquated expression. I haven't heard it since I was a kid and had to listen to my grandfather's long-winded stories. He always used that word. Everyone was a lad to him."

With an annoyed look on his face, Erik reached over and tousled Steve's hair. "Amusing. So are you saying that you have a problem dating someone who is a mere seventy years your senior?" He smiled at Steve, then turned to Rickman without waiting for a response from his young lover. "As I was saying before I was so *unpleasantly* interrupted, Mitch is a devoted friend as well as a loyal police officer. I am confident he would be willing to help with this matter."

"I don't feel quite so alone in the world, now that I know there's someone else that I can talk about this with," Rickman said. "I'll discuss it with him tomorrow and maybe between the two of us, we'll be able to come up with something after reviewing the murder cases again with a different eye—maybe a weakness this vampire possesses. My experience has shown me that in many cases, the answer is right there. We just tend to overlook it. Erik, can you stop by the station tomorrow morning? Perhaps with the three of us…"

"I am afraid that is quite impossible. I am unavailable during the daytime."

"Oh yeah, that's right," Rickman said, a disturbed look on his face. "I forgot about the sunlight thing."

Erik smiled bleakly and sighed. "I wish I could as well."

"What about Steve? How can we be sure that he will be safe?"

"He shall be staying with me." Erik said. He then turned to Steve with a stern look on his face. "*Won't you dear?*"

Steve blushed. "I promise," he said, holding up his right hand. "Scout's honor."

"It looks like I have a lot to absorb. I never expected to be having a polite conversation with a vampire tonight, that's for sure." Rickman said, eyeing Erik up and down. "This is still incredible."

"Could you do me favor?" Erik said. "It would be most appreciated if you could limit your use of the word vampire. I consider it to be a derogatory term." He sighed. "I suppose it is that the word makes me feel alienated from the rest of the world, like I am separate from the human race."

"I apologize. I didn't know."

"I am certain that you did not." Erik looked out the window and turned to Steve. "It is nearly time to return home. Dawn is not far off."

Steve nodded then turned his gaze to Rickman. "Thanks for your concern, Jon. And don't worry about me. I'll be fine. Erik won't let anything happen to me."

Rickman smiled, then pointed at the table. "Do you think I can have my gun back now?"

Erik laughed shortly and handed him the 357. "Certainly. You never know when you might be needing this." He walked over to the table, ripped a piece of paper out of Steve's notebook and scribbled. "Here is my address and telephone number. Should you come up with anything else, please let me know."

Rickman took the piece of paper and pushed it into the pocket of his jeans. "I will." Then looking at Steve, "Take care, huh?"

"You got it," Steve said, extending his hand to Rickman.

After Rickman left, Steve quickly gathered up a few belongings and stuffed them in a backpack. As he packed, he smiled to himself. To think just a few months ago he was bored with his life. Strange how things can suddenly turn around.

"Hurry Steve," cried Erik from the living room. "It is getting late."

Before Steve closed the door to his apartment, he took one swift glance around and sighed. He couldn't help but wonder if he would ever see this place again.

* * *

Steve had a difficult time keeping up with Erik on the walk home. It amazed Steve how briskly Erik was moving without demonstrating the least amount of effort. Steve was nearly out of breath and they still had several more blocks to go before reaching Erik's house. As they rushed along, Steve glanced at the sky and noticed the darkness was already starting to dissipate. What a horrible existence, Steve thought and suddenly felt sorry for Erik. He couldn't imagine having to fear the rays of the sun, much less never seeing daylight again.

It took Steve several moments to catch his breath after they had reached the house. Erik closed the door behind him and breathed a long sigh of relief. Erik stopped and stood immobile in the center of the living room, like a jungle cat listening for its prey to make the slightest movement so it could attack. His body stiffened and his eyes grew wide.

"What is it?" Steve asked.

"*Something is wrong*," Erik answered in almost a whisper. He was visibly alarmed.

Steve walked over to join him. "What do you mean?"

Erik seemed reluctant to speak.

"I am not quite sure. I sense that something is not right." He closed his eyes, as if concentrating. "There has been an intruder."

"Victor?" Steve asked, shaken. His eyes began frantically searching the house.

Erik seemed to sniff the air. He then lunged forward. "Mitch!" he cried out. "Mitch!"

Erik suddenly vanished. Steve could hear him dashing throughout the house, calling out Mitch's name. From the crashes, Steve guessed that he was overturning furniture in the process. All at once, Erik returned to Steve's side and his eyes met Steve's in a penetrating gaze.

"He is not here."

"Could he have just gone out?" Steve asked, afraid to speak.

Erik shook his head. "He is always here when I get home without exception. In all the years we have been together, he has never gone anywhere without letting me know." He walked to the living room and sat down. Steve followed. "No, I just cannot explain it Steve, but I feel that something has happened to him. What it is, I do not know."

"You mentioned an intruder. What did you mean?"

"I sense there has been an invasion of the household." He sighed. "And I do not believe it was a human invasion."

Steve noticed that Erik all at once looked tired and seemed to be slowing down. He guessed it was because of the approaching sunrise.

"If he's not back by morning, I'll call the police station to see if he went to work." Steve didn't know what else to say.

Erik nodded weakly. "I can do no more tonight." He leaned over, kissed Steve and hugged him tightly. "It is time for me to rest."

"Goodnight," said Steve, holding onto Erik's hands. "I'm sure Mitch is okay."

"I certainly hope so. I just cannot shake this feeling…" He kissed Steve lightly on the forehead then drifted upstairs.

A moment later, Steve heard a loud cry coming from upstairs. "Steve! Quick!'

Steve found Erik's sanctuary without any difficulty. The open coffin in the middle of the windowless room startled him at first sight but he tried to ignore it. Erik has standing over the coffin, holding a note. His entire body was shaking. He handed the note to Steve.

"The handwriting. It is written in blood. Mitch's blood. I thought I could smell it when we first came it. It was too faint for me to be sure."

Dear old friend,
If you wish to ever see your lackey alive, meet me at the Grayland Metra Station tomorrow night at midnight. Bring the boy with you.
I am simply dying to see you again.
Eternally yours,
Victor

Erik threw a quick panicked look at Steve.

"Call Rickman. Tell him to be here at sunset—and to bring the guns!"

Coming Together

◆

Rickman gulped down the last of his cold coffee and sifted through the file once again. Steve's phone call this morning had sent him into a frenzy. He groaned as he tried to work out a plan in his head but his mind wouldn't let him. He could barely digest the fact that actual vampires exist and now he had to work out a strategy to try to catch one—with the help of another vampire, of course. Focus, focus, he told himself. This would not be a matter of catching a mere criminal. He needed all of his metal resources to be as sharp as possible. His thoughts were interrupted by a highly offensive voice.

"There's someone to see you," the voice grumbled at the door to his office. Rickman looked up. Officer Peale was squinting at him as if he were extremely irritated. "And he sure is a pretty one too."

"Fuck you asshole," Rickman muttered as he walked past the cop. Peale looked taken aback, shocked at Rickman's comment. But Rickman didn't care. He was in no mood for Peale this morning and wouldn't hesitate to let him know it.

He shuffled out to the front desk and looked around. Sitting in a chair with his hands clasped was a young blond kid who appeared to be in his mid-twenties or so. He was thumbing through an issue of Time Magazine with a nervous urgency. Rickman eyed him up and down before approaching. He was more than pretty—this kid was downright beautiful. Rickman guessed that he must have stood about 6'2 with a body that was obviously well taken care of, as his skin tight Levi's and t-shirt demonstrated. His shaggy blond hair brushed loosely at his shoulders. The kid looked up and noticed Rickman staring at him and broke into a warm smile, revealing a set of pearly white teeth which flashed along with his aqua blue eyes. He stood up.

"Are you Jon Rickman?"

"The one and only. And to whom do I have the pleasure of talking?"

"I'm Jamie, the friend of Steve's who called you yesterday. I've heard a lot about you." He held out his hand. Rickman shook it, keeping it in his own for a little longer than necessary. He could feel that the kid was trembling.

Rickman remembered the call. The kid had only said that he had an important matter he wanted to discuss with him and it might have something to do with a murder case.

"Oh yes, I remember." Rickman pulled the boy off to the side. "You mentioned you might have some information on a case we're working on?"

Jamie glanced around nervously, as if to ensure that nobody was listening to their conversation. He began wringing his hands as he spoke. "I think so. I'm not sure. I don't know. It's my friend Steve Mitchell. He is messed up in this somehow and now he's missing. I've been trying to call him all night and this morning, but there's no answer. I've afraid something might have happened to him. I don't know where in the hell he could be."

Rickman eyed him suspiciously. The kid looked like he was trying to hold off tears. "He's fine, I assure you," Rickman responded with a soft voice. "He's staying with a friend."

Jamie breathed a sigh of relief. "So he did go to the police after all. Thank God. I was worried sick. Where is he? Is he staying with Erik?"

Rickman jerked unconsciously at the sound of Erik's name and hoped Jamie didn't notice. Just how much did this kid know?

"Erik? Yes, he's staying at his boyfriend's house for the time being."

Jamie's voice fell to a whisper. "Did you find out anything about," he looked around again, "the vampire?"

Rickman's face went white. "Listen Jamie, I don't think it's a very good idea to talk here. Too many big ears lurking about." He glanced at his watch. "I know it's still early but what do you say we grab a burger somewhere and talk over lunch? I'd really like to hear what you have to say." He hoped the kid would say yes.

Jamie flashed a big smile at Rickman. "Sounds great," he said enthusiastically.

Moments later, they headed out the door together. Officer Peale whistled as the door closed.

* * *

Steve paced back and forth in the still unfamiliar house. No matter how hard he tried, he couldn't sit still. His mind was racing. He prayed for sunset yet dreaded it as well. Tonight he would finally meet Victor and hopefully this ordeal would be over one way or another. He shivered. How would the evening end? With his and Erik's death? Maybe they both should just leave the city and try to find someplace where Victor wouldn't find them. But Erik was probably right. There was no escaping Victor. He also knew that he would never leave without Erik. And Erik wouldn't leave without Mitch.

Steve thought of him sleeping in the coffin upstairs and shuddered. "I won't let you down Erik," he said out loud and walked to the window. It was only a little after one in the afternoon. He had been pacing the floor for hours and dusk was still a long way off. He wanted to try to get some sleep, as he knew full well that it was going to be a long night. But he was much too nervous for sleep, even as sleep deprived as he was. After the discovery of Victor's note, he had been unable to nap more than a couple of hours and it was not a very restful sleep.

Even though it was daytime and he was safe, he found himself constantly looking over his shoulder, half expecting to find Victor standing behind him, fangs bared. Every little noise made him jump. He now wished he had taken Rickman up on his offer to come over. After he had called him, Rickman was ready to come right down but Steve had told him that it wasn't necessary and that he would be all right at the house by himself. Since they had little time before the confrontation with Victor, it made more sense for Rickman to stay at the station, study the files and hopefully come up with a plan.

Steve threw himself into a chair and, after pondering his uneasiness for a couple of moments, decided that would walk down to the station instead. He could bring Rickman that note. That's a good excuse to go. He didn't want Rickman to think he was some kind of nervous nelly. But being alone in this house was driving him crazy. He needed to be around people—he needed to feel safe.

A knock at the door startled him causing him to nearly fall out of his chair. Who could that be? Rickman said he wouldn't be over until after four. Did he dare answer it or should he just ignore it?

He got up and crept up to the door slowly. One would think that with Erik being a vampire, he would at least have a peephole on the door so one could know who was standing outside. Gathering up his courage, he slowly opened the door.

"It's about time you got your tired ass to the door, Steven Mitchell!" a familiar voice said to him.

"Jamie!" He didn't notice the man standing behind Jamie at first as the door was open just a crack. Steve flung the door open and was surprised to see Jon Rickman as well.

"You naughty, naughty boy," Jamie said as he brushed past Steve and entered the house. "You should know better than try to keep secrets from me."

Steve laughed nervously. "I certainly didn't expect to see you two together."

He flashed Rickman what he hoped was the evil eye but Rickman didn't seem to notice. The only thing Rickman seemed to be noticing at the moment was Jamie.

"Jamie came to see me late this morning," Rickman explained. "He was concerned about you Steve. I tried to assure him that you were fine but," he said turning to face Jamie, "he certainly is an insistent fellow. I had no choice but to fill him in on the situation." He looked at Jamie sternly. "Mainly for his own protection."

"His own protection?" Steve asked.

"I'll explain to you later," Jamie said, averting Steve's eyes. His face was crimson. "Jon brought me over here just so I could be assured that you were okay."

Steve looked confused. Did Rickman tell him everything? "Yeah, I'm fine. As good as I can be expected under the circumstances, anyway."

He looked over at Rickman with quizzical eyes and Rickman nodded, and mouthed the words, "he knows everything" behind Jamie's back.

"Do you have the note?" Rickman said. "I want to take it back to the station and look it over."

Steve reached into his back pocket and produced a crumpled piece of paper. "Here it is," he said as he handed it to Rickman.

Rickman read it then sniffed the piece of paper. "You're right Steve. It does appear as if it's written in blood."

"I have to admit that I'm really scared about tonight," Steve said.

Rickman crammed the note in his shirt pocket then gave Steve's shoulder a squeeze.

"Don't feel alone Steve. I'm scared shitless myself. I've never had to battle a vamp before and don't feel too good about walking into a situation like this without backup. Goes against everything I've ever learned since being a cop. I just sure as hell hope that Erik knows what he's doing." He reached in his pocket and pulled out a Marlboro. "This is all so fucking strange."

"You think it's strange?" Steve said. "I've only had two days to digest the fact that my boyfriend is a vampire and that we're both being stalked by another vampire who is evil and wants to kill me." He then forced himself to smile at his two companions. "I sure am glad that you two came by, though. I was having a bad case of the jitters right before you stopped over."

"I don't blame you," Jamie said. "This is all pretty weird. I would be an absolute wreck! By the way, just how are you dealing with Erik? I mean being a vampire and all. That night you introduced him to me at the bar I got the feeling that there was something unusual about him."

"Not quite this unusual though, hey?"

Jamie giggled, glanced at Rickman and then back at Steve. "Never would have guessed it in a million years." He then looked serious and lowered his voice. "You okay with it?"

Steve nodded. "Erik is a wonderful guy. I've finally met someone who I feel is my soul mate and I'm not about to let him go." He grinned at Jamie.

"I can't believe that you're so comfortable with it. You act like it's nothing out of the ordinary."

Steve shrugged. "What choice do I have? I love him and he is what he is. If I want to stay with him, I have to accept him for his—differences." He smiled. "And I do want to stay with him."

Jamie laughed. "I wonder if I would have been as understanding as you if I was in your shoes. Actually, I think it's cool. My best friend is dating a vampire. Wow!

Rickman stared at Jamie. "Remember Jamie, this is just between us. The last thing we need is for this to get out."

"Don't fret. Besides, whom would I tell? Nobody would believe it anyway."

"Jon," Steve said. "Were you able to come up with anything new?"

Rickman shook his head. "Not really. I reviewed the files on the murders this morning but nothing jumped out at me. But now that I know who and what the killer is, I was able to read them in an entirely different light. It's amazing how much sense everything makes now." He flicked the ashes from his cigarette into his hand. "What we have to be concerned with right now is getting Mitch back alive and putting an end to Victor's reign of terror on the city without getting ourselves killed in the process."

"If Victor hasn't already killed him," Steve said. "I feel horrible for Erik. He is quite close to Mitch."

"I hope that isn't the case," Rickman replied sadly. "But now knowing what Victor is capable of, I really do wonder what the chance is that Mitch is still alive? As far as we know, there has not been anyone who has been spared after an encounter with this creature." His hands suddenly balled up into fists and his eyes flashed. "We gotta kill this fucker, that's all there is to it."

"Have you worked out any plan?"

"I have a general idea on how to approach this. The trick will be to show up without Victor noticing me. If he suspects that there's a third person, he might kill Mitch outright." He sighed. "I checked out the train station right after your call. It's fairly secluded but there's a parking lot on the bottom, below the tracks that you can't see very well from on top. I'll wait there in the car and approach when the time is right. Hopefully, Erik can distract him enough so he wouldn't notice my advance. Erik may have his own ideas on the best way to handle this. We just gotta make sure that he doesn't detect me waiting below."

Steve shuddered. Jamie grabbed his hand and looked him in the eyes. "I'm sure it will be okay Steve. Jon will make sure that nothing happens to you."

Steve nodded weakly. "I'm sure it will all work out somehow." He squeezed his friend's hands, then let go. "Besides," he added, looking at Rickman, "we have the 357 on our side."

Rickman laughed. "Make that two 357's. I got one for Erik as well. Not only that, but it's also three of us against one of him."

"I still think I could be of help too if you would let me come along," Jamie said, almost pouting. "Four against one is even better odds."

"We've already gone over this," Rickman said, looking sternly at Jamie. "This is just too dangerous to risk another life. Besides, I need you to notify the police station if you don't hear anything from us by morning. Somebody has to fill in the department should…" he hesitated, "the mission not go as planned. It's a very important role you'll be playing Jamie. I really need you to do this."

Jamie nodded. "Yeah, yeah. I'll do it. But I'm going to lose my mind just sitting there all night, waiting for the phone to ring. Make sure you call me the minute it's over."

Unconsciously, Rickman ran his hand up and down Jamie's back, which looked to be more than a friendly rub. Steve noticed, but said nothing. There was definitely something going on between the two of them, an obvious mutual interest. He smiled. It would be nice if Jamie ended up with Rickman. Maybe he could even tame Jamie down a bit. Or maybe it was Rickman who needed the taming.

"I think I better be taking you home," Rickman said to Jamie. "It'll be dark in only a couple of hours and I still have some preparations to do." He thought for a moment, then added, "If you can get in contact with your friends, you might want to warn them to stay off the streets."

Jamie glanced nervously at Steve then turned back to Rickman. "I'll do that. I'll take a walk tonight and let them know what happened to Skip if they hadn't already heard and suggest that they take a little break."

"Just make sure someone's with you when you go out. Do not under any circumstance go out alone."

"What in the world are you two talking about?" Steve asked.

"Now is not the time," Jamie said. "I'll tell you later." He tickled Steve lightly on the ribs. "You're not the only one who has secrets, you know."

Rickman patted Jamie on the back then turned to Steve. "I'll be back in about two hours. After I drop Jamie off, I need to run to my apartment and get the guns. I should be back well before sunset."

"Is there anything I should do in the meantime?"

Rickman shook his head and squeezed his shoulder. "Just sit tight. And if I don't make it back by dusk, tell Erik not to do anything until I get here. Without the guns, we won't have much of a chance."

"I wouldn't exactly say that," Steve said. "Remember, Erik almost put Victor down once."

"You're right. I forgot for a moment exactly what he was and the abilities he possesses. Shit, having him with us is probably better than having ten 357's."

Jamie walked up to Steve and hugged him tightly. "Be careful, hey?" he whispered in Steve's ear. "I need you around for a long time yet."

"I will," Steve whispered back. "I'll call you as soon as I can."

They left, and Steve found himself alone again. He paced back and forth, all the while looking at the clock. The sun will set in a little over two hours. A heavy apprehension filled him and he did something he hadn't done since he was a child.

He prayed.

The Plan

◆

Darkness swooped in like a large bat, wrapping the city in its black leathery wings. Steve watched the darkening sky with a dread he had not yet experienced in his young life. At last the waiting was over. The night would come to an end and with it, the mysteries of events yet to unfold. At least he was no longer alone. Erik had risen, and stood by his side also watching the black sky, both of them wordless, hands clasped together. There was nothing to say. All they could do now was wait.

Erik was quiet and his face held a blank expression, an expression that told Steve that his thoughts were a million miles away.

"Are you okay?" Steve asked.

Erik looked at Steve then smiled weakly. "Not really."

"Mitch?"

Erik nodded. "I just hope to God that for once, Victor will be true to his word and not kill him. Losing Mitch would rip me apart." He turned his gaze back to the window and added, "Please let him still be alive."

The next several minutes were filled with silence, as Erik and Steve continued to stare out the window at nothingness.

"It is so typical of Victor to set a meeting for midnight," Erik said, finally breaking the nerve raking quiet. "He always did find it necessary to make a production out of everything—dramatizing even the smallest event to monstrous proportions. He will pay for what he has done, and pay dearly. It is he who shall perish tonight."

Erik's tone of voice caused Steve to instinctively take a step back. The words, or rather the manner in which they were delivered, caused the hairs on Steve's neck to stand up on end. Erik spoke like a vampire—a true vampire—and one not to be taken lightly.

Erik turned to face Steve as if he could sense Steve's alarm. "I apologize Steve. I did not mean to frighten you."

"That's okay. You just startled me a bit. I guess we're all a little on edge knowing what is going to happen later."

"Or rather not knowing what will happen tonight." He sighed deeply and returned his gaze to the window, as if patiently waiting for guests to arrive. "The last thing I ever wanted was to put my friends in danger. Now Mitch is gone, very likely dead, and Victor wants me to bring you to some godforsaken place at midnight. We must not fail tonight."

Steve said nothing, watching Erik's back as he spoke. Erik turned, smiled at Steve, then walked up to him and wrapped him tightly in his arms, burying his face in Steve's neck. They stood for several minutes in the center of the floor, their bodies wrapped in a strong embrace.

"Ah, Jon Rickman has arrived," Erik said, pulling away from Steve.

Steve had not even heard his car pull up. But sure enough, within moments, there was a loud knock at the door.

"Boy, do you have good hearing!" Steve said in amazement.

"And a good sense of smell as well," Erik added and he walked to the door and opened it. Steve frowned.

Rickman strolled in. "Sorry I'm late boys. I had a few things to tend to before coming."

"Or perhaps someone to tend to?" Steve asked.

Rickman blushed briefly then smiled at Erik's confused look. He turned to Steve. "Just exactly what are you implying?" he asked innocently.

"You don't think I'm blind, do you?" Steve said. "I saw the way you and Jamie were looking at each other. It wasn't hard to figure out that there was something going on between you two."

"Jamie?" Erik asked, confused. "Your friend from the bar?"

Steve filled him on his earlier visit that afternoon from Jamie and Rickman. "But don't worry Erik. Jamie is cool about everything. He would never breathe a word of this to anyone."

"Plus," Rickman added, "he is playing a critical role in our plan for tonight."

Erik crossed his arms and shook his head. "In all these years, I have kept my secret completely safe from humans. Now in a matter of a few days time, it has become almost common knowledge." He turned to Steve. "You are sure this Jamie can be trusted?"

Steve grabbed hold of Erik's hand. "Positive. He and I are close friends and I know that he would never do anything to betray me." Steve then turned to Rickman and flashed him a mock dirty look. "Well, until today that is."

"Now Steve," Rickman answered, "you can't blame him for coming to me. He cares about you and was afraid that you were in some kind of trouble. Friends like him are hard to come by, you know."

Steve nodded. "I know. He is a great guy—as I'm sure you have dis-covered. Nudge nudge, wink wink."

Erik smiled as Rickman blushed again. "There will be time to discuss Jon Rickman's love life later. Now, we must put together a plan of action for tonight. Did you bring the weapons Jon?"

"Have them right here," he said, pointing to one of the paper bags he was holding. "I also brought something for you Steve. I stopped at Checker's on the way over here and picked up a couple of burgers. Thought you might be hungry."

Steve smiled, taking the small white bag from Rickman. "Thanks! I could smell it when you came in and was hoping it was for me." He opened the bag and took a deep whiff. "Come to think of it, I haven't eaten a thing today."

The three went into the kitchen and sat at the table. As Steve gulped down his dinner, Rickman reached into the other bag and produced three guns.

"They're all loaded," he said as he laid them on the table. "Don't worry. I have the safety on now so they won't accidentally go off."

"Cool!" said Steve. "You brought one for me too!"

Rickman reached over and gave Steve's arm a quick rub. "Especially for you. Do either of you know how to use them?"

"My father has a ton of guns at home and he taught me how to shoot when I was younger," Steve said. "They were all rifles though. I've never used a handgun."

"There's not that much of a difference. Aiming is pretty much the same." He looked over at Erik. "How about you?"

Erik shook his head. "I have never used a gun." He picked it up and studied the weapon. "I assume it cannot be too difficult."

"It's fairly straightforward," Rickman said. "Here, let me show you." He then gave Erik brief instructions on how to hold the gun and how to aim. "There will be a pretty good kickback after the gun is fired. It takes a little getting used to." He then pushed the third gun towards Steve. "The important thing to remember is when it comes time to use it, don't forget about the safety. You have to move this lever here before you'll be able to fire the gun."

Erik and Steve listened carefully as Rickman explained the proper use of the weapon.

"Very good,' Erik said. "Let us hope that these guns will suffice should they be necessary. Now in regards to a plan…"

"I've thought about the best way for us to proceed against Victor tonight," Rickman interrupted.

Erik nodded. "Very well. Let me hear what you have in mind."

"We can go in my car. In order to pull this off, we'll have to arrive early so that he doesn't detect me. Since he is only expecting you and Steve, I'll hide in the car, crouched down, while you two wait for him on the platform. The parking lot is hidden enough from the station that I think we can get away with it. There's a stairway leading up to the platform. Shortly after midnight, I can sneak up the stairs and take him from behind."

Erik listened closely then creased his brow. "Very good in theory, but there are several other things to consider. First of all, how will you know when he arrives? It is also important not to forget that being a vampire, he has an extraordinary sense of smell, especially if it has been awhile since he has fed. He will be able to smell you from a long distance off and will be able to easily discern the difference between your blood and Steve's. If I personally am in the company of humans, I can distinguish the various differences in their blood with little difficulty and am always aware when another human is approaching. In order for you to arrive undetected, it would be essential for us to somehow divert his attention. Only then could you possibly get away with approaching. You see, if he detected you, he could have the gun out of your hands and your throat ripped out before you so much had the time to move your trigger finger."

Rickman swallowed hard then nodded. "Understood. But I still think it's the best way and I'm willing to take the chance. This fucker has to be put down."

"I agree with you Jon," Erik said, "but I'm not willing to jeopardize your life to do it. I simply will not allow you to take a foolish chance for which your probability of survival is next to nothing. There must be another way." He placed the gun firmly on the table and creased his brow. "I need to battle him myself and bring his death by my own hands. Should he by some remote chance overpower me and Steve's life becomes in jeopardy, only then must you take the risk and attempt to execute Victor yourself. I will let you know somehow should I end up in trouble."

Rickman frowned, looked at Steve then turned his gaze back to Erik. "What about Steve? Do you honestly think he will be safe during all this? If my chances are limited, what would his be?"

"Much better than yours would be. I will be there to protect him and will destroy Victor before he gets a chance to even get near Steve. It would be much too difficult for me to watch over both of you and battle Victor at the same time."

"But how will you destroy him?" Steve asked. "I thought only fire or sunlight could harm a vampire."

"That is true," Erik said. "Though it is only those two things which will completely extinguish a vampire's life, or so I've been told, I can easily render him helpless and weak. We feel pain such as you do and can be injured in much the same way, although it takes somewhat more effort. If I can get him by the throat or cause him a head injury, he would be powerless to prevent any further destruction of his body. It is then we can administer a bullet to his brain and burn his body." He paused. "This my friends, will be our best chance of defeating him."

Rickman and Steve looked at each other in silence. Rickman fingered his gun on the table. "I just don't know. I really think that if I…"

"I'm afraid I must insist," Erik said in a cold tone of voice. "You are to only approach should I fail. Understood?"

Rickman nodded weakly. "You're the boss. I just hope you know what you're doing."

Erik rose and walked up behind where Steve was sitting. He wrapped his arms around him. "I know precisely what I am doing. Victor shall die and Steve will be safe."

"And Mitch?" Rickman said.

Erik frowned. "What about Mitch?"

"Do you think Victor will be true to his promise and bring Mitch along?"

Erik shook his head sadly. "I pray more than anything that Mitch is still alive. But I have learned that a promise made by Victor holds little value. Although if he wants his revenge badly enough he might be true to his word and show up with Mitch—in exchange for Steve."

Steve raised his head slowly to meet Erik's eyes. "Thanks! That's just what I wanted to hear. It's a lovely thought—being traded like farm cattle."

"You will not be exchanged for anyone or anything Steve. If Mitch is still alive, then you and he shall both walk away unharmed. Victor will be killed before he has the chance to attack either of you."

"I wonder why he chose to meet at a train station?" Steve said. "Wouldn't there be a lot of people around?"

Rickman shook his head. "The Grayland stop really isn't a train station but rather a platform with a small shelter without any doors. There is nothing much around at all. I was there this morning during rush hour and even the nearby streets were empty. It actually makes sense that he would want to meet us there. The chances that anyone would be hanging around the platform at midnight, in a neighborhood that is not too good to begin with, is unlikely."

"I prefer it that way myself," Erik said. "I would rather not battle Victor in an area where there is a chance of being seen by humans. I have my secret to protect as well. Although it does seem to be getting around these days."

"Yeah, but remember it's safe with your friends."

Erik smiled. "Of course it is and I have complete trust in you." He stood up. "I think we should go into the living room and try to relax before our adventure this evening. It could prove to be a very long night."

Battle

◆

Mitch's eyes adjusted to the darkness allowing him to make out vague shapes in the room. Where was he? He tried to remember but couldn't. The hammering in his head had at least subsided and his mind was clearing. For most of the day, he had drifted in and out of consciousness, barely able to lift his head from the hardwood floor. He moved towards the wall and sat up. God he was thirsty! What had happened to him? Slowly it came back. He had been watching television alone at home. Erik had gone to Steve's earlier to try to convince him to come back to the house. All of a sudden there was a noise behind him. He turned and was face to face with a man he had never seen before. From the red glow of his eyes and the paleness of his skin, it didn't take too much to guess it was Victor.

"Erik is not here," he managed to stammer. His gun was unfortunately up in his room.

Victor smiled, disclosing a mouthful of sharp fangs. "It is not Erik upon whom I have come to call. It is you."

A flash of light sparked in his brain as Victor struck him. Then blackness.

He reached up and felt his swollen head. At least he was alive. For how much longer, he didn't know. But why had Victor taken him? The only explanation he could think of was that he is to be a part of Victor's revenge against Erik. Which means that Victor most likely planned to kill him. The pain in his head began hammering again. He tried to lift himself up but was too weak. Every ounce of his strength seemed to have left him and he maintained his present sitting position with difficulty. He heard a shuffling noise, then a click. Light flooded the room. He rushed his hands to his eyes to protect them from the attack.

"Good morning," Victor said at the door with a sickening smile. "It is so nice to have you awake at last. I was afraid that I had killed you and that simply would not have done."

Mitch raised his eyes to meet the vampire's face. He was surprised at how attractive Victor was. He somehow had the impression that Victor would resemble a demon more than anything else, or at least not be so human in appearance. He could now understand how this creature had seduced Erik so many years ago.

"Where am I? What have you done with Erik?"

Victor laughed, standing immobile in the doorway. "You shall see your beloved Erik soon enough. If he cares at all about your safety that is. If he does not show up for our meeting, then," he paused for a moment, "you shall die."

Mitch stared at the vampire wide-eyed and wondered what sort of deal he had made with Erik. As he broke the gaze with the vampire and looked down, he noticed for the first time that he was completely naked and that both of his legs were covered in large gashes. Bright red scabs had formed around the wounds. He turned his head away in disgust. Victor had drunk from him. His stomach flipped and nausea overtook him at the thought of it. He shivered.

"Could I get some water?"

"How inhospitable of me to neglect the needs of my guests! You must pardon my rudeness. It has been so long since I have had any callers."

Mitch could hear him laughing as he vanished. He returned moments later with a glass of cold water. With trembling hands. Mitch greedily gulped down the liquid, draining the glass. Rather than hand it to the vampire, he placed the glass on the floor next to him.

"Would you tell me what is going on here?" he said. "What do you plan on doing with me?"

Victor glared at him and rubbed his hands together. "An even exchange. You for Erik's boy. I want Erik to see me kill his human lover right before his eyes."

"You expect Erik to give you Steve in exchange for me?" Mitch asked.

That hateful smile once again planted itself on the vampire's face. "Exactly. Although your blood is so delicious that I hesitate to give you up, I am sure the blood of Erik's little boyfriend will be equally tasty and fulfilling." He licked his lips in mockery.

"He'll never do it," Mitch said defiantly. "He would never make such a deal with you."

What little color there was drained from his cheeks. He looked at Mitch sharply. "Then that would be most unfortunate for you."

"He'll destroy you."

Victor raised his eyebrows. "He has not the power nor the strength to accomplish such a task. He has walked among mortals for too long. He is weak. He has tried to become one of them and it is this fact that shall cause his demise. How could he possibly battle me when he had forgotten what it is like to be a vampire, move like a vampire, think like a vampire and fight only as a vampire can? No. Tonight he will fall at my hands."

"I thought you only wanted Steve."

Victor threw his head back in insane laughter. "Do not be a fool! Did you genuinely think I would spare Erik's life or even yours for that matter? You shall all be mine." He ran his cold finger along Mitch's cheek. "You might make an admirable vampire though. I think a set of fangs would be becoming on you."

Mitch flung his head away from the vampire's touch. Victor chuckled again.

"I must apologize for departing so abruptly but shall return to you shortly. It is time to step out for dinner. I must have full strength for tonight."

Before closing the door, he turned off the lights, leaving Mitch once again in utter darkness.

* * *

It was nearly eleven-thirty when the three men arrived at their destination. Steve looked around as they pulled into the nearly empty parking lot. Rickman was right. The area was desolate. The train platform, located on top of a small hill, was several blocks down a lonely street which contained nothing but a few factories, now closed for the day. Next to the parking lot was a small Irish tavern with only one or two customers, judging by the number of cars in the parking lot. Steve could hear screaming and the screeching of tires in the distance. Most of the nearby buildings were run down with broken glass scattered on the snowy sidewalks. He would hate to find himself here alone at night. The gun that he had in his coat pocket gave him at least some reassurance. He snuggled up close against Erik.

"This is the place," Rickman said in a flat voice as he shut off the car. He reached in his pocket and produced his own gun. "I think you two better go up before he arrives. There isn't too much time left."

Steve and Erik both took a deep breath. Erik opened the car door and stepped out. Just as Steve was about to follow suit, Rickman grabbed him by the arm.

"Don't worry Steve. We'll get this bastard."

Steve swallowed then nodded. "I'll be okay. I have faith in Erik—and in you."

"Be careful, okay?" Rickman's voice was thick and course.

Shutting the car door, the two slowly climbed the snow-covered concrete steps, a crunching noise echoing in the still night as they ascended towards the deserted platform. All was quiet.

"I can barely see it's so dark." Steve said, trying to break the silence.

Erik held tightly onto his hand then released it, draping his arm around Steve's shoulders, pulling him as close to him as he could. "It is certainly dark and deserted. I can understand why Victor chose this place to meet."

They both stood right outside the little shack next to the tracks. A broken down blue newspaper machine stood empty on the side of the building. The glass on the door had been smashed and the sides were sunken with large dents where people had frequently kicked the machine. Next to it stood a four-foot high pay phone booth, the interior laced with shards of wires were a phone had once been. Across the tracks next to the steps was a massive billboard, advertising Walt Disney's World on Ice. The cheerful sign seemed to mock the seriousness of their situation. An odor of urine and popcorn hung heavily in the air. The platform was littered with broken glass and cigarette butts.

"I'm cold," Steve said, shivering. "Maybe we can step inside the shelter for a bit to get out of the wind?"

"That would not be wise," Erik said. "The last thing we want to do is find ourselves cornered when Victor arrives."

"You have a point there," Steve said, still shivering. Erik pulled him close to him.

The minutes dragged as they both stood silently—waiting, listening. Every now and then a scream would echo into the empty night. Steve glanced at his watch. It was now five minutes to twelve. His heart began thrashing wildly in his chest as fear began to well up inside of him. He could feel himself start to shake, ever so slightly.

"I am here and I will not allow anything to happen to you." Erik whispered into Steve's ear.

True to his word, Victor appeared out of nowhere precisely at midnight. He stood facing Erik and Steve, who were still wrapped up in each other's arms. He held what appeared to be a body wrapped in a shroud.

"How tearfully touching," Victor said, sneering. His face and clothes were covered in blood.

"You bastard," Erik said through his teeth. "What have you done to Mitch?"

"What? No warm welcome? I would think you could greet me in more of a civilized manner after all these years. It is so good to see you old friend. In case you're wondering, I am fine and yes, I have missed you terribly. And you know—"

"If he's dead, I will…"

"You will do nothing!" Victor sneered.

He laid the body gently on the ground next to the tracks. "Your lackey lives. You should know dear Erik, that I am a man of my word."

"It is a blasphemy to refer to yourself as a man."

Victor roared with laughter. Erik gently pushed Steve behind him. "You have not harmed him then?"

Victor smiled a deadly smile. "He is alive, as promised."

Erik clenched his fists and stared at Victor. He could smell Mitch's living blood as it flowed through his body. His heartbeat was feeble. Too feeble. The blood splattered on Victor's face and clothes did not belong to Mitch. Erik breathed a sigh of relief.

"What do you want from me?"

Victor ignored the question. "I was true to my word. Now hand over the boy." He looked down at Mitch on the ground. "Or I will kill your lackey."

"You are insane," Erik said.

Victor's eyes grew wide and he grinned. He crossed his arms. Waiting.

"You shall be killing no one tonight," Erik said.

"Oh? And who is going to prevent it? You?"

"If I must," Erik said. "Why have you come back after all this time? The past is the past, Victor. For God's sake, let it die."

"Did you think that I would let you live after what you have done to me and to what was rightfully mine?" Victor answered with a sudden explosion of fury. "You betrayed me and now you shall pay with your pathetic life and that of your mortal spouse. Your boyfriend will be taken from you just as you took my Jason from me."

Erik took a step back, pushing Steve along with him, his eyes never leaving Victor's face for a moment. "No, my friend, it is you who shall perish this night. The world shall be finally rid of the likes of you."

Victor's eyes glittered like stars. "Do you think I have not made others? My, my Erik, how naive you are!"

"If there are others, then they shall be destroyed as well," Erik said matter-of-factly. "Just like I killed Jason seventy years ago."

Without warning, Victor lunged at Erik and Steve. Erik was too fast for him and swooped Steve up, moving them both out of Victor's path before he could make contact. Erik and Steve stood inside of the platform.

"Stay here," Erik whispered urgently. "I will not let him near you. I must fight him alone, in the open."

Steve nodded and said nothing. Erik vanished from the shack. Steve retrieved the gun from his coat pocket and with trembling hands, undid the safety latch. He held the gun tightly and pointed it at the two figures standing on the train tracks.

Erik and Victor stood face to face.

Victor's fangs were bared.

Erik approached slowly, ready to spring but Victor beat him to it. He smashed unexpectedly into Erik's chest, knocking him down. Victor stood above him, a huge rock in his hand. He brought his arm down towards Erik's head in one quick swipe but met with empty air.

"What?"

Erik rematerialized and reappeared behind Victor.

Victor swung around.

"You have slowed with age, old friend," Erik said, a tight smile on his face.

Victor glared at him, hands clenched. "I see you have picked up some new tricks since we last met. Interesting. I was not aware of this power. No matter. It shall take a lot more than a simple disappearing act to save you now."

Barely had the words escaped his lips when Erik lunged forward, hands outstretched. He slammed into Victor, knocking both of them to the ground. He grabbed Victor's throat and squeezed. With all strength he could muster, he crashed Victor's head against the hard steel train tracks. Blood ran down Victor's face as Erik continued to pound the vampire's head against the sharp steel.

The next thing Erik knew, he was sailing through the air, landing near the small shack. Before he could get to his feet, Victor was over him, bringing his mouth to Erik's throat. Erik kicked him squarely in the chest, sending him sprawling backwards several feet. He smashed into the broken down newspaper machine. Victor got up and brushed himself off. His eyes glowed with rage.

He continued to rub his hands against his clothes. Blood trickled from the recent head wound, causing him to look all the more frightening. His bloodstained face broke into an eerie smile.

"Now, my dear, dear, sweet Erik. Prepare yourself to die."

His eyes opened wide. He reached inside of his long coat to produce a shiny kitchen knife. He waved it wildly over his head.

"I have always wondered whether a vampire could live with a severed head. Call it scientific curiosity, if you will."

Erik took a step back, bracing himself for the impending attack. He stood motionless, waiting. All at once, Victor vanished. Frantically, Erik turned his head. Not possible. Victor would never flee from battle. All at once, a penetrating searing sensation rammed through his body as the blade of the knife sunk into his back. Then again.

And again.

Erik shrieked in agony as he turned around to face the crazed vampire, the bloodied knife now on the ground. Pain soared through his body as he struggled to remain upright.

He was weakening fast.

"You coward!" Erik gasped. The pain traveled throughout his body. He stumbled. "I should have figured you would attack from behind."

Victor approached him. Erik clumsily took a step backwards. It would be impossible to dematerialize at this point. From a distance, he saw a bright light and then heard the rumbling. A train! He must finish Victor off before it arrives. There must be no witnesses.

Victor took advantage of Erik's momentary loss of attention. He clasped his hands together tightly, stretching his arms out then swung with all his force towards Erik's head. Erik turned his head just in time to catch a flash of movement before the fists made contact with his skull. There was a sickening crunch as Erik's body powerfully propelled backwards.

For the first time ever, Erik actually saw stars. He blinked his eyes and tried to fight off the blackness that was trying to overtake him. Losing consciousness now would most certainly mean the end of him, Steve and Mitch. He tried to raise himself up, but could not. The pain in his head was almost too much to bear. It was time.

He filled his lungs up with fresh air and gathering up his strength, shouted. "Rickman!" The raw power of his vampiric voice echoed and shook in the quiet night.

He lifted his head. What he saw next filled him with an unnamable horror.

Victor was in the shack, his face buried in Steve's throat! The gun Steve had been holding was lying on the ground.

He grabbed the bloodied knife that lay on the ground next to him. Where the strength came from then he did not know, but he found himself rising off of the ground and literally flying towards the small building.

The train was approaching, the whistle growing ever louder. Victor was still drinking from Steve when Erik reached him. He grabbed Victor by the hair, yanked his head backwards, and slid the sharp knife along his throat. The skin split. Blood poured out like water streaming from a faucet.

The surprised vampire took a step backwards and looked at Erik in wide-eyed amazement. A strange gurgling sound escaped from him as he tried to talk. Instinctively, his hands then flew up to the throat wound in an attempt to stop the rapid gush of blood.

With what little strength Erik had left, he jammed the knife to the hilt into Victor's chest. Victor stepped back, the knife sticking out of his chest. Erik slumped onto the ground, depleted. The train was almost upon them. Its vibration and bright lights were splitting Erik's injured head in two. All at once, five shots rang out. Victor screamed as the bullets tore into his body. Rickman stood on top of the steps, the smoking gun pointing at the blood drenched vampire. Victor turned to face Rickman, opened his mouth as if trying to speak, swaggered once, and then fell onto the tracks. Blood gushed out of his body, staining the wooden beams between the steel rails. With both hands, he attempted to lift himself up but failed. With one final effort, he raised himself into a squatting position, just long enough to face the train as it rushed down the tracks and over his body. The only thing that remained after the train passed were freshly painted long red streaks along the tracks.

Erik crawled to where Steve was lying. Steve's vital juices ran out of the open gash on his throat onto the concrete floor. As he reached his lover, Erik looked down at him and listened. The sound of his heartbeat was barely audible.

Steve was dying.

The smell of his blood caused Erik's head to spin but he tried to ignore it. He slowly lifted Steve's head.

Steve was still conscious but his eyes were growing dimmer.

"Can you hear me Steve?" Erik asked through his tears.

Steve nodded slightly. Erik could hear Steve's heartbeat slow considerably.

Erik sobbed. Burning tears rolled down his cheeks.

"I cannot let you die Steve. I cannot lose you this way." He gently stroked Steve's face and pushed back his hair. "Do you know that I love you more than anything?"

Steve nodded. He had begun gasping for breath.

"I can save you Steve. But there is only one way and you know what that way is. I would never wish my existence upon anyone but I am prepared to do what it takes to save you. I need you in my life." He swallowed, then continued. "Never would I transform you against your will. It is up to you. Steve, the decision is yours."

Tears flooded Erik's face.

Steve's eyes opened wide as he understood the meaning of Erik's words. He brought up his hand to touch Erik's. He closed his eyes then opened his mouth in a feeble attempt to speak.

"Do it," Steve rattled. His head fell back to the ground.

In one swift movement, Erik slashed his wrist with his fangs and brought it up to Steve's mouth.

"Drink Steve," he whispered. "Drink deeply. It is your only chance."

Steve locked his mouth on Erik's wrist and allowed the vampire's blood to flow into his mouth. As the warm blood filled Steve's stomach, Erik could hear his heartbeat grow stronger. Erik had bent his head down and placed his lips on Steve's neck. He lapped up the youth's blood. There must be an even exchange.

Rickman was crouched over Mitch's body when he looked up saw Steve drinking from Erik's wrist and Erik's face buried in Steve's throat.

"What in the fuck are you doing?" he nearly screamed, and ran towards the shack.

Erik lifted his head, his eyes meeting Rickman's. Steve still was drinking.

"Victor got to him. This was his only chance of survival. Otherwise, he would surely have died." His voice broke off into a whisper. "It was his choice, Jon. I gave him the option. It was he who made the decision."

Erik suddenly pulled his wrist away. Steve lay on the floor, gasping for breath. The corners of his mouth stained with Erik's blood. His eyes closed. His body convulsed.

"What's happening to him?" Rickman asked, not breaking his gaze from Steve. "Is he turning?"

"The blood which he took from me is fighting to keep him alive," Erik explained weakly. "If his body can survive my invading blood, then he will live."

Rickman took a step towards Erik. "He'll be like you then?"

Erik nodded. "If he can survive the transformation."

Erik's head was starting to swim from weakness but could feel his body begin to repair itself. The gash on his head had nearly healed.

He picked up Steve and gestured to the body on the ground with his head. "And Mitch? Is he…?"

"He didn't make it," Rickman said coldly. "He was already dead when I got to him."

Erik nodded. "Victor. He is dead as well?"

"I would think so. I planted five slugs in his back before the train ran him over. There's no sign of his body though. Probably dragged along by the train if it wasn't pulverized underneath it."

"I pray to God that you are right," Erik said, staring directly into Rickman's eyes. "Let us hope that he never returns."

Erik walked over to the shroud-wrapped body next to the tracks and crouched down beside it. Rickman followed.

"My young Mitch," Erik whispered at the corpse, still holding Steve's shaking body. "My companion. I am so sorry. So sorry this happened. You will never know." He wiped his wet face with the sleeve of his coat "You were a good friend and will not be forgotten. Farewell my companion. Farewell Mitch." Erik rose to face Rickman.

Rickman grabbed hold of Erik's arm. "I'm sorry about Mitch. He was a good cop."

Erik nodded in response and took a final look at the body on the ground.

"Will you see that he is properly taken care of?"

"Don't worry about anything, I'll see to it all. But now we have to get Steve to a hospital," Rickman said.

"No,' Erik said gently. "Nothing can help him now. If he is strong enough, he will awaken, newly born as a vampire. If not, then nothing with prevent his death." Another tear rolled down his face as he spoke. "I love him Jon. I just couldn't bring myself to let him go. I hope you understand."

Rickman slowly nodded. "Let's get out of here," he said. "I have to get down to the station to fill out a report."

"What will you say?"

"I have no fucking idea."

Erik and Rickman slowly descended the steps. Rickman carried Mitch while Erik held Steve in his arms. When they reached the car, Rickman gently placed Mitch's body in the back seat of the car and closed the door. "This is going to take some explaining."

Erik nodded. "I shall be in contact with you."

Rickman looked confused. "You're not coming with me?"

"I will get home faster on my own. I want to get Steve safely in bed as quickly as possible so he can begin what will hopefully be his recovery." He paused and his face grew solemn. "Now, about your report...."

"No need to worry," Rickman said. "Your secret shall remain safe. Our serial killer has just been killed by a train."

Erik nodded in understanding. He reached out and touched Rickman's arm. "When you call Jamie, please tell him that Steve will be fine and he and I will come to see him soon."

"Shit, I forgot all about Jamie! You do realize that I will have to tell him everything that happened tonight?"

"Naturally. I would expect nothing less."

"And if Steve doesn't survive?"

"I shall contact the both of you either way."

Rickman looked down. "Jamie and Steve are very close, you know."

"I know," Erik said. He held out his hand. "Good-bye for now Jon. Thank you for your support and understanding. It will not be unrewarded."

Before Rickman could answer, Erik had vanished. His hand still remained extended in mid-air as if he was shaking hands with a ghost. He sighed and a slight shiver crawled up his spine. He started the car, screeched out of the dark parking lot and headed towards the police station. A high-pitched scream boomed in the distance—and then all was quiet.

THE END

0-595-20713-8

Made in the USA